Praise for Crosswind

"In *Crosswind*, Patricia Boomsma does what we fiction writers always hope to accomplish: she makes the reader crave whatever happens next. She creates a genuinely gripping plot. As chapters roll, the stakes get higher, the danger more intense. At one level, it's a mother/daughter tale. At another, it's a story about decisions: bad ones, good ones, and those made so long ago their value has accumulated meaning beyond categories. These pages are jam-packed with consequences, the real stuff that happens to people who've lost their way, who've lost a sense of home, who've forgotten that our mothers are waiting, every moment, to walk us back from the brink of doom. It's a page-turner in the best sense. You'll need to blast through it because you'll want to know who gets saved, who doesn't make it, and who gets forgiven." — John Mauk, author of *Where All Things Flatten* and *Field Notes for the Earthbound*

Other books by Patricia Boomsma

Flotsam
The Way of Glory

CROSSWIND

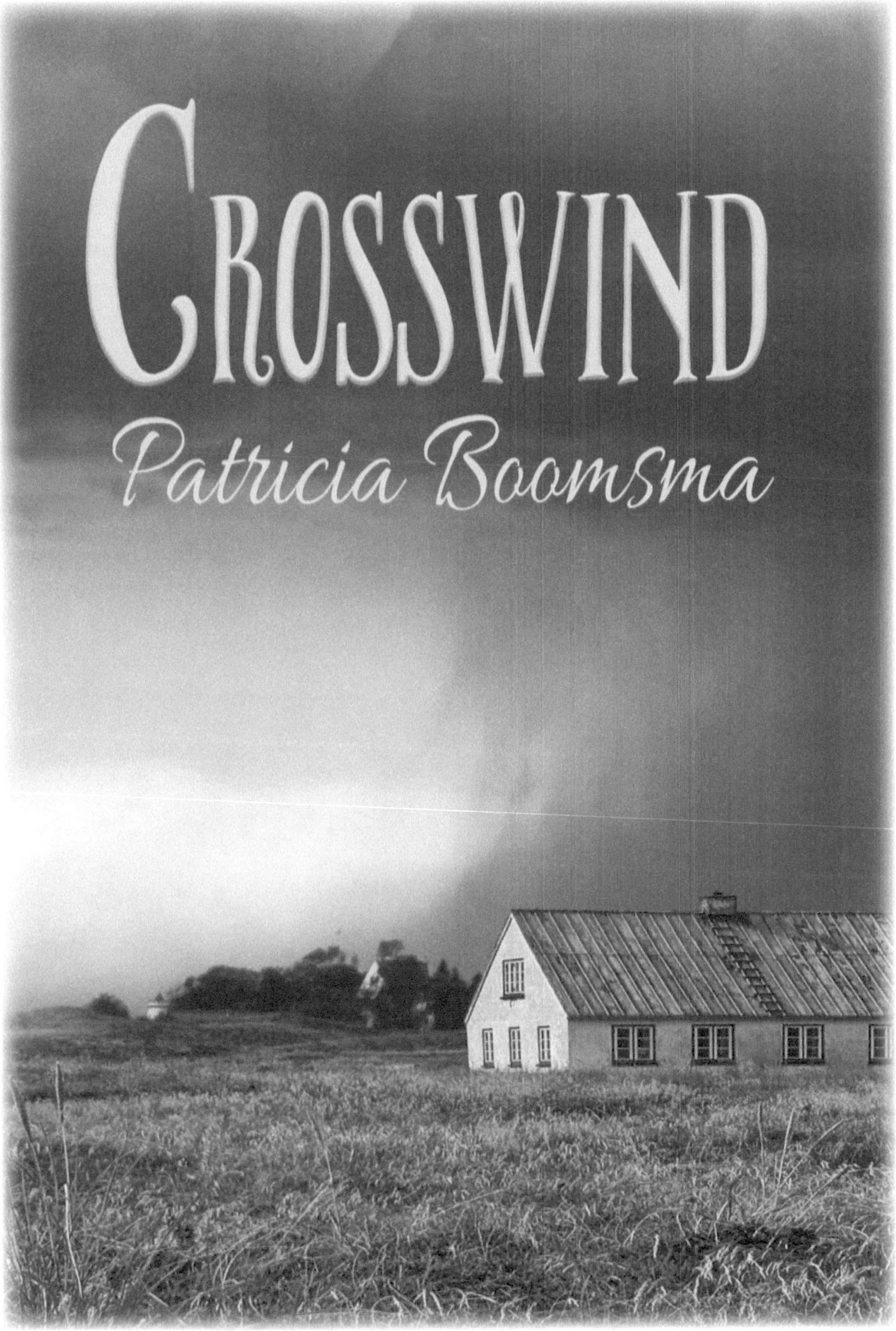

CROSSWIND

Patricia Boomsma

Bink Books

Bedazzled Ink Publishing Company • Fairfield, California

978-1-960373-60-1 paperback

Cover Design
by

Bink Books
a division of
Bedazzled Ink Publishing, LLC
Fairfield, California
http://www.bedazzledink.com

To my chosen family

CHAPTER 1

Amanda

I AWAKE WITH a start, disoriented. The room, the color of the dark, off-kilter. Someone is sleeping in the bed a few feet away. As the fog in my head clears, I recognize my new striped towels draped over a chair and remember. College. Indiana. Fifteen hundred miles from the only place I've ever lived. I relax. No more Mom rifling through my stuff, no more Grandma Beane clucking that dying my hair black doesn't suit me.

Kelsey, my new roommate, hugs her pillow, her long blond hair falling over the edge of her bed. She's tiny and cute and being near her yesterday made me feel huge, awkward, dull. As we unpacked yesterday, my long-sleeved size twelves dwarfed her size two sundresses in the closet, and she fit twice as many jeans and yoga pants in her drawers as I did in mine. When we went to dinner, Kelsey charmed everyone, my mom, the server, the men at the next table, as I nodded and smiled and tried to be sociable. Kelsey wants to teach kindergarten, join the cheerleading squad, volunteer for the local food bank. I almost asked her to explain her plan for world peace.

Ominous thoughts prowl in my half sleep. What was I thinking coming here? I'm going to flunk out. I have no friends. No one will ask me out. The need to calm myself, cut myself, grips me, crushes me, makes my ears ring. But the only razor I have is the electric one Mom bought me. No. I'll be different here. Everything will be fine.

Daytime is better. In the afternoon, I read under the big leafy trees near the fountain and watch people. A skinny guy with a blond ponytail plays his guitar. I fantasize he walks over, sings to me, takes my hand. Kelsey's shown no interest in including me in her plans with her friends from high school and she seems to have a date every night. The busyness once classes start helps, and at night I hang around the dorm lobby with whoever else is avoiding their roommates and the papers they're supposed to write.

On my way to my room after supper the second week, I recognize Felicia from my choir class opening a door down the hall from mine. Felicia's navy beret sits on her kinky light brown hair like a UFO on a tumbleweed. I offer to share the brownies I'd snagged from the cafeteria, and she smiles and invites me in. Piles of books clutter her nightstand, and literary posters fill her side of the room. My favorite is a Great Gatsby poster dominated by enormous eyes behind wire-rimmed glasses. I bet she'd like the Goya poster hanging in my room back home. Mom said it was bad enough to have *Saturn Devouring His Son* hanging in her house, and she refused to let me pack it. "Don't let that be people's first impression of you," she said. It seems like truth to me.

When one of Mom's "care packages" arrives the next day, I bring it to Felicia's room to share its chocolate chip cookies and caramel corn. In her card, Mom reminds me I promised to call her at least once a week. As if I could forget with her constant texting.

Felicia lifts the pair of socks Mom sent with a twenty-dollar bill inside and scrutinizes the rattlesnakes and gila monsters pictured on them. "Are these for real?"

"Yes," I say.

This sends Felicia to her laptop, where we look up images of diamondbacks and sidewinders and the strangely beautiful, beaded lizards.

"How do you live there?" Felicia asks.

"I don't anymore, do I?"

FELICIA WANTS ME to go with her to a party some guy in her math class told her about. She decides my clothes are trendier than hers, so we spend Friday afternoon debating who will wear what. Felicia borrows my oversized blue shirt with black trim but rejects my skinny jeans ("Too tight!") or the patterned wide-legged ones ("Pajamas!"), opting instead for her own yoga pants. She straightens her hair into soft waves. I choose a long-sleeved red-and-black lace dress that hides the scars on my arms.

Wandering students fill the streets near campus after dark, some gravitating toward open doors where loud music pulses, others congregating on the outdoor patios of the many coffee shops and micro-breweries. The streets darken and crowds thin as we near a warehouse, its doors propped open. Light spilling into a crowded parking lot and the driving beat and bass of music welcome us.

More and more people fill the cavernous room until it's hard to move. Someone shouts, "Over here!" and Felicia pushes me toward the voice. She's all smiles and nervous laughter as a tall guy with emo glasses and messy dark hair that curls at his ears hands her a large red cup. Next to him is a shorter, clean-shaven guy with hair that's short on the sides and the middle swoops into a brown wave with white tips. When he smiles, dimples crease his face. His eyes appraise the red bow in my spiked black hair, my dress, my short red boots with black laces. They introduce themselves as Ken and Bert.

"Bert?" I ask.

"The Third." He bows. "Your first kegger?"

"In college," I say.

While Ken and Felicia flirt with each other, Bert points out the frat boys and sorority girls and tells me which Greeks throw the best parties and which are known for studying or style. The music is deafening, the beat dominating any lyrics or melody. Someone hands me a beer. One sip of the bitter, skunk-smelling stuff is enough.

Bert suggests we go outside, so the four of us push our way to the door and lose our red plastic cups on a window ledge. A police cruiser pulls into the parking lot. We hustle to the street as officers start checking IDs.

Giddy with relief, we recount other narrow escapes at past parties.

"So, this one time," Bert says, "My friend Screech . . ."

"You had a friend named Screech?" I ask, laughing.

"Yeah, yeah. He had a weird voice, and somebody decided he reminded them of that kid in *Saved by the Bell*. Anyway,"

"Did he have curly hair?"

Felicia and Ken slow down a bit.

"Hey, let me tell my story," Bert says.

I pretend to zip my mouth.

"Screech's parents went away to Florida, so he invites all these people over. There are cars lining the block and he plays the music loud and all the popular kids have decided why not, let's check this out."

I nod. I think I've been to this party.

"So, everybody gets there, but Screech doesn't have any booze or dope . . ."

I must have been at a different party.

" . . . and the football guys call him lame and the girls roll their eyes, and everybody leaves taking their six packs and spliffs with them. And Screech yells in his weird high voice, 'Buuuddeeees.'"

"Was that when people started calling him Screech?" I ask.

"Might have been," Bert says. "Anyway, the neighbors called the cops, but everybody was gone so fast by the time the cops came it was just me and him sitting on lawn chairs in the back, drinking Mountain Dew. They looked at us, said 'Keep the sound down boys,' and left."

"What was his real name?" I ask.

"Did you even get the point of this story?" Bert asks, laughing.

"There was a point?"

"Look at him," Bert says as a skinny guy with a long braid cycles past. "Sixties are over, buddy."

"Yeah, get a man bun, loser." I can't stop laughing.

Felicia frowns at me and pulls me aside. "Are you drunk?"

I find this hilarious too. "No. Bert makes me laugh. I can't help it."

Felicia and Ken put distance between us. When we get to campus, they announce they are going for a walk. Bert recites his favorite Stephen Colbert riffs as we head for the Union.

"You haven't asked me my major yet," I say.

"Oh, so sorry. What's your major?"

"I don't know," I say, and we both laugh. "What's yours?"

"Astrophysics," he says, suddenly somber.

"Really?"

"God no," he says. "But it sounds impressive, doesn't it?"

After several cups of remarkably strong coffee, I tell Bert I should head back. He helps me into my jacket. He opens the doors for me. Inside the lobby, he takes my hand and tells me how much fun he's had. I wait for him to ask for my phone number or to suggest doing something later, but he walks out.

At breakfast the next morning, I ask Felicia if her evening turned out as she hoped.

"Yes," she says, reddening.

"Bert was great," I say.

"Ken says he prefers guys," Felicia says. "Just so you know."

I'm disappointed and happy at the same time. "He's still fun."

It bothers me they were talking about me. It bothers me Bert didn't tell me himself. It bothers me I may never see him again. Fuck that. "Can you get me his number anyway?"

That afternoon Bert calls and asks me to go to the old movie night in the Union. *Bill and Ted's Excellent Adventure.*

"Party on, dude," I say.

"Excellent," he says.

"Why didn't you tell me?"

"If you haven't noticed, this is a conservative place. I had one girl send me conversion therapy pamphlets."

"I admit to being disappointed. I hope you take that as a compliment."

"If you mean it that way, I'll take it that way."

"Are you seeing someone?"

"No. Like I said, it's a conservative place. I don't get invited to many frat parties."

"Fuck them."

"I wish," he says, and starts into a riff of John Belushi and *Animal House.* I wonder if his parents have stacks of DVDs of old movies like my dad does and feel sorry for those whose film history begins with *Superbad.* Kelsey's favorite movie.

BERT IS FUN, and he never judges my dates until after somebody ghosts or stops calling me. Then he lets me rant about how "I was good enough for him last Friday but now he doesn't call," or makes jokes ("He had a man-bun? You're better than that"), or demands I attend the latest old movie the engineers are showing at their lecture hall for two dollars. I help him with his profile on Grindr, and he takes my picture for Tinder, then sweeps left on all my matches.

Besides old movies, we bond over our parents. His dad "doesn't want to hear about it," and his mom gets way too excited when Bert tells her about a female friend. "Bring her over for dinner, we'd love to meet her," his mom said when he mentioned me. I tell him about my mom's constantly wanting a phone call or an email, and how my dad never does. "Which is better?" he asks. I shrug. All I know is Mom enrages me more.

"She doesn't even like me," I say. "She said that once. Said if I wasn't her daughter, she wouldn't like me much."

"What had you done?" Bert asks.

"Yes, okay, she was mad about something when she said it, but, really, if you don't like me, you can't love me either. That's how it works."

Bert says nothing.

I don't say I'm a little hurt at Dad's silence since I started school. At least he trusts me. I never worried about hiding my pot at his house. He never searched my room, or checked my phone, or read the stories on my laptop. Even after the school nurse called to tell him about the cuts and burn marks on my arms, all he said was "Don't do that," while Mom went crazy and cried and made me go to counseling. Like I'd ever tell my secrets to a stranger she hired.

When I tell Bert I was a cutter in high school, he looks at me sadly and shows me some burn marks on his thigh.

"Promise me if you think about cutting again, you'll call me," Bert says. "I'll talk you down."

"OK. You promise me too," I say.

"I promise," he says, giving me a quick hug.

Someone tags Bert and me in a picture on Facebook, and that night Mom calls, asking if I'd met anyone special. "Lots of people," I tell her. Let her guess.

CHAPTER 2

Susan

THE HOUSE FEELS different with Mandy gone. Quieter. Emptier. Calmer. Not like when she was staying at Tony's. Those days were times to read and pick up the clothes and dirty towels in her room and make ready for the day she would burst into the house and fill the kitchen table with her laptop and assignments. It's been a month now, and I'm not sure what to do with my new-found freedom after so many years of organizing my life around her.

I hate it.

I call Corey. She sympathizes for about five minutes before saying we need to set up a birthday happy hour. Fifty-one, I think, how can that be?

"Karaoke?" I ask.

"No way," Corey says. "No one will come."

By the afternoon, Corey arranges for us to meet Hallie and Brenda Friday night after work. We clerked at the appellate court when I first moved to Phoenix, arguing legal issues during long afternoons of research, getting to know Phoenix as we looked for new lunch places during the day and happy hours after work. After two years, we scattered. Corey and I ended up at one of the bigger firms, Hallie went to a small firm before starting her own, and Brenda went to the County. We saw even less of each other once Corey stopped being a lawyer and I switched firms and got so busy with Mandy I had time for little else. We tried to get together for birthdays at least, and they helped me through many rough times, like my divorce. They helped me move, invited me for Thanksgiving so I didn't need to be alone when it was Tony's turn with Mandy. Laughed at my dating fiascoes. I'm not sure I would have survived without them.

We meet at the rooftop bar at Ruth's Chris. Hallie had grabbed a table near a fireplace in case it got cold once the sun set. I got there second, so we had time to commiserate about our teenage daughters.

"I miss Mandy," I say. "But it is nice not to feel like I'm doing something wrong every minute. Is that awful?"

"God, no," Hallie says. "I'd like a break once in a while from the sour looks and the fear when she's late."

Corey arrives and sits next to me on the couch. "Happy Birthday, beautiful. How're you holding up?"

"Good."

Brenda joins us as the waiter delivers our margaritas. She grins when she sees we've ordered one for her. She drops a pink bag on the table in front of me and kisses my cheek.

"I thought we agreed no presents," I say.

Brenda shrugs. "Sue me. It's something I got at the shore this summer. No big deal. Open it later."

Corey complains how her new guy, Steve, doesn't seem to know when to go home. Brenda and Hallie laugh a lot, complain how their husbands ignore them until they want a Friday night with us. I try my best to make light of the drama at work, Mandy's joy at leaving, the guy on the internet dating site who sent me a picture of his hairy chest. Brenda says she's not sure she'd date again if she and Andy broke up. I tell her I'm not sure why I keep trying. I guess there's a part of me that still hopes.

Corey and I order food once Hallie and Brenda leave to make supper for their husbands.

"How are you really?" Corey asks.

"It's weird being all alone in the house," I say.

She nods. "Maybe you should get a dog? Having Cole around helps me, gets me to take a walk every day."

I smile thinking about Cole, her goofy lab-border collie mix shivering in delight whenever I, or anyone, visits. He's sure we're there for him and Corey is a distraction. Corey runs with him. Probably how she stays so thin as I put on the pounds year after year.

"I don't have your energy," I say. "I'm at work all hours and go out of town a lot. I think I'd be a bad dog mom."

Corey scoffs. "So get a lap dog. I'll watch her when you go out of town."

"Maybe," I say.

Corey gives me a sideways look. "Then let's find you a man. Tonight."

Dread fills me. "I'd rather hang out with you."

Corey piles our plates and stuffs birthday cards into the pink bag. "I know you're doing the internet thing, but it's fun to catch someone's eye and not just be all what books do you read and do you check the right boxes on my list. How about we start with a nice quiet place, move on to someplace more hopping next week?"

I groan inside, but maybe she's right. "OK."

Corey tells me to meet her at a quiet bar she knows along Scottsdale Road. When I arrive, the place is dim, the only bright lights in the center over the bar that forms a rectangle in the middle of the room. Booths line the windows and I sit in the first one I see.

"For this to work, we have to sit at the bar," she says when she appears.

"Can I fortify myself first?"

"One glass of wine, then we move."

I nod. Anything to put this off.

Before we order, the waiter places a glass of white wine in front of each of us, small bubbles rising in the glass. "The gentlemen at the bar hope you like Prosecco," the waiter says.

Corey raises her glass to the smiling men. "We do."

What do I say to them? What could I possibly have in common with strangers bold enough to offer a drink to two women at a bar?

They introduce themselves, and the shorter, darker one sits next to me. His name is Stan. He says he's a property developer, and part of me wonders if I can bill this as client development. He likes to talk, so I let him tell me about the unreasonable demands a city is making, requiring fire sprinklers and gray water systems. He's friendly. Self-assured. Nice looking and fit. Well-dressed in a pressed shirt, khakis, loafers. I can't seem to make myself interested.

After a half hour, they invite us to go somewhere else, a different bar or one of their places. Corey looks at me, a question in her eyes.

"I'm sorry, I need to get home," I say.

"Yes, me too," Corey says.

They don't ask for our numbers. I don't give him my business card.

Corey calls as we drive away. "They seemed nice enough," she says.

"I wasn't feeling it," I say.

"No matter. Practice is always good."

I put on my nightgown when I get home and turn on Netflix, finally able to relax.

I TOLD MYSELF I wouldn't look for online dates anymore, but here I am scanning pictures again. Online dating is a series of humiliations. First you have to put up a "profile" with a catchy phrase and a picture that will attract attention. The right kind of attention, so a face shot with me in a plain blue blouse that matches the color of my eyes, my recently highlighted hair in a smooth bob, wearing a camel blazer to show I'm a serious person. I got more emails when I took my job off the profile. Lawyers make people nervous, I guess.

Corey talked me into it, says it's how she met Steve, and despite her complaining, he seems like a good guy. "Expand your horizons," Corey says. I can't date clients or coworkers even if they ever asked. Which they haven't. I could go to church, but it seems disrespectful to use church to find dates when my doubts about, well, everything overwhelm my belief that something other than mere chance or natural selection accounts for the universe. And "one way"? God, if there is one that pays attention to whether I have the flu or who takes away the love of my life to teach me some unknown lesson, must be bigger than that. And yet, every church I've ever been to says theirs is the true and complete and only way, and I can't keep my doubts to myself for long.

Looking online is easier than going to places hoping to exchange glances with a stranger like that night at the bar with Corey. The anonymity is nice, not too risky. A guy sends me a naked picture? No thanks. Too many spelling mistakes? Get spell check, loser. Doesn't have a favorite book? Next. I know the guys have their own deal-breaker lists, although I have no idea what they might be.

A week later, I'm getting ready for another first date, having made it through the gauntlet of picture-swapping and emails. Al's emails were funny and self-deprecating and grammatically correct. He said he works at HealthCo, although he was vague about his job. No naked selfies. His favorite books are the Harry Bosch novels. I haven't read them, but if this works out I will. I like a good mystery.

I should be more excited. All I feel is dread.

What is wrong with me? Fifty-one and going on a first date when I should be, I don't know, seeing the world or writing the Great American Novel. No, I should be married and discussing with my doting husband where we'll live in our retirement. Calculating how much we'll need and when we can quit the daily grind. Instead, I'm buying Spanx and considering Botox. Ridiculous.

I take a selfie and send it to Corey. The long, loose sleeves and swirly red colors of my tunic top disguise most of the bulges. That and the Spanx. I scrutinize my makeup. Is it too much? I usually stick to a little face powder and lip gloss, but tonight I went all out: mascara, eyeliner, concealer, foundation, and a bright red lipstick that matches my shirt. I feel like a clown. How do people do this every day?

Corey texts, "Looking good!" She sends a picture of her dog with his tongue hanging out. "Cole agrees."

Should I wear perfume? I never wear perfume. Some people are allergic to perfume. I spray a quick spritz of my newly purchased *Coco* and walk through it. Can't put it on my skin, it makes me itch.

I arrive early, so sit in my car listening to Sarah McLachlan. I open the window a crack and the smell of diesel from the freeway rushes in. A nearby movie theater's neon signs draw laughing people toward its wide doors. I realize when I start pulling on my cuticles that Sarah's making me even more anxious than I am already, so turn on the oldies station and smile when I hear "Devil with a Blue Dress." When it finishes, I take a deep breath, open the car door, and dawdle toward the OPEN sign flashing in the window. I'd suggested a coffee shop, but Al wanted a bar. This pizza place was the compromise.

I look at the tables near the door, not sure I'd recognize Al. The only pictures I've seen are the two on his profile: a head shot that looks like an employee ID and a blurry one where he's standing in front of a Harley. The restaurant is small with metal tables. I'm not sure what the point of the candles is, but maybe they turn the lights down later. A young woman in a red apron rushes toward me.

"Is anyone waiting?" I ask.

"No. Would you like a table or to wait here?"

"I'll wait," I say.

Too jumpy to sit, I read the menu then examine the mural of an Italian cafe, the top lined with balconied windows and out-of-perspective tables served by waiters in tuxedos. I look around. No tuxedos here. This restaurant has a more industrial vibe. Out of the corner of my eye, I see a man outside looking in. It's dark outside and light in here, so I know I'm more visible to him than he is to me. He soon leaves.

I wave at the hostess, and she seats me at a booth with a view of the door and a promise to seat Al when he arrives. He hasn't texted to say he's running late, and doubt blooms as the seconds click by. I run through our emails in my mind. I was honest. The pictures were from last spring, not three or more years ago as I suspect his were. I'm not particularly photogenic, so I think I look better in person. The restaurant voyeur couldn't have been him, could it?

After half an hour, I order a glass of wine and a pizza for one. May as well, I don't feel like cooking. I console myself that at least this is an improvement over the guy who made me pay for dinner and fell asleep at the show for which he later admitted he'd received free tickets. And the one who borrowed one of my DVDs then didn't show up for our next date and never answered my emails or texts. I close my eyes to stop thinking about all these little indignities.

Happy hour with my friends was so much fun, laughing, talking, remembering. Easy, relaxing. Women have always been more support to me than any man has ever been. More forgiving of my oddities, my gaining weight, the stupid things I sometimes say. Maybe it's enough.

Corey calls from the car on her way to work the next morning. "How'd it go?"

"Not so great," I say. "He never showed."

"Bastard," Corey says when I explain how he may have taken one look at me and left. "Let's go somewhere Friday night. Rebuild your self-confidence."

"I need a break, Corey. And I need to get the house ready. Mandy's coming home for Thanksgiving."

"Sounds like avoidance to me," she says.

"Might be," I say.

CHAPTER 3

Amanda

AFTER THANKSGIVING BREAK, Felicia begs me to come with her to a Messiah singalong.

"There must be a party somewhere," I say, "something better than joining a lot of people singing loudly off-key."

"C'mon. I went last year, and it was fun, put me in the holiday spirit."

"Didn't our choir's Christmas concert do that?" I ask.

"That was last week," she says.

I can't believe the line to get into the Student Center. None of my friends in Phoenix would even consider this, and here we are in the cold on an icy sidewalk with probably three hundred other people. Inside, students hand us single sheet programs. I buy a score from the tables off to the side, even though Felicia says we can share. I like to hold my own music.

"Now you can sing at home," Felicia says. "Messiah karaoke."

A man in a clerical collar directs us to sections: men in the center, sopranos to the right, altos to the left. We go left but pick seats as close to the center as we can. I wave at two guys from University Choir. I elbow Felicia, and she waves too.

"They're sort of cute," Felicia says. "Let's happen to bump into them after."

"What are their names?"

"Connor's the one with the glasses, and I think the other guy's name is Tim," she says.

"Dibs on Tim."

"Works for me."

The auditorium is a hum of voices punctuated by laughter and voice-clearing. I side-eye Connor and Tim as they page through their scores. Tim's uneven brown hair keeps falling in his eyes as he bends over the music, while Connor pushes his wire-rimmed glasses up to the bridge of his nose every time he looks up to watch the orchestra tune. They seem nice. I'm pretty sure it will never work out with me and Tim.

The orchestra and choir stand and clap as the conductor walks in, elegant in his tails, red cummerbund, and red bow tie. Three giggling girls come in late, and they want to sit in our row. We try to shift, but there's only room for one, so they try the next row and the next until they've distracted everyone.

The conductor turns to face us.

"That's it for the ritual, folks. This is a sing-along! Let me introduce our soloists and tell you how this will work."

The conductor lifts his program.

"Our Community Choir is here as backup, but don't be afraid to join in. This is supposed to be fun! Laugh if you want. Sing as loud as you want. There will be no recordings."

I laugh with everyone. Maybe this won't be so excruciating after all.

The overture is glorious, drawing me in with joy and expectation. How had I never heard this? So much better than the Nutcracker my parents took me to every year until they split. Halfway through the tenor's solo, my eyes tear. Felicia has my hand. I glance toward the center of the room and see a man I don't know looking at me. He gives me a crooked smile when I catch his eye, then turns back to his score. He seems self-assured, older than most of us, and has the most wonderful face I have ever seen. Dark eyes, dark hair falling over his high forehead, a narrow face with a short beard, and full, eminently kissable lips. I feel a different kind of anticipation, and when it's our turn, I sing my heart out.

I'm light-headed when the final "Amen" crashes to its finish. I need to get up now, I tell my dazed legs as the women down my row stare at me in frustration. I let go of Felicia's hand, trying to appear like a normal person. Felicia slows down as Connor and Tim approach, but I want to find the beautiful man. Did I imagine him?

"A bunch of us are going caroling on the way to Starbucks," Connor says. "Would you like to join us?"

"Yes," Felicia says, and I smile.

"I thought caroling was only in movies," I whisper to Felicia as we join the group.

"Welcome to Indiana," she whispers back. "Think of it as an impromptu flash mob."

It snowed while we were inside, enough to outline the bushes and cars in white and slick the sidewalks. I feel cozy and cute in my new fluffy sweater with a big-eyed owl on the front, the long, hooded red coat I got at Thanksgiving, and the UGG boots Dad bought me. Having doting, contrite parents is nice sometimes. As we slide our way from house to house, our group of singers grows, and I find myself next to the beautiful man. This close, I notice his long dark lashes and knowing eyes, and a few lighter hairs at his temple underneath his knit cap.

The people around us sing and laugh. We know all the words to five songs and the first verses to several others, so we repeat those over and over, some singers adding a new harmony or descant, mostly badly. Sometimes a deep bass voice tries to start something new, and if we catch the tune, we tra-la-la along. Eventually we end up at a coffee shop, where someone pays for us all.

"I'm Philip," the beautiful man says as I stand at the condiment counter adding extra cream and a shake of vanilla to my cup. A rush of warmth runs through me as he stands close, reaching for the napkins. "You have a lovely voice."

"Thank you, Philip, so do you. I'm Amanda."

Philip pulls off his gloves and stuffs them in the pocket of his navy pea coat. "Where are you from, Amanda?"

"Arizona. Phoenix. You?"

"Near here. Hebron." He holds out his hand. "Nice to meet you, Amanda from Arizona."

I take off my mitten and reach for his hand, slightly dizzy from his quick touch. I've never had such an immediate attraction to anyone. I want to throw my arms around him and bury my face in the fuzzy blue scarf wrapped around his neck, but I keep myself together and try to smile. "Me too, Philip from Hebron. You can join us if you'd like."

We make our way through the crowd. Felicia looks at me questioningly as I introduce them. Philip seems so much more mature, so much more attractive than Tim. There are no empty chairs, so we stand until Philip snags a couch near the door. Occasionally someone sings, and the baristas join in. The crowd is noisy and hearing each other difficult, but it gives me an excuse to sit close and for him to talk into my ear. His breath against my skin is overwhelming even if all he's talking about is a farm he lives on. Mostly he asks questions, and I try to make Phoenix summers seem funny and my parents' divorce no big deal.

It seems too soon when Felicia comes to say they're heading back.

"I live in Quimby dorm, the one closest to the Union, if you're ever near there. And my last name is Beane."

"See you around," he says. There's a promise in his eyes that makes me catch my breath.

"Who was that?" Felicia asks once we split from Connor and Tim. "And what happened to dibs on Tim? You left me stranded."

"I'm sorry," I say. "Philip was by himself. And gorgeous."

"He seems a little old."

"Really?" I say, not caring.

PHILIP CALLS MY room from the lobby the next Thursday. I quickly comb my hair, frown, and grab a hat, hoping I look stylish instead of goofy. I put on my jeans, a long crochet sweater over my t-shirt. A few small scars show through the open weave of the sweater. I'll keep my coat on.

Be cool, Amanda, I think. Be cool.

Philip wears the same navy pea coat he wore the night of caroling, and his beard is carefully trimmed. My skin prickles when I see him smile.

"It's exam week, isn't it?" he asks. "Thought you might need a break and some coffee."

"Aren't you a student?"

"I graduated," he says.

"And what do you do now? I'm sorry if you've told me already. It was noisy."

His smile is generous. Kind. "I live and work on a farm. An organic farm with sustainable farming practices, thank you very much."

"Sounds exciting. Must have a lot of free time in the winter."

"More than in the spring, for sure, but there's plenty to do in the winter. We have cows. Cows need year-round attention."

"So, not a vegetarian organic farm with sustainable farming practices," I say.

"No," he admits.

"My grandfather was sort of a farmer. He had a couple of acres of flowers and produce he sold at a stand and to restaurants, but no cows. Summer was his slow time. It's too hot in Phoenix to do much besides sit in the pool."

"Would you like to see the farm sometime?" Philip asks. "Not now–too much snow, and not much to see other than the cows. But when we start planting?"

"I would love that!" I particularly love that he's planning to see me in the spring.

Students staring at their laptops, sorting through photocopies, drinking huge cups of coffee, looking tired and stressed, fill the Union. As we walk toward the line, several people wave at Philip, and a short, burly, gray-haired man stops to ask him about how his animals are handling the cold. I am impressed by how many people he knows, and how few I do.

"How long did you study here?" I ask as I dump a second sugar in my cup.

We head to the only open table, near a door that sends a freezing blast toward me when someone opens it.

"It took me five years to graduate. I worked the whole time, so took it slower than some do," he says. "And besides, who wants to leave college and work full time?"

I laugh. I'm laughing too much. Stop it. "Not me. Is it your family's farm?"

"No, I live with a group of friends out in the County. We all work the farm."

I sense there's more to this story but know it's too soon to pry for details about who he lives with and why.

"And what are you studying?" he asks.

"I'm undeclared," I say, "but I'm leaning toward history."

"Ah, a practical degree," he says, bending toward me, his hand on the table.

"You sound like my mom," I say, leaning in and holding my cup loosely with both hands. "In high school I thought about pre-med. Doesn't everyone? But my grades aren't good enough."

"I thought this was your first year. How can you know that?"

"Midterms."

"What about vet school?"

"It's even harder to get into vet school."

"Probably right," he says. "Everybody wants to take care of puppies."

"And kitties and rabbits," I say. "Cows, not so much."

"Sweetest, stupidest animals in the world," he says.

He's still smiling. Good. I haven't offended him yet.

We talk for what seems like ten minutes, but when I check the big clock on the wall, it's been two hours.

"Whoa," I say. "I need to get back to studying."

He springs up. "I'll walk you back."

Outside the dorm, he takes my hand, and its warmth runs through my body. "When are you leaving for winter break?"

"Next Wednesday."

"May I call you?"

"I'd like that," I say, and we exchange mobile numbers.

He gives me a quick hug. "Have a great Christmas, Amanda from Arizona."

I put my cheek next to his. His beard is softer than I expected. "You too, Philip from Hebron."

CHAPTER 4

Susan

I TRY TO evade the doubt and dread that fill my nights as I lie in bed unable to sleep, but they always surface. I'm failing at work. At motherhood. At life. My life is small. Tony's gone. Mandy's gone. I knew she'd get busy at school, and she's only been away three months, but I didn't know I'd feel so abandoned.

I should read, but can't make myself interested in the large pile of books on my nightstand. Sometimes I long for the forgetfulness age is supposed to bring. These days almost anything can trigger a memory or a regret. A red car. A bird calling. The smell of water. On sleepless nights I want only pleasant memories. The fun of college, the exhilaration of meeting Tony, the day Mandy was born. The ones that will let me rest.

What has happened to me? I used to laugh. A lot. Could make other people laugh. People I'd meet would tell me their life stories, and I would comfort them. Now I fill my days with the busyness of work and laundry and my once-in-a-while book club where hardly anyone reads the book. I should join a gym or a real book club or a choir. Invite people over. Take a trip.

Next week.

I hope Mandy is having fun, has met someone.

Mandy.

How did we end up this way?

I remember making excuses when Tony's absences grew longer and more frequent, telling Mandy how hard Daddy worked. I ended up being the one who had to tell her we were separating, the coward. She refused to believe me, blamed me, accused me.

I remember the awful trip to my parents to tell them.

Trips to Chicago were a highlight of my year after Mandy was born. Grandma and Grandpa took her to the park, to the zoo, to the oceanarium. We had dessert every night, and I never had to cook. But that year before the divorce all I felt was panic. Mom and Dad wouldn't understand. Would say marriage was for life and I must do whatever it took to keep my marriage together.

I sat at my parents' kitchen table the day we arrived, trying to figure out what to say while my dad read the Bible and prayed. A grackle looked at me through the window, reproach in its yellow-eyed stare. I lowered my eyes when I recognized the familiar refrain to his prayer.

"Susie, stay and talk with me a while," Mom said when Dad finished. "The dishes can wait."

Mandy rushed from the table with her cousin Nadine, intent on getting back to whatever secrets twelve-year-old girls share.

"Amanda Sue," I said. "Bring your dishes to the sink."

Mandy looked at Nadine and rolled her eyes. They goose-stepped to the sink with their plates and glasses, dropped them with a thud, giggled, and ran off, bursting through the screen door.

"Any coffee left?" Dad growled as he rumbled toward the kitchen.

Mom rose and patted my hand. "I'll be right back. You want any?"

I shook my head and lifted my cup to show her I still had some.

"How's Tony?" Mom asked when she sat.

"Busy," I said. Tony never came on the annual trip to visit my parents, and "busy" was always the reason. I hesitated. "We're getting a divorce."

Mom stiffened and took my hand, the smile she had since Mandy and I walked in the door now gone.

"This can't be a surprise, right?" I asked. "You commented he was gone a lot the last time you were in Phoenix."

Mom dabbed the corners of her eyes with her napkin. "I was hoping all that counseling would have helped."

"It did," I said, scraping a tiny blue flower on the worn vinyl tablecloth with my ragged fingernails. "We know we can't work it out."

"Have you told Mandy?" she whispered.

I nodded, tears filling my eyes. "She won't talk about it. Says she doesn't believe me."

Mom sat back against the wooden slats of her chair, looking suddenly old, the soft wrinkles around her eyes sagging and her manicured steel-gray hair bending where she twisted it around her finger. Silence filled the room. I felt like I was suffocating.

"It's my fault, isn't it?" she said, tears now streaming down her cheeks.

"What? No. Why would you say that?"

"You don't want to end up like me."

True, but Tony's and my problems were nothing like my mom's and dad's. I didn't know what to say.

"I complained too much," she continued. "I was a bad example of a wife. I'm sorry."

She wiped her eyes, got up, collected plates and silverware. I followed her to the sink and rinsed the dishes while she put them into the dishwasher, both of us pausing often to wipe our eyes and noses with our sleeves.

I looked out the window over the sink into the backyard. Dad sat on a lawn chair in the middle of a large swath of grass, smoking a cigar and reading. Strands of his thinning white hair moved in the wind, exposing the bald spot he so carefully tried to hide.

"I guess I should talk with him," I said.

Mom nodded and dried her hands as I went outside.

I put a lawn chair next to Dad's, both of us facing the church my family attended all my life. It was a typical summer afternoon in the Midwest—hot, sticky, a little windy. On the telephone wires three black birds shimmered purple and green and squawked.

"Tony and I are getting a divorce," I said. "I don't expect you to approve, but I hope you can accept that."

Dad chewed the stub of his cigar. He put his rough palm on my hand. The brown spots on his crumpled skin stretched as he squeezed my hand. "If you believe divorce is the only solution, then I support you."

I'm shocked. I expected a lecture on the sanctity of marriage. "Thank you."

"Maybe he's hit you."

"Never! That's not it," I interrupted.

"Marriage is hard. Your mother and I have our problems, but we're from the old school. People from the church will criticize; so what? It's none of their business. People can always find reasons to criticize. If you need money, tell me."

We sat silently, my mind racing between relief and disbelief. Who is this man? I wondered.

I stared at the cracked asphalt in the church parking lot. I could think of nothing worth saying, nothing that would make him understand how I felt lonelier now than I ever had. How simmering anger and rejection filled the house. How afraid I was of the example we were to Mandy. I decided to be glad he'd chosen to be forgiving. Hell, I don't understand, how could I explain it to him?

When I came in the back door, Mom stood by the sink. She turned to look at me, her eyes glassy. Mandy and Nadine burst into the room, holding hands and laughing.

Mandy stopped when she saw us and dropped Nadine's hand. She looked first at Grandma, then at me. Her smile turned into a grimace.

"I hate you," she said, stabbing me with the glare of her narrowed eyes. She pushed Nadine toward the door and rushed outside.

My chest aches as the memory fills me with grief. I won't get much sleep tonight.

ANTICIPATION MAKES ME smile at everyone who passes as I wait at the airport for Mandy to arrive the week before Christmas. Holiday travelers crowd the terminal. The usually empty gift shops are doing a brisk business. Mandy's plane is late, so I buy a cappuccino and wait on the black vinyl-and-chrome chairs outside the airport security line, close enough to check the Arrival boards every couple of minutes. Flashes of Christmases past keep intruding, buffeting me with fear and hope. The happy times when Mandy was young and tearing open each brightly colored package. The last Christmas we spent as a family with Tony's silences and my anxiety and Mandy pretending nothing had changed. The bad times after the divorce when Mandy said she didn't "do" Christmas anymore.

I glimpse Mandy's Mickey Mouse roller bag breaking through a knot of slow-moving white-haired women. Her purple-streaked hair is flat on one side, its length hidden by her green and gray striped scarf. She looks tired, then wary when she sees me. She almost trips when two little girls rush past her toward a woman in a wheelchair being pushed by an airport employee.

"Welcome home, Mandy," I say, hugging her. "I've missed you."

"Amanda, OK, Mom?" she says.

"Sorry. Welcome home, Amanda." She'd decided last summer that heretofore she would be called Amanda. When I asked why, she said because she was not that innocent and naïve Mandy anymore. I'd asked her if I could call her "Moon Unit" instead.

I can make her laugh sometimes.

The sun blinds us as we pull out of the parking garage.

"There's a pair of sunglasses in the glove box," I say to no response.

"How were your exams?" I ask after a long silence.

"OK."

I search wildly through my brain, trying to figure out what might get her to talk, that won't offend her, that she'll see as supportive or interesting. I've got nothing. If I ask about her dad, she'll think I'm criticizing him. If I ask her what happened since the last time we talked on the phone, she'll decide it's a rebuke. If I ask about her roommate, she'll say she's told me already.

"I'm staying at Dad's," she says as I drive past the exit to his house.

What? When did that decision get made? And why am I picking her up if she's staying with him? "I thought you were staying with me," is all I say as I get off at the next exit.

Silence.

"When will you be coming to my house?"

"I'm not splitting my time, if that's what you're asking."

I try to stay calm as the voice in my head screams.

"Christmas Eve?" I say in my calm, lawyer voice.

"We'll see."

I will not let her see me cry.

"If I'm not going to see you on Christmas, I need to make other plans. I can't be alone on Christmas. You know that." Memories of that first Christmas after the divorce come flooding back. Looking at the empty tree, its colored lights mocking me. Crying when my mom called to say Merry Christmas.

I park in Tony's driveway. A familiar pang of anger and regret slams into me. This used to be my house. I drove around with the agent, found it, decorated it, left it when he refused. I admire the huge clay pots it took so long to find and silently criticize him for the dead plants.

Mandy hands me her wallet, a hairbrush, a wad of tissues out of her purse as she searches for her key.

"How about dinner tonight?" I say. "We can go out or I can cook."

"Not tonight. I need to sleep. Let's meet tomorrow after work?"

"OK. Sixish?"

She nods, and I hug her. As I drive away, I pull a tissue out of my purse and smash it against my eyes when the road becomes too blurry.

At home, all is dark and silent. I throw my keys on the kitchen table and turn on every light I pass. I should have flown to Chicago for Christmas. Let Mom make all my favorite cookies and smile whenever I enter the room. Be with somebody who wants to be with me. I refuse to open Facebook with its pictures of friends and relatives with their smiling kids and grandkids, all their talk about how great it is to see everyone at this happy time of year. Does anyone else have a daughter who hates her? Not if you believe everybody's posts or Christmas letters. For my Christmas card I included a picture of

Mandy as a toddler in front of the tree opening presents and say: "Mandy's coming home!"

We were happy once.

I nuke a single-serve microwave meal from the freezer and take it outside to sit by the pool. I watch a brown leaf drift toward the side. Such an adventure it was moving here from the Midwest. Like a foreign country. Tony and I built a house on what seemed the edge of civilization, nothing but sandy dirt and tumbleweeds behind us, flat until a black rock mountain cast its shadow toward us. Every morning I watched the play of sun and shadows against the mountain, and every evening the colors of the sunset made me stop whatever I was doing and watch, amazed at the size of the sky. I remember a beautiful spring day, pillows of cloud careening in the sky, pregnant me sitting on a lawn chair as Tony sat on the steps smiling at me. My life is perfect, I thought. In the summer, dust storms would engulf us, dropping a thin layer of red on our patio furniture and drifting somehow under the doors or through the windows. We had to be vigilant to sweep the black widows and scorpions from Mandy's play areas.

Year by year, the desert receded, replaced by houses and lawns and engineered washes, the cacti placed to enhance the desert look without compromising sight triangles. Year by year our lives became routine, and the silences grew.

I want a cigarette, but not badly enough to leave the house. I quit before Mandy was born, but the desire still haunts me. Especially when I'm sad or lonely or anxious. So, lately, a lot.

I call Corey instead.

"Hi," Corey says. "I was going to call, but thought you'd be hanging out with Mandy."

"She's staying at Tony's." I burst into tears.

"Aw, honey, I know how much you were looking forward to this. Want me to come over?"

"Yes, please. And bring cigarettes."

"You got it."

Tony's mom calls to say they are having all the cousins and aunts and uncles over on Christmas Eve, and they want Tony and Amanda over Christmas Day too. They say I can come to either or both. They seem irritated when I suggest I'd like to spend time alone with Mandy. Tony calls a little later, but I don't pick up. Then Mandy calls.

"Hey, Mom. Grandma says you don't want to come to their party. Dad wants you to know he gets it, and it wasn't his idea. He says he wishes he had a good excuse to skip it."

"I saw he called. I was afraid he'd tell me I had to go 'for your sake.'"

"You don't get him at all, do you?"

"Will you be coming over either day?"

"Yeah. Dad will be spending Christmas day with Paige, his new girlfriend. He'll drop me off Christmas Eve after the party and then pick me up on the way to his parents' house Christmas night. Does that work?"

"It does," I say, hopeful again. "Want to go to church in the morning? Always lots of singing on Christmas day."

"No thanks. I'd rather sleep in."

"OK, see you tomorrow, sweetheart."

Corey arrives with a bottle of wine, a carton of ice cream, and a pack of cigarettes. We listen to the Rolling Stones, watch *Saturday Night Fever*, try out our disco moves and sing "Staying Alive" after a few glasses of wine.

THE RESTAURANT MANDY picks the next night is dark and crowded and smells like beer and fried dough. The rhythm of classic rock mixes with the orders of bartenders and waiters and the shouted conversations at the tables. I wait at the front door, lifting my head every time a shadow passes.

When Mandy arrives, she gives me a quick hug. "Sorry I was so crabby yesterday. I was really tired."

I smile and kiss her cheek.

A waitress carrying a tray of beers shouts, "Anywhere you want!" before rushing past. Mandy heads toward the outdoor patio.

We always get the same thing, so we order instead of looking at the menus.

The server brings two huge mugs, spilling a little on Amanda's shoulder as someone behind tries to wiggle through the narrow passage between the tables.

"It was snowing when you flew out of Indianapolis yesterday," I say.

"Not bad."

"Tell me all about your first semester."

Mandy hesitates, and I know there's something she's not ready to tell me.

"Classes are good. I spend a lot of time with Felicia and Bert. I've told you about them. How're things with you?"

The server sets a basket in front of each of us, and I pierce the crimped end of my pot pie letting out the steaming chicken, potatoes, and gravy. I breathe in its comforting smell.

The outside tables are entirely shaded now, the cold sneaking in. I move closer to the patio heater, staring at its soft glow. A waiter must have seen me hugging myself because soon he's turning up the propane and the lamp turns a brighter orange.

"Nothing much changes with me," I say. "I stay at work longer now. I put up a profile on an internet dating site."

Mandy laughs. "You go girl."

"I find out what I can before I meet anybody. People lie."

"Anyone you liked?"

"A couple, but they never called again."

"Sorry."

"I'm ambivalent. I might be too old for dating."

"You're not that old!"

"It takes so much energy. I suppose that's why my mom and dad stay together. Weariness. Afraid to be old and alone."

"Grandma and Grandpa?"

I nod. "I said to her once, 'Mom, if you're that unhappy get a divorce. Otherwise figure out how to deal with it.' She looked at me with such sadness. And didn't bring it up much after that. Not that it was a real option for her. She had no money, no job skills, and three kids. And her church forbade it. It was hard needing to be her shoulder to cry on and her mediator with my dad."

"You do that too, you know," Mandy says.

I feel as if she stabbed me. "I'm sorry. I try not to put my anxieties on you. I know you have enough of your own."

I see a glimmer of understanding in her eyes before she changes the subject.

ONCE I HEAR the shower start on Christmas morning, I sing along with Pentatonix and put cinnamon rolls in the oven with the ham and sweet potatoes. Despite the sun shining through the French doors, I light a few candles and plug in the multicolored lights on the fake pine tree heavy with unmatched ornaments—a pair of porcelain booties with Mandy's name and birth date, filigreed Mickey Mouse ears from a long ago trip to Disneyland, a crystal bell, a misshapen snowman Mandy made in elementary school.

I make a mimosa for myself and pour a glass of orange juice for Mandy. Mandy falls onto the couch, her hair still wet. "Coffee, I need coffee," she says, and I bring her a cup.

"I may take this robe back with me," she says, wrapping it tighter. "I'd forgotten how warm and comfy it is."

"It's yours," I say and hand her the plate of cinnamon rolls. "Take as many rolls as you want."

"All of them," she says. "Well, I guess you can have one."

"Two," I say.

"In exchange for my stocking."

I bring it to her. Mandy empties her stocking on the couch, unwraps one of the chocolate bells, sticks the Starbucks' gift card into her pocket, then pulls out cash wadded into a pair of red-and-green striped socks.

"Can never have too many socks," she says.

"Not in Indiana," I say.

Mandy's pile has one large and several small boxes, all wrapped in colorful foil, the largest with a huge bow. She grins at the *Nightmare Before Christmas* mug and fills it with the cash and Macy's gift card from my parents. She shakes a small, heavy box, and looks surprised when she sees a blu-ray player.

"Old school," she says.

"You can take some of my DVDs with you to watch with Bert," I say.

"*Dr. Strangelove*?" she asks.

"Any," I say.

Mandy opens the biggest box last and pulls out a navy satin bomber jacket with white and red roses embroidered near the shoulder. "Mom! It's perfect! How did you know?"

"I saw you fingering it when we went shopping at Thanksgiving."

"I did prefer the green one with the embroidered skull and crossbones."

"You can exchange it."

"No. I love it. Thank you. Now open yours."

She hands me a small box wrapped in colored comics. It's a small purse, intricately beaded, and inside a beaded bracelet.

"They're beautiful! Thank you."

"I made the bracelet, but not the purse."

I put on the bracelet and hold my arm out for her to see. "Now I need to get invited to a ball."

"It's fine for happy hour too." She laughs. "Or one of your internet dates."

She's in a good mood, so I decide to bring it up. "Can I ask you again to call or text me more often?"

She sighs.

"I'm concerned that you're OK," I say. "You do have a history."

"And you will never let me forget that, will you?" she says, her eyes thinning. "I keep telling you, it was no big deal."

My heart grieves every time I remember. The school nurse thought it was a big deal, called Tony to say Mandy had cuts and infected burn scars on her arms, and he doesn't tell me? "I don't care if she wanted you to keep it secret," I'd said to him. "We have joint custody and I have a right to know!" I still get riled thinking about it.

The school nurse demanded we see a counselor. Most of the articles I read said girls who harm themselves are trying to cope with emotional pain. I don't get it. How does slicing or burning your arm make you feel better? Mandy would never explain. Wouldn't talk about it at all. I knew she was having a hard time and blamed me. Hell, I blame me. *But not just me,* I want to scream.

"Please. I worry. And I love you," I say.

"Didn't you tell me once you had a poster hanging in your dorm room that said something like 'If you love something you must set it free' and see if it returns?"

Despite the knot in my stomach, I laugh. "Pretty sure that's about romantic love."

"Still." She pauses. "Let's shop the sales tomorrow. I need new jeans."

CHAPTER 5

Amanda

"READY, AMANDA?" DAD asks for the tenth time. He's dropping me off at the airport and wants to get to work. I know he's irritated I didn't have everything packed and sitting by the door before I went to bed last night. What can I say? Everything always takes longer than I think it will.

"Just about. Put these in the car and I'll be out."

I fill my clear quart bag with as many mini mouthwashes and shampoos as I can find in Dad's medicine cabinet and throw a bottle of ibuprofen in my purse. I grab a banana from the kitchen and rush out the door. I can't wait to get back to the University, the misery of exams and staying up all night writing papers a memory, a small price to pay for my new life.

He drops me off curbside and hands me a twenty. "Eat breakfast. Learn lots."

"I will. Love you." I give him a hug, and he leans in.

"Love you too."

I'm swept in by the airport's excitement. Everyone rushing toward people and places, starting new lives. And the airport reminds me of my grandparents—picking them up, flying to their house. I guess I was eight when Mom first let me take a plane alone. I was so excited. Mom waited at the front of the line until a flight attendant put on my badge and took my hand. I had a window seat and saw her standing, watching, along the big windows, and felt suddenly homesick. I'm glad only ticketed passengers can get through security now. She'd probably still do it.

The heaviness of obligation and guilt I've felt all winter break starts to lift. I suppose it was mean to suddenly decide I was spending all winter break at Dad's, but I can only be with Mom a few hours at a stretch. The musk of her anxiety leaks from her pores, charging the air.

I text her, "On my way!"

"Be safe xxxooo" immediately shows up on my phone.

So, Mom is internet dating. I try to think about her as a potential date might. She's smart. Has a good job. What might an old man like? She's nice enough looking, I guess, wears expensive, if boring, dresses and suits. A little overweight. How do I know if she's attractive? She's my mom.

I relax near the gate with my grande cappuccino, its warmth and aroma calming. My phone pings. I sit up straight when I see it's a text from Philip: "When r u coming back?"

"At airport in Phx," I text back.

"U need a ride?"

"Taking shuttle."

"Arrival?"

"3:50. American. Dallas to Indy."

"Call. Will be in cell lot."

"THANK YOU"

"Ur welcome. CU."

He doesn't call all break and then offers to pick me up from the airport? I'll never understand men.

I TEXT PHILIP when my plane lands, and he's waiting at the baggage claim exit by the time I get there. On the drive to the University, Philip asks if I'd like to go to church with him Saturday night. I say sure, but how about some food now? We stop at a place made to look like an old wooden house with rocking chairs on the porch. The smell of roast beef and fried chicken is intoxicating. I order a grilled chicken salad.

"How can you not order something fried here?" Philip asks after he chooses the catfish and corn. "Go with the specials is my motto."

I shrug. "It does smell good. I'll try yours."

"Hands off my tater tots," he says. "Next time order something I might be willing to trade."

We talk about our holidays. He's spent most of it working on the farm. I tell him about the drama back in Phoenix with my mom and dad and grandparents. I grab the check when it comes.

"I'm paying," I say. "You drove all the way to the airport to pick me up."

"OK," he says. "I should have ordered dessert."

Philip drops me off at my dorm. As he pulls my suitcase from the trunk, he kisses my cheek. "I'll call you tomorrow," he says, putting my roller bag on the snowy sidewalk.

I give him a quick hug, then watch him pull away. A frisson of joy sparks as I remember I'll be seeing him Saturday night. I hope then I'll get a real kiss.

When I turn back toward the dorm, Bert rushes toward me. He drags my roller bag up the few stairs to the door and gives me a bear hug once we're inside.

"I could have picked you up," he says. "You didn't need to call that guy."

"He called me," I say and wiggle my eyebrows.

"Oh," Bert says. "Love the new jacket. Want to do something?"

"Sure. Let me get rid of this stuff and I'll be right back." I changed my shirt and primped in the airport rest room before leaving security, so I don't need to change again. Besides, it's Bert.

It's trivia night at BB's Pizza and Wings. The place is dark and loud, filled with smoke and the smell of stale beer. I peer around the booths and tables, but don't see anyone I recognize. We head toward the sound of someone calling our names and find Felicia.

"Welcome back," she says as we sit down.

I point out the group of engineers sitting near the front. "We're screwed. They always win."

"But we're better company," Bert says, putting his arm around my shoulder. "Right, Felicia?"

"And we're not here for the prizes," Felicia says. "Or the beer. They're carding everybody."

Bert leans toward her. "Guess who drove Amanda back from the airport?"

"You?"

"No, that old guy," he says in a loud whisper.

"Really?" Felicia asks, looking at me wide-eyed.

I nod and can feel my face warm. "His name is Philip."

"You're a thing now?" she asks.

"I don't know. He invited me to church Saturday night."

"And you're going?" Bert says, withdrawing his arm.

"Why not? I like him."

Bert looks toward Felicia. I'm guessing he's rolling his eyes.

"Philip doesn't talk all crazy religious," I say. "I can't imagine him blockading a Planned Parenthood or refusing to sell cake to a gay couple, so I figure his church won't be all radical right either." I'm defending Philip but I worry too. When my parents were together, we went to a church my grandma thought was too liberal—"No standards," she said, but even in that youth group lots of kids said gays and Muslims were going to hell, and some of those kids were the meanest ones in high school.

"It's Indiana, sweetie," Bert says.

"Don't be condescending," I say. "You're being just as prejudiced as you think he is."

"Well, isn't this fun," Felicia says.

"I'm sorry," I mumble. "Let's enjoy each other's company."

"You're right," Bert says, putting his arm back around me.

SATURDAY NIGHT, PHILIP drives for quite a while along empty rural roads. I ask him what was his favorite course at the University, and he tells me about an Agriculture class where the professor helped birth a calf by putting his arm inside the cow and pulling the calf out feet first.

"I think I'll skip that course," I say.

"It was great. Practical. So many courses are all ideas and theories, but this one helped me become a farmer. I guess I'm not one of those people who likes to argue. One guy I knew took a philosophy course and the whole time they discussed 'What is a thing?' Really? Like, you don't know?"

I laugh, but the philosophy course sounds more interesting to me than sticking an arm up a cow. "No wonder you mocked me about wanting to be a history major."

"I wasn't mocking you," he says. "OK, maybe a little."

We pull into a parking lot filled with a beat-up old bus and several cars next to a square, warehouse-looking building. Philip introduces me to his friends in the band, Nathan, Patrick, Lisa, Rachel. I'll never remember. They're welcoming, but not all like I was their best friend already—just hello and where am I from and how do I like my classes. Folding chairs form a semi-circle around a table covered with a white cloth.

I recognize some of the songs we sing from my old youth group, but most are new. Pastor Mark has an easy way about him, pushing his sandy-colored hair out of his eyes or scratching his beard when he pauses. He talks quietly and calmly, sometimes pacing, sometimes sitting on a chair or even the table. Somehow it seems like he is having a conversation with me, answering my questions before I ask them. He looks directly at me a few times, his dusky blue eyes calm and friendly and kind. He explains it isn't our role to judge others—only God can judge. He talks about faith and the impossibility of certainty.

The sermon focuses on how to be happy with simple joys instead of wanting constant highs and good fortune. How to bring peace by setting aside anger and forgiving each other for little slights no one probably meant in the first place. How doing these things fulfills the only commandments that matter, to love God and one another.

I've heard this before. But it's different somehow when Pastor Mark talks. More intense. More real. More personal. I promise myself I'll listen more closely next time, to stop looking at what people are wearing or wondering what brought them here.

Afterward, Philip says they have a discussion group that meets in a few minutes.

"Would you like to go? No pressure, I'm asking in case you do," he says.

"Next time?" I say.

On the ride back we discuss the sermon, and I say how different it was from the ones I remember growing up. I tell him I've lost my religion, and he says, no you need to find the right community. I should ask him their position on same sex marriage and social justice, but all I want is to bask in feeling warm, feeling content, feeling welcome. I can ask the hard questions another time. When he drops me off, he leans across the console and kisses me, lingering a little. I feel heat rushing through my body and loss when he stops.

AFTER A FEW weeks of Saturday night services, Philip says I should try a Sunday morning, see what I like better. I hope that means we'll have an actual date on Saturday night, but I end up going out for pizza with Bert and Felicia. We squeeze into a booth with some guys Bert recognizes from his dorm. They ignore us and we ignore them.

"I'm glad you're finished with that churchy guy," Bert says. "Jesus freaks are so last century."

Felicia elbows him and frowns.

I laugh despite my irritation. "We're going to church on Sunday morning like regular people."

"Oh," he says. "Sorry. He's really good looking for a straight man."

"That's not why," I say.

"Liar," he says.

"Well, maybe that's why at first, but I like him."

"OK," he says, taking the last slice of pizza then offering it to me.

I get up at seven the next morning, now wishing we'd gone the night before. The drive is more interesting in the morning, great expanses of white interrupted by ice-covered trees and the occasional corn stalk poking through. The old bus is in the parking lot with newer cars and minivans. Inside, I see children and families and a few older people as well as about twenty people I recognize.

The children give a rousing, off-key, rendition of "Jesus Loves the Little Children," then run off to another room with one of the mothers. Pastor Mark waves and shouts, "We love you!" until the last one is out the door.

"Do you sometimes wonder," he says once the room quiets again, "what difference it could possibly make whether you or I or anyone is a Christian? Why not follow one of the other great religions? Or none at all?"

I wonder that all. the. time.

"One of my college friends is a Buddhist," Pastor Mark says. "One time we challenged each other to say in one word the central message of our religions. His word was 'wisdom.' Mine was 'love.'"

"Amen," someone in the back says.

"We then spent a couple of hours trying to convince each other that ours was the better approach to the same thing, him saying love was the natural expression of wisdom, and me saying the only true wisdom was love."

Mark opens his arms wide. "How insufferable we were!" He drops his arms and puts his hands on the Bible. "But in our way, we were struggling with the most important questions: what is the foundation for the choices we make? What should we believe and how should we live?"

Yes, I think, this is what I need to know.

Mark talks about love through forgiveness. Grace. Says church history has filtered, hidden, that simple message. Says we should separate ourselves from the theological arguments about original sin, free will, predestination, and focus on loving each other as Christ loves us. He talks about sin, how we may all be good people with good intentions then asks us if we have ever been selfish or unkind. Put our own needs above the needs of our family, our neighbors, our country, the world. Didn't do what we knew to be right because we didn't feel like it. Thought somebody else should do it.

Of course we have.

"Jesus said from the Cross: 'Father, forgive them for they know not what they do.' If anyone legitimately had a claim to righteous anger at that moment, it was Jesus, am I right?"

"Yes," several people say.

"But instead, he forgives and prays for his murderers. In his final words, Jesus surrenders to God. As we all must. Freely. Gladly. It's not easy to forgive. We need help—from God and from each other. Let's ask for that forgiveness with a humility that celebrates the unity and community of us all." Mark folds his hands and bows his head.

The band leads the congregation in singing a rousing song about how they want the whole world to experience the fire of God's love. The beginning of the last verse makes me unable to stay standing:

I wish for you my friend this happiness that I've found.

I dig in my purse for a tissue, hold it to my nose, and wipe my eyes. I feel lonely among all these happy people. Why am I so disconnected, so angry? Suddenly Lisa is hugging me, then Philip covers us both with his arms. They keep holding me as Mark ends the service and people start to leave. Some pat our shoulders as they pass.

"What is it?" Lisa says. "How can we help?"

"I want that too." I sniff between sobs.

"Say yes," Lisa says. "That's all it takes."

Lisa listens as I cry incoherently about being alone, misunderstood, unlovable. After about a half hour, Mark and Philip ask if everything's all right. No, I think but say yes.

"You want to go back, or stay?" Philip asks.

"Go back," I mumble.

"Come talk to me," Mark says. "Any time."

I nod, unable to speak.

"Wednesday, then," he says. "Philip will pick you up."

Philip puts his arm around me as we walk to his car. I cry and apologize during the ride back, and Philip holds my hand and tells me everything is all right. Tells me how this community has changed his life. I feel humiliated and weak and strangely elated.

CHAPTER 6

Susan

MANDY HASN'T RETURNED my calls for several weeks now, only once to say she arrived back in Indiana on the day she left. The worry nags at me, makes it difficult to get to sleep, and when I finally do, sometimes I jolt awake from some dream or premonition. I look on Facebook to see what she's doing. There's nothing new, hasn't been for a month. I check her friends' pages to catch a glimpse, a picture, a comment. Lately, nothing. When she first went off to school, there'd be almost daily postings—Mandy in the rain, Mandy with a group of girls, Mandy tagged at a party making odd faces. "Stop stalking me," she said when she first found out I did that. What? Isn't the point of social media to see what people away from you are doing? "Get a life," she told me. "Your own life."

But she *is* my life. I've had this protectiveness for her since the day she was born. That doesn't go away when she decides she doesn't need me anymore. I'm surrounded by traces of her: the blue plaster fish she made in second grade now holding soap in her bathroom, a picture of her at age two in sunglasses and a scarf on a sunny, hot Christmas Day, Disney videos on the bookshelf.

Is a text or a call once in a while so much to ask?

I work longer hours now and try to focus on my career. I need a big push, something that will distinguish me, encourage the firm to finally make me a partner. The men my age are all partners, even those who, like me, came from other firms. Most of them have wives who don't work, who do the laundry and pick up the dry cleaning and make nutritious meals and make sure the children get to day care or school or soccer or music lessons on time.

We all make choices. Mine is Mandy.

I pass the pictures of Mandy hanging on the wall. I straighten the one with all her school photos, her graduation pose in the center. She's smiling in them all. So beautiful. How could I know she was that unhappy? I remember a little girl so full of life throwing herself at me when I came back from a trip. Grinning at me while telling Grandma to push her higher, higher on the swings. Smiling and singing at the front of the church with her friends. An eighth grader looking through summer dresses on the store rack, wanting something for her first dance and rolling her eyes at me when I told her one was too skimpy.

Am I still missing the signs?

I call Corey to quit obsessing. "Let's go somewhere this weekend."

"Oooh. Short notice girlfriend. What do you have in mind?"

"Vegas? I've never been."

"That could work," Corey says. "Let's go to a show. And stay someplace ritzy."

I do some quick research and email her my suggestions. *Jersey Boys* or *Rock of Ages*. Venetian or Bellagio.

"If we're seeing *Jersey Boys*, we should stay at the Four Seasons," she texts.

"Ha. Check the prices." I text back. We end up booking *Jersey Boys* and the Venetian. I've always wanted to ride a gondola. Venice isn't looking likely any time soon.

THE LATE FRIDAY flight to Vegas is quick. We spend more time at the airports than in the air, then take the shuttle to the hotel. Two other couples at different hotels share the ride, and we get a close-up view of Lady Liberty in front of the first drop off. I've never been to New York City either, but in all the pictures I've seen of the Statue of Liberty she's surrounded by water and boats, not cars and desert. *Spotten,* I hear my grandmother's voice say in my head. A mockery. The weather and terrain of Phoenix and Las Vegas may be similar, but the other differences shock me as the shuttle slowly travels the brightly lit streets lined with huge hotels and masses of people. I know there are homeless people and addicts hiding in the shadows, I watch *CSI*, but the glitz and theme park atmosphere makes it easy to ignore, to act as if we're in a playground instead of a city with problems of its own.

A gilded globe and mermaids greet us as we enter the hotel.

"Close your mouth." Corey laughs as I gape at the frescoes everywhere.

I stare at the ceilings and run into a couple ambling in front of us. "Sorry, sorry," I say, but they seem not to notice.

I pick the bed closest to the window and check for bed bugs as Corey gets ready. The noise outside and in the casino below is a constant din. I find a pack of earplugs next to a Gideon Bible in the nightstand drawer.

Even in daylight the next morning everything seems excessive. The individual Chihuly glass flowers are fabulous but overwhelming. The Bellagio Conservatory is set up for the Chinese New Year, the dim red globes, flowers, water lilies, fountains, and soft flute sounds a welcome change, but the huge plaster doll heads, hands, and feet protruding from flower bodies and the laughing tourists mar its peace. We eat, walk, ride the Big Apple Coaster, eat again.

Our gondolier sings as he pushes our little boat past huge window displays of televisions and expensive wrist watches. I doubt this is anything like Venice, the brick too new, the restaurants and stores too close to the edge. Diners stare at us over the wrought iron fences protecting them from the canals. Kitsch, but fun. We make no time to sit by the pool or gamble. I decide Vegas is a good place for people like me. Not in the least relaxing and hardly any time to think. Perfect.

After dark we ride the elevator to the Eiffel Tower's viewing deck, unable to get reservations at the restaurant on top before the show. At night, the city glows, the Venetian outlined in white lights, the Paris balloon multi-colored. When we get to the theater, some people are dressed in sixties outfits and others in all sorts of outrageous evening wear. One man with spikey black hair wears a black leisure suit with a leopard print collar that matches his shirt.

"We're clearly underdressed," I say to Corey, fingering my wrinkled blue shirt.

"No, we're not," she says, pointing to two older men wearing shorts, their spindly legs covered up to their knees with white socks.

The show is lively and fun, a little sad sometimes. The music reminds me of summers at the beach and first love. On the way back to our hotel, Corey and I sing "Big Girls Don't Cry" at the top of our lungs.

"Thanks for coming with me this weekend," I say.

"Thanks for inviting me. I'm having a blast."

We take a midday flight back to Phoenix on Sunday. I crash when I get home, and don't wake up until it's time to go to work Monday morning. My body tenses for the start of another week.

CHAPTER 7

Amanda

PHILIP DROPS ME off in the church parking lot Wednesday afternoon, promising to be back in an hour. A row of grackles on a power line squawk as I pass underneath. I'm not sure anymore I want to be here. Lisa assured me these sessions are freeing, uplifting, but what do I know about any of these people? The minister in my parents' church sat in his big chair behind his desk tenting and flexing his fingers like he couldn't wait for me to leave. All he said was "God never gives you a burden you can't handle."

Right. Thanks.

Pastor Mark opens the door, and his smile and the warmth of his office invite me inside. Book-lined walls back a large desk that looks out over the empty fields. Another wall holds a medieval-looking print of an angel bowing before a woman. I step closer and see that the beam of light shining toward the woman's face holds a small white bird. The painting is filled with detail—a man and a woman leaving an orange grove, fruit at their feet, as another angel rises from the trees.

Mark stands next to me, hands in his pockets. "Do you like Fra Angelico?"

"If that's who painted this, yes, I do."

"I look at that painting when I need comfort or inspiration, and it usually works. That's why I have it in here. Would you like to sit?" He points to two beige chairs set at an angle to each other, an end table with a lamp and a box of tissues between and a large cross behind.

"What? You're not going to sit in the big comfy chair behind your desk?" I ask.

Mark's eyes scrunch into a puzzled look. "Should I?"

"No, sorry, that's what my parents' minister did when they sent me to him for my 'teenage issues.'"

"Do you want to talk about that?"

"I do not."

I take the seat where I don't need to stare at the cross. "What does the painting mean?"

"It's called the Annunciation, so it's about angel Gabriel announcing to Mary that she would have a baby. But there's so much more, isn't there? I'm not sure I can even say what it means. To me, it's joy and hope."

"I see a little fear, don't you?" I say. "Look how stiff Mary's fingers are, and how withdrawn her expression. And the other woman with her hands clenched as she looks at the man next to her."

"That's Eve," he says.

"Oh." The painting transforms for me. "I guess they both had a lot to fear, as well as hope for."

"Don't we all?"

I hesitate. "I need you to know I'm not sure I buy all this religious stuff. I mean, I like what you say in church, but I'd be lying if I told you I was a believer."

"You must believe something," he says gently.

Do I? We sit silently for a while. "I know what I don't believe."

"OK, let's start there. What don't you believe?"

"I don't believe in a God who decides before we're born who is going to heaven or hell and nothing any of us do can change that. I'd rather believe in no god at all."

"Wow. You jump right into theology. Don't you see the comfort of accepting grace instead of having to work so hard to be perfect?"

"I do, I just can't believe it." I turn my head to look outside at the icy landscape.

"Why not?"

"I guess I wasn't chosen."

"You think your doubts exclude you."

The kindness in his voice draws me back, and I look at him. His eyes are gentle, his hands relaxed on his knees. "I asked our minister once how to know if you were chosen, and he said, 'you just know.' It made me so mad."

Mark leans toward me. "Because you didn't know, so that meant you weren't chosen."

"Exactly."

"Did you ever think maybe that man was an idiot?"

I bark a laugh and shift in my seat. "That was my conclusion."

He looks toward his bookcase. "I'm going to give you a couple of books to read, famous believers who struggled with doubt about a lot of things."

"Please don't give me anything that tells me to believe because it's absurd." I grip the arms of my chair.

"No, not a good place to start."

His teasing warms me, makes me feel safe. He takes my hand and holds it lightly.

"Something draws you to our community despite your belief—see? you believe in something—that you are not one of God's chosen. Any idea why?"

I've been asking that same question for weeks now but have no good answer. "I want what all of you seem to have—peace, a sense of purpose, a community. But sometimes it seems like believing in what I can't is the only way to have that."

"So once again you're excluded. First God, now us. And all for something you have no control over."

I pull several tissues from the box on the table as the tears stream. I can't say a word.

"There are other ways of looking at this. You seem to think you have to earn people's—and God's—love. I'm here to tell you, you don't need to earn anyone's love in our community. We give it to you. My experience is that when someone's need for love is met, they give it to others freely and it builds. That's what you're seeing here, what you envy. And I say, welcome."

I nod, mute, dabbing my eyes and nose.

"And you can come talk with me, or anyone, any time you want."

"I'd like that," I croak.

"Until next time then." He goes to his shelves, considers a few books, pulls out two and hands them to me. "Here. Read these when you get a chance. I hope they'll give you a new way of seeing, or help you understand that doubt can be a good thing when it pushes you to open your heart."

I feel a quick shock when he touches me. The book on top is *Night,* by Elie Wiesel.

"Would you like to come next week at this same time?" Mark asks.

I nod.

As I get into Philip's car, I realize Lisa had been right. I do feel uplifted, free.

"How'd it go?" Philip asks.

"Good," I say. "Really good."

"So, you'll be going again?"

"I'd like to," I say. "If you don't mind picking me up all the time."

"I'm glad." Philip leans over and kisses my cheek. "And I don't mind."

FELICIA WARNED ME about the February snows, told me the professors never canceled class. I know now I should have let Mom buy me those snow cleats I scoffed at. And the wind. I wear many layers and a thick scarf over my nose and mouth as I walk to class, but still it gets through. Then I have to unwind it all once I get to the overheated buildings, my coat and sweater over the back of the chair, my gloves and scarf underneath, all of them dripping as the snow from them melt.

Not many open places in the cafeteria this evening, the snow making the inside more inviting. The view through the large windows reminds me of the static we used to watch on my grandma's old TV. Sometimes I see shadows of people trudging along the edges of buildings, but mostly it's a blur of white forming higher and higher drifts along the windows. Everyone lingers over coffee or cocoa or anything warm and likely won't leave until the staff turns off the lights. Felicia and I join a couple of Resident Assistants. They're deep in conversation, and barely nod as we sit down.

"You and Bert going to *The Big Lebowski* next Saturday?" Felicia asks.

"The church is having a retreat that weekend, and I told Philip I'd go."

"You've been spending a lot of time with those people," Felicia says.

I shrug.

"I get that Philip is hot, but you've never seemed like a church person. Is he the reason you go, or is it something else?"

"I suppose he's the reason I started going, but not the only one. It's hard to explain—I like the feeling I get there. It's like I don't have to pretend to them, they take me in, no questions asked."

"Don't you have to pretend to believe all that crap?"

"I thought I would, but I don't. We have these discussion groups after service, and I say all the things that bother me about Christians and all the things I'd never say to my family or at my old church and they listen and tell me why they see it differently."

"Doesn't sound like the church I grew up in," Felicia says. "They think there's only one way. Theirs."

"Come with me some time," I say.

"I don't know."

"Bert's been asking questions too," I say. "We could all go together."

"If Bert goes, I'll come too," Felicia says as we put our dishes on the conveyor belt and throw paper in a bin.

Bert is even more reluctant than Felicia, saying the last thing he needs is another group of people trying to convince him that he's sick or broken. When I tell him they're not like that, he says they're all like that. It's the biggest argument we've ever had. He says, "You're not a gay man so you don't know." I tell him he should stop using the gay card to avoid anything he's uncomfortable with. He hangs up on me.

Bert and Felicia are my best friends, and I'm driving them away. No, that's not it. They don't want me to change. It's all fine when I laugh at Bert's jokes and try to pick up guys with Felicia, but if I go outside the little circle they understand, they think there's something wrong with me. They're what's wrong. I've gone outside my normal, but they sit back there smoking weed and looking for their next hookup.

I can't sleep for all the anger and hurt roiling around in my brain. Kelsey comes in the room about two a.m. giggling and shushing some guy who's already started unbuckling his jeans.

"If you make one peep, one noise, one little yelp, one little squeak of a bedspring I will tell the RA where you hide your weed," I say in my most steely voice.

"Bitch," Kelsey says, but they both leave.

TWO WOMEN ARE in the car with Philip when he picks me up for the retreat. I recognize them as students who regularly stop at the church's campus activity tables on Friday. One of them, I think her name is Shirelle, flirts with Philip every time, and she has claimed the front seat.

I stuff my duffel and sleeping bag in the trunk and hold my pillow and purse on my lap.

I nod to the woman in the back seat whose name I can't remember.

"Amanda, you remember Shirelle and Nan, don't you?" Philip asks.

"Of course," I say.

"This will be fun," Philip says a little too heartily.

I stare through the fogged windows as we overtake a freight train running alongside the two-lane road. Shirelle and Philip talk incessantly, but Nan and I are silent. We pass the occasional house with a barn and a pickup truck, but mostly miles of flat farmland covered in snow. We enter a wooded area where six small cabins surround a large one. I can see the blue of a lake through the trees. We pull into a ragged parking lot as the church's faded yellow bus lumbers in. I wave to Lisa when she steps off, and she rushes to hug me. Philip, Shirelle, and Nan head toward the largest cabin. Lisa picks up her faded denim backpack and my sleeping bag.

"That's all you brought?" I ask, balancing my duffel bag and purse on one arm, my water bottle and pillow on the other.

"Sure," she says. "One change of clothes. The cabins have sheets, blankets, and pillows."

The main room quickly fills. I recognize several people, but many I don't. Pastor Mark, looking comfortable in his worn blue jeans and plaid flannel shirt, waves. "Put your things along the wall and take a look around. We'll get back together around four—everybody should be here by then—and have a group activity before we eat." He waves at several other newcomers.

"I'd like to see the lake," I say to Lisa as I drop my sleeping bag next to a pile of others. I'd like to see it with Philip, but he seems to have disappeared.

"Good idea," she says.

My coat and hat are no match for the icy wind tearing across the fields. We stand silently watching the water peak into little white caps.

"I'm so glad you've joined us," Lisa says. "I love what a seeker you are, how determined you are to find answers to whatever is troubling you."

Gratefulness washes over me. I was afraid I was driving her and everyone crazy. Other people always seem so much more content than me. "Thanks," I say. "I'm glad you don't think I ask too many questions."

"No, no," she says. "That's your gift! To make us reflect, to help us express what we believe, and why. It tells me you're serious about finding the truth. And this retreat will help. I remember my first retreat. I kept thinking, 'What are these people going on about all the time?' But these retreats help us become a community, willing to stand with each other no matter what. You'll see. There's so much love here, and love's not a limited commodity—it multiplies as our numbers grow."

"How long have you been with the group?" I ask.

"Almost three years now," she says. "I grew up in Michigan and came to the University to get away from home more than anything. I spent my first two years partying every weekend."

I nod.

"Then in my junior year I came to church. I could feel the love and energy the first time."

"I feel it too," I say.

"Amazing, isn't it? And at that first retreat I decided: this is where I want to be."

I want to ask her all sorts of questions, but a loud bell starts ringing.

"Is it time already?" Lisa asks. I show her my phone. "I guess it is."

As we enter, Philip hands me a bag and a notecard. "Put your cell phone in the bag, write your name on it, then put it in the box next to Pastor Mark. A distraction-free weekend; won't it be great?"

I feel a spark of dread. If I'd known, I'd have sent out a few texts first.

The room is loud with noise and confusion as everyone gives Pastor Mark their bags and looks for a chair in the double circle.

"Grab your pillow and sit in front of the first row of chairs," Lisa says into my ear. "It lets the older people have the chairs and I like being in the center of things anyway."

Pastor Mark stands in the center of the circle, beaming at everyone. He exudes a sense of authority and benevolence. When the noise lessens and most people have found a place to sit, Pastor Mark raises his arms, and closes his eyes.

"The Lord be with you!" he shouts, opening his eyes.

"And also with you!" the room shouts back.

"Seeing all of you here give me so much joy. I know we'll grow together this weekend," he says in a quieter voice. "But if you don't yet feel that joy, I pray that by Sunday you will, and we can go back into the world with a renewed sense of purpose."

A few "amens" scatter around the room.

"Right now, we're all coming from different places—some of us part of the group for a long time, some just joining, and some here to observe. But it's my job to disabuse those observers that they can just sit and watch." He pauses and looks around. "Did anyone come here planning to sleep in, read books, be alone?" The room is silent. "Great! Then we'll have our first get-acquainted game!"

There are a few groans.

"It will be fun," he says. "I promise. Everyone should have been given a 3x5 card—if you don't have one, raise your hand and someone will bring one over." Hands shoot up around the room. "Now, write down the name of someone you would like to be—living, dead, biblical, fictional—someone at least a few people in this room might have heard of. Then put your card in this bowl."

There must be a book somewhere of icebreaker games, because we played this one in high school. I'd picked Bathsheba, to the scandal of the leaders. Which was the point. Guess I should be serious this time. Jane Eyre? Too mousy. Queen Elizabeth? Nah, too matronly. Adele. Yes, that works. How great it would be to have that voice!

It takes a while as people ponder, laugh, and whisper to each other, but finally Mark lifts the bowl and asks if there are any more and no one comes up.

"OK. We'll take turns pulling cards. When it's your turn, read the card you pick then guess who it might be and why. If you guess correctly, we'll clap. If not, the person who chose the name will give a quick explanation. Either way, whoever's card it is goes next."

The room buzzes as everyone tries to explain the rules to each other.

"I'll do mine first to show how it works." Mark reads his own card. "Martin Luther." He puts his finger to his chin as if he's puzzled. "I think that's from Pastor Mark." Laughter sparks across the room. "Why, yes, it is. I picked Martin Luther because he believed so strongly the Church had gone astray, he risked excommunication to protest and ended up inspiring the world into a new direction. I have similar notions of grandeur."

Everyone laughs.

Pastor Mark picks another card. "Hermione Granger. Hmmm. I guess a young woman." He scans the room, lingering for a few seconds on me, then points at one of the college students I hadn't met yet. "You? Tell us your name and if I win."

"I'm Sandy," she says. "And no, not a *Harry Potter* fan."

"It was me." Lisa stands up. "Hermione is smart and powerful and even though she was born a Muggle, she still believes in magic."

"Your turn to pick, Lisa," Mark says.

The game goes on for a while, and I'm surprised at some of the names and explanations. Only a few people have picked Biblical characters so far. There's been Korra, Sherlock Holmes, Helen Mirren, Michelle Obama, Pocahontas, Solomon, Betty White, and a bunch of people I've never heard of.

"Adele," a voice behind me says. "That must be Amanda because she's got the best voice in church."

I turn around and smile at Rachel, both at the compliment and because mine is the first one anybody guessed. I stand up and admit that was me, then pick a card out of the bowl. Eric Liddell. That must be Philip. Philip went with Bert and me to *Chariots of Fire* on campus. Couldn't stop talking about what a great role model he was. Bert was not impressed.

"Philip," I say, "because he's as much like Eric Liddell as anyone I know."

Several people clap as Philip stands up. "Got me."

"Two correct choices in a row," Pastor Mark says. "That must be a sign our pool is shrinking. Since it's almost time to eat, how about the remaining people take turns saying who they are and explaining their choices?"

Afterward, I stand in the food line behind the woman who wanted to be Helen Mirren. "I think my mom would have made that same choice," I say. "Why did you?"

"She's beautiful for one, and talented, and shows that older women can be both. And you might hate me for saying this, but she seems to be a feminist and still a lady. If that makes any sense. I'm Nicole, by the way."

"And I'm Amanda. It makes sense to me. My mom would say the same thing—she was so proud one time coming home with what she called her Helen Mirren haircut."

Nicole laughs. "I've asked my stylist to give me that haircut, but it never looks the same. And, by the way, I agree that you have a beautiful voice. As fine as Adele's. No need to envy her."

We have a short service before heading off to our cabins, mostly singing. I feel an inexplicable closeness to everyone. People who I thought were strong cried, and we told them we loved them. Everyone told me too when I cried about my fears and loneliness and doubts. The songs calm and energize me.

Lisa, Shirelle, Nan, and I share a room with a noisy space heater attached to a rough wood wall, and we groan every time it screeches on.

"I'm glad it works," Lisa says. "And I'm glad we're here together." She walks to each of us, sits on our beds, hugs us. "I love you."

I crawl into my sleeping bag and cover it with the cabin's scratchy sheet. Love and acceptance blanket me, and I fall asleep easily despite the hard bunk and lumpy mattress. That love and acceptance surrounds me all weekend during lively group discussions about the retreat's theme, the fruits of the Spirit: love, joy, peace, patience, kindness, goodness, faithfulness, gentleness, and self-control. I'm amazed at how seriously everyone takes this. When guilt or depression about how far I am from these ideals start taking hold of me, Mark tells a story about how he's failed and been forgiven. How we all fall short. Our meals are basic and small as we remember how many people in the world are hungry and poor. We stay up late, get up early, take walks with each other, eat with each other. We are never alone.

I grab the front seat on the way back to campus. Philip smiles at me but shakes his head when I try to take his hand. He drops me off first.

Chapter 8

Susan

THE SKY STARTS to lighten as I pull out of my driveway, the outline of Camelback Mountain emerging out of the dark. Frustrated drivers on the already crowded freeway refuse to let me merge into their lane.

"Where am I supposed to go?" I yell at the third driver who has shimmied up behind the car in front of him to close any possible gap. In my mind I hear his silent reply: behind me.

No matter how early I arrive in the morning, I'm never first. All the associates' and many of the partners' offices are lit, and industrious men and women in drab suits stare at their computers or sort through piles of paper on their desks.

Tomorrow I'll leave my house a half hour earlier.

I deposit my frozen meal in the break room's refrigerator, pour a cup of coffee, and grab a donut from the counter. The firm provides snacks, coffee and soda on each of its six floors in a downtown high rise. Wouldn't want anyone to have to stop billing hours to walk to the Circle K.

My supervisor, Mike, sees me pass and calls me into his office.

"How's Mandy doing at college?" Mike asks.

"She loves it," I say. He doesn't need to know how few details I have.

"Must be strange, her being gone."

"It is. We spend so much time organizing our lives around our kids, and suddenly they're gone." Mike's two boys graduated several years ago. One is married and the other in law school.

"Isn't that the truth," he says, as if it wasn't his wife who did all the organizing and driving their boys around. "Now that you have more time, I'm wondering if you'd like to try something new?"

Sixty hours a week isn't enough? a voice inside me screams, but I smile and try to look eager. I've been here eight years and twice passed over for partner. This might be my last chance. "Sure. What do you have in mind?"

"The litigation department could use some help with the rush of real estate development cases we have, and your land use background fits well."

I'm confused. "I'm already working on motions and appeals for most of those."

"We're thinking you could be the lead litigator in the Petrel Homes case."

My body freezes. I've spent my career as a transactional lawyer and the thought of cross-examining witnesses and trying to persuade a jury scares me. Always has. "I'm a little rusty on the Rules of Evidence," I say. "Maybe I should start as second chair?"

"That case won't go to trial for at least a year. Plenty of time to refresh your skills. Sign up for a trial advocacy course." He smiles, and I realize I'm being dismissed.

Dread blooms in my gut as I return to my office with my cold coffee. Is this a ruse to get me to quit? I love working with developers and city staff to get a project off the ground, usually a cooperative endeavor where the city tries to get some free infrastructure and appease their citizens who never want change while we try to find a profitable plan for our clients that doesn't create large scale public opposition. I fear becoming a litigator will damage my relationships with city staff as they start to see me as the enemy. Should I mention this to Mike? I should have. I will. Later.

Bev, my office neighbor, stops by at noon to see if I want to join her for lunch. She seldom leaves her desk for lunch, so I'm both flattered and fearful that she's asked. I think about the frozen meal I'd brought and decide getting out of the office is better. The box will keep, and I want to talk to someone about Mike's suggestion.

Bev is an imposing woman with a quick smile and a kind heart, tall, muscular, with a short, severe haircut so different from the rest of the women in the office who either have a smooth bob like me or long hair tied into a loose bun. No one works longer hours than Bev. "I love what I do," she tells anyone who asks. "It's fun. I don't need hobbies, and I don't have a family." And despite her crazy work ethic, she never criticizes anyone who needs to leave early for a sick child or takes a two-week vacation.

We walk to a nearby restaurant that serves breakfast all day, Bev saying she's got a craving for pancakes and bacon. That sounds great to me, but I order a salad to make up for the two donuts I've already had today. When I tell her Mike wants me to move to the Litigation Section, she puts down her fork and looks me straight in the eye.

"And what do you want?" she asks.

"I like what I do now," I say. "What I don't know is if this is an ultimatum."

Bev sits back in her chair and pauses before she speaks. "It might be, but you should ask him. Your name comes up at partner meetings, as you must know since you've been passed over twice. I won't tell you who says what, but there's been some grumbling about your billable hours and how few clients you've brought in. Everyone agrees your work is good, but you must know that isn't enough."

I did know. Mike had told me essentially the same thing during my last review. "But why litigation?"

Bev frowns a little and I know I'm making her uncomfortable. Mike isn't always straight with me, and I know Bev will be.

"Some people think you need to be more aggressive and litigation will force you to do that," she says. "And we hardly ever write off hours in a litigation practice, except maybe for research memos written by new associates. You write off a fair amount of your time."

It's true. My hourly rate seems obscene to me, so when I review my monthly billings, I often feel compelled to eliminate short phone calls and shave time from traveling or waiting or other less productive time. Colleagues tell me I should appreciate my value, take credit for every possible second, let the partners do the trimming. And billing too few hours is a sure way to lose my job.

"Has the firm thought about making me a senior staff attorney?" I ask.

Shock flashes across Bev's face. "Why would you want that?"

"If I don't make partner soon or if I resist litigation, I'm afraid I'll be asked to leave."

"You can do this, Susan," she says, her eyes steeling. "I am totally opposed to putting women into lesser roles because they have families. This is your chance. Take it."

We're both quiet on the walk back. I sense she sees my hesitation as a lack of ambition, even a betrayal, to her, to the other women in the firm, to women in general. I fear I've lost one of my few advocates.

"Thanks for being honest with me," I say as we reach our offices. "I'll talk with Mike."

She gives me a quick smile and closes her door.

I try to ignore the anxiety eating away at my gut. I can't lose this job. A mortgage, a car payment, out-of-state tuition don't pay for themselves. I'm already a failure at marriage, at motherhood, at dating. And now this. I'll work harder. Longer. I'll go to events where potential clients go, give them my business card, tell them about our firm's successes.

Do I have to?

Yes. Yes I do.

I microwave my box for dinner and eat it at my desk as I review the Petrel Homes file and draft a motion for summary judgment. Now I have more reason than ever to hope the case won't go to trial. I call Mandy from my car on my way home, the traffic finally thinning now that it's almost eight. Eleven her time. Not late for her, she never goes to bed before midnight. It's after classes, after supper, not a date or party night. She always has her phone with her. No answer. Again. She probably saw it was me and put her phone back in her purse. I'd seen her do it to her friends when they annoyed her, or to a boy who no longer interested her.

I pour a glass of wine, grab several cubes of cheese, watch *Glee*, and sing along with "Come Sail Away." I'll try, best as I can, to carry on. Oh, stop with the self-pity.

I set my alarm for an hour earlier.

Chapter 9

Amanda

CROCUSES SEEM TO come up overnight, first the small lavender and white ones, then the more brightly colored purple, orange, and yellow. Today they surround the church buildings, their thin green leaves and vibrant flowers set against the ice crust achingly beautiful.

My Wednesday counseling sessions give me a sense of belonging I've never experienced before. Mark's office is a haven from the irritations of my roommate, my classes, my mom. Mark and I argue sometimes, but it's a seeking kind of argument where our differences open a new way of seeing to me. I sense he's had and worked through the same doubts and questions as me, found a way to balance puzzle and mystery. I've admitted things to him I've never dared speak about, and he always listens carefully and kindly. He takes my hand when I tell him about what I needed to do in high school to feel included, smiles when I tell him my hopes. I suddenly understand about doing things I don't love, even hate, like shoveling snow and knitting and changing diapers because I love my community. And I do love them, even irritating people like Nathan, who responds to every single thing someone says, or Shirelle who uses every excuse to be near Philip.

I haven't talked about Philip, though. How confused and hurt I am over how little our relationship has changed these past months. Shirelle or Nan are almost always with us when we go to church now, and Philip lends me the car for my Wednesday sessions instead of taking me. When he takes my hand or hugs me it's in such a friendly way, I fear I've misunderstood.

I should talk about my growing feelings for Mark, but that's the scariest topic of all. How can I explain without seeming utterly idiotic that the best part of a service now is when he smiles directly at me? I see him look at others too, it isn't special, but it feels special. And it hasn't escaped me that several women seem to follow him around, volunteering to help at the food bank or visiting the hospitals with him. I want that too, but resist. Instead, I volunteer to babysit his kids so Hannah can go. She thanks me, says it's easier to stay home and keep the kids settled, but it would be great if you'd stay and help me some time. Three young kids. No wonder she wants some help and some company. So, this Sunday I join her and the others living at the Grange on the bus after church while Mark and Philip and their groupies drive to Hebron for a service at Philip's home church.

At the entrance to the farm is a sign that has "Welcome to the Grange" woodburned onto a piece of old gray wood. A gravel driveway leads to the big farmhouse, a huge gray barn, a square one-story building with aluminum siding, two small houses, and, in the center of it all, a low, flat masonry building with windows surrounding the front third.

We eat lunch together in the large central building which contains a commercial-style kitchen leading to a dining area surrounded on three sides by windows that look out onto a pasture and the barn. Afterward, Hannah shows me around the farmhouse where she, Mark, and their kids live. She tells me Mark's grandparents built it. Once inside, I can see the footprint of the original house, a large central room painted blue, an adjacent dining area, and a crowded kitchen. A small bathroom and office near the front door appear to have been added later as the floors don't meet evenly and the ceiling is lower. A steep staircase leads upstairs. Worn curtains cover most windows and children's drawings cover the wall. I like it.

Matthew wants to show me the cows, so Hannah and I and the three kids tramp toward the barn. A huge black lab they introduce as Jax greets us at the barn door and follows us around. The manure smell is strong, and I pull my scarf over my nose. Hannah leans toward me and whispers we won't stay long. I pet a heifer's rough skin as Matthew informs me of how often they must be fed, milked, brushed. He knows a lot for such a little boy. Then they show me the other buildings. The two small houses are dorms, one for the single men and the other for the single women, and the square building with siding for the two other married couples and their children.

"Did all of you buy the farm together?" I ask.

"No," Hannah says, "we built it over time. Mark's grandfather farmed the Grange. Mark's dad built the second house when Mark and I married. We built the other ones as the need arose. This isn't the life for everyone, but a lot of the young people wanted to live in community and help with the farm."

"You're OK with that?"

"Any time a group of people decide to live together, married or not, there are conflicts, but I believe in Mark's ministry and it's a big help to have so many good people to do the farm work. It frees Mark to minister to the congregation. We first held services in the smaller house, but it became clear the ministry would have a broader appeal if services were held somewhere else. Nathan's uncle owns the land and building where we meet now."

"I'm surprised the whole church doesn't want to live here," I say.

"You are? I'm always surprised when someone does," Hannah says. "Most people want their independence, keep God on Sunday."

After supper, Lisa invites us to the women's house. Most of the other women went with Mark and Philip. Lisa makes us tea and gives the children oatmeal cookies she'd brought back from the dining hall. After Matt and Becky smash their cookies beyond recognition, Hannah decides it's time to head back.

"Amanda, are you going back to the dorms tonight?" Lisa asks, and I nod. "It might be late, and black ice is a problem out here. Why don't you stay? It will save Pastor Mark or Philip an hour too."

"I didn't bring anything," I say.

"We have everything here a woman could need," Lisa says.

I look at Hannah and she smiles.

"All right. Thank you. I'll come back after everyone's in bed."

Becky falls asleep on my shoulder as we walk back, and Hannah tells me to check her diaper and put her to bed—she can go tonight without a bath. I read Angela a story out of the illustrated Bible she had next to her bed, one with a picture of angels climbing up and down a ladder above a sleeping person's head.

"I'm named after angels," she says.

"Yes, you are a little angel," I say, kissing her good night.

"Tell Mommy to kiss me too," she says.

"I will," I whisper. "Good night."

AT BREAKFAST, EVERYONE treats me like a guest, bringing me coffee and offering me pancakes and bacon and toast and anything I want. I take a yogurt and some scrambled eggs with my coffee and wonder if they always eat like this. Although the room is big, the individual tables are pushed together, and we sit around it like a family. Not like my family, where even when we lived together dining was more a grab-what-you-can affair. Philip heads to the barn and Mark offers to drive me to campus. Hannah waves me off when I start clearing the table and offering to do the dishes, so I grab my purse from under my chair and follow.

"Did you enjoy staying at the women's house last night?" Mark asks once we're buckled in.

I nod.

"Hannah and the kids enjoyed your company. Angela couldn't stop talking about you this morning."

"You have a great family."

"Anytime you'd like to stay, you're welcome," he says. "What time's your first class?"

"I've already missed it. On purpose, don't worry. I'll be back in time for my next one." Except I have no intention of going to that one either. I sat up most of the night talking with Lisa about why she decided to live at the Grange.

"If you have the time, why don't we talk?"

"Instead of Wednesday?" I ask.

"Or both, whatever you prefer."

Mark pulls into the church parking lot. "I'll put on some coffee. No one gets here until ten."

We sit in our usual places. A rush of warmth rises when I blow on the hot coffee.

"How was Hebron?" I ask.

"Good. A much more uptight crowd than here, but still nice."

"What do you mean?"

"Oh, less singing, less hugging, and certainly no hand raising. More than one person told me how much they preferred hymns as they shook my hand."

I have to talk to him about my forbidden feelings. If any time is right, it's now. No, I should not. I spent the evening with his wife and kids, for Christ's sake.

"Something seems to be on your mind," he says. "Do you want to talk about it?"

"I don't know if I should. It's some feelings I don't approve of."

"And you don't think I'll approve either," he says, shifting forward in his seat.

"I'm sure of that." I can't look at him, so look at my clenched hands instead.

"You won't know until you tell me, and anything you say will be fine." He takes my hands and smooths them straight. "Really."

Does he feel me tremor? I look at the floor. "I have—improper—feelings about you."

"What kind of improper feelings do you mean?" he asks quietly.

"Are you going to make me say it?"

"Sometimes saying things lessens their power, releases them. And there's nothing wrong with thoughts, it's bad action you need to worry about."

"I seem to recall Jesus saying that lust is the same as adultery."

"Are we talking about lust? Or something else?"

"I don't know," I say much too loudly, finally looking at him.

I want to run out of the room or throw my arms around him or pull my hands away or scream. I do none of those things, but I do cry. He releases my hands and takes a tissue to my face. When I calm, he kneels in front of me, puts his hands on my thighs and his head in my lap.

"Let's pray about it," he says.

I put my hands and head on his. He might be praying but I don't hear it. My entire body is on fire. I feel deliriously happy and guilty.

Eventually he stands and wipes my eyes with his fingers. "You should move to the Grange."

I nod.

THE DORM CASTS long, hazy shadow onto the parking lot glazed with melting frost when Philip arrives early Saturday morning. Not much color greets us today, only a few orange berries and small green leaves clinging to bushes lining the dorm's brick wall. Philip gives me a quick hug, then loads my suitcase, pillow, books, and laptop into the space behind the seats in the pickup. My stomach is roiling, whether from hunger, nervousness, or anticipation I'm not sure.

"Philip, is this going to be awkward?" I ask as he pulls onto the highway. "My living the same place as you."

"No," he says. "Why would it?"

"Well, we haven't been seeing each other that long."

Philip looks at me quickly, and I can see surprise or maybe panic written in his eyes and raised eyebrows.

If it wasn't awkward before, it is now.

"Philip, is this, are we, going anywhere at all?" I blurt as he drives. "I mean, are we friends or is it more?"

Philip's mouth smiles, but his eyes have no sparkle. "I love being with you, but it's not about you and me. I'm—we're—part of a community."

"I know that."

"I've committed to the community to submit to its care any serious relationship. That's what you're asking, right?"

"They decide who you date?"

Philip steers with one hand and takes my hand with the other. "We—I—believe that our culture's emphasis on feelings and attraction misses the most important parts of a relationship: friendship, common goals, commitment, honesty, loyalty. Love at first sight and other physical attractions are a trap. Half of marriages end in divorce—I'm sure all those people were in love when they got married. In our community we try not to act on simple attraction but wait for the call."

Why didn't he say anything like this before? He had to know I had a crush on him. I stare at the empty road. "What's 'the call'?"

"When you know, and the community agrees."

"Are we headed in that direction?"

"I don't know," he says.

"Are you even attracted to me?" I ask, fighting tears.

"You know I am," he says, releasing my hand to drive double-fisted, silently, for the rest of the trip.

I wanted us to be something. Something that would distract me from my feelings for Mark. I'm humiliated it isn't.

When we arrive at the Grange, Lisa runs to take my suitcase. "You're with me," she says. "I'll help you unpack."

I fight the tears I won't give Philip the satisfaction of seeing.

"We'll talk later, OK?" he says, and I nod.

In the daylight, the women's house looks uninviting. I see the faded beige paint peeling along the sides, and the cobwebs crowding underneath the stairs of the porch. Have I made a big mistake? Should I turn around now, ask someone to bring me back to the dorm? After we hang a few things in Lisa's tiny closet and put the rest in the two drawers she's emptied for me, I lie on the single bed Lisa tells me is mine.

"I'm so happy you're here," Lisa says. "I've been praying for this."

Her excitement lessens the pain of Philip's rejection. "I'm glad too. Although I wish I didn't have to get up so early."

"Better get used to it. You're living on a farm now," Lisa says. "But you're tired. Rest a while. Lunch is in a couple of hours—you'll probably hear the bell, but I'll come get you." She kisses my forehead as she leaves.

It's quiet. Everyone must be working, doing their part. I think about the love I feel from Lisa and Pastor Mark and even Philip, remind myself that this is about growing closer to God, not to Philip. I want both! My mind argues back. Why can't I have both? And why doesn't Philip give me a straight answer? Does he think I'm fragile? I am not. I'm not going to spend any more time worrying about what he does or doesn't feel about me, I tell myself, knowing I'm lying.

Sleep eludes me, so I walk around the farm. I let the wind's hushing in the trees and the birds' songs seep into me. Tree limbs near the main house reach haphazardly every which way with small bursts of golden green. As I approach, I see new small stems lined with tiny buds, little spikes of brown, and inside some of the leaves are many small buds with a silvery sheen, others larger with green tips, and some larger still, reddish, with a hint of bright pink on top. I watch a robin hop from branch to branch then fly away, and I search to see if there's a nest nearby. I don't hear Mark until he's next to me.

"Are there robins in Arizona?" he asks, putting his arm around my shoulder.

"Yes, although I haven't seen many. It's more of a quail and hummingbird kind of place."

"Growing up, we always looked for that first robin, sure it meant winter was almost over. Now I know some robins stick around most of the year."

"Not much winter where I'm from. The snow and cold here were a little hard to get used to. But every day I'm surprised by some new beautiful thing. Like these buds."

"When they blossom, it's glorious."

"I bet. I look at these and think there's probably some lesson here I don't want to learn."

"Want to talk about it?"

"Not right now," I say, putting my arm around his waist. I'm content.

SUNDAY MORNING, PHILIP drives all of us to church in the faded yellow bus, its gears grinding on every turn. When we join the band, I make a point of smiling and talking with him to let him know I'm fine. Patrick gives us the order of songs, and we file to our places in the front. Bryan sets up more chairs, anticipating latecomers. I fall into the rhythm of the service, the songs, the greeting, the prayers, the children's sermon, the children leaving in a rush of noise and song. The room quiets as Mark begins to speak.

"Wouldn't it be nice to be kids again, sure of Jesus' love and, for many children, your parents' and grandparents' and friends' and neighbors' love?" Mark asks. There's a murmur of assent. "But as we get older, we start to question all of that, don't we?" A few amens and yesses respond. "We keep looking for that love, for proof of that love, for anything that makes us feel loved. And once we figure out the attraction of the opposite sex, we look for it there."

Several people laugh, nervously I think.

"Parents fail us. The church fails us. Friends fail us. If only we could find that one person to rely on, the one who will complete us, make us whole and happy again. We cite bible verses to back us up: 'the two will become one flesh.' The Bible wants us to find our soul mate, right?"

I think that. I want that.

"Romance novels are some of the best-selling books," Mark continues. "And for the most part their plots are simple: a man and a woman meet, have troubles, realize they're soul mates, get married. In fairy tales, the princess marries the prince and lives happily ever after. Most of us have heard the Beach Boys' sing 'Oh we could be married, and then we'd be happy.'"

He pauses. "Wouldn't that be nice?"

I remember my parents' long silences those few times they ate together, or how Dad would read a book in one room while Mom watched TV in another. How, toward the end, we'd go on vacation without Dad. I remember Mom telling me Tony had been the love of her life, and when I asked what happened all she said was, "I don't know."

Mark talks about the hopeful lie of romantic love. How many cultures ignore romance when it comes to marriage, making marriage contracts when children are young, marrying people they've never met. He says our need for romance makes us believe when romance fades it's time to move on. Or stoically persist, growing ever more desperate and angrier at our spouses, thinking ourselves better than the rest of the world because we keep our promises.

"We burden other people when we ask them to complete us, to be our happiness. No person can do that for us. Only God can. 'But God's love is too abstract,' some of you may be saying, 'I need something physical, someone I can see, hear, taste.' Yes, we are physical beings who need each other, and that is what our community can provide."

As Mark talks, I begin to see what Philip was trying to tell me in his way. The family of God is larger than a nuclear family. God is present in the group. My hurt and anger fade.

"We are God's presence to each other," Mark says. "I feel this all the time and hope you do too. I feel God's presence when we sing together, and when we go on retreat together. I feel it when we share our hopes and doubts and dreams and fears. When we touch each other. That is what we as a community can do for each other—be Christ's presence. But it's not the person facing you that gives you comfort and power, it's from God."

Mark talks about Godly romance. How in the fourteenth century "romance" referred to heroic tales of adventure. King Arthur, Sir Lancelot, Guinevere, the hunt for the Holy Grail. The quest was central, whether searching for a holy object or proving a knight's honor, these adventures had a spiritual goal. And the hero often failed.

"An adventure, the search for spiritual truth no matter what life throws at us—that's the romance that should inspire us. We are the heroes who bring God's kingdom to the world. Each of our stories is different but important, and we do it together. Some of us are called to be teachers, some healers, others counselors. Some are called to be married, others to be single; some to be parents, others to give up their families. And what an adventure each calling can be. Let's get excited about our own journey and how we can help others with theirs. Let's stop spending our time looking for that one person to complete us and accept God's promise to be all we need. How freeing that is. Now we have time to feed the hungry, comfort the sad, give hope to the forgotten. Time to tell the world about the love and joy and peace that comes from God. I can get excited about that; can you?"

I raise my hands in the air as we sing the final song. No one says much as we gather our things and line up for the bus. Pastor Mark gives each of us a hug and a word of encouragement. To me he says, "Still want to meet on Wednesday?"

"I wouldn't miss it," I say.

CHAPTER 10

Susan

BOUGAINVILLEA RIOT MAGENTA along the fence line as I drink my coffee, trying to ignore my anxiety. I know I shouldn't worry. Mandy's told me a million times she's old enough to take care of herself. But I can't help it. The worry is like a buzzing in my head I can't shake or ignore, and it won't go away. Sometimes it's unbearable, and I have to talk to her, make sure she's okay.

When I can't stand sitting anymore, I pace around my yard, my pool, walk to my mailbox and back, trying to decide what to do. Over a week ago I left a message: "Hi sweetie, this is Mom. Haven't heard from you in a while, could you call me, please? Love you!"

That's innocuous enough, isn't it? She would have called back if she were OK, wouldn't she? She must have had five free minutes since then.

I try to give her space, not make demands. I do, in fact, remember what it was like to be eighteen, away from home, away from the expectations, the demands. Away from a mother whose love feels like constraint. But the need to know she's all right is a physical need, like hunger. Like desire. I need to know she hasn't fallen into one of her dark spaces, hasn't started cutting herself again, knows I love her.

I've sent several emails and texts offering to fly her home for Spring Break. She's got to be sick of all that snow. The weather is perfect in Phoenix right now. People from the Midwest are flocking here, clogging the streets and crowding all the restaurants. The Renaissance Festival is bigger this year; she always loves that. Or she could drive to Lake Havasu with some of her friends. Or California. We could stay at Disneyland if she wanted. If she'd call, we could plan. I already asked for time off work.

The babble in my head is unbearable. I resist the specters, but they find the cracks and fog my brain. If she were hurt or was missing, the University would call me. I'm not sure I believe that.

I stare at my phone. I could call Tony. I hate calling him, it's always so awkward, especially if his girlfriend picks up. I'll be hurt if Mandy's called him and not me.

Too bad. I need to know.

He has caller-ID, so I'm relieved when he answers.

"Yeah?" he says.

"I haven't heard from Mandy for weeks. Have you?" I run my finger along the edge of my cup.

"Nope," he says.

"I'm worried . . ."

"She's in college. She's fine. Leave her alone."

A sudden empty silence. He's hung up.

He's probably right. I don't care.

I call Corey. "I can't stand this. Not knowing. What should I do?"

"Call the University tomorrow morning," Corey says. "Ask them to check on her welfare."

"Mandy'd get mad," I say.

"So? Then she should at least text you once in a while, return your phone calls."

I get up early to call the University first thing. They transfer me to her dorm.

"Nope, don't know Amanda Beane, but I can connect you to her room," a young man's voice says.

"I've tried that already," I say.

"What floor's she on?" he asks, and when I tell him he transfers me to that floor's Resident Assistant, Tammy.

"Haven't seen her lately," Tammy says in a groggy voice.

A wave of panic slams into me. "When was the last time?" I ask, trying to sound pleasant, but I hear the steel entering my voice as I try to resist nightmare scenarios.

"Um, not sure. I'll talk to her roommate and call you back, OK?" I hear the wariness in her voice before she hangs up.

I log into the parents' portal at the University's website. I read the disclaimers about the Family Educational Rights and Privacy Act and why no one but the student could have access to anything worth knowing. I call the registrar. Tell them the people in the dorm haven't seen her, and I want them to check on her welfare. Now. They promise to get back to me. I know Mandy would hate my making all these calls. Too bad. I can live with her disdain more than I can live with not knowing.

I barely function when I get to work, the words of a contract or a court case incomprehensible as my mind keeps darting toward Indiana. I wait until noon for the registrar to call, but no one does. I call again, ask if she's still registered, tell them I have a right to that information because she's my dependent. After being on hold for twenty minutes they tell me there's no FERPA waiver on file, and if I want access to Mandy's academic records, I should send them proof of dependency, or, if I wish to file a missing person's report with the local police I should do so.

Knowing Mandy will hate this even more, I call the local police and talk to a Detective Taylor who is more interested than anyone I've talked with so far.

"I know all about her right to privacy," I say. "But something is not right. All I want to know is if she's OK. If she wants to hide, I'll live with that."

"I can tell you no one else has reported her missing to us," Detective Taylor says. "That's a good sign. Someone would have noticed if she'd gone missing for as long as you think. The University Police sends us a missing person report, usually within a day."

I remember my conversation with Tammy and decide to book a flight.

"Thank you, Detective. I'm flying in tomorrow; would it be all right for me to come by?"

"Sure. I'm in the office most afternoons. But you can talk to anyone."

I call Mike, tell him I have a family emergency, book a flight, spend the evening filing my taxes. Luckily, this is my year to claim her.

I call her high school friends, call the dorm to see if anyone knows who Mandy hung around with, Facebook-stalk in earnest. Nothing. I call Tony.

"Mandy's missing," I shout through my tears.

"What do you mean, missing?" Tony says.

"Her Resident Assistant can't remember the last time she's seen her. And the school won't tell me anything, they say she's an adult and has a right to privacy,"

"Which she does," he interrupts.

"And she hasn't signed the waiver to let us know anything. I thought we made her sign that?"

"I don't remember, but she could revoke it," he says.

I know that. Why does something that seems so right in principle seem so wrong when reality hits? "Yeah, but I looked it up. They can tell me if she's my dependent. Which she is."

"OK," he says.

"I have to prove it."

"Then prove it."

"I will. I'm going out there. Tomorrow. You can come if you want, or not," I say.

"Why don't you file a missing person's report and let the police handle it?" Tony asks.

"I did," I say, weeping so hard I can barely speak. "But I have to do something."

"I know," he says, and I hear a kindness in his voice I haven't heard in years.

THE FLIGHTS TO Indianapolis take all day and give me far too many hours to worry with nothing to distract me. There's no way I'll make it to the University before the offices close. I wait in line at the rental car counter, its vacant whiteness doing nothing to cheer me. I check my phone for messages again. Eight of us wait, weary from our flights and leaning on our luggage. I review my notes from the conversations with campus police, Detective Taylor, the Registrar, Tammy. They all told me to be calm, not to worry. They must not have children.

The clean-cut man at the counter takes pity on me, upgrades me to an Accord instead of the economy car I'd booked. Consumer Review said not to buy all their insurance, but I do anyway. If something happens, I want a new car, no questions asked, and that's what he said would happen. Done.

The sun fades behind clouds lining the horizon as I drive the freeway past the flat emptiness of fields covered with patches of snow. Wheat-colored grasses wave in the gray sky. I see a house now and then in the distance, but the traffic and buildings thin the further I get from the airport, and my only company is the occasional semi barreling past. The darkening landscape crowds again as I near my exit. The two-lane road toward the University passes abandoned sheds near a railroad track, a town with one traffic light swinging on a cable above an intersection, rusting cars lined up near a barn before I see a tower rising in the distance.

I park near Mandy's dorm, not caring how late I check into my room. It's dinner time, so after finding out that Tammy isn't in, I hustle to the dining hall. Not that I'd recognize Tammy, but maybe someone there would know Mandy. I don't dare hope I'll see her. The cafeteria lets me buy a meal for cash. The room is filled with chattering students, some laughing, some staring intently at each other or their laptops, their plates filled with french fries and hot dogs or fried chicken. Only a few skinny girls have plates of salad. I look at my plate of meatloaf, mashed potatoes, and gravy. I need comfort.

I scan the room, aware of how little I know about Mandy's life here. Who might have known her, missed her? As the tables fill, two girls, one tall with stringy blond hair wearing an over-sized parka and the other shorter, darker, wearing tight jeans and a heavy red sweater with "Lace Up" written across her chest, ask if they could join me.

"Of course," I say.

Once they sit, I ask, "Do either of you know Amanda Beane?"

"Sounds familiar," the taller one says, scrunching her forehead. "Why?"

I pull out my envelope of pictures and show them one I'd taken at Christmas. "I'm her mom, and I'm looking for her."

The two girls stare at the picture. "I've seen her in here," the taller one says.

"But not lately, have you?" the other girl says to her friend.

"No, not lately. We didn't hang around. Sorry."

"It's OK," I say, "I'm waiting to talk to her RA—Tammy something."

They brighten. "Tammy's right over there." The tall one shouts across the room. "Tammy! Over here!"

Tammy is just as I imagined her: thin, athletic, her hair in a long, dark ponytail. She has on navy yoga pants and a black shirt emblazoned with the school's mascot that I would have thought was a little too tight to be comfortable.

"Hey guys, what's up? Is this your mom, Katy?" Tammy bounces as she talks.

"No, this is Amanda Beane's mom," Katy says.

Tammy's smile drops, and she looks at me a little fearfully.

I put out my hand. "Good to meet you, Tammy. We talked on the phone."

"Yes," Tammy says, stepping back. "Like I said, I haven't seen her in a while. But we don't do bed checks or anything."

The lawyer in me stands at attention. She's afraid. She's hiding something. "I was wondering if you got a notice she'd moved out, or dropped out, or if you had reported her missing?"

"I'm not supposed to talk about my residents with anyone," Tammy says, backing further away. "I'm sorry."

"Could I see her room?" I'm begging now.

"I'm sorry, no." Tammy turns and flees. My two companions leave with her.

Something is definitely wrong. I steel myself for the job ahead. Panic and tears won't help me. I chew slowly, deciding I need to find Mandy's roommate or one of her friends.

I peer through the dorm's front doors to make sure Tammy and the two girls aren't in the lobby, then approach the front desk. A young man with wildly curly hair and a snake tattoo running up his arm is reading a Greg Bear book.

"Hi!" I say with forced cheerfulness. "I'm here to see Amanda Beane."

"You her mom?" he asks, and I nod. He types her name into the computer. "OK, I need you to fill out this guest card and see your ID."

He scrutinizes my driver's license as I fill out the card.

"Is she in her room?" he asks.

I shrug, and he picks up the phone to call the number on his screen.

"No answer," he says. "You have to be with a resident to go inside after dark."

"That's a good rule," I say, hating it.

"Where are you going?" a young woman in the line forming behind me asks. "I can walk you in."

"328," I say.

"No prob. Who you going to see?" she asks, making polite conversation as we walk toward the doors. The doors appear to be unlocked, no one is checking IDs, and the boy at the desk is back to reading.

"Amanda Beane. Do you know her?" I say. "And what's your name?"

"Celia," she says, dimpling. "I'm on the fifth floor. I'd probably know if I saw her."

I drag my pictures out of the envelope and show one to her.

"She looks familiar," Celia says.

"Do you know anyone on the third floor?" I ask.

"Sure. If Amanda isn't around, we'll ask Felicia."

The name sounds familiar and hope blooms.

The elevator arrives with a clunk, but it's a good ten seconds before the doors slowly open. We walk to 328; no one answers. A small young woman comes toward us, running her fingers through thick, curly hair.

"Hey, Felicia," Celia says. "Do you know Amanda Beane?"

"Sure," Felicia says, frowning a little.

"This is her mom."

"Oh." Felicia hesitates. "I haven't seen her in a while."

"Well, I'll get going. It was nice to meet you Mrs. Beane." Celia runs toward the stairwell.

"I'm paying her a surprise visit. Guess that wasn't such good planning, was it?" I say, digging my fingers into my palms to keep calm.

"Aren't you from Arizona?" Felicia asks.

Ah, so Felicia does know her. "I'm worried about her Felicia. She's not returning my phone calls. I didn't know what else to do. Can you help me?"

Concern flashes over Felicia's face. "Last time I saw her she was leaving with that guy she started seeing. Philip. She had her roller bag and a pillow, so I figured they were going somewhere for the weekend."

"How long ago?" I ask.

"Must have been a couple of weeks, I guess. We're both in choir, but I was sick last week. I don't think she was there the time before that."

Panic constricts my throat, and I can't speak.

"We used to be friends," Felicia continues, "but not much after she got back from Christmas break. I have a study group meeting in a few minutes, but I'll ask around."

"What can you tell me about Philip?" I croak, trying desperately to catch my breath.

"Not much. They go to some off-campus church. I've never been."

"Who's her best friend?"

"I thought I was until Philip. And Bert. I'll call Bert for sure."

I take Felicia's hand. She hesitates, then squeezes and releases it.

"I'm sure she's fine," Felicia says. Concern shines from her eyes.

"Can you meet for lunch tomorrow or something? Will you give me Bert's number?"

"Sure. I have a break between classes at twelve-thirty until three."

"OK," I say. "I'll meet you downstairs around one?"

She nods, and we walk back toward the elevator. She texts me Bert's number as we ride down in silence. I sit in the dorm lobby and call Bert, but it goes to voicemail. I beg him to call me back.

I try to muffle the nightmare scenarios filling my head from too many evenings watching crime shows. Locked in a barn somewhere. Body on the side of some road in the middle of nowhere. Lost in a forest. My smart, naive, baby girl. She has to be all right. Has to.

I can't sleep, hoping Mandy, Felicia, Bert—someone, anyone—will call with news. Out the window of my room at the Union snow reflects the moonlight and occasionally a hooded student wanders between the buildings. I doze occasionally until some dream or anxiety startles me awake.

CHAPTER 11

Susan

THE DEAN OF Student's Office opens at nine, and I'm there at eight-thirty. A student worker unlocks the door five minutes after she should have. When I tell her who I am, a tall, portly man with a crew cut and in a rumpled gray suit rushes toward me. His tie looks as if it's choking him.

He introduces himself as Sam Brown and leads me to a glass enclosure in the rear of the huge room. His office is orderly. Labeled notebooks line the wall behind his desk. A pad of paper and two pens and two pencils in a cup fill the space between the computer and the phone.

I pull my tax forms from the envelope and hand them to him. "Here's my proof of dependency. Keep them on file, please," I say. "They're copies."

He looks them over, hands them back. "No need. I'll mark Amanda's file." He punches something into the computer, I'm surprised how quickly. He must have been looking at her records.

"After we got your phone call, we sent emails to Amanda's professors. Apparently, she's missed all her classes this week, and her attendance has been spotty since late January," he says. "Although not all the professors have been taking attendance, it seems.

"More troubling," he continues, "is when we contacted the dorm, her roommate said Amanda hasn't slept there for a few weeks. Her Resident Assistant—"

"Tammy," I say.

"Yes, Tammy, says she hasn't seen her in a while. We checked her meal card, and it's mostly being used at lunch." He peers at the computer screen. "Last use, two days ago."

I sit straight, fight to keep my face still. "Could someone else use her card?"

He hesitates. "It's possible. She might be living off campus." His chair rocks as he leans back. "That's against the rules without notifying us, and I'm told Tammy is being required to undergo training about keeping an eye on the welfare of her residents."

No wonder Tammy didn't want to talk to me.

"Yesterday we asked campus police to look for her. If they can't find her in twenty-four hours, they will involve the local police. We care about our students and will do all we can to make sure she's OK."

Yeah, you care so much it took phone calls from me for anyone to notice she's skipping class and not sleeping in her room. "Thank you, Mr. Brown," I say, grasping the chair arms. "I'd still like to know where she's living and whether something's happened."

"Of course, of course. Let's call the campus police, see if they've found out anything." He reaches for his phone.

"Thank you," I say as I stand. "I'd like to talk with them in person. Will you tell them to expect me in a few minutes? Then I'll go to the local police. I'm not waiting twenty-four hours."

Officious bastard, I think as I stride past the office workers pretending not to watch.

The campus police look at me like I'm a crazy person when I visit them in their cramped little office behind the library. They repeat the same information in the same words as Mr. Brown. My anger builds at each deflection. Do something, I think.

Maybe I am crazy. She's probably fine. But what if she isn't?

WHEN I GET to Mandy's dorm, I see Felicia and a young man standing by the front doors. He's clean shaven, unlike a lot of the students I've seen with their stubble beards or even those with full beards and ponytails who look like they could have gone to school with me in the seventies. Felicia's wearing a puffy blue jacket with fake fur lining the hood she's pulled around her face, but her friend looks much more elegant in his double-breasted suede jacket with a shearling collar and trim. Felicia waves.

"Mrs. Beane, this is Bert," she says.

I grasp his gloved hands. "Please, call me Susan. Where would you like to eat?"

"How about Mackey's? Amanda always liked eating there." Bert strides ahead of us toward the Union, and I struggle to keep up. Clearly, he's a take-charge kind of guy. I see why Amanda likes him.

"Slow down, Bert," Felicia says as we fall behind. "It's slippery!"

Bert turns. "Sorry. I'm always late so have perfected the sliding power walk. Not something you need to practice in Arizona, I'm guessing."

I laugh for the first time in weeks. So, Amanda has talked to Bert about me. "No, although I grew up in the Midwest. Went to school in Michigan. I tended to avoid icy sidewalks, though. Couldn't stand the cold. Probably why I moved to Arizona."

Bert slides his arm through mine. "Felicia, take her other arm. Let's show her the icy sidewalk slide. Right foot firm, slide the left, slide the right, watch out for the dry patches."

I almost fall several times, but Bert and Felicia keep me upright. We're all grinning and breathless by the time we get to Mackey's. It's a fresh burger place with too many choices, but there's a long line and I finally decide on a quarter pound with avocado, bacon, lettuce, and grilled onions with sweet potato fries. More comfort food. "Cheese?" the cashier asks, and I shake my head. A little concession to my cholesterol levels.

We find a table in the back that's not too noisy. Bert's been smiling and nothing but nice to me, but I feel I'm being scrutinized. I can only imagine what Mandy has said.

"Do either of you have any idea where she might be?" I ask as we wait for our meals.

Bert hesitates. "Felicia told you she was dating Philip, right?"

"I'm pretty sure he picked her up that last time I saw her," Felicia says.

"And she had her suitcase?" I say. "Who is he? She never told me about him."

Felicia looks down at the table and frowns. "I should have asked her where she was going, but we'd had an argument. I feel awful. If anything's happened to her . . ."

"I'm not going to lie," Bert says, gesturing with open hands. "I always thought there was something off about that guy. But not dangerous. He's involved in some church and lives on a farm with cows. They must be a student organization because I saw Amanda talking to Philip once at an Activity Table in the Union."

I'm confused and must look it because Bert says, "The University lets campus organizations set up information tables in the Union on Fridays."

"Any idea what's the name of the group?"

"Something weird," Bert says. "But I can't remember."

"Is there a list?" I ask. "Would you recognize the name if you saw it?"

"Probably," Felicia says.

"There's a list of student organizations online." Bert pulls a silver laptop out of his backpack as the food arrives. Felicia and I eat silently as Bert types, then reads whatever he's found.

"Seventy-five religious organizations on campus," he says, staring at the screen. "I would have guessed more. Some weird names too—wait, this is it. Sower of the Word." He clicks on something and reads again. "Yes, this looks right." He shows the screen to Felicia, who nods. "I'm sure the tall guy standing on the side in the picture is Philip."

I push my burger basket toward the center of the table and pull Bert's laptop toward me. A snapshot of six people dominates the page, three women and three men, standing in front of large, leafy trees with water behind them. All hold each other's hands with arms raised above their heads. Three are looking upward, two have their eyes closed, and the man Bert says is Philip is staring at the camera. He's handsome—tall, square-jawed, dark brown hair with a short beard. He's in jeans and a plain blue t-shirt that shows his muscled arms.

I point to his picture. "This is Mandy's new boyfriend?" Bert nods his head and holds his hand in front of his mouth as he chews.

"He's too old for her," Felicia says. "And I got a bad vibe from him."

"You've met him then," I say.

"Yes," she says. "And I've seen her with him a couple of times in the lobby."

Listed next to the picture are the advisor's name and email, a few bible verses, and a quick summary of the group's mission.

"Mandy's joined this group?" I ask. Mandy, who wouldn't go to church even on Christmas?

"Yeah," Felicia says.

"Do either of you know their advisor?" I ask, pointing to his name.

Bert types the name into a search box. "He's a Professor in the Ag Department."

"Well, at least I have someone new to call. Thank you both, so much." I quickly write my cell phone number and email address on the back of my business cards and give them each one. "Please call if you hear anything. Any time."

"OFFICER TAYLOR," I say again to a woman behind a thick window at the City's Police Department. "Officer Gene Taylor. I need to see him."

"I'll see if he's available," the woman says to her microphone.

I wait in the stark lobby—white tile, white walls with black vinyl baseboards, two black plastic chairs. I roll my manila envelope in my hands, wondering if I'm being watched through the one-way window in the middle of the thick steel door that separates police staff from marauding hordes. It's hot in here. I remove my coat first, then my sweater, and drape them over my arms as I wait. I want to pace, I should sit, but instead I stand motionless looking out at the main doors to a statue of a police officer and a dog. In a few minutes, an officer pushes open the heavy door and beckons me into the small hallway.

"Mrs. Beane, I'm Detective Taylor. Let's talk in our conference room. My office chairs are filled with boxes."

"Ms. Beane, please. Or Susan. I'm divorced," I say.

"OK. Do you have a preference?" Taylor asks.

"Susan, I guess. I thought about taking back my maiden name. But it's Mandy's name, too. And the one everyone in Phoenix knows me by. But, please, not Mrs. Beane."

I see Taylor struggling to keep his face pleasant. He doesn't want my life story.

"Tell me why you think Mandy is missing, Susan," Taylor says as we settle across from each other at a blank metal table.

My spine stiffens. As if I'd come here on a whim. "Because I can't get a hold of her and I've been trying for weeks!" My envelope uncurls as I set it on the table, my right hand picking at the cuticles on my left hand. "I don't *think* she's missing; she *is* missing." As I tell him what I've found out, my eyes and nose drip. I rummage through my purse and pull out a crumpled tissue and wipe my eyes. I look at the black smudges on the tissue and snort. "I knew I shouldn't wear mascara."

"I'm wondering why no one reported her missing," Taylor says.

"Me too," I shout. "You send your kids to school, pay lots of money in tuition and dorm fees, you expect someone to pay attention."

"When was the last time anyone saw her?"

"As best I can tell, three weeks. Her meal card was used two days ago, but that doesn't mean anything." I squirm in the uncomfortable plastic chair and hear the hysteria creeping into my voice. "What if I'm buying some murderer lunch?"

Taylor sits back in his chair as if he's deciding whether to say something.

"What is it?" I ask. "I can see there's something you're not saying."

"I'm sorry. I don't want to upset you. But that group you mentioned, Sower of the Word? There've been rumors, but nothing concrete."

"What rumors?" I ask, my panic rising.

"That it's a . . . cult," Taylor says.

"Like Jonestown?"

"Nothing that extreme. I'm told they home-school their kids and no one ever sees them. Makes some people question what's going on I guess."

I can't breathe. "Have you done anything?"

"One of our officers went over there after a man reported they were holding his young daughter," Taylor says. "Turned out she and her mom sought refuge there, said the man had beaten the mom. We ended up charging him instead."

"Sounds like they were doing a good thing," I say. "Protecting her."

"That's what I think," Taylor says.

"Thank you," I say. "That's comforting."

Taylor puts his hand over mine. "If she's with them, she should be safe. Try not to worry."

I look at him and give a wry laugh. "Fat chance." I take a few more moments to collect myself. "I'm going to see their faculty advisor next. Will you come with me?"

"How about we call him?"

I nod. It takes a while for the department secretary to track him down, but after about ten minutes I hear a clatter and a gruff voice. Professor Krava swears under his breath when Taylor asks him about the group. "Can't you leave those people alone?"

"Sir, I'm sorry," I interrupt, "but my daughter is missing, and some students say she might be with them."

"Well, why didn't you say that first? They're good people," Krava says, and gives us the pastor's phone number. "If your daughter is there, they'll help you. They'll help you even if she isn't."

No one answers when Taylor calls the number Krava gave us. I cover my eyes with my hands and lean on the table.

"Where is this farm? I'm driving out there," I say.

"I wouldn't recommend that," Taylor says.

I stare at him. "I don't care."

"Tomorrow is Friday. Check out their activity table. If she's not there, I'll drive you to the farm."

"And what am I supposed to do until then?"

"We can't burst in on them." Taylor hands me the paper with the church's phone number. "Keep calling, have supper, check the Union tomorrow, and if all that fails, we'll drive out there. Together."

"You're not going to give me the farm's address, are you?"

"No."

I glare at him as I gather my things. I know where the church is. Taylor follows me to the front. Outside it's already dark.

AS I EAT my grilled cheese and fries alone at a table in the Union, I look at the church's website. It lists the pastor as a Mark Vinnar. I search County property records and find a property in his name. The address is a Rural Route number, but the map shows it located about a mile from the address for the church. I throw my utensils in a bin and drop my plate onto the conveyor belt slimy with water and other people's food. Time to find Mandy.

The GPS on my rental car leads me along dark roads bounded by railroad tracks, through empty fields, past the sporadic farmhouse and barn. Occasionally my headlights reflect the eyes of an animal alongside the road. I find the church first, three small square buildings with metal siding that looks like a warehouse complex. No steeple or light shining through colored windows like some holiday card, just a large, white plywood sign marking the entrance. I pound on every door I can find, but all are locked and silent.

I can't find the farmhouse. The GPS takes me to empty farmland. I pass several driveways as I go up and down the highway, but it's too dark to see any addresses or markings on the mailboxes or houses. The houses are lonely and quiet. If I lived here, I wouldn't answer the door to an unexpected visitor. I've read *In Cold Blood*. I give up and return to my room, defeated but determined to come back if I don't find her on campus in the morning.

Sleep eludes me, the sleeping pill I finally take giving me ominous dreams in my half sleep. Mandy screaming and I can't move. A farm on fire surrounded by FBI. Unable to dial my phone as I watch in horror. I get up and make coffee in the room's little pot. Take a shower. Open my laptop.

I google Mark Vinnar. The church's website says he graduated from Moose College in Minnesota and Carpenter Seminary in Indiana. I find an alumni website for Carpenter that lists congregations served and discover Vinnar's first and only other church was near Moriah, Indiana. But it's too early to call anyone, so I type a long email to Corey telling her what I've found out and venting my frustrations. Play some online sudoku. Wait for the sun to rise.

CHAPTER 12

Susan

I'M WAITING IN line when the Union Cafeteria opens in the morning. I buy an egg sandwich and some very strong coffee, then find a seat where I can watch the happy mayhem of students as they set up tables, tack banners to the walls, display books, and flirt with each other. It takes all my self-control not to pace the halls looking for Mandy. I don't see her, or anything called Sower of the Word, from my vantage point. By nine everyone seems ready, so I walk past table after table of campus activities—Paws for a Cause, Federalists, ROTC, many religious groups, LGBTQ Alliance—each with a clear-eyed and smiling student standing behind. I examine them out of the corner of my eye, not wanting to stare and knowing I am not who they want to attract.

I'm jittery from lack of sleep and too many cups of coffee.

As I round the corner toward the elevator, I see her, her red coat and the unmistakable curve of her head. Joy and fear flood my brain—she's alive, she's well, she's right in front of me. I'm giddy with relief and steady myself in the shadow of a pillar, not yet ready to face her. She's talking fervently to a young man, sometimes smiling, sometimes serious, sometimes touching his elbow. Next to her is a handsome dark-haired man who seems a little older than everyone else. Philip. He's charming the woman in front of him, occasionally paging quickly through a book and showing her things. Mandy is proselytizing? She gives a little wave to the young man as he walks away, then scans the hall. She sees me, and her smile hardens into a grimace. She turns toward her companion.

Well, she knows I'm here. I put on my pleasant face and square my shoulders.

"Amanda," I say. "What a surprise."

"Right," she says quietly, clearly not wanting to attract anyone's attention.

"Well, of course, I came to see you, but I'm surprised to find you here at the—what's the name of your group?" I look up at their banner. "Sower of the Word? You were never much interested in religion before."

The man thrusts his hand toward me. "Hi!" he says cheerfully. "I'm Philip. You know Amanda?"

"She's my mom," Amanda says, her voice flat. I can see the surprise in Philip's eyes as I shake his hand.

"All the way from Arizona? How exciting," he says.

"I couldn't get a hold of her, and I got worried," I say, looking at Amanda who is looking at the floor.

"Amanda," he says in cheerful reproof. He puts his arm around her shoulders, a little too possessively in my opinion. "You need to call your mom."

"Even a text would be fine." I can hear the whining in my voice.

"We're mostly to blame," Philip says. "Since Amanda joined us, she's thrown herself into our work."

"And the Dean tells me you haven't been to class in a while," I say.

Amanda stiffens and looks at Philip.

"I've missed some classes, a couple when the snow hadn't been plowed yet, and last week I was so tired and a little sick."

"Aren't you living on campus?" I ask.

"I can't stand my roommate. I told you that." Finally, she looks at me, and I'm taken aback by the anger in her eyes. "So, a group of women at Philip's church invited me to stay with them. It's on a farm about ten miles from here. I help them cook and clean and watch the kids sometimes."

This is my daughter who I couldn't get to clean her bathroom?

"Are you the pastor, Philip?" I ask.

"No, I help out with the music and on the farm."

"Can we talk?" I say to Mandy.

"I need to stay and help here," she says. "And I have class this afternoon. As you say, I shouldn't skip another one."

"Why don't you come back around eleven, and I'll treat both of you to some fine cafeteria food?" Philip says.

"OK," Amanda says.

I nod. I would have preferred some time alone with her, but I will take what I can get.

I stare at the ceiling in my room as the time slowly passes. When I come back to the table, new people are there, and when I ask about Mandy and Philip one of them hands me an envelope. The letter reads:

Mom, something came up. Why don't you come to church tomorrow night? It starts at 5:30. Here's a map. We can talk after. Amanda.

I stick the letter in my purse, feeling discarded.

I call Detective Taylor, tell him I've found Amanda, retract my missing person's report.

"I'm glad it all worked out," he says when I reach him. "So, no need for me to take you out there?"

"I'm going to the church on Saturday night," I say.

"That's good. Could you let me know if something strikes you as," Taylor hesitates, "odd?"

"You mean if I think it's a cult?" I ask. "What's odd is how Mandy has changed. I suspect it might have something to do with her handsome friend Philip."

Taylor laughs. "Oh, to be young. Well, if something concerns you, please tell me. I'm happy you found her."

I'm not entirely sure what makes something a cult, what to look for. I will keep an open mind. I will.

But it nags at me, so I call Felicia then Bert to say I've found Mandy, and spend hours doing internet searches on cults. Apparently, there are many. The more I uncover, the scarier it seems. All kinds of weirdness from Charlie Manson to David Koresh to alien saviors and yogis and sex cults. Calm down, I think. Those are the extremes. But when does an alternative lifestyle become a cult? When did Jim Jones change from a progressive social innovator to someone who would require his followers to kill themselves and others? As far as I could tell, Charlie Manson and David Koresh were always a bit violent and crazy, but Jim Jones, when he was in Indianapolis at least, ran quality nursing homes and a soup kitchen, promoted integration, was Chair of the City's Human Rights Commission.

I should call Tony.

"What," he says.

"I wanted to tell you I found Mandy, and she's fine."

"Never doubted it."

"She's joined a religious group called Sower of the Word. A policeman here says some people think it's a cult."

Tony snorts. "Some people think yoga classes are a cult. Amanda's smart."

"It's just odd to me she's suddenly gotten so involved with this group that she skips classes and cleans their house."

Tony's silence seems threatening somehow.

"Am I boring you?" I ask.

"What do you want me to say? She's fine. Let it go."

"But what if she's not fine? You say she's an adult and can make her own choices, but she isn't, is she? It's easy to manipulate the emotions of a lonely teenager far away from home. And all those studies that say kids' brains don't fully mature until age twenty-five? It was only last year that she was cutting herself, and now she joins a commune?"

"I trust her."

"It isn't about trust!" I'm yelling into the phone now. I hang up before he can say yet another thing to hurt me, make me feel inadequate.

I spend a couple of hours answering work emails and reading everyone's cheery posts on social media, but anxiety and self-doubt plague me. Was I always this anxious and obsessive? In my mind, I scan through the last years of my marriage—Tony's detachment made me try all sorts of things like hanging around with his friends instead of mine and planning vacations he didn't want to go on. And leaving made me have to stay at my well-paying black hole of a job.

I pace the room, needing to talk to someone. I remember Corey is in Utah skiing this weekend, so not her. I could call my mom. No, I can't tell her about this, especially the cult part. That would send her into a panic even greater than mine. She and Dad would be here tomorrow, and Mandy would be angrier. Instead I lie on the bed, hugging a pillow and staring through the window at the clouds rushing past the moon. Eventually I fall into a fitful sleep filled with troughs of Kool-Aid and girls with rifles slung over their shoulder. I awake more exhausted than before.

The cafeteria is closed when I leave my room early Saturday morning, but the mini-grocery store is open, so I buy a donut and a diet Coke, then pick up a double Snickers at the register. I try to clear my mind by walking through campus. The clouds hang low, the wind blasts little bits of something in my face. I miss the big sky and warmth of Arizona. I try to work again, to read, to nap, to play Candy Crush on my computer.

Finally, it's late enough to start getting ready. I'm not sure what to wear. When I was growing up, it was always my best dress, but the few times I've gone lately only the old ladies wore dresses, and some of the teenagers looked like they had just gotten out of bed. Literally. I'm sure some of them were wearing pajama pants, flannel with cartoon characters on them. I try to remember what Mandy had been wearing yesterday under her red coat— black pants and a white sweater, I think. Philip had on pressed pants and a tie. I'm guessing there won't be any pajama pants at this church.

Several men are talking to each other in the parking lot when I arrive at the big white sign in front of the nondescript warehouses, a little less bleak in the twilight than it was in the dark. I glance at the car's clock: 5:15. I stay in my car and watch people gather. Soon an old bus arrives, and several children rush out, followed by about ten adults, mostly women. They seem normal enough, no long dresses and caps, anyway. I see Mandy carrying a small child, and my heart flips. No, it couldn't be hers. Not enough time.

"Amanda!" I say, opening my car door. She waits to walk with me and introduces me to the women and children around her: she's carrying Becky, the pastor's daughter, then there's Hannah the pastor's wife and two more kids, Matt and Angela. Lisa, Rachel, and Sarah. I will never remember.

I see Philip at the front tuning his guitar, and he waves at us. He says something to the man at the drums, then comes over to hug first me and then Mandy.

"Welcome!" he says. "I hope you enjoy the service."

"I'm sure I will," I say, hoping I've hidden my skepticism.

He returns to the front as the words to a song flashes on a screen behind the band. Philip picks up his guitar, stands by the microphone, and sings. Everyone except me joins in. A man I assume is the pastor walks up to the front, hugging people as he passes. When he reaches us, he takes my hand and holds it, looks into my eyes, smiles, and introduces himself. I'm reassured somehow. At least he didn't hug me.

Three lively songs later, everyone sits. There's a charge in the air, and I see from Mandy's body she is excited, interested, involved. Did the music do that? It reminds me of when she was a child singing in front of a group at school. I'm glad she's happy. I'm jealous it has nothing to do with me.

I watch the congregation, following their lead when they stand, sing. Not when they clap or raise their arms. Like Mandy, most seem mesmerized by what the pastor is saying. It doesn't seem that special. He has an endearing way about him. He's not particularly handsome, slightly balding with his sandy hair and beard beginning to gray. Medium height, medium build, nothing distinguishing about him at all. A regular guy. How did he attract such devotion from this group? They laugh at the slightest irony; they cry when something hits close to their hearts. Mandy takes Lisa's hand at one point. She doesn't touch me.

The service ends with several obnoxiously repetitive songs. The first one repeats the word "holy" at least fifty times. It seems to put everyone in a trance except me and a few others whose eyes dart around the room. The songs get progressively livelier, and on the fourth one the pastor walks to the back of the room while most people are clapping and singing.

This is not for me.

After the service, Philip encourages Mandy to go with me back to campus and promises to pick her up after I leave for the airport. In the car, my attempts at conversation receive mostly one-word answers, Mandy having become fixated on the vacant dark expanses she must pass almost every day. She finally turns toward me when I mention I met Tammy and Felicia and Bert.

"What'd they say?" she asks.

"I think I got Tammy in trouble, so she ran when I told her who I was."

Mandy laughs. "How did you get her in trouble?"

"Well, she was supposed to alert the administration when you stopped sleeping in your room, but apparently she never noticed."

"She was glad I wasn't around," Mandy says. "I kept complaining about Kelsey."

"Is that why you started staying at the farm?"

"Partly," she says, becoming interested once again in the moonlit fields.

The campus is a beacon in the distance, and I wait until we're settled at the Thai restaurant Mandy picked before asking, "What are the rest of the reasons you stay there?"

"I may drop out of school, at least for a while," Mandy says. "The work we do is important, and I can't seem to keep up with both."

I try to hide my dismay but guess from the thin line her lips are making that I'm not hiding it well. "But at least finish out this year! You're more than halfway through. And we can't get a refund anymore." I know immediately this is the wrong approach.

"The money is the issue? Well, I'll pay you back." Amanda's eyes were a thin line now too.

It takes all my self-control not to say, "with what" or "how." Choose your battles, choose your battles. "That isn't the point," I say.

"No? I think it is," Amanda says.

"The point is you've already done so much work, and you've made a commitment to school and, frankly, to your dad and me."

"Dad doesn't care," Amanda says.

"You've told him? When?"

Amanda shakes her head. "Not yet, but he's much more understanding."

I hear the implied "than you," and it hurts. "You might be surprised about that. Shall we call him?"

"No way. I'm not getting in the middle of your finger-pointing at each other."

"When will you tell him?"

"When I'm ready."

"At least withdraw from your classes. A withdraw is better than failing."

"I know. I'm not stupid. I haven't decided yet, so I haven't done anything."

"Can I talk you out of it?"

"This is my decision. When I decide for sure, I'll tell you. And Dad. Your pushing me does not help." Amanda stabs her curry.

I force my face to remain still as waves of confusion and sadness fill me, as they do every time we argue. Every time I think "I got this; I understand her now," the landscape changes. As we eat silently, I remember before Amanda was born thinking I wouldn't be my mother, with all sorts of unspoken rules I'd find out about only when I broke them. No, I'd create a loving environment where peace and understanding reigned, where we'd talk about our thoughts and differences. I wonder for the millionth time what happened.

I know I'm an over-anxious mom, and that anxiety intensified as Mandy got older. It was worse after the divorce, when it seemed Tony abdicated all responsibility to make sure that Mandy turned into a well-adjusted, functioning member of society with his leave-her-alone-she's-fine attitude. I got handed the job of saying "is your homework done? If you're not going to practice, you need to give up those piano lessons. Empty the dishwasher." I'm aware I'm the main reason Mandy wanted to go to school so far away.

"Talk to me, please," I say. "I want to understand."

Mandy shrugs. "I spent most of the first semester studying, going to parties, and hanging out. It was fun. But this seems more real, more important."

"College should be a little fun," I say. "You'll be an adult for a long time. It's okay if you postpone taking on the weight of the world."

"You see, that's it right there. You think I'm a child."

It's true, but not the time to say it.

"I get it, Mom," she says. "You wish you could be irresponsible for a while. Well, you have my permission. And once I live here awhile, I'll qualify for in-state tuition and apply for grants. Go ahead, open that bookstore on the beach."

"When did I tell you my escapist dream?" I ask, stirring the curry with my fork.

Bert and another young man approach our table as I'm figuring out the tip. Bert leans and kisses Mandy on the cheek. "I haven't seen you in ages. Where've you been?"

"Around," Mandy says. "I understand you've met my mom."

"Yes," Bert says, turning to me. "I'm glad you found her."

"Bert wants to be a lawyer," Mandy says as she stands.

"Save yourself," I say, standing too. "But call if you ever want to talk about it."

I invite Mandy to stay in my room at the Union, but she says no, she has things she needs to get from her room anyway. My mind races as I pull the sheets over me. Unlike Mandy, I think Tony will not be so accepting of her dropping out of school. He will care. He may be easy going about some things, but not about education or money. We've both struggled since the divorce, and out-of-state tuition isn't cheap. Maybe he can talk some sense into her?

"SHE'S JOINED A religious commune?" Corey says when I call her Sunday night. "Wow. Didn't see that coming."

"Right?" I say. "Of all the terrible things I imagined might have happened to her, that one wasn't on my radar."

"A while ago I read a couple of news articles about some groups at ASU and U of A that ex-members were calling cults. I'll see what I can find out."

"I doubt they're related," I say. "This group is small."

"All the worse."

At least Corey is taking this seriously, I think as I throw laundry into the washing machine, unlike Tony who says she's only experimenting with radical ideas. I admit, after college I considered banding with friends to buy a few acres and live off the land. But Tony would have none of it, and I chose him. My friends never did it either, probably because we were all Philosophy and English majors who had no clue about farming. It would have been a disaster but was appealing then. Maybe that's all this is.

"Call me when you can," Corey texts when I'm in a strategy meeting the next day. Mike sees me looking at my phone and frowns, so I bury it in my purse. I know he's irritated about the time I took off last week. I try to listen as an eager young associate recommends we set up a deposition of a businessman's wife.

"The client says his opponent is very protective of her and will likely settle if we push that," Andy, my aggressive younger colleague says. "I think she might be agoraphobic."

"On what basis would we depose her?" I say.

"To see what she knows about their finances and spending. This is a community property state," Mike says.

"Except she probably doesn't," I say. Andy and the other young litigators at the table look at me with shock. No one questions Mike. I'm expected to smile and agree.

"We won't know until we ask," Mike says. "Schedule the deposition."

I do, despite my unease. It bothers me we're using someone's mental struggles to leverage a settlement with her husband's business. It reminds me of one of my prior firm's in-house trainings when I was a new lawyer. A partner told war stories about how to get the advantage in litigation. At one point, he stood on his chair next to the huge walnut conference table, looked around the room at our young faces lit by the sun shining through the wall of windows high above the city's other buildings, and told us it was our obligation to be an asshole on behalf of our clients.

I call Corey when I get back to my office. "What's up?"

"There's a lecture on campus a week from Thursday called Cults at College. Want to go?"

"Yes, let's."

THE CAVERNOUS LECTURE hall in one of the newer buildings on campus reminds me of a Roman Coliseum, a half circle of rows of seats ascending along stark white windowless walls. I wonder if the instructor feels more like the lion or the prey. The room looks empty and it's almost time to start, only a few groups of college kids and several worried-looking couples I guess are hoping, like me, the speaker will help them understand, comfort them. I notice a man in a clerical collar sitting in the first row. Corey and I pick seats halfway up along an aisle.

Just as a middle-aged man in a gray suit approaches the podium, about thirty students file in followed by a tall, thin, bearded man wearing a t-shirt underneath his corduroy jacket. They seem too clean cut to be Philosophy majors, I think. Religious Studies, then. The man in the suit introduces himself as the Dean of Multicultural Programs, then introduces the speaker, Professor Vozel. The Dean lists the speaker's many awards and a few of her publications. Professor Vozel breaks my stereotype of an academic—her hair is too blond and too loose; she wears bright red lipstick, and her cheeks glow as if she has a fever. She has a commanding presence as she strides toward the podium, towers over it, and stares directly toward us.

"When I first started researching so-called cults in graduate school," Vozel begins, "I quickly discovered the term is almost meaningless, often used as a derogatory label for any group somebody didn't like or that challenged the majority culture in some way. Some define it by size, others by how long it's been around. If you look at some of the cult characteristics in the literature, practically any religious group could qualify.

"The FBI issued a Law Enforcement Bulletin in 2000 called 'Interacting with Cults: A Policing Model.' It says new religious movements are often labeled cults, and most such groups are benign with only a few devolving into violence or criminal activity. Jonestown, the Branch Davidians, Aum Shinryko, and the like are the exceptions, not the rule. Because our Constitution protects the right of everyone to practice their religion, the FBI encourages police to limit their law enforcement activities to interfering only when the group threatens to or commits violent or illegal acts."

At this, many in the audience start whispering to each other. She's right. People can believe any stupid thing they want.

Professor Vozel ignores the crowd's restlessness. "But this doesn't help parents who think their children are being misled or taken advantage of, does it?"

"No!" someone behind me shouts, voicing my thoughts. The volume of side conversations increases, and Corey squeezes my hand.

"There ought to be a law, right?"

I hear yesses and see a few heads nod. The lawyer in me knows any law like that would be impossible to enforce. The mom in me thinks we should be able to do something.

"Well, there isn't," Vozel says, "so the interesting question to me is more a psychological or sociological one: when is a so-called cult a danger to an individual? The Constitution protects religions, yes even new ones, and the right of people to have ideas that challenge the existing culture. But if someone you love has joined a group that you think is hurting her, what should you do?"

Exactly, I think, hoping she has some answers.

"Telling college students their ideas are stupid isn't going to work." A ripple of laughter spreads through the group. "In fact, I would argue it won't work with anyone. Cults are groups that challenge the status quo. Shouldn't we all be doing that? Our real concern should be with the psychological effects of a group on the people in it. That's much harder to assess. If a group promotes or condones physical or sexual abuse of any kind, threatens to blow up a train or a plane, storms a government building, defrauds investors— these are crimes, matters for police. But what about the more insidious threats like psychological abuse? Because I only have an hour to talk about my life's work, today I'll talk about two red flags in potentially harmful groups: the concentration of authority in a charismatic leader and the separation of group members from outside influence. I'm not saying every group having these two characteristics is a danger to its members, but I am saying that if it does, you might want to look a little closer."

She has everyone's attention now, except for several students sitting far from their instructor who seem to be asleep.

Professor Vozel spends most of her talk discussing the group's leader, saying that a group with a diffuse organizational structure is less likely to commit atrocities. Sort of like a government with checks and balances. This can be disguised if the leader has hard-core followers who have nominal authority. Most dangerous are those groups led by charming people with narcissistic or anti-social personality disorders. My mind starts to wander as she describes in typical academic fashion the characteristics of these psychological disorders. How the hell do I know if someone has empathy or remorse? I think. Or has illusions of grandeur and doesn't accept criticism well?

"The most obvious red flag, though, is if the group members are kept separate from their non-member family and friends," Professor Vozel says. "This is a classic sign of potential domestic abuse, and the purpose and effect are the same in a group context. Limiting outside influences and relationships strengthens a person's dependence on the group. The danger to an individual comes when the member's dependence on the group leader is so complete that he or she will do anything the leader directs. Think of Manson, Jones, even Hitler. Their followers did terrible things, convinced that their leader knew more than they did, and they should follow his teachings no matter what. A healthy group allows dissent and discussion and doubt. Without that, individuals in the group are easy prey for manipulation."

When she opens the floor for questions, several hands shoot up. She calls first on the man in the clerical collar.

"I'm the pastor of a church that's been called a cult. We've been visited by the police and our student outreach program has been investigated by the University. Your talk focused on how persons on the outside of a group can identify potential dangers to their loved ones in a group. My question is, how can the group itself alleviate the concerns of its neighbors or the parents of its members?"

"An interesting question," Vozel says. "I don't think I've ever had an alleged cult leader at one of my lectures." A few people laugh. "New religious groups may always be viewed with suspicion. I think the more open you are about what's happening at your church—inviting neighbors and parents to attend, sending out newsletters, participating in activities with other congregations, for example—the more likely outsiders are to become comfortable with the group. They may still disagree with you but will feel less threatened.

Hopefully."

"Then I'd like to invite you, and everyone here, to attend this Sunday, or to come talk to me," the pastor says, waving a handful of papers. "Ask me if you'd like directions."

"I may take you up on that," Vozel says.

A couple of students ask questions that start with "I know someone who" then describe a behavior, leading to the question "does this person have narcissistic personality disorder?" The professor predictably answers it's impossible to know on the basis of even a few examples, and besides she's a sociologist and not a psychologist. Like me, the students find this unhelpful.

A man behind me, his voice quivering from either emotion or nervousness, asks, "What kind of person is susceptible to being drawn into a dangerous group? I fear my daughter may be part of one on campus."

Professor Vozel is silent for a while. "That's an important question and not easy to answer. We're all susceptible to manipulation if our most important needs are being met by a group or person. Under the right conditions, almost anyone can be attracted to a cult. College campuses are fertile ground for recruiters because there are many lonely, searching people there. The best thing to do is to talk with your daughter, find out if she's one of those lonely people looking for someone to give her the answers."

The man mumbles a thank you.

Good luck with that, I think.

A young woman near the front stands and turns to the questioner. "Which group is your daughter in?"

The Dean interrupts. "Let's not name groups here. It's not the time or place to make specific accusations when not all parties are here."

"Come talk with me after, sir," the young woman says. "I was part of a campus cult and if your daughter's in the same one I'll tell you what I know."

Uh-oh. I can see the Dean fidgeting.

"Anyone with a specific complaint can contact the Office of Student Organizations," Professor Vozel says, and the Dean nods. "Like the Dean said, we're speaking in more general terms here, and investigating a complaint requires hearing both sides. I've been researching this phenomenon for over twenty years and although I get nervous about certain groups, only observation and research about a specific person or group can give any real answers. Thank you all for your kind attention and interest."

"Feel better?" Corey asks as we file out of the room.

"No," I say.

Chapter 13

Amanda

I WIPE DOWN the huge plastic tablecloth on the Grange's dining table and smile at the children outside laughing and running with Jax. Lisa pokes at my feet with the broom, playfully telling me to hurry up or move aside.

A screen door slams, and the sound of Philip and Hannah washing and putting away dishes stops, replaced by Pastor Mark's deep voice saying something I can't quite decipher. I poke my head into the kitchen to see Hannah drying her hands on a towel whose picture of strawberries is faded from many washings.

"Did something happen?" Philip asks.

"It's probably nothing, but I wanted to let you know about an interesting conversation I had today with a Detective Taylor," Mark said. "He was asking all sorts of questions about us."

"Who's complaining now?" Philip asks.

"He didn't say, but I was wondering if we should go talk with anyone."

After a long silence Philip says, "Didn't Amanda's parents call us a cult?" Everyone looks at me.

My face burns. When my dad called last month to absolutely forbid me from dropping out of school, he said he wouldn't let me ruin my life by joining some stupid cult. To appease him, I didn't drop out, but my grades took a big drop from first semester. "My dad said that. They're both mad at me."

"And why would he think that?" Mark's voice is quieter now but has a hard edge. "He's never been here."

"Dad said some detective told my mom there were rumors. There's no reason she would think that on her own."

Mark nods. "Probably Paul Ryandowski spreading lies again. Poor Helen, bound for life to him. Well, it shows we need to be vigilant. Always kind to our neighbors, but careful around them too. Give them no cause. You all are here by choice, right?"

His vulnerability at that moment pierces me. He's trying so hard to lead this community, to help us be open to the Spirit and to our neighbors, and people spread rumors to hurt him. I feel a flash of anger for my parents' part in that.

"I've never felt freer in my life," I say. "And I'll gladly tell the detective that."

"Me too," Lisa says, and everyone nods and murmurs assent.

"The world may misunderstand us," Philip says. "But we are united."

Mark smiles. "I love you all."

"And we love you," Lisa says.

"Group hug!" Mark says, and we all come together, laughing when the children burst through the screen door and pile on.

The children quickly tire of this game and start chasing each other around the table.

"Time for bed!" Rachel announces to the sighs and complaints of the eldest children.

Matthew pulls on my skirt. "Will you tuck me in?"

I look over to Hannah, and she nods. "OK," I say. "Angela, you come too."

I hold both their hands as we climb the stairs to their rooms. "Who wants a story?"

"Me!" Angela and Matt say together.

"Brush your teeth and put on your pjs, and I get to pick the book."

I scan Matthew's bookshelf as I help him put on a large soft t-shirt. The well-worn edges of *His Treasure Map* help me choose, and Matthew claps when I pull it out. Even Angela seems content as they snuggle next to me, and we look at the map that leads to the heavenly kingdom. Despite its talk of pirates and buried treasure, it reminds me of Pilgrim's Progress, the book my grandma read to me before bed when I was six, and I understand the comfort it gives. Matthew falls asleep, but I continue until I hear Hannah putting Becky to bed. Angela moves sleepily toward her own room.

"I'll walk you back," Mark says, and Hannah nods, mouthing "thank you" as she lifts Angela into her bed.

The night is clear and cool, and I'm glad for the sweater I'd put on earlier. Mosquitoes buzz my ear, and when I slap one, I see from the red on my palm it had already drawn blood. I hug myself and rub my arms.

"Are you cold?" Mark asks.

"A little," I say, and he puts his arm around my shoulder and draws me closer.

We walk slowly and silently, a galaxy of fireflies beside us the only light until we near the porch of the women's house.

"Talk with me a while," Mark says, and we sit on the stoop, close but not touching. "Your parents are angry."

"Yes. They had big plans for me I'm not following," I say.

Mark shakes his head. "It's hard not to dream big for your kids."

"They need to let me dream for myself."

"You could invite them to stay a few days. See that we're not so bad."

Dad would never come, and the thought of Mom sharing a house with ten people, having all her meals with a group, praying, doing chores was . . . unthinkable. "That would not go well."

"Asking them might relieve some of their fears."

"OK." I smile at him. "A vacation in Indiana this summer."

"God's country, for sure."

"My mom grew up in the Midwest and my dad went to college in Michigan."

"Then it should feel like home."

Lisa peers out the screen door. "Hey guys, want some tea?"

"I should get back," Mark says, getting up and waving as he leaves.

"I would," I say, coming into the arc of light.

"What was that about?" Lisa asks.

"He was worried about my parents calling us a cult, says I should invite them for a visit."

"Will you?"

"I said I would."

"IT'S FINALLY A warm Sunday morning," Pastor Mark says at the end of the service a few weeks later. "I think we need to get ready for volleyball season. Who's in?"

Several men shout, "Me!" and an excited hum fills the room.

"In the summer we have a weekly picnic after church on Sunday and play volleyball," Lisa leans over to explain. "It's fun."

"I'm not very athletic," I whisper.

"No worries. A couple of the guys take it seriously, but most of us don't."

Philip drives Lisa, Shirelle, and I to a park next to married student housing at the University. Children burst from the church bus the second the doors open and run towards the slide that towers over the swings. Matthew climbs a large dome crisscrossed with metal bars. Sarah rushes to catch Emma just before she starts to climb the ladder, Emma shrieking as Sarah puts her in a toddler swing instead. I help Lisa carry a large box filled with plates, utensils, plastic tablecloths, two large bottles of disinfectant spray, and several scraps of towels and old t-shirts. I can tell they have a routine as they secure tablecloths to the picnic tables and fill cups of lemonade. Mark dumps charcoal in one of the park's grills while Philip and Nathan set up a volleyball net. Soon, only Mark remains near the tables, poking at the briquettes.

"C'mon!" Lisa shouts from the other side of the net. "Play with us."

I hesitate, then run to join her team. I apologize every time I miss the ball or send it wildly in the wrong direction, which is almost every time the ball comes anywhere near me.

"Stop apologizing," Lisa whispers as we pass each other during a rotation. "Really. Nobody cares."

But I care. I hate being incompetent. But at least my serves are good. My side cheers as I again and again lob the ball toward the other team's weakest player. Not intentionally, just because I have one move and that's it.

"Food's ready!" Mark yells.

I sit between Lisa and Matthew. Hannah is so busy feeding Becky she doesn't see Matthew's hot dog keep slipping from its bun.

"You want some help?" I ask.

"The hot dog keeps moving," Matthew says.

"You could cut it in half. That might help."

"Mom won't let me have a knife," he says.

"Well, she can't stop me," I say, brandishing mine.

Hannah smiles gratefully at me as I cut Matt's hot dog. I let him pick the exact sizes the pieces should be.

A couple of the dads take the children back to the playground as everyone else talks.

"Nice serves out there," Mark says.

"Thanks. I can hit a ball when I'm standing still and taking my time, but anything that requires me to be more athletic than that, well, let's just say I never get picked first."

"You're in good shape, though."

"No eye/hand coordination. At home I'd swim a lot, and the University has a nice pool where I went when I could."

"Can you lift a bale of hay?" Philip asks. "We always need help with that, and you can sure get your exercise that way."

"I have no idea," I say. "I'm willing to try. But it doesn't look like we'll be baling hay any time soon."

"Is this your first time on a farm?" Nathan asks.

"I'm definitely a city girl. My grandparents' farm was all flowers and vegetables. They'd sold most of their farm to developers before I was born. Every Fall my parents would take me to a local farm with a cornfield maze, and we'd buy a pumpkin and have chili. No bale lifting involved."

"Time for more volleyball!" Bryan shouts from near the net.

"I'll clean up here," I say to Lisa. "Hannah, Mark, go ahead and play. It won't take me long."

"Go ahead, Hannah," Mark says. "I'll douse the charcoal and pack everything back into the bus."

There's a comfortable silence as Mark pours water on the coals and throws away the paper plates with their blotches of ketchup and pieces of bun and potato salad. A lot of the tableware are metal utensils, but some are plastic. I pick up one trying to decide whether to throw it out.

"Put the metal and plastic utensils in the empty bun bags. We'll wash them back at the Grange," Mark says.

"Not very green using these paper plates," I say as I wipe down the plastic covering the tables. Most of the dinnerware at the farm are breakable, I recall, not suitable for a picnic. "Maybe we should get some cheap plastic ones?"

Mark pokes at the coals to see if there are any live embers before dumping them into a huge metal garbage can. "At least we don't use the Styrofoam ones. But I'm betting we could get a bunch of picnic-ready plates at the Goodwill. Want to go sometime and pick them out? It's where we get a lot of our clothes."

"I would." I smile as I think about how only a few months ago the thought of buying plates at Goodwill would have shocked me.

Together we pack the boxes with the picnic gear and put them on the front seat of the bus. I head toward a bench near the volleyball net, but Mark takes my arm.

"A family that plays together, stays together," he says. "And we don't want uneven sides."

CHAPTER 14

Susan

MANDY'S INVITATION TO spend a week in Indiana surprises me. I accept before she can change her mind. Summer's a good time to be away from Phoenix. It's slower at work, clients escaping to San Diego or Colorado or the East Coast, the legislative session is over, the "snowbirds" are long gone. My friends at the County Attorney's office get an uptick in cases during the hot months, but anyone who can leave does. I can't imagine what it was like before air conditioning. Or what it's like for those who can't afford it. Or for those people standing with their signs at the freeway exits asking for spare change. They must be desperate. I should give them something, but I lock my doors instead, convincing myself that donations to the Food Bank or Rescue Mission are better for everyone.

When Mandy told me her house wasn't air-conditioned, though, I told her I'd stay in a hotel. I remember Midwest summers, the humidity and mosquitoes. "Your choice," she said. I asked if Tony was coming too, and she said no, he said he'd see her next time she came home. And when might that be? I asked. She didn't know.

By June, I've given up watering my little patch of grass, now a frazzled brown. At least the bougainvillea and oleander thrive, bits of bright pink against the white-hot sky. Thorns and poison. I've always said I prefer the searing heat of the summer here to the ice and wind of a Midwest winter, but I'm not so sure anymore.

The metallic whir of the fan breaks the silence as I match pants to blouses, pack a loose-fitting dress, add another, trade it for a long skirt, count out my underwear and put them in a large plastic bag. I limit myself to two pair of shoes, pack my e-reader. If I forget something, I have a credit card.

I go to Mandy's room. I sit in the old rocking chair and hum the songs I'd sing to soothe her to sleep. "Twinkle Twinkle Little Star," "Simple Gifts," "Amazing Grace," "Do Re Mi." I hug the soft, sad looking donkey that's been waiting patiently for her since December. I won't take him. She might come home for that. I open a drawer and see her summer shorts and tops, and decide to pack those. I sort through the thin summer dresses hanging in her closet she said she'd never need until she came back, and pack a few of those too.

Her name flashes on my caller id.

"Pastor Mark says we can pick you up tomorrow," she says. "You can use our car while you're here."

"That's nice of him. OK. Yes. I'll cancel the rental. Meet me at baggage claim? And M . . . Amanda? I was going to pack some of your summer clothes. Do you want them?"

"Yes! Whatever you can fit. Especially loose things with sleeves—the mosquitoes are vicious. Get the stuff from Dad's too."

I sing "My Favorite Things" as I fold a soft red blouse she got at her high school graduation party. Was that only a year ago? I tape together a folded moving box from the garage and fill it with all the clothes I remember her wearing last summer—multi-colored wide pants, long, loose, gauzy and lace blouses, jean shorts, black capris. I'm sure she'll be on the best-dressed cult member list.

AS I DESCEND the escalator to baggage claim in the Indianapolis airport, I see Mandy near the carousels talking with Pastor Mark. He looks even less imposing than I remember, here, out of his element. But Mandy is looking at him with the same devotion I remember on the faces of the rest of the congregation. I try to tamp down my irritation as I stretch my shoulders. I wave when they look my way, and wariness takes over her face.

"Susan, welcome," Mark says, taking my hand with both of his.

I stiffen. "Thank you, Mark." I slide my hands away from him.

"Hi, Mom," Mandy says, and I throw my arms around her. She puts one arm around my waist.

"I missed you, sweetheart," I say and kiss her forehead.

Mark drags my suitcase and box off the carousel. Mandy gives me a questioning look.

"I couldn't fit all of your and my clothes in my suitcase," I say. "Can I buy you both a late lunch? Well, late for you, right for me."

"Absolutely," Mark says before Mandy can answer. "What do you have in mind?"

"Surprise me," I say.

"Perfect. I love a person with an adventurous spirit."

We pull into a strip mall in front of a small restaurant called Biuro. Inside is brightly lit and empty, with four-person tables covered in red and white checked plastic tablecloths. A thin woman wearing a colorful triangular scarf tied at the back of her head comes rushing toward us. A large man in a chef's cap waves at us from an opening behind a counter in the back. The woman hustles us to a table near the window and hands us large, laminated menus. An older woman brings three glasses of ice water. None say a word.

I scan the menu skeptically. "You're going to have to order for me, Mark."

"Me too," Mandy says.

"You're in for a treat. I found this restaurant with my mother, and we made a point of coming here whenever someone needed to go to the airport."

The thin woman returns, and Mark orders stuffed cabbage, sausage rolls, potato and cheese pierogi, and baked sauerkraut. Too much food arrives, and the older woman beams at us from a stool near the kitchen window, nodding happily as Mark puts one of each on our plates. I decline the sauerkraut. I might be adventurous, but not that adventurous.

"Have a little," Mark insists, dropping a small lump on my plate. "Add some sour cream."

Mandy grimaces at the sausage rolls as I stir a large amount of sour cream into the sauerkraut. I'm surprised at how good the pierogi and sausage are.

"You're Polish?" I ask to break the silence.

"Moravian my mom would say, but yes this is traditional food. She had cabbage growing in her kitchen garden all the time. We still grow it, can it."

Mandy nods. "We have sauerkraut with most meals." Her body leans toward Mark.

"She would buy sausage from the market," Mark says. "Said she'd done her fair share of sausage making growing up and she'd sacrifice taste for not having to do that ever again."

"Well, they do say you should never watch sausage being made," I say.

"I've never heard that," Mandy says.

"Never? Lawyers are always saying 'never watch the law or sausage being made,'" I say.

Mark sits back in his chair and laughs. "My dad would say that too."

"Must be an old person thing, then," I say.

"Let's get going," Mandy says.

"No, no. Not until we have apple pierogi with ice cream!" Mark waves at the waitress. He's like a little boy happily ordering then diving full force into the dessert, finishing mine when I can't. His smile is infectious, and he soon has us laughing about the first—and last—time his mother made sour rye soup for his dad, or the time he snuck into the cupboard to try the fermented honey drink his mother had forbidden him.

The sun is low in the sky when they drop me off at my hotel.

"You can stay with me sometime, if you want," I say as I hug Mandy goodbye. "There's a pool."

"Let's wait and see," she said, handing me the keys. "Here's a map to the farm. Call me when you're coming."

"Come for lunch," Mark says.

They climb into an older red truck parked near a large tree. I wave as they drive away.

I SWIM IN the hotel's pool, dawdle over breakfast, wash and curl my hair, and still it's only nine a.m. when I'm ready to go. Well, they live on a farm. Mandy answers her phone before I hear it ring.

"Hi, sweetie," I say. "Want to go shopping today?"

"I thought you were coming for lunch," she says.

"Sure, but before or after that."

"I promised I'd help with the kids but come around noon and we can figure out the best day for me to be gone."

"OK," I say, but I'm not sure she hears me before she hangs up.

The downtown is quiet. A woman leaves a coffee shop, balancing her purse and a covered paper cup, and rushes into a run-down office building. It's cool this early, and the few trees have broad leaves and unpruned branches tumbling over the sidewalk. I find a lovely old courthouse that's the most inviting place around despite all the police cars lining its perimeter. The white stone building fills most of a square block, the upper level a mass of pillars and carvings topped by dormers. I sit on a bench in front of a fountain until I see a scruffy man pushing a cart headed my way.

Inside, I admire the carved wooden doorways and wainscoting, the floor painted to look like tile. An old elevator with accordion doors takes me to the second floor, opening to a hallway with pink walls broken up by massive wooden doors. The hallway leads to a round, open area brightly lit from large windows on two sides. Carved and painted crown molding lines the tops of the walls meeting a green ceiling with a hole in its center. Looking up through the hole, I see lathed railings for two floors and at the top a white dome with gold stars lit by clerestory windows. So different from the bare functionality of the courthouse in Phoenix. It reminds me of a cathedral, the quiet and the mystery. Whoever built this thought the law was sacred, and the courts its protector.

I used to think that.

"There are nineteen stars, if you're counting. Indiana was the nineteenth state," a security guard who'd silently approached me says.

"Such a beautiful building," I say. "Are the courtrooms open?"

"There's a trial starting soon in Courtroom 1 so it should be open." He points toward heavy doors down the hallway where a tall man in a navy suit is talking with a shorter man in a white shirt and a tie. As I pass, the two men stop talking and watch me. Inside is more carved wood—along the walls, railings separating the public benches from the counsel tables and the jury section from everything else. Most impressive is the judge's area, a barrier of walnut protecting the clerk, the bailiff, and the judge. I can't help but wonder what my life would have been like had I stayed closer to home, closer to my classmates, closer to what I knew, instead of running off to Phoenix the minute I graduated. It seemed right at the time. Better than moving back to Chicago to be the loser everyone in high school thought I was. A chance to be somebody else.

A clerk comes in with a pitcher of water for the counsel tables and smiles at me. The two men enter the courtroom as I'm leaving, the shorter man's mouth forming a thin line as the taller man holds open the heavy door. Lawsuits bring out the anger and orneriness in people. It's not personal.

MANDY'S HAND-DRAWN map directs me to the central building in the complex behind the main house. I park next to the red pickup and an old tractor. Under the eaves of a huge barn a man appears to be showering fully dressed. Above him on the barn's roof is a large barrel, and I'm impressed with its ingenuity. A large black dog stands nearby, lapping the water as it runs toward a tree. I see Philip hanging his shirt on a line strung between two houses, and he raises his hand in greeting. Mandy and another woman come toward me, a screen door slapping shut behind them. I had no idea what to bring them. It seemed silly to bring food or flowers to a farm, so I bought them a lovely red, black, and white Navajo rug I saw in a pawn shop in Flagstaff. What if they think it's a discard? Too late to change now.

"Mom, you remember Hannah, Pastor Mark's wife," Mandy says as they help me unload the car.

"What is all this?" Hannah asks as she picks up the box, and I open it.

"I brought Amanda's summer clothes, and the rug is a gift," I say.

Hannah lifts the rug toward the sun. "It's beautiful, but too much." She folds it back into the trunk.

"Don't make me take it back to Arizona, please," I say. "It won't fit in my suitcase."

"Mark," Hannah says as we walk toward the back of the house. "Look what Susan brought us."

"Lovely," Mark says. "I'll bet there's history here."

"Probably," I say. "Sadly, I don't know what it is. It came without provenance. I liked it."

"Provenance," Mandy says under her breath, and I feel my cheeks warm.

"Where should we hang it?" Mark asks.

"I think the dining hall, where everyone will see it," Hannah says.

Mandy carries her box and leads me to a room on the second floor of the house next door. Two single beds separated by a chest of drawers fill the room. The walls and floors are bare, and the single window has ruffled blue gingham curtains.

"We could shop for some decorations if you'd like," I say.

"I'm hardly ever here, and I'd want Lisa to help choose anything anyway."

"She could come with us," I say.

"We're not into things here," she says. "Some books might be nice."

Two young women are placing bread and bowls of fruit on the table when we reach the dining hall. The rug is hanging on the back wall facing the windows. We slide in on a bench near two empty plates, but before even one dish comes our way Mark taps on his glass.

"Everyone, this is Amanda's mom, Susan," he says.

"I hope you're not planning on one of your dorky get-to-know-you-games," says a tall man with a blond braid.

"A fine idea!" Mark says. "No, but, Susan, would you like us to go around the room?"

I shake my head. "I'll have a better chance of remembering names if I meet you one at a time."

The larger group discusses the drought and a cutworm infestation while Mandy and Lisa talk about what books they want. I try to keep an interested smile on my face as conversations swirl around me.

Chapter 15

Susan

MY CELL PHONE wakes me at three a.m. the next morning. Disoriented, I reach for my phone from the wrong side of the bed, knocking my glasses on the floor. When I roll to the other side I see "Ed" on the caller-id. This can't be good.

It isn't. I wait until seven to call Mandy. I'm numb as I tell her Grandma and Grandpa were in a car crash in Ohio. Grandma is dead. Grandpa is on life support. He's not expected to live. Uncle Eddie's on his way to the hospital. He'll call when he gets there.

I feel like I'm in a play, reading lines meant for someone else. Mechanical. A robot pretending to be alive.

"I'm sorry, Mom." Mandy says. "Is there anything I can do?"

"You can come to the funeral with me," I say.

"I'll be ready in two hours," she says. I hear voices in the background, Mandy explaining and asking about a car. "Mark says we can take the car you're using. I'll drive it back."

What should I do? Who should I call? Should I post it on social media? No. Too raw.

As I put everything back in the suitcases, I wonder why I'm not crying, why the whole world seems frozen. Look, the sun is shining. Who cares? I order French toast, bacon, hash browns at the hotel restaurant, but they're tasteless. Eddie calls, and I ignore the frowns of the people at the next table as I talk with him. Dad died before he got there. He's made arrangements with the funeral home to transport their bodies. Can I come home quickly?

"I'm in Indiana, Eddie. I can make it to Tinley in a few hours," I say.

"Right, Mom told me. You're dealing with Mandy," he says.

"She's coming with me. It will be good for her to get away from these people."

I pack the car and think about how much I don't want to go home with its oppressive weight of unfilled expectations and lost friendships. Now my mother's warmth will be gone, too. I never did work out my anger at my dad. Grief will have to do.

I call Mike, hoping to leave a message. His assistant picks up but transfers me to him. He tells me he's sorry for my loss. I can hear annoyance in his voice when I request bereavement leave.

"Aren't you on vacation?" Mike asks.

"Yes, but I'll need to add on a few days. This was all very sudden and none of us was prepared. I'll need to help with things after."

"Are your cases ready?" Mike's voice is flat. He knows there's always more to do, more research, more motions, more interviews, not to mention all the new matters he's emailed me the last two days. I could argue with him, remind him about the firm's policy on compassionate leave. But what's the point?

"I'll come back the Monday after the funeral," I say. "That's when I was planning to return anyway."

"See you then," Mike says and hangs up.

I feel a flash of anger. Why did I expect any sympathy? I knew he was all about billable hours. He probably thinks I should return the day of the funeral and work through the weekend. A hard ball of resentment sticks in my chest. I wish I could leave the firm, but who will hire me at my age? I better start looking. They're going to find a way to let me go. I have no illusions anymore about becoming a partner.

I tell the hotel why I'm checking out early and probably won't be back. They look at me sadly and say they're sorry. The air is heavy with humidity. Mandy's waiting under a tree alone in front of the farmhouse when I pull in. She throws her suitcase in the back seat and signals she wants to drive. I kiss her cheek when she settles in.

Miles of corn fill the horizon. Flashes of sadness and memory threaten my ability to speak. "Knee high by the fourth of July," Dad would say every time we passed a cornfield. Or he'd read the signs, in case anyone missed them. Dad loved to drive, always up for a road trip and never wanting to stop for a bathroom break. "Oh Jim," Mom would say, "the girls need to stop." I remember countless bologna sandwiches eaten along the side of the road with warm pop, Dad too cheap and too driven by how many miles he wanted to cover to stop in a restaurant. I guess it's fitting they died on a road trip. I hope at least they stayed in a decent motel on their last night.

"Grandpa loved road trips," I say.

"He did?" Amanda says. "You hate them, don't you? Dad says you always insisted on flying."

"Too boring, too long, too little time to see the place you're headed. I prefer being there to getting there."

"He also said your idea of camping requires bathrooms with running water. I'm with you on that."

"Guys don't understand that, do they?"

A lighter silence falls on us, and I doze until the car slows. Amanda throws quarters into a toll bin.

"I probably should drive the last bit," I say. "I know the way by heart. Let's stop at the next exit, get some gas and lunch, and I'll take over."

Mandy parks in front of a diner next to a car packed with brightly colored towels and inner tubes. As we slump on the vinyl benches waiting for a table, children chase each other in the crowded entrance. The place smells of pancakes and bacon and burned coffee.

"Grandpa's idea of fine dining," I say.

"Don't be a snob," Mandy says, covering my hand with hers. "It's fine."

I slide a knuckle over my eyelid. "Both at once."

After we order, I squeeze Mandy's hands. "Are you sorry we didn't live closer to them?"

She hesitates. "I loved when they came to see us, and the few times I stayed with them they made sure we did fun stuff. So, yeah, when I was a kid, I couldn't understand why they weren't around all the time. I know now if we did live around here, it wouldn't be all ice cream and trips to the zoo. Besides, you're different around them, all tight and angry."

"Mostly around my dad, right?" I ask.

Amanda shrugs, sliding her hands under the table. "Let's talk about the good times."

We tell each other stories about the first time Mandy saw snow when my parents drove her to Flagstaff and the time she ran away from home, dragging a wagon filled with stuffed animals toward the airport. How they always showed up for birthdays and graduations. By the time we finish eating, we're both laughing and crying.

"Are you folks OK?" the waitress asks as she slides the bill underneath the sugar shaker.

"My mom and dad just died, and we're reminiscing," I say.

"I'm sorry, hon," the waitress says, patting my shoulder.

As we near my parents' street, I resist the impulse to keep driving. Several cars fill the driveway. The house is as I remember, rose bushes, petunias, and geraniums lining the perimeter, with an occasional bush pruned to fit under the windows. Two enormous maple trees hover over the roof in the back, everything surrounded by yards of bright green grass and the yellow of an occasional dandelion. I remember Dad paying me a penny a piece to root them out.

The front screen door bursts open, and my sister Diane rushes out. "Susie! Finally!" she says.

"I said we'd be here in the afternoon."

Diane hugs me and starts to cry. "I know, I know." She then hugs Mandy. "It's so sad, they're gone so soon."

"It's good to see you, Aunty Diane," Mandy says.

I drag my roller bag toward Diane's husband Ken who is standing at the edge of the stoop. He hugs me, and we stand silently for a while.

"Put your bag in Mom and Dad's room," Diane says. "Mandy can stay in your old room with Nadine."

"Nadine's here?" Mandy brightens.

"She's flying in this afternoon with Katie," Ken says.

"Any word from Eddie?" I ask.

"He's going to meet us at the funeral home, then rush off to Midway to pick up Katie and Nadine. I think he should sleep, but you know Eddie."

I nod, not sure what she means.

NO MATTER HOW bright and tasteful they try to make it, a funeral home is depressing. All those heavy dark drapes and crosses dripping from every wall. Diane keeps asking for tissues. Eddie isn't here, and I answer the director's questions, agree that a joint service is a good idea, balk when he talks about a showing.

"Oh," Diane interrupts. "Daddy wants a showing."

If that's what they wanted, then that's what they should have. Just because I hate viewing dead bodies. Does anyone like it? I guess so. Someday I'll research the psychology of that. Not today.

When we return, Mandy is sitting with her cousins Ted and Cal, a round of Ritz crackers and a can of Cheez-Whiz in front of them. Ted and Cal are telling stories of Grandpa taking them fishing, and Mandy is countering with stories of coffee cake and cigars on South Mountain.

"Aunty Sue promised everyone pizza," Diane says. "I thought we'd order in an hour."

Eddie comes in, grim-faced and tired, and silently gives everyone a hug. In a monotone he tells us about the accident and the arrangements he's made. Thankfully, he doesn't describe their injuries, says the wake won't be until

Thursday because the mortician has a fair amount of work to do. I can see we share coping mechanisms in doing what needs to be done, getting through it.

"I can pick up Katie and Nadine," I say. "You should sleep."

"I'll be glad for you to drive," Eddie says, "but I want to come too. A nap will do. Wake me if I'm not up by eight."

Mandy goes for a walk and I lie down. I sniff a few times and blow my nose so no one will think I'm such a hard ass. One more thing to pretend about. Pretend I'm happy, pretend I'm smart, pretend I'm a good mom, pretend I cry when both my parents die. Oh god. Both my parents are dead. I'm an orphan. I should have been a better daughter. I should have gone to visit them more, had them move in with me once Dad retired. Like that would have worked out. After a five-day visit I needed them to go home. And they usually stayed two weeks.

I try to read in the hopes my brain will stop careening.

THE FUNERAL HAS an unreal quality. I stand in a line shaking people's hands, trying to smile, but it's like I'm somewhere else watching what's happening. Eddie, Diane, and I take turns talking in front of the church, but the words seem disjointed. When I talk about Mom's kindness, a few people cry. I ask Mandy to come up and sing Mom's favorite hymn with me. I let Mandy lead, and everyone joins in.

As I fill my plate with ham buns and potato salad in the church basement, my parents' lawyer approaches. "Little Danny," Dad would call him, forever remembering him in Sunday School. He's a few years older than me, student council president when I was a freshman. He calls me Susie, pretends like he knows me, and asks about practicing law in Arizona, says maybe he'll retire there, winters are getting tiresome. I act like those are interesting points. I'm saved by Mom's best friend coming to hug me. Danny asks me to come by his office to talk about the will.

As we sit around my parent's living room later, Diane says she made an appointment for all of us to see the lawyer. Tomorrow. "It won't take long."

"I don't want to go to the lawyer's with everybody," Mandy tells me later. "I don't care what the will says."

I don't want to go either. "Aunty Diane says we have to."

Mandy gives me a look I interpret as her asking when I ever did what Diane wanted. I shrug.

WE TAKE TWO cars to the attorney's office the next day. Once we're seated in the conference room, Dan turns on a projector. Oh my god, he's got a PowerPoint. Mandy falls back into her seat with a sigh, and Eddie squeezes my hand.

"Jim and Betty were frugal people," Dan begins. "I think the size of their estate may surprise you. They decided to create trusts with conditions and limitations, and the most detailed limitations are on the trust for the grandchildren, so let's start there."

How like Dad to make decisions for our kids, I think, my resentment building. I remember his using college tuition as a threat anytime I wanted to do something he didn't approve of, like spending the summer working on the New Jersey shore, or going to a protest. He controlled Mom through money too, never telling her how much they had, making her ask for every little thing from a new coffee pot to presents for the grandkids. I understood when he cut us all off once we graduated from college, although there were many times a little help would have made life easier. I said that to him once. He said it wasn't his job to make my life easy—it was his job to make sure we were independent. He took credit for our successes. "See?" he said when I graduated from law school and got my first job. "Tough love works." It took almost fifteen years to pay off those loans. I dread what sort of restrictions he's put on us from the grave.

"Your parents asked that Edward be the executor." Dan looks at Eddie, who nods. "The grandchildren's trust will be administered by Edward, Susan, and Diane. Two hundred thousand dollars for each grandchild to be transferred, with interest, on the earliest occurrence of one of the following." Dan moves to the next slide. "First, graduation from college, second, the first anniversary of the grandchild's marriage to a person of the opposite sex to be used for the purchase of a home, or third, reaching age thirty-five."

The room is silent, each of us with a look of disbelief on our faces.

"They also made specific bequests to their church and other charities. The remainder of the estate is to be divided equally between Eddie, Susan, and Diane, with $250,000 to each as soon as possible, and the remainder for the purchase of separate annuities for lifetime monthly income." Dan pauses and looks around. "Does anyone want further explanation or a copy of the will?"

I'm not sure what surprised everyone else, but an anger I've suppressed for many years grows in me. He still wants to control me. And everyone. Thinks we can't make our own investment decisions. Eddie and Diane whisper with their kids.

"I'd like a copy," I say.

"Couldn't we create our own trust and take a monthly stipend instead?" Eddie asks.

"No, the will says it must be purchased," Dan says.

"Dad doesn't trust us with money, that's obvious," I mutter.

"What does it matter?" Eddie asks.

"What's the current value of the estate?" Diane asks.

"Two years ago, your father estimated it at four million."

Mom had to ask for money for socks when they had four million? This spark of rage is the first strong emotion I've felt in days. I need to be alone before I burst.

"We'll be collecting liabilities and liquidating assets for a while, so don't expect a check any time soon," Dan says.

We leave the room together, but no one speaks until we reach the parking lot. "Who wants ribs tonight?" Eddie says. "Dad's treat."

Chapter 16

Amanda

MOM'S MADE COFFEE when I stumble into the kitchen early the next morning. She offers to cook breakfast while I finish packing, but I tell her a bowl of cereal is fine. Her eyes are red, and she holds a scrunched-up tissue in her hand. I put my arms around her and kiss the top of her head.

"I'm sorry, Mom," I say.

She nods and sniffs and grabs another tissue. "Can we talk? Or are you sick of talking with me?"

I am sick of it, but now is not the time to say so. "What do you want to talk about?"

"I came to visit you in the hopes we could understand each other better, put aside any bad feelings." Tears drip down her cheek. "And then this happens. And all the old feelings about my dad come crashing and I get angry and you get mad at me. I'm wallowing when I should be comforting you. I know all this but can't seem to stop."

"It's okay, Mom, I know you're having a hard time," I say.

"Please talk to me. Tell me what you think about home, about the farm, about me. We can't have an adult relationship if you keep hiding from me."

"Mom, two days after your parents' funeral is not the time to argue, and we'd end up arguing." Let me leave in peace, I think. I'm grieving too.

"Then when? Will you come home for a visit? Don't lie to me."

"I don't know."

"Tell me why you prefer living on a farm with all those strangers than living at home?"

"They're not strangers to me. And you left home, too, Mom. You complain that Grandpa was controlling. Well, you can be too. You didn't like my friends in high school, you set a ridiculous curfew . . ."

"Midnight is not ridiculous!" she says.

". . . you wouldn't let me stay at Dad's whenever I wanted, you absolutely forbid me from getting a tattoo. Do you want me to go on?"

"You were sixteen," she wails. "You thought you knew more about the world than you did. I don't apologize for setting boundaries. I bet there are rules on the farm, aren't there? Oh, your dad was easier on you I know. Well, I think it's because he hates confrontation. Don't forget, you were cutting yourself when you were at his house, not mine. I made sure I was home the nights you were with me, not off at a bar or playing video games with the door closed."

How dare she say those things? I stand and put my bowl and cup in the dishwasher. She follows me to the room where Nadine is still in bed, a pillow over her ears.

"Please don't leave like this," Mom says.

"Talking now, when we're both upset, won't resolve anything, Mom."

"OK," she says hugging me.

"I'm an adult now. I'd appreciate it if you'd treat me like one."

"I know, I know," she says, hugging me tighter. "I love you, please remember that."

I load my duffel into the back seat. She waves until I'm out of the driveway. When I look in the rearview mirror, I see her sitting on the stoop, head in her hands.

I stay angry as I drive through morning traffic, honking my horn at the inevitable driver who thinks weaving in and out of lanes will get him to work faster. Idiot. I need to calm down. What is it about Mom's family that makes the air feel as if a spark might blow up the whole room? So different from the peacefulness of the Grange. Maybe the difference is we chose to live with each other as adults, instead of being thrown together by fate and DNA. Mom, Aunty Diane, and Uncle Eddie are so different. Or maybe their sameness makes them irritate each other. What would Mark say? "Leave other people to their anger and selfishness. You remember the gifts of the spirit." Peace, patience, kindness. Peace, patience, kindness. I repeat this for miles until calm comes over me. The wide expanse of farmland helps too.

Don't let the family's trauma make me bitter, I pray. Help me to be patient and kind to Mom. I decide I'll call her when I get back to the Grange. Yes, that's the right thing to do. Mark will agree. The decision makes me happy, and I wave at the trucker who's been following me too closely as I let him pass. He waves back. I'm even forgiving of the naked women emblazoned on his mud flaps.

I pull into a rest stop to take a break, get a pop, stretch my legs. As I get back in the car, I notice a trucker watching me. He's a short pudgy little man in a loose-fitting gray uniform with wisps of blonde hair escaping from under his cap. He gives me a leering smile, but I look away and lock my doors.

I wonder what Mark will think when I tell him about the will. He'll probably tell me to finish my degree. Something more useful than history though. Something I can use on the farm. Maybe a nurse? I wouldn't want to move, though. Or a nurse practitioner? They do a lot of the same things doctors do. I'll check into it.

I look into my mirror, and there's a truck following too close again. What's his problem? I slow down and glare at him as he passes. I recognize the trucker I'd seen at the rest stop. Shit. He slows way down. What the hell?

Peace, patience, kindness.

OK, I'll pass again, and this time go really fast. That big truck can't be as fast as my car.

But it is, and I can't bring myself to go more than twenty-five miles over the speed limit. I slow to ten miles over, and he passes me again pulling at his cap as he does. I slow to the speed limit, then ten below, then twenty. Finally, I don't see the truck anymore. I consider pulling over, but don't want to be sitting on the side of the freeway. I decide it's all over, and I'm imagining things. Then I see the same truck ahead of me, going far below the speed limit.

I panic now. What if he tries to drive me off the road? He knows I'm alone, knows cell service is spotty out here. I've watched enough *Criminal Minds* to be scared. We're approaching an exit, so I slow, figuring I'll take it once he passes. Instead he starts waving at me, seems to be telling me to exit here. Is he crazy? He pulls into the exit lane and I follow. When he's committed but I'm next to the gore, I swerve back onto the freeway as he heads down the ramp. I go as fast as I'm able, watching the return ramp. He must have caught the light, as I don't see any truck getting on. Five miles to the next exit. If I speed, the state police might pull me over. Not all bad. I pull in front of another big truck, hoping it hides me, then speed up again because I hate not seeing what follows. The exit is one mile away now. I pull into the exit lane at the last possible moment, glad for the light traffic here in farm country. I drive into a town and park as hidden from the street as I can at a rundown little restaurant. And then I cry. For fifteen minutes, I cry.

I call the Grange. Mark gets on the phone, and I tell him what happened. His calm, reassuring voice is a blessing. He tells me he's coming, wait in the restaurant. I order fried chicken and mashed potatoes. They serve it with okra. I've never tasted anything so wonderful. Mark arrives as I'm finishing and orders a cup of coffee. He walks me to the car. We stand in the parking lot and he holds me for a long while, brushes my hair with his hands, and my fear slowly dissipates.

WHEN I ARRIVE for my Wednesday session, a great weight lifts. For the next hour at least the pain and lethargy I've felt since the funeral will be gone. Mark says eventually I'll be able to get to that place through prayer and reflection, but he's happy to be my support until then. I like spending time alone with him. At home he treats me like everyone; here I'm special. Here in this room nothing else matters.

Mark hugs me before we sit, takes my hands once we do.

"What would you like to talk about today?" he asks.

"Mom called again this morning. Part of me wishes I could be more help to her, but most of me wishes she'd quit calling. I'm a terrible person."

"It's hard to help someone else when you're full of grief."

"Doesn't she get that?"

"From what you've said, it sounds like she doesn't have much support. She's rejected the church, she's divorced, she lives alone. Her need may be greater than her understanding right now."

"I guess."

"It's important to have a community to rely on. You have us. Keeping busy isn't a way to avoid grief, it's a way of finding purpose. You told me last time you want to take up nursing at the University. That's purpose. Once school starts, you'll be so immersed in the joy of helping people that your own troubles will fade."

I have found myself almost happy playing with the kids at the farm or baking in the kitchen with the women. I need to be busier.

"My advisor says I need to retake two of my courses from last semester before I can apply to the nursing program. But I'd like to be more involved with the work here too."

"I've been discussing that with the Council, and we've agreed that when you're ready, you could be co-director of campus outreach with Philip. Would you be interested in that?"

"You mean more than staffing the tables on Fridays?"

"Yes, I mean helping Philip plan what is the most effective way to reach students. And meeting with them individually. Everyone needs someone to listen."

I nod. Loving listening, Mark calls it. It's what God does for us, but sometimes we need a person to show us. To respond in ways we can understand. "I'm not sure how good I'll be at that. Look how I am with my mom."

"There's a lot of history to get past in families. It's easier with someone you've just met. You need to care enough about them to listen." Mark goes to his shelf and pulls out a book. "Here, this book talks about how to be a good listener and why it's important. There are even exercises we can do together. Why don't you read through it and we can talk about it next time?"

He strokes my hand, and my desire for him builds. When I stand to leave, he pulls me into his arms and kisses me. The light touch of his tongue on my lips releases something inside of me. I open my mouth and let the ardor I've bottled up for a long time release into my kiss. I know he's married. Right now, I don't care.

A LIGHT BREEZE moves the sheer curtains and keeps my room from getting too hot. I remember July in Phoenix, the sun searing my eyes and skin, unlike the soft gray haze that seems ever-present here. I push the curtains back so I can watch the trees. A few dark clouds build towers in the distance. I hear the tractors coming toward the barn and the shouts of men calling in the cows from the pasture. Soon everyone will huddle inside to play games or go to their rooms to take a nap during the storm. Storms here are nothing like the monsoons back home, where sometimes all we'd get was a wall of dust moving toward us, making it impossible to see, and, if we were lucky, the violent, short-lived, rain and thunder.

Lisa comes in, peeling off her shirt before heading to the shower. I barely notice when she returns, combing her long, wet hair. She sits on the end of my bed.

"Did you go to the library today? I need a new book too," she says.

"No, Mark gave this to me at our session earlier. I was telling him how hard it was to listen to my mom. He says I need to work on my listening skills."

"Don't we all? I should read that when you're finished."

"OK."

"I miss my sessions with Mark," Lisa says. "I think I'll try to set up a regular time again."

"He seems busy," I say. "Mark suggested I work with Philip on the student outreach when school starts. Should I?"

"Why not?" she says. "You'll be there anyway. Are you afraid it will be uncomfortable?"

"Yeah, a little. I did have quite the crush on him."

"Still?"

"No, I can honestly say I don't. He's more like a brother now."

Lisa shrugs. "He's probably lost his mystery, what with seeing him up to his boots in manure."

"That's for sure," I say. "Do you ever consider going back to school?"

"No," she says. "We can't afford it, and I like watching the kids and cooking and practicing with the Band. Especially now that we have a rock star like you singing."

"I'm not sure if my parents will pay after last year. I haven't asked them yet. I'll probably have to take out student loans."

"Hah. Don't play poor. Your mom inherited a bunch of money. She'll send some your way. And even if she doesn't, once you graduate, you'll have plenty to pay off any loans."

I nod. Is she jealous?

"Do you think you'll stay once you graduate?" she asks.

"I don't have any plans to leave," I say.

"I wonder how you'll feel when you come into all that money and there's feed to buy and roofs that need repairing. This farm is poor. What we sell is never enough."

I'm filled with guilt. "I wish I had some of that money now so I could share it. It's not right I live here for free."

Lisa hugs me. "You're not a burden—you help a lot. And you don't eat that much."

"I'll be spending gas money once school starts. And I'm not sure if my dad's still paying my health insurance."

"You'd better find out," Lisa says, and I nod.

I can't imagine Dad cutting me off, or Mom either. But Lisa's right. I'd better find out.

AFTER SUPPER, PHILIP and I walk around the orchard to check for storm damage. The rain was heavy, but there hadn't been much wind. A few unripe nectarines and peaches lie on the ground, and we put them in the compost sacks. The setting sun glistens off the wet leaves and fruit and creates long shadows in the paths between the rows.

"Looks like a good year," Philip says. "We'll have plenty of fruit to eat and to sell."

"Do you set up a farm stand?" I ask.

"Some of the big orchards have markets as well as pick-your-own days. We make jams and apple butter and pies to sell there, and if we have a great crop, we sell bushels. They take a cut, but we don't have enough people to run a market of our own, and I'm not sure we'd want to anyway. You'll be conscripted into jam-making soon."

"I have to say, if anyone told me last summer I'd be living on a farm, baking pies, and canning beans I would never have believed them."

"Life can be funny," he says. "And wonderful."

"Lisa says the farm has money issues. Would setting up our own stand help?"

"We tried to figure that out one year and decided the best use of our time was making fancy jarred fruit to sell. People love homemade organic foods. We can make decent money from being the supplier—so the more you help us make, the better. We bring a lot to the food pantries and homeless shelters. At least a tithe, but usually more."

We've reached the apple trees now, the apples still mostly green. We pick the few we can reach that have insect holes.

"Mark says he suggested we share responsibility for the campus ministry this year," Philip says. "Is that something you'd like to do?"

"I'd like to try. I'm sure I'll be mostly learning and following your lead. Who helped you before?"

"Sarah did for a couple of years before she dropped out and had Emma. Becoming a student organization and setting up tables on Fridays were her idea. A good one, although I'm getting tired of doing the same thing all the time."

"How about we have students staff the tables most of the day and only one of us there for a couple of hours. After a few weeks we'll know who we can count on."

"Good ideas already." He puts his arm around my shoulder. "We'll make a good team. Still going to major in History?"

"No," I say. "Nursing seems better. If I get admitted to the program. My advisor says I can take the nursing biology and psych courses even though I'm not admitted. I'm taking that as a good sign. Should we have something planned out for the first week?"

"Probably. How about I leave that to you?"

"Oooh. Pressure. I've been thinking about it, though. The hardest thing for me was fitting in. We could do something like I saw on the news once, where some kids in middle school made it a point to invite the kid sitting alone to play or eat lunch. We can go to the orientation picnic and the Union and talk to those people sitting alone looking forlorn."

When we're standing in front of my house, he kisses my forehead and walks quickly toward the men's house. He hasn't done that for a while.

Chapter 17

Amanda

LISA AND I spend most summer mornings picking fruit or making peach pies and jam, switching to apple pies and jam once the early apples ripen. I've never been much of a morning person, but it is glorious to fall out of bed and trudge to the kitchen where the smells of coffee and cinnamon greet me. Hannah wants us to know all the steps, so some mornings I pit the peaches and on others measure out the sugar, stand over the stove stirring, strain the cooked fruit, roll out pie crust, pour jam into mason jars. We sample the morning's batch on the waffles or pancakes before Lisa and I go to work at the Pick-n-Eat market that sells our fruit and jams. Someone always asks if I made the jam, and I'm proud to point out which ones I did. Inevitably they smile and buy at least a couple. We decorate the cooled jars after dinner. Lisa's artistic, so she does the lettering and draws little pictures (a tree, an apple, a grove, whatever moves her at the time) while I cut strips of gingham into ribbon. I never knew how much was involved in making those pretty little jars my grandpa used to sell at his flower market. No wonder they cost so much more than supermarket jellies.

The market's busiest times are Saturdays when families come to pick fruit themselves. The market has air conditioning, and the hot, muggy afternoons drive the older women into the store. The shop has a small refrigerator with lemonade and unfermented apple cider next to a row of baked goods with pies and breads and cupcakes and fudge wrapped in cheese cloth or gingham and tied with a bow. Then there's the row of jams and jellies and fruit butters and barbecue sauces and an area of what they call gourmet items—dried figs and dates and a variety of nuts. Lisa prefers the cash register to stocking, so I'm the person to ask when someone's looking for a particular item. In the front of the store is a section with craft items like apple dolls, straw brooms, metal sculptures, quilts, and souvenir thimbles and mugs. Lisa says some of it is art from students at the University, but most of it is from nearby farm wives. During slow times, we talk about what arty things we could make this winter.

The last Saturday before the dorms open is particularly busy. Lisa and I roll our eyes every time some man in a silk shirt says "Americana" or "how quaint." It's no wonder those guys aren't outside picking fruit. I try to talk to their embarrassed children often hiding near the sample fudge, ask them whether this is their first year, what's their major, and tell them I'm a student, too, maybe we'll see each other on campus. They seem grateful. One mom asked whether there were any nice churches around. I looked at the manager—he had forbidden us from talking about ours—and he came over and told them about the find-a-church website. I could have told her that.

Bert walks in with an older man and woman about an hour before closing. The woman smiles and chatters and the man looks at the floor. I slip into an aisle where I can watch them on the big convex mirror. The woman I guess is his mom looks older than I'd expected, her white hair clipped severely from her pale face and her flowered sack of a dress hovering loosely just below her knees. How different from my mom. How different from Bert, who even today has taken great care to look good with his slim-fit t-shirt, tight jeans, and carefully mussed hair. You never know who'll you'll meet out and about, he once told me. Well, at least his mom is comfortable. I glance toward his dad, who seems almost invisible. Faded baggy jeans, short-sleeved plaid shirt, a crew cut leaving bare his large red ears and face. He's still looking at the floor.

Bert looks up at the mirror and surprise bursts on his face. I quickly move toward him.

"Hi, Bert," I say. "Are you folks looking for something in particular?"

"You work here?" Bert asks and I nod. "Mom, Dad, this is my friend Amanda."

"Lovely to meet you," his mom says, and his dad mumbles what I take to be agreement. "Do you make any of this?" She waves her hand to take in the whole store.

I take her to the aisle with the Grange's items. "I had a part in all of these."

"How nice," she says and puts a jar of peach jam into the plastic basket hanging over her arm.

Bert looks uncomfortable, so I give him a quick hug. "Good to see you," I say.

"Yeah," he says, looking away.

"I should get back to work," I say, shaking hands with Bert's mom and dad. "It was nice to meet you."

"Absolutely," his mom gushes. "I hope we see you again."

When I return from the back room with a large box and begin stocking shelves, I overhear bits of conversation between Bert and his mom.

" . . . nice . . . told us about? . . . invite her . . ." his mom says.

Bert's voice is deeper, clearer. "We don't hang around anymore."

His words hurt, but it's true I haven't spent much time with him or Felicia these last few months. Am I one of those girls who abandons her friends when she meets a guy?

Apparently, I realize, vowing to be better.

ON THE WEEKEND before classes start, Philip drives with me to Orientation Game Night at the University. He plans to hang around the Union, looking for anyone who seems lost and alone while I play. I climb the stairs to a conference room on the second floor where several Resident Assistants with bright blue tags stand near tables filled with game boxes and snacks. I see Tammy, my old RA, and decide that's as good a start as any. She'll be looking for her charges and so won't stick with me long. I fill a small paper plate with some carrots and celery sticks, then drift over to say hello.

"Hey, Tammy," I say. "Remember me?"

"How could I forget," she says. "Your mom got me into a lot of trouble. I wasn't sure I'd get an RA position again this year."

"Sorry. My mom is the anxious type. I started texting her more often after that so she doesn't come storming out here again."

"Good." Tammy heads toward a group coming into the door.

I look around to see if I recognize anyone else, but all I see are new faces. Many of the newcomers are standing in front of the boxes of games as if mesmerized by them. I approach a timid-looking girl with limp ash-blond hair who's picked up a beat-up Monopoly game. Unlike most of the others, she isn't dressed in tight or revealing clothes, or in a t-shirt advertising some band or political cause. Instead, she looks like her mother dressed her—a shapeless yellow top over Bermuda-length jean shorts with white socks inside brown loafers.

"Want to play?" I ask. "My name is Amanda."

She looks at me with wide, frightened eyes. "Yes."

"What's your name? Are you a freshman?"

"Yes," she says. "My name's Trudy."

"I'm a freshman too, although I started last year. Which dorm are you in, Trudy?"

I'm already tired of this one-sided conversation but feel sorry for Trudy. A young man looks at me with interest, but I suspect Trudy will stop talking if we invite him to play. As we set up at a card table in a quiet corner, two young women approach us and ask if they can play too.

"Fine with me," I say. "But I get the race car."

"I'll take the iron," Trudy says faintly.

"Top hat for me," one says. "And I'm the banker."

"I'll take the Scottie dog," says the other.

"I'll bet our pieces say something about us," I say. "I'll start—I'm Amanda, and I picked the race car because I love to drive."

The girl with the Scottie dog smiles. "I'm Caryn, and I picked this because he reminds me of my dog back home, Angus."

The other girl claims the seat with the best view of the door. She has all the style Trudy lacks, casual, but striking—a long, thin white jacket over a black-and-white striped tunic on top of black leggings. She even wore jewelry, a necklace with clunky white beads separated by smaller black ones. I take a quick look at her leggings tucked into short black boots. This is a rich kid looking for a date. Sort of like me last year.

"Hi all. I'm Missy, and I picked the top hat because it matches my outfit," she says, laughing.

Yes. Yes, it does. We look at Trudy.

"I'm Trudy. I picked the iron because it's retired in the newer games," Trudy says in her quiet, hesitant voice. "I'm glad they still have it in this one. I like antiques and old stuff."

"When did they retire it?" I say in my kindest voice, sensing this may get her to talk.

"2013. It was one of the original pieces," Trudy says. "So were the race car and the top hat. The dog came a few years later."

"How do you know all this?" Missy asks.

"My grandma told me. She still has a set from when she was a kid."

"The iron reminds you of your grandma," I say.

"Yes," Trudy says, looking away.

"Classic or Speedy?" I ask. Missy and Caryn say "Speedy" almost in unison. Trudy nods.

Monopoly doesn't take much skill or attention, so we spend most of the game asking each other about our majors, where we're from, and why we picked this school. Missy and Caryn haven't decided on their majors, but they heard this was a fun school. Trudy said nursing.

"Me too," I say. "Let's see if we have any classes together."

We play for about fifteen minutes when the young man I'd seen at the buffet comes to watch. Missy gives him an encouraging smile, and he asks if he could be the banker. To make sure Missy doesn't cheat, he says. She gives him a soft punch in the arm but moves her chair to give him room. After a half hour, Missy looks at her meager holdings and Trudy's hotels and folds. She and the banker head outside to look for more exciting times.

"Yeah, I'm done too," Caryn says. "Looks like Trudy is going to win."

"OK, Trudy wins," I say. "Go ahead, I'll pack up."

"I'll help," Trudy says.

After we put Monopoly back, I ask Trudy if she'd like to play something else or go get a coffee. She chooses coffee. Downstairs, I see Philip talking to a large guy in a t-shirt that says, "Deny Everything." Philip smiles, and I wave.

"You know him?" Trudy asks.

"Yes, he lives the same place I do."

"He's cute."

"Yes, he is. Do you want to meet him?"

"No, please no. You live off-campus or in one of the co-ed dorms?"

"Off-campus," I say and tell her a little about the church and the farm.

"That sounds better than a dorm. I hope I can find something like that next year."

Philip and his new friend, Bob, come up to us as we're clearing the table. We walk Trudy back to her dorm. Bob's dorm is a little further, but he waves us off when we offer to walk with him too.

"Tonight went well," Philip says.

"Yes. Trudy is painfully shy, but sweet and smart. And it looks like we have a class together this Fall."

"Nice," Philip says as he opens the car door for me.

ONE MORNING AFTER class during the third week of the semester, I have time to kill and decide to see if Bert's in the same dorm as last year. He is, according to the guy at the front desk. I walk the hallway, loud bass sounds surging from behind many doors. A woman in a ponytail wearing pajama pants and a loose t-shirt hovers near the microwave in a kitchen area. The smell of onions and tomatoes and garlic waft my way. Two guys run around the corner laughing, the one behind snapping a towel at the one in front.

Bert's room is toward the end of the hallway. He's scored a single this year. I knock loudly.

"Just a sec," Bert says, and I hear rustling papers and other noises that sound like an attempt to straighten the bed or throw clothes in the closet. He opens the door and looks at me in surprise.

"Amanda," he says. I see an open laptop and several books—*Western Civilization, Elements of Style, Invisible Man, Paying Guests*—in a pile on his desk.

"Hey," I say. "Can I come in, or are you too busy?"

Bert opens the door wider. The fluorescent buzz of the overhead lights keeps a melodic line to his neighbor's rhythmic bass. I see a new poster of Sam Taylor.

"How've you been?" I ask. "It was nice to finally meet your parents."

"You don't need to keep coming around," Bert says, looking out the door. "You'll never convert me, and you're always busy with those holy rollers."

"I do have less time living off-campus," I admit. "But we can still be friends, can't we?" His words hurt, probably because there's truth to them. I did want him to join the church, but it's because I like having him around.

"Pretty sure they don't approve of me," he says. "And you've changed."

"OK, I'll leave if you want me too." Tears sting my eyes.

"I want the old Amanda back," he says, touching my fingers. "The one who liked to have fun and laugh. Who was smart and kind and not all so pious and judgmental. Who had time to go to a movie once in a while."

"That's what you think of me?" How dare he?

"I miss that girl who couldn't stop laughing."

I flop onto the scuffed blue bean bag chair in the middle of the room and Bert drops to the bed. We stare at each other for a bit.

"Well," I say. "I'm not sure what to do. The church has given me something to believe in. Why isn't that a good thing?"

Bert looks down at a dark blob on the mottled gray carpeting. "Because you're gone," he mumbles. "You're never around, never have time, and I'm sure those people are filling your head with ideas about how I'm bad. Unnatural. Need to be saved." He looks me in the eye. "It's condescending and hurtful. You were such a change from all the people around here who are either condemning or wasted. We had the best conversations. I miss that."

"If I've made you feel like I'm judging you, I'm sorry. I'm not. But I need you to be happy for me. Can we talk about that? It's a different conversation, one where we're not always agreeing with each other and making fun of everybody else."

"You don't think I wish I could believe? But forget about all the irrationality and inconsistencies for a minute and look at one big thing. I can only be accepted if I deny who I am."

"I don't think that. Not all Christians think that."

"But many, probably most, do."

I shrug. I don't want to admit he's probably right. "Forget about them. Or show them how wrong they are."

"It's hard to be around people who don't accept you, who treat you like a Sinner with a capital S. It's tiring to pretend you don't know what they think."

"Come on, you are so much more. Most of these people have never been around outspokenly gay people and that allows them to keep their prejudices. Don't let them! And if I act that way, call me on it."

Bert sits next to me on the beanbag and takes my hand. "You don't make me feel that way, but I'm afraid they'll get to you."

"They won't," I say. "I'm far too enlightened."

Bert gives a scoffing laugh. "I'm still not going to church. But come around more. If you want."

"I will," I say. "And how about we go get some of that high-octane coffee in the Union. It looks like your paper is going to take a while."

Bert stands, then pulls me up. "Let's go."

CHAPTER 18

Susan

I STARE AT the letter and check from my parents' lawyer. I knew it was coming, but the unreality of suddenly being debt free astounds me. I could buy a bigger house, a new car, put a down payment on a place in Flagstaff.

I could get a different job. Work for people with a social conscience. Teach at the University. Join the Peace Corps. My mind drifts to thoughts of opening a bookstore with a coffee shop and wine bar, a dream of mine ever since I visited Boston when I was in college. Independent bookstores are dying, I remind myself, but then bask in the fantasy a while longer. I wonder how much income that annuity will provide? A voice inside my head that I recognize as Dad's says, "Don't count your chickens before they're hatched."

The possibilities brighten the next morning at the office. I decide today I don't need to eat at my desk and call Corey to meet me for lunch. The sun and cooler September air make my walk to a vegan café across from the ASU downtown campus invigorating. The downtown is so much brighter, feels so much safer, than when I first moved here. And a lot more food choices. At the restaurant, even the outdoor tables are crowded, but I grab the last one with shade as I wait. Other people take a break for lunch. Why don't I ever? I resolve to be more social. Meet people for lunch, for happy hour, for breakfast if that works best.

"It's good to see you smiling," Corey says as she drops into her seat and leans toward me. "Good news?"

"It's a beautiful day," I say.

"Have you heard from Mandy lately?"

"Not since she asked me to pay her tuition about a month ago. I'll call her soon to see what her plans are for the holidays. But I got a check from my parents' estate, so I'm feeling flush."

"Let me guess, you're going to pay down your mortgage."

I laugh. She knows me too well. "Probably."

"We should plan another trip. More than a weekend this time. And not Vegas."

"I can't make any plans until the partnership vote in a few weeks, but after that, yes."

"Any idea how it will go?"

"I've started sending out my resume. And dreaming of opening a bookstore."

"You know I think you should leave that place no matter how the vote goes."

"I know," I say. Maybe Corey's right, but part of me wants them to offer me a partnership and then leave. I'm not sure why I need that affirmation of my worth, but I do. "What's going on with you?"

"I'm done with Steve."

I repress a smile and reach for the breadbasket. She's been done with him several times now. "Oh? What did he do now?"

"The usual. Eats my food, leaves my house a mess, never invites me to his. He says we're at the comfortable stage of our relationship. I told him it looks more like the I-do-all-work stage. Who needs it?"

"Not me," I say with a little too much emphasis.

"Where have you sent your resume?" Corey asks as our lunches arrive.

"A couple of small firms and the U.S. Attorney's Office. And there are some judgeships opening up soon, I hear."

"You'd be great at that."

"I'm not well-connected enough. Haven't done enough networking or been on enough committees. And part of me wants to do something completely different."

"Like what?"

"There are a lot of great nonprofits. Maybe something will open up at one of them. And I could move pretty much anywhere, now that Mandy says she's going to stay in Indiana."

"You wouldn't move out there, would you?"

"Chicago, maybe. I still have some ties back there."

Corey crinkles her face. "You've always said you're glad to be out of there."

"I am glad, but I'm trying to be open to possibilities. I'd want to live downtown, not in my old neighborhood."

"I hope you stay. I suppose that's selfish, but I do."

"I'd miss you, but my roots aren't very deep here anymore. And I'd only leave if I could get a job where I wouldn't need to take another bar exam. You made the switch look simple, but it wasn't, was it?"

"No, it was scary. But those first two years in the law firm convinced me this wasn't the life for me. So I lived cheaply and paid off my student loans as quickly as I could. That last year of work when I did my post-bac certification is sort of a blur, but I did what I had to do. Luckily, I didn't have anyone else depending on my income."

A wave of respect and sorrow washes over me. I was too involved in my own life to understand what Corey had done, had given up. Was that why she avoided commitment? "Do you ever regret it?"

"Nope. I love teaching, and working at a magnet high school lets me teach interesting classes and work with dedicated kids. Always something new."

"Do you worry about after you retire?"

"Sure. But I'll have a pension and I'm saving. Inheriting a bunch of money would be better, but I'm not counting on that."

I wasn't thinking about money but decide to let it go. Getting married and having a kid didn't protect me from ending up alone.

We hand the server our credit cards and tell her to split the bill. On my walk back, I try to decide if I'm feeling free or adrift.

THE PARTNERS' MEETING is set for the first Monday in October, the beginning of the last quarter and the start of the Supreme Court's new term. The three associates being considered for a partnership are asked to be available, so we sit at our desks pretending to work. Or at least I assume Courtney and Tim are pretending too. The restaurant on the first floor of our high rise delivers a pizza, but spicy food won't work for me today, so I eat the breadsticks and salad and the candy bar I have stored in my desk drawer. Everyone else here knows what day it is, what's at stake for me, so I keep my door closed. I have no desire to commiserate with anyone.

Time drags by. The meeting started with dinner at six, but it's eight and no one has asked me to join them in the big conference room. I wonder about Tim and Courtney but don't want to ask. Do I dare get up to get coffee? Go to the restroom? What if that's when they call? By ten, fewer people pass my office windows and the lights in the hallway are dimmer. I hear a vacuum somewhere in the distance. Did they forget about me? My neck is stiff, and my stomach roils. I decide to make a list of what my options are if they turn me down again. They would have let me go already if I wasn't profitable for them. Will I be able to stay? Where will I go? What will I do?

It's 10:23 when Mike knocks, comes in, and closes the door. I see from his hooded eyes and the thin line of his mouth the news isn't good. But how bad? My throat constricts. Will I need to pack up tonight?

"Susan," he says as he sits in the plush sage chair in front of my desk. "Sorry it took so long. There was a lot of discussion tonight, not about you but about the future of the firm and partner compensation and possible mergers. The firm will make announcements about all of that eventually, but I wanted you to know you won't be a partner."

Tears spring to my eyes, and I know if I speak they'll fall, so I just grimace until the burning subsides. "So, what now?"

"Being turned down three times is the end of the partnership track, I'm afraid. But we're going to offer you a contract position based on your billings. Is that something you would consider?"

NO! I want to scream, but I can't just leave without a backup plan. I wish I had an offer somewhere, but the government jobs I've applied for are moving very slowly and I haven't heard one way or another from the few private firms where I've interviewed.

"Depends on the terms," I say. This will buy me some time anyway.

Mike nods. "Everything stays the same until the end of the year, so we have time to work that out. I need to warn you, though, other things happened tonight that will affect everyone."

"Can you give me a preview?"

"No."

"How about Tim and Courtney? Are they partners now?"

Mike hesitates. "You should ask them."

"When will everyone know?"

"Soon," Mike says as he gets up to leave.

I call Corey from my car on the way home. "They said no again. Offered me a contract instead."

"Bastards," she says. "I hope one of your other leads works out."

I smile. It's nice to have someone on my side.

When I arrive, late, the next day, small groups whisper in the hallways, in the break room, behind closed doors. Conversations stop when I walk by. Courtney stands by the coffee machine and by her slouch I'm pretty sure I know she's received the same news I did.

"They turned me down," I say to her.

"Me too," she says, wiping her left eye. "I hear Tim made income partner, though."

That's not really a surprise. He's been the top billing associate for the last three years. And he's a likable guy, damn him. Easy to talk with, smart, funny. I'd have voted for him too.

"Glad one of us did," I say. "Have you heard what else was decided last night?"

"No," she says. "But I got an email announcing an all-attorney meeting for Thursday night."

I hope the rumor mill reaches my office before then.

By the afternoon, it's clear something big had happened. A named partner hadn't come in and files in his office are being removed. I overhear one legal assistant tell another about shouting overheard in a partner's office on the eleventh floor. Once everyone heard I'd been turned down, a steady stream of young associates come to talk to me about what I thought their chances were. What can I tell them? How would I know?

I think about skipping the dinner meeting on Thursday night, but my curiosity gets the best of me. The firm reserved the conference room on the top floor of our building. The room is set up with tables of eight spread out in front of a raised podium. The management committee has the two tables in front, but as far as I can tell there are no other assigned places. The equity partners sit together, and the income partners and associates gather into practice groups. I notice several partners are missing. I take a seat next to Courtney, figuring right now we have the most in common.

For such a large group, the dinner is eerily quiet. During dessert, Samuel, the Managing Partner, introduces Tim as the newest partner, and talks about the notable successes of the past year. By the time he starts discussing trends, almost everyone has turned their chairs to look at him, cups of coffee warming their hands.

"The last few years have been a struggle for our clients and most law firms," Samuel says. "But we've survived the recession and hope for better days ahead."

A smattering of applause and a noticeable easing of tension surrounds me.

"What these last two years have shown, however, is that we cannot keep operating as we always have if we want to stay in business."

The tension level rises again as some sit straighter and begin to fidget. My neck and jaw tighten.

"On Monday night we had a long, difficult discussion about the way forward. Not all the partners agree with the decisions that we made. Tonight we want to explain to all our associates our way forward to avoid misunderstandings and rumors. The partners know what changes we are making to their income distribution, so we won't discuss that tonight. And we will let your supervising attorney explain how these changes affect you individually.

"We have seen a significant drop in our income and profits per partner, and for the last several years the partners have taken compensation cuts. It has become clear we must make other changes. We will need to reduce our workforce at all levels. Yes, some partners will retire, and others will move on. In addition, we will have much smaller classes of incoming lawyers and law clerks, and we will be letting go about ten percent of our associates and support staff. Your supervising partner will come speak to you tomorrow about whether or not you are being asked to leave."

Icy lightning shoots through the room, freezing people's faces and causing many to gasp. I was pretty sure I was safe since Mike told me they were offering me a contract, but I knew now my negotiating position was weak.

"Some of you will be offered contract work, so think about whether that is acceptable. I know this is a surprise to many of you although if you've been reading the trade publications, it isn't. The partners are committed to making these transitions as painless as possible, so be sure to talk about any issues with your supervisor."

Samuel leaves the podium and then the room, followed by most of the equity partners. The room erupts in conversation and many leave, their faces grim.

"It'll be hard to sleep tonight," I hear a young associate say as we take the elevator to the parking garage.

The mood in the office the next day is somber. By late afternoon, many offices are dark, and I wonder if Mike is coming. He arrives around five, exhaustion obvious in the slump of his shoulder and the sag of his chin.

"A hard day," I say.

Mike drops into a chair. "Yes. Here's the firm's offer for your contract. Basically, you change from a salaried employee to one who's compensation depends on your billed and collected hours. You can stay on our malpractice policy and health insurance. You keep your office and place on the letterhead. Take a look at it over the weekend and we can talk next week."

I nod, and Mike pushes himself up from the chair and out the door.

I scan the proposal for its termination provisions, but don't find any. I already know I want to move on but keep my job until I do. Courtney told me at lunch she was taking the three-month severance package. I sit back and rock on my chair as I think. It's time to decide what I want going forward. I can't see retraining for a new career like Corey did. But I could work fewer hours, take a class Spring Semester. Maybe this won't be so bad after all.

Chapter 19

Amanda

IT'S NOT QUITE dark as the Church's leadership meeting begins in the farm's dining hall.

Jerry Andersson, one of the older members of the church who doesn't live at the Grange, opens a tin of cookies. He gives it to Hannah as she fills cups with coffee from the huge urn we use at group meetings. "Nicole made these for the meeting, but she said to be sure the kids get some."

Hannah smiles and puts several in the pocket of her dress before placing the tin on the middle table. I pick a seat where I can watch the clouds outside change from yellow to pink to gray, even a little orange. Not as gaudy as the sunsets in Phoenix before a storm or on a smoggy day, but pretty in its softer way. We won't get to anything important for at least fifteen minutes, time enough for the twilight to creep over the trees. Philip sits next to me and gives me a quick hug.

"You got mail today," Mark says. He hands me a letter then leans over me to grab a cookie.

It's from my grandparents' attorney: "Upon comparing the value of the estate's assets and liabilities, the court authorized the estate to send the initial check to each of the decedent's children. The estate has mailed notice to all known creditors and published notice for unknown creditors. The date for creditors to file claims is October 20. The estate will purchase annuities and fund the stipulated trusts once the claims period has passed and all liabilities have been paid. The court's order is enclosed."

The money is still unreal to me. I don't feel like any of it is mine. I only feel relief that at least Mom won't be so worried about tuition now, and my disastrous last semester might not be such a big deal. I wonder if she'll finally quit that job she hates so much. I hope so. I miss my grandparents, but it would be nice for Mom to be happier.

The Church's Treasurer, Bryan, hands out a financial report with the yearly budget and actual expenses. It's obvious the Church and the Grange are losing money. Donations to the Church barely cover the electricity, heat, and maintenance, with little left to begin to cover the pittance assigned to Mark as his salary. It's a good month if he gets fifty dollars. The statement for the Grange is more robust this quarter, but the bottom line is negative and has been for quite a while. I want to cry, thinking how hard everyone works, knowing we'll need to talk about lowering expenses or increasing income. Where? How? The mortgage is small, taken out to cover building the dorms and kitchen. The taxes on the Grange and insurance on both properties are high. I don't see how we could eat less, and I remember being cold all last winter. What could we change?

Dark surrounds us as Bryan explains the details. His reddish-brown hair falls over the edge of his black-rimmed glasses as he talks, not looking at any of us as he shares the bad news. Mark gets up to pace and the rest of us fidget or watch Bryan for some sign of a solution. I draw little pictures of flowers and apples in the margin of my report. When Bryan finishes, he looks to Mark. I see despair in Bryan's eyes.

"So," Mark says, almost cheerfully, "not that different from the last quarter?"

"No," Bryan says, a little smile cheering his face. "But we have to make some changes or sell off some property or apply for grants or something. We can't keep bleeding."

"I agree," Jerry says. Jerry matches my stereotype of an Indiana farmer, a large man with a perpetually sunburned face usually wearing a John Deere cap with a flat brim. He's taken it off tonight, showing the white fringe surrounding the bald center on top of his head. His blue chambray shirt is wrinkled and partly covered by denim overalls spotted with white bleach spots and an occasional dark blotch. His big, rough hands clench the edge of the table. "We have no denomination to help us through the rough spots. The only reason we survive at all is because Nathan's uncle lets us use the church buildings for the insurance costs. Mark's farm provides most of the rest. We can't keep abusing Mark's inheritance."

"It's freely shared, Jerry," Mark says.

"Yes, but at the very least the Church should support itself. And give you a salary. What you do with your property is your business, but the Grange should be self-sufficient too. If that means you need more or fewer people living here, well, figure that out! I move we separate the finances of the Church and the Grange."

"We do keep them separate Jerry," Bryan says. "We'd get in a lot of trouble with the IRS if we didn't."

"You know what I mean," Jerry says. "The church should give Mark a fair salary and the people at the Grange should tithe, but other than that . . ."

Mark interrupts. "I thank you for wanting to be fair to me and my family. But please try to understand I see things differently. The ministry is my calling, my life's work. I would do it for free. Some months I do." A few people laugh softly, but not Jerry or Bryan. "A lot of pastors have other jobs and ministry is a side job. I'm blessed I can spend all my time in ministry. And the people living at the Grange allow me to do that, taking care of the farm while I write sermons and counsel people. Besides, in my view, the Grange belongs to the family of God, not to me. It's not a burden, and I don't see unfairness."

I'm stunned by this discussion and Mark's words. Not his property? Believing in his calling enough to work for free? I've never met anyone so selfless and feel honored to know him, to be a part of his life. Could I be that generous? I guess we'll find out when I graduate. I hope I'm strong and committed enough to turn over my inheritance to what I believe in instead of keeping it for myself. I wonder if I can talk Mom into giving a tithe of her inheritance to the Grange.

Probably not.

"You and Bryan are right, though," Mark says. "We need to make changes. We are the leaders of this community, and so must decide what sacrifices are needed or if we need to take a new direction. Does anyone have suggestions?"

Bryan hands out a new report with individualized expenses. Bryan comments that there are large transfers of food from the Grange to church activities. Everyone agrees we should move to more potlucks where the cost of food is shared with those who don't live here. Philip points out it will always be unlikely that students will be able to participate, and I nod in agreement. Mark vehemently refuses to consider eliminating the student ministry, but he concedes we could talk about scaling it down if needed. Philip says students need us more than anybody. Jerry responds angrily that this is why the finances of the church and the Grange must be kept separate. Nathan points out that eventually his uncle or his cousins will want to take back the church site, so we should at least start some kind of building or capital fund.

"Mark, I know you hate to preach about tithing or to berate people about increasing their gifts to the church," Nathan says. "But the loss of the church building is a reality we need to plan for."

"We can meet here, at the Grange, if we need to," Mark says. "It's where we started."

The sometimes-heated discussion goes on for another hour. I'd heard my parents talk enough about separation of church and state to understand that Jerry and Bryan are concerned about the church's losing its tax-exempt status if Sunday worship returns to the Grange, while others see them as inextricably linked. What's important? I wonder. I realize for me it's this community. And the student ministry is what saved me. I never would have known about these wonderful, loving people if I'd never met Philip. Philip told me he had "seen a seeker" in me and that's why he introduced himself. He wouldn't have been at the sing-along if he hadn't been the campus ministry leader. I want this community to survive, not only to support me but to give others the acceptance, love, and joy I now have. But what can I do now? Not four years from now when I graduate. Right now.

That's when I decide.

By the end of the meeting, the leaders vote to have the Grange reduce its food donations to church events by moving to potlucks or fees, and Mark would emphasize the importance of charity in his sermons. Postponed for another day is a discussion of starting a building fund. I ask Mark to walk me back to my house.

"I have another idea, Mark, but want to discuss it with you first," I say.

"I wondered why you were so quiet. I hope you understand you can say anything to the group? No one will judge even if they disagree."

"Yes."

"What's your idea?"

"I think I should get married and claim my inheritance."

Mark stops and looks at me. "To who?"

A heaviness fills the silence. The man I love most here is not someone I can marry. "I will leave it to the community. Philip? We've gotten closer since we started working together on campus. He told me once that marriage here was a decision for the community, and I've heard you preach that, too. We could build a house here, pay the Grange for the land it's on, invite more people to live with us. Have a second kitchen and start our own farm stand."

Mark pulls me into the dark of some trees, strokes my face, and kisses me on my temple then my neck then my lips. His voice quavers a little when he speaks. "I'm glad to hear you're willing to marry Philip. He's a good man and cares about you. I was afraid our relationship would make you want things we can't have, and I can't bear the thought of your ever leaving. I'll talk to him."

PHILIP AND I meet with Mark in his study at the Grange instead of the office at the church. This more neutral ground is calming with its walls of books and the sounds of children playing and Hannah vacuuming. Here I can think about community. Be rational about the future.

"During the ceremony I'll read the usual passages about leaving your parents and becoming one flesh," Mark says. "What does that mean to you Philip?"

"It means we're not two separate people anymore."

I squelch a small spark of fear.

"And yet people get divorced all the time and they're still walking around," Mark says.

"They're still joined whether they admit it or not," Philip says.

"So, my parents are still married?" I ask. "My dad's probably going to marry his new girlfriend and I'm sure he's slept with her."

"We shouldn't judge what other people do," Mark says. "But marriage is a lifetime commitment and not an experiment. You're young, Amanda. Can you do that?"

"Absolutely. I've already left my parents," I say.

"Going to college is one thing, but leaving your family means never going back," Mark says. "This will be your home in every sense. Jesus tells us if we are to be his disciples, we must give up everything for God and follow the path Christ shows us."

As Pastor Mark talks, my mind races between remembering the loneliness I felt before and the love I have with these people, my new family. Here I'm part of something bigger, something important.

"Leaving Mom and Dad to be part of God's family seems like I'm gaining, not losing," I say. "I'm getting married younger than I thought I would, younger than my parents want, but I've never been more sure of anything in my life."

Philip leans over and kisses me. "I've been living here a while already, and this community is my family. I believe God has called me to marry Amanda, have children with her, and keep on with our ministry together."

Mark walks around his desk and hugs us both.

MARK INVITES THE Church to the Grange for Thanksgiving. Each family is asked to bring enough at least for themselves and two additional people. Philip and I invite several students who can't go home for the weekend, and they're asked to help clean up. The Sunday before Thanksgiving the church is full of people making deals on who would bring turkey, who dessert, who salad, who potatoes.

Wednesday night, several families show up with decorative gourds, paper plates, plastic ware, and a few pies and thawed turkeys. Philip and Nathan set up grills, and Jerry brings a fryer. Most families will cook at home and bring the food in time for dinner.

About a hundred people come to the Thanksgiving morning service. Will we have enough? Mark opens the service with a prayer thanking God for this year's good harvest, then suggests we sing one of his favorite old hymns, "Come Ye Thankful People, Come." The older people seem pleased. The keyboard player starts the familiar chords after projecting the lyrics on the projector screen.

I sway as I sing, swept away with joy and love. At the song's close everyone is smiling. Tears burn the edges of my eyelids as I look around. My family. I can't wait to tell everyone Philip and I are getting married. Mark invited the regular attenders to come to the Grange an hour before everybody else, and only a few people know why—those who live at the Grange and the leadership team. Who probably told others. Who am I kidding? Everybody probably knows. Mark says this is like the old church banns. Give people a chance to voice any objections before the day. It's silly, he says, to wait until the day of the wedding. I wonder if my parents might want the chance to object. I hope not. I hope they can be happy for me.

"My friends," Mark begins. "God has blessed us this year."

"Amen," most people say.

"What should be our response to God's great generosity and grace? Christ has told us that much is required from those who have much. And who has more? Plenty to eat, shelter, family, friends. A community that supports us when we have hard times. And God's grace that protects and saves us. So, thank God and thank your neighbor. Stretch out your arms in prayer and then use those arms to hug the person next to you, behind you, in front of you. Hug your family, your friends, that person in the back row you've never met, the people you recognize but can't remember their names."

Mark raises his hands high, a look of joy on his face. I raise my hands and close my eyes, but soon feel Philip's familiar arms around me. He kisses me and I open my eyes, then we both turn to the people on either side. Soon the room is filled with hugging, laughing people. Philip and I leave our row to include the people in the back, some of whom put their hands in front. To them we give a short bow, touching their shoulders or cheeks as they allow.

My heart is bursting when the band begins playing a jazzed-up version of the opening hymn. Many of us sing as we move around the room, taking one another's hands, forming a circle to smile and sing with each other. We sing several more songs until Mark breaks the circle by raising his arms again.

"And all God's people say," he begins.

"Amen!" the room responds.

"Food at three!" Mark says. "See you then."

I don't want to leave, and few people do. Instead, we hug and hum and talk. Many come up to Philip and me with congratulations. Several ask what we need.

"Nothing," I say. "I have everything I've ever wanted or needed."

Finally, Philip puts his arm around me and whispers, "There are turkeys to baste and potatoes to mash." I'm sad to leave, but happy this love will continue all day and for the rest of my life.

I see unfamiliar cars parked near the main house when the bus pulls into the driveway. I kiss Philip's cheek, then run to the kitchen. We'd put out plates and dinnerware before leaving this morning, and Hannah and Sarah stayed back to put in the turkeys and lessen what needed to be done during that hectic time between getting home from church to placing the food on the tables. I thank them, and Hannah smiles and tells us what to do next. We hear car doors slamming and watch as new tables and chairs are set up wherever there is available space. Women with bags of bread and rolls or carrying pies surge into the kitchen.

"Put everything on the counters," Hannah says. "We'll have to do a buffet in the kitchen today. Sarah, can you help everyone set up?" Sarah nods and herds the women into the dining room.

Then come the waves of children looking for their mothers, diversion, something to eat. Their happy, excited noise matches my emotions.

"We should give them some crackers or bread and cheese." Lisa says.

"Good idea," Hannah agrees. "Keep them out of the kitchen as best you can."

I see dishes piled in the sinks and start to work on them. Finally, all that's left is the waiting.

"There will be another rush at two-thirty," Hannah tells us, "when we'll carve the turkey and mash potatoes and pull out the pies, but until then let's enjoy each other's company."

Mark comes in. "Most of our regular members are here. It's time for Philip and Amanda's announcement."

Hannah puts her arm around me, kisses me on my temples. "Yes, let's do that."

About thirty people gather in the dining hall. The women smile at me as I join Mark and Philip.

"Most of you know Amanda and I want to marry each other," Philip says. "But this isn't a decision we make alone. Not only do we want your blessings and advice, we want your agreement. Some of you may think we're too young. Others of you may think our getting married will put a burden on the Grange. So, please, let's talk about it. We submit ourselves to the judgment of the community."

I nod and smile, but inwardly pray everyone will agree.

"Where will you live?" Nicole Andersson asks.

"Here," Philip says. "The family house is full. For now, we'll live in the farmhouse with Mark and Hannah."

Jerry Andersson stands up slowly. "Well, that's crap. These young folks are getting married. They deserve a place of their own. My son-in-law sells those tiny homes on wheels, and I'm sure I could get a good price on it. Let's all pitch in and see what we can come up with. Bet we can get good financing on the rest."

"Or we could build onto the existing family house. Wouldn't need another bathroom then," Rachel says.

It will only be for a year, I want to say. Should I? I look to Philip and Mark for some hint. Philip shakes his head.

"There's room in the farmhouse for now, but I agree we should eventually build. We welcome any contributions," Mark says.

"Amanda," Nicole says, "what do your parents say?"

What should I say? That I haven't told them? That they'll think the "commune" is stealing my inheritance? Mark looks at me with a warning in his eye.

"My parents want me to graduate college first," I say as best I can with tears in my eyes. "But I know what I want, and I don't want to wait. God has led me to this."

Nicole gives me a hug. "Your parents aren't church-going people, are they?" I shake my head. "They think you've got yourself caught up with a bunch of Jesus freaks, don't they?" I nod. "Well, never you mind. Philip's a fine man, and this is a godly community."

I hold Nicole tightly, and the relief is like a letting go.

"Sadly, sometimes our own family is our stumbling block," Mark says. "There are plenty of examples in the Bible when a believer had to turn away from family because they heard Christ's call."

For the next several minutes, as different people pray aloud for blessings and direction for us and themselves, I try to organize my jumbled emotions. I'm making a lifelong commitment. Whenever doubts make me waver, I remember the instant I decided and how it felt like a sign from God. Peace comes over me. These people love me. Philip loves me. I love all of them. Yes, this is where I'm meant to be. I am home.

I lean on Philip's shoulder as Mark says, "Amen."

CHAPTER 20

Susan

SEEING TONY'S NAME on my caller-id rouses me as I doze in my chair. I can't remember the last time he called, or even returned one. Mandy. I grab the phone, and before I even say anything, he starts talking.

"Did you know?" Tony demands.

"Know what?"

"Amanda's getting married."

"What? To who? No, I didn't know." The sun glares in my face as I stand.

"To some guy at that farm she lives at. Philip." Tony's voice is breathless with anger.

"I've met Philip. He seems nice enough."

"She's nineteen! If she thinks I'm paying her tuition once she's married, she needs to think again."

"Maybe it's about her inheritance?"

"What inheritance? She got money from your folks?"

I hesitate, the anger at my father threatening to erupt again after months of tamping it down. What my parents gave Mandy is none of Tony's business. Unless that's why she's getting married. "She inherits two hundred thousand dollars on her first wedding anniversary, so long as she marries a man."

"What? This guy, this farm, wants her money?"

"They may not know." Well, this is a switch. I'm the one taking the calm, rational approach.

"Of course, they do."

A million questions race through my mind. When is it? Why did she tell Tony and not me? My phone buzzes. Mandy's calling. "Tony, she's calling. I have to take it."

"Get some answers!" he says as I switch to Mandy's call.

"Mom?" she says.

"Amanda," I say. "I was talking with your dad."

"Sorry. He must have called you right away."

"What's this about your getting married?" I dangle my feet in the pool, its cold water bracing. Sun glints on the ripples.

"You've met Philip. You liked him, right?"

"He seems nice, a little too nice for my taste, but I would never suggest you follow in my romantic footsteps. But why now? Didn't he dump you? I thought you were committed to getting your nursing degree?"

"I'm marrying him because I love him and it's the right thing to do."

"Are you pregnant?"

"No, Mom."

Every muscle in my body tenses as I try to sound calm. "But he did break up with you not that long ago."

"In his mind we weren't dating, we were friends. It was me who wanted something more than he was ready for."

"And now, a few months later, he's suddenly ready? You'll have to excuse me for questioning his motives coming so close to your finding out you inherited a lot of money."

After a long pause, Mandy says, "I guess it was too much to hope that you'd be happy for me."

I sag. I can't lose her, and I can't stop her or save her from her choices. Let it go, my rational mind says. Protect her, my mother mind screams. "If you're happy and sure he loves you and not your soon-to-be net worth, then I'm happy."

"I'm sure."

I kick my feet in the water as she gives me the details, the sting of the cold water lessening. Not the elaborate wedding I'd been saving for, a small service at the farm with what sounds like a potluck after. No dates invited. Not that I'll have one, but Tony might. His problem. Three weeks from now. "Your dad is upset and wants me to call him back. I told him about the inheritance, and it kind of set him off. What should I say? That you'll call him again?"

"I'm not calling him again," she says in a flat voice. "I'm getting married. I don't care what you and Dad think." She hangs up.

Damn. I wish we could have a calm conversation about this. Oh, who am I kidding? Neither one of us could be calm on this topic.

I wait a few minutes, shading my eyes with my hand as I watch a flock of birds drift then swoop in the cloudless sky. When my composure returns, I call Tony.

"Well?" Tony says, picking up on the first ring.

"She says it's not because of the inheritance."

"And you believe her?"

"Yes." I hope she's truly in love and that will carry her through. Marriage is always risky.

"I'm calling her," Tony says, and the line goes silent.

I dry my numb legs and enter the gloom of my shuttered kitchen. Well, Dad, you thought you were so clever, assuming getting married would keep them from squandering their inheritance. Bet you didn't anticipate your grandkids joining a commune. I can't help worrying over Detective Taylor's rumors about the farm, and I wonder if he's learned anything more.

I ALWAYS IMAGINED planning for Mandy's wedding would be busy, exciting, fun, but instead I'm left out. Tony and I offer to hire a caterer for the wedding, but Mandy says send money because the church women want to do it. I call caterers in Indianapolis and get a quote for a buffet for a hundred and fifty and send her a check. I buy a blue silk suit with a white silk blouse. I don't care if Philip's mother bought blue. I'm the mother-of-the-bride, I get first pick. I offer Mandy my wedding dress, and she says that seems like bad luck. Hurtful, but not wrong. She said one of the church women was making the dress as a wedding gift. I hope it's not gingham like everything else at that stupid commune. Oh, pardon me, Grange.

Nothing but money for a wedding gift either. I don't know what Tony will do. He's told her once she's married, she's on her own, she'll have to find her own way to pay for school. I agree with him, but I'll pay her spring tuition as her wedding present. I'm not all that convinced this is going to last, and I want her to have a way out if she needs it.

For a while I thought Tony might not even go, he is so angry. None of his family are coming, and his girlfriend's not invited. I'm glad his love for Amanda beat out his anger, though. I fear if I don't go, she'll cut herself off from me completely.

Diane and Eddie weren't sure about coming, but I told them if they didn't, I would never attend their kids' weddings either. I mean, my word, Diane's in Chicago and Eddie's in Ohio, they can do a day trip.

Happy. I need to be happy for her. Why can't I? Philip's nice, Pastor Mark is nice, everyone is so damn nice. Now all she talks about is her calling and purpose. But isn't that better than cutting herself or experimenting with drugs and sex? Happy. I should be happy. But I miss her dark humor and her love of John Stewart and Harry Potter. I fear she'll become a Stepford Wife. Or, worse, Posse Comitatus.

No, she's too smart for that. She's not a different person, she's simply chosen a new direction. I have to believe that.

Eddie and Katie invite me to spend Christmas with them this year since it's right after the wedding, so I fly into Columbus and drive to Indiana with them. Nadine and I sit in the back seat and she tells me about her classes and roommate at Ohio State. It hurts to hear how normal it all is. I ask Nadine if she's met anybody special, and I can tell by the expression on her face that she has but isn't ready to talk about it yet. At least not in front of her parents. Katie turns around, wanting to hear the answer, but Nadine shakes her head.

Amanda stays with us at our hotel near the University the night before the wedding, and she and Nadine go out for what Nadine calls a bachelorette party.

"Have fun," I say. Have so much fun you decide you're too young to get married.

They're back by eleven, and head straight for bed. No motherly advice the night before the wedding. I understand she's afraid she won't like what I have to say, but I would have liked one more chance to breach the chasm.

Nadine and Amanda leave early, and the rest of us follow two hours later. A heaviness overwhelms me. All my movements and facial expressions take an insurmountable amount of energy. I stare out the car window, remembering the day she was born. So much hope and wonder. And the first day of kindergarten. I was afraid she'd be excluded or bullied, but right as we walked in, one little girl took her hand, brought her to the science center, and they stayed friends for the next two years until her parents moved to Scottsdale. I remember her first dance, my refusing to buy her that bare midriff dress, wanting her to be in style in a more restrained way. Those high school years were part of growing up, separating. She would have come back to me. Only now I fear she never will.

Cold air blasts me when I open the car door when we arrive at the farm. Everyone at the hotel kept remarking about how warm it was for December. Only a light dusting of snow in the shade. But I can't seem to get warm. The gravel crunches beneath my shoes, and I skid on the slick sidewalk. Eddie grabs my arm. Silk won't stand up to either gravel or wet, and I smile my thanks. The older men are in suits and ties while most of the younger men wear shirt sleeves. "Guess I'm getting old," Eddie whispers and tugs at his tie as we enter the farmhouse.

Inside, sofas and chairs line the walls of a large room filled with brown metal folding chairs facing an adjoining room. There's no center aisle. The pastor's family and others who live in the commune are in the front rows. A youngish man in a bow tie directs us to a row about three back, and I claim the end seat. Nadine peeks out of a doorway and waves at us. She's wearing the green satin blouse and black velvet pants I'd bought for Amanda.

Tony comes in with Diane and Ken. They sit behind us. Tony leans toward me and asks, "Aren't we supposed to sit in the front? Hell, shouldn't I walk her in?"

I shrug and see the sadness in his eyes too. "This is where they directed us," I whisper, "I told them who I was." Tony sits back in his chair with a thud.

Two young men tune their guitars as more people file in. All the band members and many of the guests have flowers or bows pinned to their jackets or dresses. Was I supposed to wear one? No one offers.

Several young children run to sit on a green flowered sofa along the back wall, followed quickly by two women who pick up and place the youngest on their laps. People are sitting on stairs and lined along the wall next to the front door. The chords the band plays start to form a song, what seems to me a sad song with hopeful lyrics about always being here, no matter whether the sun appears, or the seasons change.

I will not cry.

Nadine and Lisa appear in front with two young men, and Lisa and the young men join the band.

I will not cry.

Amanda, Philip, and Pastor Mark come to the arch between the two rooms as the band starts the chords of a new song. Mandy's wearing a cream-colored dress with what appear to be clusters of holly embroidered all over the fabric. Her brown hair falls loosely around her shoulders, held behind her ears with a matching ribbon. The sun streaming through the windows highlights the red in her hair. She is so beautiful. She seems so happy. I can't see anyone else.

Mandy begins to sing, softly at first then growing louder, her beautiful voice filled with emotion. She sings about love being their home. Many guests start singing softly with her during the rest of the song, and soon the band joins in too. Tears run down my cheeks, making little blotches on my suit. How I hope all this is true, that life and marriage will give her nothing but happiness. That vows are never broken, her children always smiling, that the words "family" and "home" keep meaning something warm and wonderful.

A hand squeezes my shoulder, and I know it's Tony's. Why couldn't we be that family for her? We started out with so much love and promise. And she seemed happy. Guilt that the disappointments in our lives are all my fault overwhelms me. Dear God, I pray, let her be happy, always. Let this be the love, the family she needs. Forgive me. Let her forgive me. Let Tony forgive me.

By the time I get it together, Pastor Mark is speaking about how all marriages need a community to support them and the community is strengthened by their love for each other. He asks us to participate, not just listen to their vows: "We've set up the rooms as best we can to create a circle surrounding Amanda and Philip. Please join hands to bind that circle."

I take Eddie's hand, and Tony takes mine. Both look uncomfortable. Amanda, Philip, and Pastor Mark hold each other's hands.

"Will all of you surround Philip and Amanda with love, offering them the joys of your friendship, and supporting them in their marriage?" Pastor Mark asks.

"We will."

"Philip and Amanda," he continues, "you are making a lifetime commitment to love, trust, and help each other. So, I ask you this. Do you promise to be loving friends and partners in marriage, to talk and to listen, to trust and appreciate, to respect and cherish each other? Do you promise to support, comfort, and strengthen each other through life's joys and sorrows? Do you promise to always be open and honest and love each other, in sickness and in health, in times of scarcity and of plenty, for as long as you both live?"

"Yes, I will," Amanda and Philip say to each other at nearly the same time.

"And will you share your strengths and weaknesses, your joys and sorrows, your hopes and dreams, your love with this community that has promised these things to you?"

They turn to us and say, "We will."

"You have made a covenant with God and this community and each other. God's blessings be on you and the family of God."

"Amen!" several people say, as others clap.

There's no recessional, only a mass of people, some moving forward to hug Amanda and Philip while others move to the door. I try to move forward, blocked by people in the front rows. I feel abandoned despite their promises to include us in their community. I've never been to a wedding that paid so little attention to the moms and dads who raised these children to become the adults they are. Sure, it takes a village, and we were that village. Not you. Not you.

Not me anymore.

When I finally reach the front, I shake Philip's hand then hug Amanda close. "I love you, and I pray you are always this happy," I say.

"Thank you," Amanda says before I'm shoved away.

I'm surprised, comforted too, when I see Detective Taylor wandering outside trying to be inconspicuous. As if he could ever look like anything but a cop with his short hair, muscular build, and the wariness about him. I'm sure he wasn't invited, so he must still be investigating this group. When I called him two weeks ago, he was cautious, said he had nothing new to report. I intercept him before he gets to the food line.

"Detective Taylor. This is a surprise," I say.

"Susan, hello. Do me a favor and act like we're together. Remember I told you I was looking for a way to get inside the commune, see what's going on? I'm using this as my reason. I hope you're OK with that? If not, I'll leave."

"I'm happy you're here." I take his arm. "I'll explain to my family later."

I see Bert and Felicia sitting at a picnic table, no one talking with them, so I steer Taylor that way and introduce them to each other.

"I take it you're not part of the community," Taylor says.

"No. I saw Amanda on campus a few weeks ago and she invited us," Felicia says.

"Little did she know, we have no life and would be able to come," Bert says, and Felicia laughs.

"Are you thinking of joining?" Taylor asks.

"Hell no," Bert says. "Excuse me. Heavens no. Whatever. Amanda used to be cool. Then she met Philip and joined the Higher Power Grangers and got all weird. Sorry, Susan, but it's true."

"No apologies necessary, and some time I'd like to hear more about that," I say.

"We wanted an excuse to check it out, and this is it," Felicia added.

"Me, too," Taylor admits.

"Why?" Felicia asks.

"My office gets the occasional complaint about the Grange, so this looked like a chance to see for myself."

"Gene was the detective working Amanda's missing person case last March," I say.

"What kind of complaints?" Felicia asks.

"I can't talk about that," Taylor says.

"Do you think they're a cult? Because I do," Bert says.

"The only thing we care about is if anyone's getting hurt."

"People do get worked up about other people's religion," Felicia says.

"What have you heard?" Taylor asks. "Anything that makes you worry for Amanda?"

"Other than I think she's brainwashed?" Felicia asks. "If it weren't for what little Amanda's told us, I wouldn't know anything. They stick to themselves. When I see Amanda at school, Philip or someone is always nearby. I don't think I've had a real conversation with her since last semester."

Bert nods. "She's pretty much cut us off. Pretends to be all happy to see me and invites me to come to church or here, but that's it."

"She seems happy. That's all I care about." I hope if I say that often enough it will become true.

"There she is," Felicia says, pointing toward the dining hall. "We should at least say hi and congratulations."

"Yep." Bert bounces up. "And I hear they make great pie."

I introduce Taylor to my family as "my friend Gene."

"Do you live in Phoenix?" Diane asks.

"No, I live here," Gene says.

"How did you meet?" Diane asks, looking confused.

"I'll tell you later," I say. Tony seems particularly dissatisfied with this answer. It can't hurt to have Tony think someone is interested in me, even if it only lasts until dinner tonight.

I feel strangely isolated. People stare at us, some say hello, but no one starts a conversation. When we look for a place to sit, a family gets up and gives us their table and rushes off. No one joins us.

"I always heard this was such a friendly group," Taylor says. "Not today, I guess."

"People who join cults are introverts," Tony says.

I wonder where he got that piece of information. I wonder if it's true.

Taylor doesn't stay long. Almost immediately Rev. Vinnar joins us.

"I see you've met our local constable," he says.

"We became friends when I thought Amanda was a missing person," I say.

Tony sits back in his chair. It's the first time I've seen him smile all day. Eddie and Diane look at each other with raised eyebrows, but keep quiet.

Amanda and Philip join us briefly, thanking us for coming, apologizing for not having more time to talk, telling Rev. Vinnar his wife needs him.

"There's a weird vibe here," Nadine says after the three leave.

"Yeah," Tony says.

"What do you mean, sweetheart," Eddie asks.

"Well, when I came this morning it was like I was invisible to everybody. I thought, well, Mandy's the bride. I tried to talk to her friend Lisa, ask her why she joined, but the only answer was she likes it here. Seems like she avoided me after that. In the car on the way here Mandy said lots of students go to their church, but I don't see many. I can't explain it. It's like they're super friendly but don't really talk."

"They're after her money," Tony says.

"Let's not talk about that here," I say. "It looks like people are leaving."

Tony bullies his way through the crowd surrounding Amanda and drags her toward us to say goodbye. She thanks us for coming and rushes away as soon as we each hug her.

The car is quiet on the way back to the hotel.

Chapter 21

Amanda

PHILIP MAKES NO attempt at quiet when he gets up at dawn to milk the cows the morning after our wedding. He's signaling I should get up, too, but I keep my eyes closed. I knew we weren't having a honeymoon, but I'd hoped we could take a day to unwind, have sex. He barely kissed me last night, said he was tired from the stress of the wedding and how late everyone stayed. I was tired, too, but looking forward to exploring each other's bodies and relaxing in his warmth. If not last night, then this morning.

I roll toward the side of the bed where he's sitting putting on his socks and slide my arms around his waist. He kisses my temple and brushes my cheek, then stands.

"Stay," I say, sitting back against the headboard. "Let someone else be in charge today."

He sits back down and takes my hand. "I can't do that. Tonight, OK?"

I don't want to be one of those women who uses tears to get her way, but I can't stop the drips. I wonder if he saw them before he shut the door. I huddle under the heavy blankets, confused and cold. I thought guys were always ready. He said he finds me attractive. Is he gay and won't admit it? It pierces me that I don't know Philip well enough to answer that.

I get up to look at our closet stuffed with my clothes. Most of them aren't suitable for farm life. I probably should box them, bring them to a consignment or charity store. I finger my favorite cream lace blouse and imagine wearing it this morning, then layer a t-shirt under a worn blue oxford shirt, under a sweatshirt from my high school swim team. Blue jeans, thick socks, hiking boots. I leave my hair loose, knowing it looks better that way, hoping someone will notice.

Lisa looks at me when I arrive for breakfast, a question in her smile. I smile back as if everything's great.

"Welcome, Mrs. Morivan," Mark says, inviting me to sit next to him.

Hannah gives me a quick hug before going to the kitchen and returning with my usual egg and yogurt and toast. We talk about what needs to be done today and who will do it. I offer to bake bread with Hannah. I can tell Lisa's disappointed I didn't offer to help her clean the houses, but she would want to talk, and I feel humiliated. I'll volunteer with her tomorrow, once Philip and I have been together. When my fears have passed.

We should have used a little of the wedding money to take a trip instead of turning it all over to the Grange. Not Hawaii or Paris like I dreamed before I got my priorities straight, but a few days away somewhere close. Gotten to know each other better without being surrounded by everyone here. Taken our time. Am I being lazy? Self-indulgent? I watch Philip through the window as he trudges from the barn to the house, his jeans and boots muddy and bits of hay clinging to his legs and jacket. I feel a rush of affection. He works so hard. He's so committed. I banish my selfish thoughts. We're in this together, for life. Plenty of time.

AT SUPPER, MARK says Philip and I should come talk to him. A tension in the room makes me feel off balance. I picture the many things I've done today, questioning Philip's love and attraction, resenting the lack of a honeymoon, hoarding my unnecessary clothes. Can Mark see all those little sins? I'll be better. I will.

Philip and I stare at Mark over the scattered papers on his desk. Philip seems worried. Does he, too, have something to hide?

"Probably a little early to ask," Mark says, "but how are things going?"

"Great," Philip says.

I nod.

"There's something I need to get off my chest," Mark says. "Remember right after you decided to marry we talked about family?"

Philip and I nod.

"I noticed some things at the wedding that showed me the wisdom of God's rule to reject our families to follow Christ. You were surrounded most of the time and probably didn't see, but, Amanda, did you know your mom invited a local detective to the wedding?"

"What? No, I didn't. I told her no dates." How dare she? It's one thing for her to call the police when she thinks I'm missing—ridiculous, but understandable. But invite a policeman to the wedding?

"And when he was here, he didn't stick by her. Nathan saw him peering into the barn, and I saw him talking to two of the students who came."

"I am so sorry." I stumble on my words, a cold anger fogging my brain. I clench my fists, fearful of what Mark and Philip will say.

"It might be best to tell your family that since you can't trust them, they shouldn't call or come around," Philip says, and I nod in agreement.

"I'd stay away from those two students, too," Mark says. "I asked them what the detective said, and they were forthright—he wanted to check out what is happening at the Grange. It seemed to me from their attitude they think we need watching."

How could my family and friends humiliate me so? I didn't need to tell any of them I was getting married, but I thought they cared about me. I look at the floor, trying not to cry. Mark and the Church give me nothing but love, and I give them trouble. I resolve to tell my family how disappointed I am. How I don't plan to call or write them ever again.

That night in bed, I cry a little as I apologize again to Philip. He puts his arms around me and says he knows it wasn't my fault. I promise to call Mom and Dad one last time, tell them to stay away. Philip kisses me gently, then more insistently until my sorrow turns into desire. As our hunger for each other intensifies and climaxes, I know he and the people of the Grange are all I will ever need.

ON NEW YEAR'S night, the house is finally quiet, the children asleep after endless cups of water and requests for stories. Our next-door neighbors were shooting fireworks until past midnight, waking the kids and making Jax howl. I can't tell if Mark or Hannah are still up. All I hear is the occasional house creak or the wind blowing branches against the side of the house. My nose is cold despite covering it with the blanket, the quilt, and my hands. I wonder if I'll ever get used to winter or setting the thermostat at sixty. When I suggested an electric blanket, Philip said I should stay close to him. But his feet and hands are freezing, and he throws off the fluffy red blanket my mom bought me before I left for school. It seems so long ago.

A little moonlight sneaks through a crack in the blinds, highlighting the shoes I left in the middle of the floor. I consider getting up to kick them under the bed before Philip sees them and complains again about my leaving my clothes out, but I don't want to wake him. Morning is soon enough. Tonight I told him as we were lying in bed that I'd called my parents to cut off all communications. He said he was glad, then turned away. I'm finding it hard to sleep. Feeling guilty, I guess. My usually easy-going dad lost it, started screaming at me saying that no damn religious cult was going to cut him off from his daughter. I guess I sort of lost it too. Called him and Paige adulterers. Well, they are. He told me to send back my cell phone if I wasn't going to call him anymore. Philip said that was a good idea, said I didn't need one.

Mom was calm. Too calm. Other than saying no, she did not invite Detective Taylor to the wedding, she didn't say much. When she said, "please don't do this," it almost sounded like she was talking under water. I thought it would be easier. I knew it would hurt them, but they deserved it. I wish I could talk with Philip about it, but he gets all prickly when I mention them, as if thinking about them is weakness.

A new year, a new beginning. I pray for my parents then force thoughts of them out of my mind and snuggle closer to Philip.

Chapter 22

Susan

I'M STILL SHAKING from Amanda's call last night. I remember the panic I felt when Amanda was missing, a searing pain and fear. This is different. A dull ache. More than sadness. Amanda says she isn't going to call, won't answer my calls, I'm not welcome to visit. And all because of something I didn't even do. I told her I didn't invite Detective Taylor. I admitted I told him about the wedding. She quoted that stupid scripture about needing to hate your mother and father to be a true disciple. You hate your dad too? I asked. She hung up.

I wander my empty house, looking at the pictures of happier times on the walls, open Amanda's empty closet. What should I do with all her mementos? She's made it clear she doesn't want them. I pick up one of her many Beanie Babies, a bear with stars and stripes I bought her one fourth of July. Some little girl would love this like she used to. Goodwill? I can't bring myself to empty her room yet. What would it become? I don't sew. I have an office. I don't get many out-of-town guests. Probably none now that Mom and Dad are gone.

I consider calling Tony to see if she cut herself off from him too, but what difference would it make? I must accept this, but I can't. Maybe she'll understand when she has a child that a mother can't just say "OK, fine if you never want to see me again." Or at least I can't. I should let her be, wait until age and life's disappointments mellow her a bit.

I know this is the work of that damn commune. Afraid I'll convince Amanda she's made a mistake sometime before the year is up. I can't deny I think she's made a mistake. Tony is even more vocal about it. I have to believe they love each other. She's an adult. Sort of. I need to let her find her own way. As long as no one's hurting her. How will I know?

Tony calls. I don't have the energy but decide I'd better answer.

"What's the name of that detective again?" he says.

"Eugene Taylor," I say.

"Well, I'm calling him. What's his phone number? Something bad's going on. She said she hated me! Called me an adulterer. We've always gotten along. They're poisoning her mind."

I give him Detective Taylor's number and wish him luck. I can't help but wonder if Tony had been this outraged last year when it all began would things be different. Or if my parents hadn't left her all that money. I'll never know.

Work seems pointless all week. These petty little disputes. Why does the Homeowners Association care that somebody has three cats instead of the allowed two? All the things I used to get energized about, like the business owner selling off his assets despite the court order or the hospital trying to shake down an elderly couple, seem routine. People treat each other badly. What else is new?

I wonder if I can get the second semester tuition back.

Oh, don't be petty.

I lie in bed most of Saturday and Sunday, looking at the thorny, frost-burned vines of the bougainvillea outside my window.

By Sunday night my thoughts swing between depression and anger. I've failed at everything important to me: my marriage, my job, motherhood. What have I done wrong? What could I have done differently? I still don't know. All I know is whatever I've done wasn't good enough.

Tuesday is the first night for the University Community Chorus I joined. I don't feel like going, but decide I should. I leave work before five, knowing it's hard to find a place to park on campus and I need to eat. It's dark as I walk to the Music Building, students whizzing by on skateboards and bicycles or walking to the beat of the earplugs they're wearing. The auditorium is a big white pit with a piano at the base. I buy a score from the student at a table in front and he points out the alto section. Those already here appear to be about my age. I pick a seat two chairs away from a dark-haired woman in a purple jacket and navy sweatpants. Next time I'll change my clothes, I decide. Who wants to be in a business suit longer than necessary?

As I drape my coat over my chair, the dark-haired woman looks at me, smiles, and extends her hand. "Hi, I'm Katya," she says. "I don't remember seeing you before. Is this your first time?"

"It is," I say, shaking her hand. "Anything I should know?"

"Not really. It's fun, but people take it seriously. The director gives us practice tapes. Expects us to practice during the week."

"Hard core," I say. "But I heard your December concert. I'd say the work paid off."

"Thanks," she says. "Are you single?"

I nod.

"Then join several of us after. We go out for a drink most Tuesdays."

"I'd like that."

The seats fill quickly. There's a mix of ages now, mostly women but a lot more men than in any other choir I've been in. A thin woman wearing a green dress well below her knees sits at the piano and fluffs her hair into loose gray curls. A balding man in a black suit rushes in, speaks to the pianist, and pulls papers from his briefcase. He looks up and grins.

"Welcome," he says. "Are we ready to sing?"

"Yes," almost everyone shouts. I look at my neighbor.

"That's his signal to be quiet, we're starting," she whispers.

The director looks at us. "Altos, are we ready?"

We nod and open our scores.

Time passes quickly. I'm glad I came. We're practicing *St. Matthew Passion*, and it's clear most of us have sung it before. I'm swept into the haunting melodies and precise rhythms. I forget the world for a while.

Katya walks with me to the parking lot. I feel an energy, excitement, that's been lacking for a long while. She introduces me to three other women.

"I see why you go out after," I say. "I feel a little light-headed. In a good way."

One of the women, Naomi, says, "The wine won't help that. We'll order fries, too."

"As if we needed an excuse," Katya says.

Chapter 23

Amanda

OUR GARDEN AT the Grange is finally producing after months of winter, giving us a few greens, asparagus, spinach, parsnips, and rhubarb. Meals have been sparse, and for the first time in my life I know hunger. I crave pizza, burgers, Oreos, anything but another dish of yogurt or sauerkraut. When we stored the potatoes, squash, carrots, onions, and apples in the Fall, I was sure we'd have plenty, and Mark had encouraged us to sell more to help pay the bills, but we ran out of almost everything by February, and Philip made it clear we were not to touch the seed potatoes. We made lots of soup with our dried fava beans, the soups getting thinner as the months dragged on. March was the hardest. We worked long hours in the garden getting ready to plant, and that's when the soup was the thinnest. When the church ladies heard Matthew complaining in Sunday School about being hungry, they started bringing us an occasional casserole, and one man brought us a side of venison from a deer he'd taken during hunting season. Trudy bought Philip and me lunch at least once a week.

I'm beginning to understand why Lisa dropped out of school. It's a lot easier to write papers and read huge assignments when that's all you have to do in the evenings and weekends. There's no break at the Grange. Between preparing and cleaning after meals, helping with the children, and tending the garden, free time is nonexistent. I've fallen asleep in class several times, making a little noise as my head drops and causing nearby students to titter and whisper. One instructor called me aside after class to ask me what was going on. When I told her, she said I need to choose. I've been staying at school as late as I can to finish my homework, but the days Philip comes he always wants to head home by three. When I told him I was afraid I'd be put on academic probation, he shrugged.

Mark will be more understanding.

I see Mark's and another car in the lot at the church and decide now is the time. The door to his office is closed, so I wander around outside looking at the patchy, unmown grass and the birds swooping in the low gray sky until Mark comes out with one of the young mothers. Mark gives her a hug as she leaves and waves me inside.

"Amanda, this is a surprise," Mark says, taking my hands. "Is something wrong?"

I burst into tears. "I'm failing at everything. School. Marriage. Everything."

"How are you failing? Because I don't see it," he says.

"I can't keep up with what needs to be done at home or school. I stay up late and fall asleep in class. My grades are dropping, and my professors complaining. And when I try to talk to Philip, he gives me a 'that's life' look and walks away. I knew it would be hard, but lots of people have jobs and go to school full time. I guess I'm not good enough."

Mark pulls me out of my chair and holds me against his body without talking until I stop crying. Then he steps away a little, brushing the tears from my face with one hand and encircling my waist with the other. I lean my head on his shoulders, my mind racing.

"Your instructor is right, you do need to make choices," he says. "And this close to the end of the semester, your choice needs to be to finish your courses. I'll tell Hannah it's only for a few weeks, and I'll help more in the kitchen and with the kids. This summer we can talk as a community about whether you should continue with your studies or take a break. OK?"

I nod. I want the nursing degree, but maybe I could take fewer classes.

He kisses me gently, and it takes all my energy not to kiss him back fiercely in return.

PHILIP AND I meet in Pastor Mark's office at home weekly now. Philip seems to resent it, as this used to be his time. I offer to stay away, but Philip waves me off. "We're one flesh now, remember?" Sometimes we talk about our marriage, but most times it's about the student ministry or farm issues. Mark's decided we need a newsletter. It seems like a lot of work to me, but Mark's excited, so I say I'll help. We already have a website, but there's not much on it. I promise to show him how to post his sermons, but he needs something shorter, more visual for a blog. Pictures of us planting or harvesting or baking pies. Something that shows we're regular people working hard together, not a bunch of hippy types living in tents, growing weed, and singing kumbaya around a campfire. He also thinks we should hold open houses for the community once in a while. Inviting people to church is one thing, inviting them for a pancake breakfast might be less threatening.

I'm tasked with coming up with ideas for the newsletter and open houses to present to the leadership team.

"We need to talk about building you a house," Mark says at today's session. "We won't have the money until Amanda's inheritance comes through in December, but it would be nice to be ready to go when that happens."

"We could do the same kind of house the other marrieds have," Philip says. "It's mostly pre-fab so easy to put up, which will save us money."

"I was hoping for something a little bigger, something that might accommodate all three couples plus children. As the children grow and we have more we're going to need some kind of school, and the four rooms and two bathrooms of the existing house could work well for that," Mark says.

"True," Philip says. "Another option is to add on to the existing family house and put up some modular classrooms as we need them. What do you say we get a builder out here to go over some ideas and estimate costs?"

"We should have a kitchen in the house," I say. "Things get crowded in the one we have on baking days."

Mark frowns. "Kitchens are expensive, and we have a big one. Sleeping quarters and bathrooms are the real issue for expanding."

Philip nods. "I'd also be afraid that there'd be less interaction with the single men and women if there was a kitchen in the family house. Sort of goes against the idea of communal meals."

I don't see why as long as we still eat in a central dining room. But it's true. Sometimes I would like to eat alone or with a couple of others instead of making a big production about every meal. I've gotten spoiled living in the farmhouse, making my own sandwiches to bring to school, raiding the refrigerator for fruit or milk between meals.

"We can only spend the money on a house, not on classrooms, though," I say.

Mark and Philip look at me with surprise.

"What do you mean?" Philip says.

"The way I remember it is I get the money a year after marriage for the purpose of buying a house. I'm guessing my family will be strict about that," I say.

The air seems heavy as the two of them stare at me.

"Will you need to own the land the house sits on?" Mark asks. "Will you need title to the house?"

"I'm not sure about the details," I admit. "I can get a copy of the will. Once the house is ours, we can share it with everybody. Seems like if we do a lot of the work, we'll be able to build a big place?"

"I would think so," Mark says slowly. "But we'd better find out before we commit to anything. Get us a copy of that will, OK?"

I nod, feeling scolded. I try to take Philip's hand as we leave Mark's office, but he walks quickly out the door toward the barn. I was sure I'd told them, although even now I don't know what the significance is. I wish I could talk to Mom. She could explain the legal ins-and-outs. But I can't, won't, call. The lawyer said we could call him with any questions. I guess I have some now.

I SET UP a conference call with Mark, Philip, and my grandparents' lawyer for the next day, and we gather again in Mark's study. The lawyer confirms I must use the money to buy a house and promises to send me a copy of the will.

"Do you have one in mind?" he asks. "It's eight months until your anniversary, but we can get the process going. The trustees will need to approve the release of funds."

"It's not automatic?"

"No, although so long as you're still married on your first anniversary and you buy a house there are no grounds for them to refuse. And why would they?"

"My family is unhappy about my choices," I say.

"None of their business who you choose to marry or what house you want to buy," Dan says. "But I guess they could refuse to sign. A lawsuit could get expensive."

"Could we buy a modular home and put it on someone else's property?" Philip asks.

"Hmmm. As long as it's a house it should qualify. Not sure why you'd want to do that. Two hundred thousand dollars should get you something decent in rural Indiana."

"We want to share our house with some friends who have land," I say.

"Ah. You've discussed this with your mom?"

"Not yet," I say. "And please don't say anything."

"Of course," Dan says. "Call me when you want to start the process."

After we hang up, Mark begins pacing. He stares at the fields for several minutes before turning around.

"The easiest thing might be to sell you a piece of my land and then draw up building plans. Once it's paid for you can deed it back," Mark says.

I nod.

ONCE THE SEMESTER ends, I try to make up for how unhelpful I was the last few weeks, but now I'm tired all the time. I refuse to be sick. I sneak a nap when Philip is in the fields. Today it seems even harder than usual to get up, get to the kitchen to help with breakfast and yogurt production. I wallow in the troughs of our mattress and double up the blanket on my side. When I force myself to get up, get dressed, go downstairs, trudge to the community kitchen, the smell of the warm milk cooking, usually sweet and comforting, makes me nauseous. I can't bear it and turn away. Too quickly, apparently, because the room spins, and I falter.

Hannah sees and grabs my arm to keep me from falling. "Are you sick?"

"I've been so tired since the end of the semester, and now the smell of milk heating is making me queasy."

"Sit down a while, and if you don't feel better go back to bed."

That sounds so inviting that I do, returning mid-morning to help with lunch and the garden.

"Feel better?" Hannah asks.

"Much," I say. "Sorry about this morning. Maybe I ate too much yogurt this spring."

"Didn't we all?" Hannah laughs. "Still, it's good for you."

I wrinkle my nose.

For the next week, my tiredness increases, and my breasts hurt a little. I wonder if I could be pregnant and realize I haven't had my period for a while. I could ask for a kit from the drug store, but I need to decide how I feel about it first. Plenty of women are nurses and mothers, I think, but fear Philip may not agree. So many changes. How different things are from my life plan: college, career, maybe get married, maybe have kids but not until my thirties.

When I throw up after breakfast, Hannah sends me to rest. She shows up a few hours later with a drugstore pregnancy kit in hand. I have a hard time focusing on the little pink plus sign on the stick. My stomach tightens. I'm finding it hard to catch my breath.

"I'm so happy!" Hannah says, hugging me. "Let's tell Philip and Mark, OK? They were downstairs a few minutes ago."

I hold on to the banister as we descend, not sure if I'm glad or not. It seems too soon. I'm not ready.

Hannah taps on Mark's office door. Her nod and the look she and Mark exchange let me know he was aware she'd bought me a test kit.

"Good news, Philip!" Hannah says. "Tell him, Amanda."

"I'm pregnant," I murmur.

Philip's face begins in shock, then quickly changes to a smile. He strides toward me, kisses me. "For real?"

I nod, and he hugs me again. "I wondered, with your being so tired and sick lately. Why didn't you tell me?"

"I wanted to be sure," I say, looking at the floor.

"Go back and lie down," Hannah says. "We'll tell everyone at supper tonight."

Philip puts his arm around my shoulder as we walk upstairs. "Mine?" he whispers next to my ear. A thrill of fear and desire runs through me.

"Of course," I say.

"Of course," he says, pulling me toward him so tightly it hurts.

CHAPTER 24

Susan

AT THE SEMESTER'S last rehearsal in May, a reduced group sings our favorite choruses from the final concert. Most of the student members have skipped, choosing to study for their exams, but my new friends are here. I will miss them during the summer. I've invited Corey to meet us after, hoping she'll like them too.

It's dark and cool enough to sit on the outdoor patio when we get to the bar. No one else is outside, which is just as well as our conversation gets noisier and our laughter louder the longer we stay. Katya and Corey bond over their stories about teaching high schoolers.

"At one teachers' conference the superintendent, God bless her liberal out-of-touch soul, said we needed to do what we could to break up the groups, get different kids to work together. She pretty much commanded me to pick some outsiders for leading roles in the next school play." Katya straightens in her seat and salutes.

"How'd that go?" Corey asks, repressing laughter.

"About as well as you'd expect. I chose a sweet, shy boy with an unfortunate amount of acne for Hamlet." She looks at each of us as she says, "That seems good casting, doesn't it?"

"Was he any good?" Naomi asks.

"As good as any high schooler once I got him to speak loudly. Anyway, first I was besieged by the guys who usually played the leads, and then my Ophelia threatened to quit."

"Hamlet seems like an ambitious choice," I say, taking one more fry.

"How'd you get them in line?" Corey asks. "I had a rebellion on my moot court team when I tried to choose partners for them. I gave up."

"I played the imperial director. Said the director gets to choose and if they wanted to boycott, go ahead."

"Did it work?" Naomi asks. "I mean, did they start being friends with each other?"

"No." Katya sighs. "Not so far as I could tell. But, the show must go on. And the next term I had fewer people at tryouts."

"Everybody wants to be with their friend group," I say.

The table quiets, and everyone looks at me.

"Especially teenagers," I say. "But not just."

"It's true," Katya says, her eyes thoughtful. "Disrupting their, our, comfort zones can be threatening. Necessary, though."

I feel guilty how I changed the mood all of the sudden, unsure how to return to fun. "Joining this choir was a stretch for me. Now I want all of you in my chosen family."

Katya grins and lifts her glass. "Here's to new friends."

"And to old." I lift my glass and smile at Corey. "Reminds me of an old girl scout song."

"Susan and I have been talking about a trip this summer," Corey says, clinking her glass to Katya's and then mine. "Anybody want to join us?"

I grab and squeeze Corey's hand under the table as the women talk over each other about where and when and whether they'd like to go.

"I have a place in Flagstaff," Naomi says. "I invite everyone to come Fourth of July weekend. I'll tell my free-loading relatives to pick a different weekend."

"I'm in," I say.

JUNE IS HOT and dry, and Northern Arizona aflame. Clouds of ash hang in the distance and turn the sky gray and the sun orange. In the afternoon, dark clouds make empty promises of rain, creating instead huge walls of dust whose yellow haze swallows the landscape with a scent of burning wire. The sunsets are spectacular. Naomi emails us to say fireworks are unlikely in Flagstaff this year, but we're welcome still. At least it's cooler.

Corey, Katya, and I drive together, the rest of the women making other plans for the weekend. I'm glad for the smaller group and the fact I won't need to sleep on an air mattress on the floor. Naomi's condo is on a little lake in the middle of a golf course. Two hours from Phoenix and a different world altogether.

Naomi stands next to me on the deck and points toward the nearest mountain. "Last weekend there was fire on the other side, and at night I could see an orange glow lining the peak."

I look at her, alarmed. "How close is it?"

"There are a lot of miles and developed areas between there and us. The rain last week and the Forest Service contained it. I guess it's still smoldering."

"Are the fireworks on?" Katya says as she joins us to watch the water.

"Yes." Naomi brightens. "We can see them from my deck or go to the party at the Country Club."

"I'd just as soon watch from here," I say, and everyone agrees.

"And there's a parade downtown in the morning," Naomi says.

This excites everyone but me. I can't remember the last time I went to a parade, not a fan of crowds and usually too short to see anything much. I smile and nod as we make plans to leave by seven the next morning, hoping to get a parking spot. We eat on the deck, and once the sun sets, the air is cold. We talk and laugh and drink as the moon's reflection ripples on the water.

I awake early, disoriented until I see Corey in the twin bed across the room. I put a sweatshirt over my nightshirt, still wearing socks from last night. I move as softly as I can down the stairs. Naomi is looking out the window over the kitchen sink and points. A family of deer wanders along the edge of the lake. We take our coffee and muffins outside, silent as we watch them cross the street into an open area behind a stand of aspens. I point to a heron standing on a rock peering into the water. Several ducks swim to the opposite shore where two children stand with a woman.

Crowds already line the streets when we arrive downtown. Everywhere is red, white, and blue: on the bunting on the second floor of a hotel, flags in shop windows, on trees, and in every child's hand, face-painted on children and adults. A huge flag and band start the parade, followed by politicians in convertibles, fire trucks, floats celebrating a variety of organizations, more bands, decorated trucks and trolleys, baton twirlers, bagpipes, more bands, more floats. After an hour we start going into the stores, put our names onto a list for an outdoor table at a restaurant. By two we're ready to relax back at the condo.

Clouds gather and darken to the west, and I hear low rumbles of thunder as we reach our car. We make it to Naomi's before the rain starts. A nap sounds perfect, and I doze to the sound of rain that shifts between sporadic drops and heavy torrents. When I awake, I see blue sky through the spaces in the blinds. Corey is reading when I turn to look at her.

"Having fun?" Corey asks.

"I am," I say.

"Me, too."

Naomi is bustling around the kitchen when I go downstairs.

"How about I pick up a pizza for tonight? Easier than cooking," I say.

Naomi looks at me gratefully. "That would be nice." She starts rifling through her purse.

"No, I'll pay. You've been more than generous already."

"I'm glad all of you came. You're easy guests."

The fireworks don't last long, but they're free and aren't so loud as to stop any conversation. Contentment washes over me to the sound of the waves lapping nearby until my bare arms start to itch.

"I'm cold," Katya says. "And something's biting."

"Yeah, me too," Corey says.

"Oh, you lowlanders." Naomi laughs. "Let's talk inside."

Naomi's living room looks like a shabby lodge, her mismatched chairs comfortable and each has a faded blanket or afghan thrown over the back. In front of the fireplace is a geometric blanket in greens and brown, and on the mantle are a wooden mallard and a carved bear.

"How long have you had this place?" I ask Naomi.

"It was my parents' for thirty years, and mine for five," she says. "I lived here with a couple of women when I went to NAU."

"Nice," Corey says. "What did you study?"

"I was a music major. Got my teaching certificate too."

My mind wanders as they talk about how their lives took unplanned directions.

"Susan's thinking about changing careers," Corey says. "Right?"

"Yeah, but I still don't know to what," I say.

"Why?" Katya asks. "It sounds like you got a great job."

I don't want to complain to my new friends. I'm embarrassed I wasn't good enough to make partner, and I fear my contract won't be renewed. "It is, but sometimes I think it would be nice to have a job where I didn't worry about it all the time. On vacation, when I'm in the shower, when I wake up in the middle of the night."

"Most jobs are like that I think," Katya says. "Or at least the ones that pay enough to live on."

"I got married in my twenties, worked since I was sixteen," I say. "I can finally afford to ease up now that nobody's relying on me anymore. Take some risks. Do something weird."

"Like what?" Naomi asks.

"I've heard there are some programs to help developing countries establish court programs. Not sure I have the right background for any of that, but it would be interesting." I pull on my hair, then sit on my hands to stop. "Or maybe get a Ph.D. in something fun like Comparative Literature, take a year off to travel the world. An old lady gap year."

"You're making me jealous," Katya says, leaning toward me. "Especially the year of travel."

"What would you do after the gap year?" Naomi says.

I lean back into my chair and look at the high ceiling near the loft where I've been sleeping. "I don't know. I've spent my entire life with a clear goal ahead of me, and right now I have no idea where I'm going or what I want to do."

"You'll figure it out," Corey says. I see kindness and encouragement in all of their eyes.

Chapter 25

Amanda

AT SUPPER, MATTHEW'S upset about something. He throws a carrot and sticks out his tongue at me when I ask him to pass the potatoes. When Hannah tells him to apologize, he screams until she carries him out. The noise rattles me, sets my teeth on edge, but everyone else keeps talking and eating as if nothing had happened. I fear I'll be a too anxious mom. Like my mom. Oh Lord, please no. All kids throw tantrums. This has to be the best place in the world to raise a child-even if I'm at wit's end, someone will be there to help and provide gentle discipline.

Afterward, the front room is quiet as Hannah, Sarah, Rachel, and I work on our projects. It's a warm night, and we've opened all the windows and the screened doors in the hopes of catching any slight breeze. I hear the cows lowing in the distance and think it a lovely accompaniment to the sound of needles clacking. Hannah's knitting a little brown sweater while Sarah and Rachel mend socks and shirts. I'm trying to knit a baby blanket in soft shades of the rainbow, but I pull apart almost as much as I finish. A sewing circle. Who'd have thought I'd be in a sewing circle?

The women at church assure me I'll be a great a mother, but I live in fear and doubt. One minute I'm excited, the next, fearful that I've eaten or done something that will hurt the baby, the next sure I'm too selfish to be a mom. All the men stop me from doing anything strenuous, which seems silly since mothers all over the world work in the fields until they give birth. But it's nice. The people at the Grange act as if they're having the baby, talking to the kids about their new sibling, sewing onesies, talking about who will do what. I should be happy I won't need to do this alone, but sometimes I want to say, "It's my baby, mine, mine, mine." I guess that's my old self coming through, the one who wants to be in control.

Philip seems subdued. I wonder if he's afraid of being a father. I hope Philip learns how to be a dad from Mark. Sometimes I wish Mark were my child's father. Many times I've wanted to be with Mark, when desire for him overwhelms all the nerve endings in my body and all my good sense. Is that what Christ meant when he said everyone who looks at another with lust has already committed adultery? I'm not sure how to stop those thoughts.

I'm still knitting when Philip comes in, his hair wet and buttoning his shirt. A sudden wave of desire hits me, and I hope that's why he's come looking for me.

"We should talk," he says. I happily put away my bundles of yarn in a ragged paper bag.

When we get to our room, I kiss him and begin unbuttoning his shirt. Being with him seems urgent now.

He doesn't kiss me back. "We need to talk."

Frustrated, I sit on the bed. He sits on the chair next to the window.

"I'm going to tell the leadership team you won't be going back to school in the Fall, and they should pick someone new to work with me on the campus ministry," he says.

My body stiffens, my feet seem frozen to the floor, and all desire flees. "Why?"

"Because you're pregnant," he says.

"The baby isn't due until February," I say. "I planned to stop going second semester, but if I'm ever going to get my nursing degree I need to do as much as I can now, before the baby comes."

"Your parents won't be paying tuition anymore, and it's expensive."

"I can get loans," I say.

"Which become due when you drop out. We don't have that money, Amanda."

I start to cry. How stupid. I cry too easily these days. "I could talk my parents into paying. Especially if I tell them about the baby."

"No," Philip says. "Keep them out of it."

"Can we present both sides and let the Council decide?" I say.

Philip bristles. "You're my wife."

"But you've always said we're part of a community. You wouldn't even date me without the community's permission!"

"It's not the same."

"If you think I'm going to let you decide for me, you're wrong."

Philip jumps out of his chair and hovers close to my face. "Love, honor, and obey. Those are the vows."

"Respect and cherish," I hiss back. "I never said obey."

"Wives, submit to your husbands, as to the Lord. For the husband is the head of the wife, even as Christ is the head of the church," he shouts.

Something inside me breaks. Two can play this game. "Husbands should love their wives as their own bodies. He who loves his wife loves himself. For no one ever hated his own flesh, but nourishes and cherishes it, as Christ does the church," I say in a steely calm.

There's a knock on the door, and Mark slides in.

"I couldn't help but overhear," Mark says. "Don't let this disagreement drive a wedge. Will you let me bring the issue to Council tonight?"

We nod, and the anger drains from me, replaced by embarrassment. Philip storms out, and Mark follows.

"I'M SORRY," I say as I take the seat next to Philip when the Council convenes in the Grange's dining room. The room is hot from the sun streaming through the windows. He nods and takes my hand.

"I'm sorry too," he says. "You were right. This is a decision for the whole."

Bryan begins the meeting with the usual gloom about finances. Nathan brings up the possibility of expanding to two services on Sunday morning, but Mark argues the Saturday service reaches a different crowd and we don't have the attendance for three. When all the ordinary business is finished, Mark reminds the group about my pregnancy and asks whether the group thinks I should continue with my studies and participate in the campus ministry in the Fall.

"Isn't that Amanda's decision?" Rachel asks.

"Amanda's and Philip's?" Jerry says.

"They've asked for your guidance," Mark says. "There's the issue of tuition. And does it make sense to start a nursing program and then take a break for several years?"

Several years? The women share every other childcare duty. I'll work hard.

I promised to let Mark handle this, so I keep quiet.

"If you want my opinion," Jerry says, "it makes more sense for her to start the program when she can finish it. It's a stressful, busy program. Stress can hurt the baby. Just ask Nicole."

"And we don't have tuition budgeted," Bryan says.

The consensus builds. I will not enroll in the Fall term. Trudy will work with Philip. I understand the decision but feel discarded.

On the walk back, Philip holds me close. "It's for the best, even if you don't agree now."

I nod, glad the dark is hiding the desolation I'm sure shows in my eyes and on my face. Why am I so sad? Last year I was ready to quit school forever, and this is simply a delay. As we get ready for bed, Philip hugs me from behind and kisses the back of my neck.

"Not now," I say.

He shrugs and picks up his book from the nightstand.

WHEN THE FALL semester starts in August, my life retains its rhythm of cooking, cleaning, mending, working at the Pick-n-Eat, helping with the children, each day except Sunday nearly the same. I help the older children with their reading and math. Trudy's moved into Lisa's room, and at supper she talks about her classes and her and Philip's successes with students. I do my best to hide my jealousy as the weeks pass and Philip and Trudy begin to finish each other's sentences.

One night in early October, the sky seems strange as I set the table. Clouds have been building and shifting all afternoon, but right now it's still, and the sky is an eerie, almost olive, green. The harvester rushes toward us, and Philip swats the cows toward the barn. I hear a faint siren in the distance and Jax barking nearby. I've never seen a green sky before and turn to point it out to Mark when his phone starts shrieking.

"Tornado warning," he says, reading a text. "And with that sky, it's close. Tell everyone to gather in the basement of the farmhouse. We'll eat dinner there."

A thrill of panic and adventure runs up my back. I'd seen the wreck of houses on television, one house flattened while the one next door was intact and listened to the concerned voices of newscasters warning people of another one to come, but never experienced one. I start shutting the windows.

"No," Mark says. "Go. We need to leave the windows open a crack."

I see Rachel and the children leaving the family house.

"Tornado!" I say. "Everybody in the basement."

They nod, and I see the front window is open a little so rush on to the women's house.

When I return with Lisa and Trudy, I see Hannah carrying a huge pan of meatloaf and Sarah with a basket of plates and utensils.

"Hurry," Hannah says. "We may not have much time."

Philip's lighting propane lanterns, but the room is well lit from bare light bulbs hanging from the ceiling. We never had a basement in Phoenix, and this one is nothing like my Aunt Diane's with its pool table and big screen TV. This basement is more like a storage cave, gray cement walls and floors lined with plank shelves filled with boxes. The children sit on a blanket in the middle of the floor, away from the wet in the corners, playing a game while everyone scurries to set up chairs. Jax whines and paces, unused to confinement and the increasing noise of the storm. Hannah sets the meatloaf with the rest of the food on one of the plastic event tables someone has already cleared.

Mark looks around. "Anybody missing? I don't see Bryan."

"He was calming the cows," Philip says. "Should be here soon."

"Don't want anybody landing in Oz," I say, trying to brighten the mood. Hannah touches my arm and shakes her head, looking at the children.

Mark turns on a radio, but it tells us what we already know: the conditions are right for a tornado, and people should take cover. It's strange to eat a meal this way. The adults are quiet, listening to the news. Matthew senses something is wrong and keeps leaving the group of children to ask Hannah for a different toy or book, one that's upstairs in his room and he can get it in two seconds. Rain pounds above us. Wind whistles through the windows high above our heads, and tree branches slam against the house. After a loud crack, the lights go out, and one by one the children start to wail. Jax barks until Bryan pets and speaks soothingly to him. In the dim light of the lanterns, I see fear on everyone's faces. I put Matthew on my knee and tell him as calmly as I can that everything will be all right, God is watching over us. He sticks a thumb in his mouth and lays his face on my expanding abdomen. He looks up at me when the baby kicks, and I whisper that his new friend is saying hello. Hannah smiles at me as she rocks Becky.

I hear the sound of a train and wonder how that could be, when suddenly the train is above us, shaking the house. Tree branches crack and every window rattles. Then the sound of breaking glass. I rock Matthew, partly for him, mostly for me. I hear mumbled prayers throughout the room.

And suddenly it passes. It seems almost silent, although the rain is still heavy, branches still scratch at the windows, and there's a roaring in the distance.

"Let's sing a song," Mark says. "Any ideas?"

Every child picks a song, and by the time we finish the rain has lightened. As we pile out the back door into the yard, moonlight highlights the clouds to the west, but the north is still black. I see a big maple toppled in the front yard and debris littering the lawn. All the buildings seem intact. Philip and Bryan leave to check on the cows, and Hannah goes upstairs with Angela, Matthew, and Becky, who are anxious to check on their rooms. I bring the dirty dishes to the kitchen and grab a trash bag, then pick up the bits of hay, paper, and other garbage caught in the corners and window wells surrounding the house.

At breakfast, Mark tells us how God saved us from the brunt of the storm. A few neighbors were not so lucky. A trailer park along the freeway had heavy damage. The church is organizing relief efforts. Part of me wants to get in the car and see, but instead I volunteer to cook extra meals while Philip and most of the men gather their tools, garbage bags, and what lumber and roofing material we have to go see what needs to be done. They come home in the late afternoon, tired, hungry, and with glum faces.

"It's bad," Philip tells me. "So many homes destroyed. Part of the roof is off the Ryandowski's house next door and the interior's damaged and filled with debris. The Red Cross has set up a shelter in the high school, but it will take months to make all the repairs."

We gather the food we've been making all day into the truck and drive to the high school. It's filled with bedraggled people with shell-shocked looks on their faces and others, like us, wanting to help. Food tables fill the stage in the auditorium overlooking the room lined with cots and blankets and laundry baskets piled with whatever people had grabbed. As we serve chili and cornbread, more and more people arrive. A truck from a local grocery store delivers cheese, peanut butter, fruit, and many loaves of bread. The Red Cross leader thanks us and asks if someone can help with water distribution. The food line doesn't end until almost ten, and we pack whatever needs to be kept cool into the school's refrigerators.

As we leave, Philip points out three people huddled along the opposite wall. "Those are our neighbors, the Ryandowskis. The man, Paul, is the guy who told the police we abducted his daughter." The man has long legs stretching out in front of him, dirty blue jeans, and the scruffy start of a beard. His arms surround the shoulders of a middle-aged woman on one side and a teenaged girl with her head on his chest on the other. All three have their eyes closed, but the tension in their bodies make it clear they're awake.

"Should we say something?" I ask.

"We're going out there tomorrow," Philip says. "Let them sleep."

Hannah and Mark are waiting for us when we return. "We should put up some people here," Mark says. "The high school is fine for a night or two, and they're talking about canceling classes Monday, but eventually they'll need something else."

"We could take a few people," Philip says. "Are you thinking of anybody in particular? Are there church members who need a place?"

"The Ryandowskis," Mark says.

"Really?" Philip asks. "After the trouble Paul caused?"

I share Philip's concern. I don't want an abusive man near my baby. "They probably need our help more than anyone," Mark says.

THE RYANDOWSKIS ACCEPT our invitation, Paul grumbling under his breath that they didn't have much choice. Helen and Sue Ann are lovely, helpful people, but Paul does little but complain when he's around, which isn't very often. Angela moves with Sue Ann to the women's dorm so Helen and Paul can have her room. At night I hear Paul moaning about the mattress being too small, too soft, too lumpy. And he snores. Loudly.

When we prepare meals together, Helen is full of motherly advice about what worked and what didn't when Sue Ann and her older brother, Paul Jr., were young. Every kid is different, she tells me, describing how right from the start Paul Jr. was active and refused to sit still while Sue Ann would happily watch other kids' activity from the safety of her mother's lap. Junior moved away the day he turned eighteen, and they seldom see him now. I wonder if Paul Senior took out his many frustrations on his son, too.

It turns out they were renting the farmhouse while someone else farmed the land. Paul works on the production line at the auto plant, but says they liked living in the country far away from people. Far away from nosy neighbors, I think. After the third time Mark reprimands him for coming home drunk, Paul doesn't come back for three days, and then only to demand Helen and Sue Ann leave too. They refuse and he leaves, swearing, angry, vowing to return for them.

Bryan and Mark meet with the Ryandowski's landlord, an accountant who lives in Indianapolis. He and his sister inherited the farm from their dad, and Mark told the Council both seem eager to sell at least the damaged house. The owners will use the insurance money to fix what they can but tell Mark more will be needed to bring it up to Code. Mark quickly calls a Council meeting to discuss purchasing the house with the money from my inheritance. Bryan questions using all the funds for a house until he learns the will's limitations.

"Who will live there?" I ask.

"There are three bedrooms, so Helen, Sue Ann, you, Philip, and your baby." Mark says.

"What if Paul comes back?"

"Paul's OK if he stops drinking. If he does, he's welcome," Mark says. "I don't expect he'll be back."

I hope not, I think, then scold myself for such an unkind thought. "It'll be hard to get to the dining hall in the middle of winter. Especially with a baby."

"Amanda's right," Hannah says. "Maybe we should have someone else move there until summer."

"Let's see how it goes," Mark says. "It may not be ready before the snow stops."

For the next week, the talk at dinner is all about how to fix up the house.

"Whatever room you're in, you can pick the color," Mark says to Sue Ann.

Sue Ann nods, her lips in a tight line.

"'We can run a path or sidewalk to the dining hall past the orchards to make it easier to push a stroller," I say.

"And a wheelbarrow," Rachel says.

"Are you going to make it bigger?" Helen asks.

"Eventually," Mark says, "but not right now. The barn's in decent shape and has water and electricity. We could partition that to house transitional families or use it for services if we need to move from our current location."

I don't want to move there. Too isolated, too rough. What's the point of communal living if you're away from everyone? A new house was my idea, but I thought we'd build a new one here, next to everybody.

Sue Ann cries as we wash the dishes. "My life is such shit. I should stay with Daddy. At least I'd be close to town. People my own age I can talk to."

"I'm not that much older than you," I say. "And you can talk to me. Lisa and Trudy too."

Sue Ann snorts. "I am not drinking the Kool-Aid."

I ponder this as we finish putting the dishes away in silence. We're good to her, protect her from an abusive father, and all she has is disdain. Then I remember me in high school, the terrible things I said to Mom, the hypocrisy I saw in everyone but myself. She needs to find out for herself, I think, pitying Helen in that moment. I think about Bert and Felicia, figuring they think I've drunk too much Kool-Aid, too. It's been a long time since I've seen them, and part of me misses the laughter when we watched hokey old movies like *The Day the Earth Stood Still*. ("I come in peace," Bert said for the next week. "Take me to your leader," I'd reply.) It's been a while since I've laughed, I realize. Bigger fish, I think.

Sue Ann flees the moment she puts the last dish away, leaving me to wipe up the counters, turn off the lights, lock up. I look toward the orchards, invisible in the dark, and am glad I can walk to the welcoming light coming from the back door to the farmhouse. My baby kicks a few times and I'm suddenly aware of a fierce protectiveness. I want this baby to live among my friends here, not among whatever strangers Mark gives shelter to. I chastise myself for selfishness but am filled with a new dread.

"NO, DON'T COME here," Helen shouts into her phone as we sit in our sewing circle in the farmhouse's front room. I hear Paul yelling, his anger if not his words clear. "No, Sue Ann's not here." Helen pauses, listening. "No, I'm not going with you." She hits the end button fiercely and thrusts the phone into her pocket. "Paul," she says to me. "Says he's coming."

Mark says we won't answer the door, will call the police if he's threatening.

We take turns watching out the window. Rain darkens the stoop and puddles on the sidewalk. It's black outside the reach of the porch light.

I hear rather than see a truck coming. It swerves into our gravel driveway, lights sweeping into our eyes and along the living room's walls. When it stops, I hear a horn beeping over and over and Paul shouts, "Get out here Helen. Now!"

"I'm calling 911," Mark says.

"I'm going out," Helen says. "The police won't get here quick enough."

"No!" I say, clenching my jaw. All Paul's snide remarks directed at Helen, at all of us, run through my mind. He's hit her before. Who knows what comes next? She can't leave with him.

"If I go with him, he'll leave," Helen says.

"We'll protect you," Philip says.

"Do you have a gun?" Helen asks, and Philip shakes his head. "Didn't think so."

My eyes burn with anger at all the hurt this man has caused. No. He can't do this. Bully us. Take Helen and beat her again. This must end. Blood rushes to my brain, blocking out all sound and reason, and I'm outside before anyone can stop me, before I know I'm going.

"Amanda!" Philip yells, rushing out, but I'm already waving my arms into the glare of the truck's headlights. I hear an engine roar. A jolt of pain at my hips, a scream. Small rocks piercing my head.

When I awake, noise and flashing lights surround me. A young man is leaning over me. "She's awake!" he yells over the sirens and the clatter of something pulled over the gravel. Something hard is shoved underneath me. They lift me onto a gurney, and we rattle toward the red and blue lights.

The pain in my abdomen comes without warning, and I scream. "Baby," I gasp.

"We know," he says, as he clips something on my finger and inserts a needle into my arm, "we'll do everything we can."

Philip climbs into the ambulance after me and holds my hand as they inject something. "Oh, Amanda. Why did you do that?"

Do what?

The pain comes in waves, and each time I yelp and squeeze Philip's hand. When I open my eyes, I see he's crying.

The emergency room is a shock of light and noise. A policeman follows the gurney. "Leave her alone," the paramedic says. "She's not dying. You can talk with her later."

I'm not dying. That's good. The baby. Is the baby dying?

They roll me into a room with several machines and monitors. The paramedics shift me to the bed and hang a plastic bag of clear fluid on the attached hook. One nurse unbuttons my blouse and places little squares of something on my chest, then attaches wires to each. Another nurse pats my hand and asks, "How many weeks along are you?"

I try to sit up but the room spins, so I lie back down. I feel a liquid warmth between my legs. "I'm not sure. Five months?"

"Who's your OBGYN?"

"I don't have one." Why don't I have one? I should know the answers to these questions.

"We'll contact the on-call doctor." She rubs a cold gel and then a rounded object on my stomach. I hear the staccato sound of a heartbeat. "The baby's alive," the nurse says, and a wave of relief washes over me. She lifts the sheet covering my legs. "Are you in any pain?"

"My legs hurt, and I get these waves of pain in my stomach," I say.

"Don't worry," she says, but I hear in her voice something is wrong. She goes into the hallway to talk with a woman in a white coat.

Philip takes my hand.

"What happened?" I ask.

"You went outside to talk with Paul," he says. "Paul stepped on the gas and hit you, knocked you to the side, yelled for Helen. Mark had already called the police and called back for an ambulance, so they were there quickly. Do you remember any of this?"

"I remember being angry and walking toward the driveway. Stupid, huh?"

"A little bit." He leans over and kisses my forehead as the nurse returns with the woman in the white coat.

"Hi, Amanda, I'm Dr. Cortez. I need to check a few things." She glances at the monitor, then presses gently on my abdomen. "We need to consider an emergency C-section."

I close my eyes. Let everyone else make the decisions for me. Their conversation murmurs around me. Risks, outcomes, alternatives, I don't care. I say yes to everything when they make me answer.

"I want my baby to live," I say. "Whatever it takes."

Eventually they wheel me down a hall, up an elevator, and into a room filled with monitors and people wearing scrubs and hats and masks. One of the masked men explains to me why general anesthesia is best for my situation, and I say fine. He inserts something into the IV, and I drift away.

CHAPTER 26

Susan

Do-not-reply@Innewsonline
Re: Accident in rural Indiana
BIII@university.edu sent you this article. Subscribe at Innewsonline.
A local man was detained by bystanders after striking a pregnant woman at a house along State Route 52. One witness said, "he stepped on the gas and headed right for her." The suspect, Paul Ryandowski, had a blood alcohol level of .15 at the scene. The woman, who through her husband requested anonymity, is recovering at University Hospital following surgery. The baby remains in Neo-Natal Intensive Care in critical condition. "If the baby dies," Police spokesman Eugene Taylor stated, "Mr. Ryandowski will be charged with manslaughter and feticide."

I'M NOT SURE why I open this email when I should be redlining opposing counsel's overreaching settlement agreement. The email has all the signs of being junk—from an unknown address, referring to a link. I guess I'm starved for news about Amanda, and the word "Indiana" sucked me in. As I read, panic numbs my hands, my legs, and squeezes my chest. Is Amanda the woman? Wouldn't she have told me if she were pregnant? How do I find out? Who's BIII? Nothing comes to mind. I need to call someone, no way I'm waiting for a return email. I could call Detective Taylor. Could he be BIII?

I call the hospital instead.

"Hi, could you tell me the status of your patient, Amanda Morivan?" I ask in my sweetest voice.

After a pause, the operator asks, "What is your name and relationship to the patient?"

Fear grabs my throat. It is her. "I'm Susan Beane. Her mother."

"I'm sorry. You're not on her list. If you'd like to be placed on her list, please have her or her husband include you."

"OK. Can you connect me to her room?"

"Let me check," the voice says.

I'm on hold for an excruciating amount of time, listening to how great the hospital is. Suddenly the announcements stop. I wait in case they don't have the annoying list of announcements to fill in the gap during a transfer, but soon it's clear I've been cut off. I call Detective Taylor, glad when he answers.

"Detective, this is Susan Beane," I say. "Did you send me that email about the accident?"

"What email?" he says.

"The one I know is about Amanda because I called the hospital, and they won't tell me anything and they won't let me talk to her and I need to know what's happening."

"Calm down, Susan," he says. "Yes, Amanda was in an accident. She's alive. That's all I can tell you."

"I didn't even know she was pregnant," I wail.

"I'm sorry," he says.

"Can you send me the police report?"

"Yes," he answers. "But it will be the redacted version we gave the media."

"OK," I say. "Did you email Tony too?"

"I didn't email anyone, Susan."

Then who did? When I check my phone, I see there's another email from BIII:

Did you get the article I sent you? When I saw it on the news the house looked like Amanda's place. Was it Amanda? Is she OK? In case you don't remember, this is Amanda's friend Bert.

I write quickly back:

Thanks for the article—I wondered who sent it. I'm flying out in a few hours. The hospital won't give me much information, but she's alive.

I receive an immediate response:

Thanks.

So, it's not only Tony and me she cut off. Oh, Amanda, couldn't you have had fun for a couple of years with your college friends and not become a wife and a mother so quickly?

I wonder as I stare at my phone if I have to call Tony. Yes. Yes I do.

Tony wants to leave on the next flight. I agree. There's one leaving in a few hours. I wince at the price but buy it anyway.

I throw random clothes into my carryon. Text Mike. Park in the expensive lot.

Tony waves at me to join him in the security line. The people behind him frown and grumble. We have middle seats, several rows apart. Just as well. I prefer to fret alone.

It's nearly midnight by the time we rent a car and drive to the University, so we go to the hotel closest to the hospital. Tony's up and drinking coffee when I wander into the breakfast area at six a.m.

"When do you want to go?" Tony says.

"I'm ready."

"Eat something. It may be a long day."

The information desk gives us her room number and directs us to the elevators.

We're somber as the elevator doors close against the brightly lit wide aisles of the entrance. A slight smell of disinfectant permeates the small space, and the loud voice of a woman paging doctors and emergency personnel punctuates our silence.

The floor is a mass of activity between breakfast and doctors making their rounds. Amanda's door is open, and she's pushed away her food tray. She's alone. Her face is slack, her eyes closed, her hair matted close to her head.

My beautiful girl.

Tony stops too, and I see tears in the corners of his eyes.

Amanda must sense us because she looks in our direction and starts to cry. We rush in and each take a hand.

"You're OK, everything will be fine," Tony says.

"Oh, sweetheart," I say.

"You shouldn't be here," Amanda says, but she tightens her grip on my hand.

"Yes, we should," Tony says.

"Where else would we be?" I say.

"Did Philip or Mark call you?" she asks.

"Neither," I say.

Amanda lifts her head. "Then how did you find out?"

"Your friend Bert sent me an email with the news article," I say.

"They weren't supposed to give out my name," she says, her head dropping back on the pillow.

"They didn't. But the article named the hospital, so I called," I say.

"I'm glad he sent it," Tony says.

Amanda shifts her body, winces, closes her eyes. When a nurse enters, she adjusts the bed to sit upright. "I want my baby."

"I'll get a doctor," the nurse says, scurrying out.

Amanda closes her eyes again. I'm afraid to ask, so I sit silently, hoping she'll tell us something. Tony turns on the television as we wait, and I read emails on my phone. Rev. Mark knocks on the door frame, looking surprised.

"Susan, Tony, good to see you again," he says. "Sorry it's at such an awful time."

"Where's Philip?" Tony says, and I can hear the anger in his tone.

"Philip's been here all day and night since it happened. We sent him home this morning to sleep and take a shower," Pastor Mark says. "We're all concerned for Amanda and the baby."

"A girl or boy?" I ask.

"A girl. She's in neonatal intensive care."

"I want to be there," Amanda says.

A doctor wearing a white lab coat enters. "Are you the father?" he asks Mark as he pulls a monitor toward him. We shake our heads, and the doctor turns to speak to Amanda. "We estimate the baby is at twenty-four weeks. Honestly, I doubt she'll make it, and if she does, she may experience severe disability. Say the word, and we'll stop trying."

Does this doctor have no empathy at all? I think.

"I want her to live," Amanda whispers.

Mark brushes the hair out of Amanda's eyes.

"We're setting up for you in NICU," the doctor says, leaving as quickly as he came.

I look up "24 weeks fetus" in my phone. The results confirm what the doctor told us, but in much greater, sadder, detail. Maybe he was being kind in his own brusque way. I hand the phone to Tony.

"What's it say, Mom?" Amanda asks.

"Same as the doctor," I answer and Tony hands her my phone. "Does she have a name?"

"Not yet," Amanda says. "Philip and I hadn't talked about names yet."

"Plenty of time," I say, patting her hand.

"I need to sleep and can't seem to do that when you're all watching me with those sad eyes," Amanda says. "Can you come back later?"

"Sure," I say. "I could use a nap. How about we come back after lunch?"

We retreat to our rooms to phone our relatives, friends, employers. Eddie and Diane want to come, but I tell them not yet.

"We need to come sometime anyway, Susan," Eddie says. "The lawyer got a formal request from Amanda for her inheritance so she and Philip can buy a house and five acres next to the Grange property."

"They're moving next door?" I ask. "Well, that seems better than giving the money to the Vinnars."

"Housing prices are depressed in rural Indiana, but even so the price seems low. If it turns out to be unlivable and it's just five extra acres for the farm, we as trustees need to decide how to respond."

"I can't talk about this right now, Eddie. I'm glad she's alive. I'm a grandma. All that can wait."

"You're right. I'm sorry. Keep me updated, OK?"

I open the window shades, pull back the bedspread, try to nap. I have a clear view of a wing of the hospital and count the floors to what might be Amanda's room. She's buying a house. I should move back here, help with the baby. My mom and I got a lot closer once Amanda was born. I know it was hard on my mom being so far from her grandchild. One year they came out four times, and every year she begged me to move back so we could be closer.

Tony calls. "Think we can go back yet?"

"Let's go," I say.

Philip and a timid young woman I recognize from the wedding are in the room when we return. Amanda is dressed and sitting on a couch between them. Philip shakes our hands with a solemn look and introduces us to Trudy.

"Are you being discharged?" I ask Amanda.

A nurse hurries in. "The parental space in NICU is ready." She looks around the room. "We limit visitors in each suite, but there's a waiting area nearby."

The nurse pushes Amanda in a wheelchair through the corridors painted white and pale blue, down the elevator, into a lobby filled with huge living plants on its marble floors, down a long hallway leading to the lobby of the children's hospital painted in bright primary colors with murals of giraffes and elephants and horses, up the elevator, opening to a floor painted soft yellows and greens. It might be calming if it weren't for the staccato of pagings, codes, and announcements that fill me with panic. The nurse leads us to a central monitoring area surrounded by glass room dividers sheltering babies in clear capsules with wires leading to more monitors. Behind the sliding door in each of these rooms are daybeds and recliners, some with women or men holding infants too small to be real.

"The waiting area is here," the nurse says, pointing to an open area lit by large windows. A few people sit in the pale green club chairs and love seats, coffee cups lining the nearby tables. Most are silent, but one woman loudly tells her life story on the phone.

"Can we see her?" I ask.

Tony, Trudy, and I stand outside a glass wall, watching the nurse hand Amanda and Philip masks and blue-checked robes. They huddle around a capsule surrounding the smallest baby I've ever seen. A tube runs from the baby's mouth to one machine, and another from her abdomen to a clear sac filled with fluid. Little wires run from her chest, feet, wrists, arms, and legs. Amanda puts her hand through an opening and pets the baby's tiny hand. The baby doesn't move.

My heart is breaking. I remember Amanda's loud cries the day she was born, her eyes demanding then comforted as she lay on my breast. I can see pain and worry in Amanda's eyes as she turns toward the monitor. We watch silently for a while, then go back to the waiting room.

We have nothing to say, and the silence grows uncomfortable.

"I'll call someone to pick me up," Trudy says. "Do either of you have a phone I could use?"

I hand her mine, wondering what she'd expected. She's young. Give her a break.

Philip comes to us a few minutes later, talks with Trudy, then sits next to us.

"It's kind of you both to come, but Amanda and I will want to stay with the baby the rest of the day and they only allow two in the room at a time," Philip says. "I hope you understand."

"Sure," Tony says, and I nod. "We'll wait here in case either of you want to go get something to eat."

"Can you tell us anything?" I ask.

"Only that it doesn't look good," Philip says. I move to take his hand, but he moves away. We all stare at the floor.

"Will you name the baby?" I ask.

"Amanda wants to call her Iris. Says she looks like a little iris bud wrapped in her green baby blanket."

"Iris," I echo. "Our little flower."

My head is full of questions, but none I dare ask.

"I understand you're buying a house," I finally say.

Tony looks at me in surprise.

"My brother Eddie told me," I say.

"We've picked one out, anyway," Philip says. "We're still working out the details."

We stay all day, leaving only to eat a quick supper in the cafeteria. Philip stays with Amanda and Iris, coming out occasionally to tell Tony and I we need not stay, and he'll call us if anything changes. I look at Tony, and he shakes his head. It's nearing ten p.m. when we see a lot of movement in the unit. Several white-coated people rush in. We watch by the doors and listen to Amanda wail as the nurse turns off the monitors.

As the doctors and nurses leave, we enter. Amanda looks at no one but Iris, rocking and singing. Amanda clutches Iris, refusing to leave or let go. We watch for a half-hour, helpless, then return to the waiting area. Tony puts his arm around me, and I lay my head on his shoulder. The nurse looks at us with pity. I ask her what happens next, and she tells me they'll let Amanda and Philip stay until morning if they want. She offers Tony and me blankets, and we nap intermittently. Just before shift change, she touches my shoulder to say goodbye. We look through the window at Amanda, still rocking, Philip asleep on the daybed. I knock lightly, but neither of them moves.

"What should we do?" Tony asks.

"We should be here," I say.

A new nurse approaches. "She asked me to call their pastor. He should be here soon."

When Mark arrives, he kisses Amanda on the top of her head. When I reach to touch Iris's tiny face, Amanda starts to wail again.

"We need to go, Amanda," Mark says, lifting Iris out of her arms and giving her to the nurse. He pushes her wheelchair toward the elevators. Philip stays with the nurse and Iris, but Tony and I follow. I understand Amanda's blank face and slumped posture because I, too, feel paralyzed by grief.

FUNERALS. I CAN'T bear them. The last time I was in this room was for a wedding. Now it's silent and filled with closed faces. The service is nearly as crowded as Amanda's wedding, but we stand for the short message. What can anyone say? It's the usual, how we'll all see Iris again in her glorified body. Finally get to know her. I want it to be true. We sing no songs. No one else talks.

I want to hold Amanda forever, but she won't let me touch her. Won't let anyone touch her, not Philip, not Mark. A little boy clings to her waist now, but she doesn't seem to notice. Her face is blank, as if she's somewhere else. Maybe she is. Maybe she took the drugs the doctors offered.

All that's left of Iris is a pretty green urn with an iris painted on its side sitting on the mantle above the fireplace. Fresh cut irises surround it. I never got to hold my first grandchild, never got to kiss her goodbye. My daughter is oblivious to my desire to help her. Paige arrived for Tony, and Diane and Eddie and their families came too. Amanda doesn't notice.

When Mark finishes, people crowd toward Amanda and Philip, say how sorry they are, and leave. There's coffee and cake in the kitchen, but no one stays. Too sad. Too hard to say anything comforting. Philip does all the talking as Amanda stands glassy eyed at his side. Bert and Felicia hug Amanda, but she doesn't react. They come to the back where I'm waiting and hug me. I fight the tears as I embrace Bert, thank him for letting me know about this tragedy. He squeezes tighter, then lets go.

When the crowd thins and I reach them, I take Amanda's limp hand. A million possible things to say run through my mind, but they all seem worthless, trite, unhelpful. "Oh, Amanda," I finally say and squeeze her hand. "I'm so sorry." She looks at me, her eyes bloodshot and dilated. Philip puts his arm around her and leads her up the stairs.

CHAPTER 27

Amanda

"IT'S BEEN OVER a month, Amanda," Philip says, standing above me, hands on his hips, as I lay in bed tangled by blankets and pillows. "You have to start helping around here. I know you're sad but keeping busy will help."

I bury my head in my pillow. "I don't have the energy."

"Lying in bed twenty hours a day is not going to help that."

I sit up, then quickly rest my head against the headboard and close my eyes. I hear him sigh and walk away.

I'm driving him away. I drive everyone away.

It's so much easier to sleep.

I force my legs over the side of the bed and look toward the dresser where Iris' urn should be. Philip moved it back downstairs to the fireplace mantle, said I'd have to get up to see it, but I want it back. I can't escape the mirror and see the woman I've become. A woman with ratty hair in a crumpled shirt that hasn't been washed in weeks. Take a shower! I think. You are stretching everyone's patience. I want to stop feeling this way. I don't know how.

Mark comes to talk to me almost daily. I want to suggest we talk back at his church office, to have him just hold me in his arms for an hour, but what would be the excuse for that? He tells me how work is going on the house. Today he told me Mom, Uncle Eddie, and Aunt Diane are coming after Christmas for the closing. Who cares? I try not to resent Philip. He's grieving too. I bet Mom would have let me wallow as long as I needed. Who am I kidding? She would have demanded I see a psychologist and get some meds. Philip doesn't believe in pharmaceuticals. He believes in prayer and work.

Nicole Andersson has been the most comfort. She lost a baby several years back, and she sits and cries with me. I know she's crying about her baby, not mine, but at least she understands. It's a little scary, though, thinking I may still be this sad in twelve years. I consider that as I shower, the hot water rolling over my head and down my back. I guess you never forget. She says time takes off the sharp edges, turns it into a dull instead of a searing pain.

I look at the red scar on my flabby abdomen and lift my sagging breasts. I'm disgusting. No wonder Philip has taken to falling asleep on the couch downstairs.

I drag myself to the dining hall for lunch, and everyone claps. Helen and Sue Ann smile hesitantly. I know they feel guilty. Helen moved to the women's house after the accident. I've told them I don't blame them, but they are a reminder. I wish everyone would ignore me, pretend I'm normal. I feel like there's two of me now, the grateful one who accepts their encouragement and sympathy, and the angry one who would happily scream all day. Except when I'm sleeping. Mark tells me it's OK to be angry, and he's willing to listen to me scream. But how can I? If I let out all the venom in my soul right now there'd be nothing but scorched earth around me.

ON CHRISTMAS EVE I stay home with Rachel to watch the kids while everyone is at the evening service. Matthew climbs on my lap and hugs me.

"I'm sorry you're so sad, Aunty Amanda," he says, and I start crying. Again.

Rachel reaches for him, and I hug him tighter. "I'm sorry too, Matthew. Thank you for the hug."

"I miss your stories."

I wipe my eyes and grab a tissue. "How about I read you a story now? The Christmas Eve story?"

Matthew claps, and the other children sit at my feet as Rachel brings over the Children's Bible. "Are you sure?" Rachel whispers in my ear and I nod. I decide to tell the story my way instead of reading it, so let Matthew use the book to show the pictures.

"Mary and her husband Joseph took a trip to Bethlehem when lots of other people did too. Mary was going to have a baby."

"Like you were," Matthew says.

"Yes, like I was. When they got to Bethlehem, there was no place for them to stay, but one man felt sorry for them and put them in the barn with the cows so they could keep warm."

"I like cows," Matthew says, and all the children agree.

"I like milk from cows," Ben says. "But the barn is kind of stinky."

"Tell us about the angels," Emma says.

"In a field nearby, shepherds watched their sheep. All of a sudden, a great light, like fireworks bursting in the sky lit up the fields and thousands of angels appeared. The shepherds were scared."

"Why were they scared of angels?" Emma asks. "Because of the noise?"

"Maybe they didn't know if they were good angels," Angela says.

"Then one of the angels said, 'Don't be afraid. I have happy news. Today your Savior was born in Bethlehem. You'll find him in a barn wrapped in towels and sleeping in a box.' Then all the angels started to sing."

"Jesus was in a manger," Matthew says.

"Yes, a manger is a feeding trough. Like we put the hay in for the cows when they can't be in the pasture."

Most of the children giggle, but Ben starts to cry. "Poor baby Jesus. He had to sleep in a stinky barn with the food and the bugs."

I consider using this as a teaching moment about how poor many children of the world are. Nah. It's Christmas.

"Can we sing the angels' song?" Angela asks.

"That is a great idea," I say, lifting Matthew off my lap and standing up. We are singing Gloria for the seventeenth time when everyone returns and joins in. Philip smiles at me, and I realize I'm smiling too.

MY CHRISTMAS HIGH doesn't last. Nicole was right; I think about Iris every day, even when I'm doing OK, like while we were singing on Christmas Eve. I barely remember the funeral, it's an empty space in my head. I don't think I cried. I know I didn't talk. Bert and Felicia were there. I might have teared when they said how sorry they were and rushed off.

Soon Mom and Aunty Diane and Uncle Eddie are coming to see the mess of a house I'm buying. I dread their reaction and their pity. They know the tornado damage is why we're getting a good price for the house and five acres, but I'm sure that they also know we could buy a much nicer house with a small lot somewhere else. Uncle Eddie already sent us a letter about what a bad investment it is "unless significant improvements have been made." Well, nothing in the will said we had to make a good investment.

Chapter 28

Susan

A LETTER SITS in my office inbox when I return from Iris's funeral. The firm has decided not to renew my contract for the next year. They thank me for my eight years, tell me if I want to leave early something can be worked out. They require as a condition of receiving my final check that I work with Mike on a plan for closing or transferring my cases, remind me of the provisions of my contract and the ethical rules concerning client contact.

Bastards. I think. *Hit me when I'm down.*

I look at my calendar, cancel all my meetings, go home to feel sorry for myself. Crawl into bed and sleep.

It's dark when I awake. Eight p.m. Four voicemails from people at work and one from Corey register on my phone. A text message from Katya wondering where I am.

Couldn't make rehearsal tonight, I text back. *Will explain later.*

Hope you're okay, immediately appears.

I'll be fine, I type, although I'm not sure when.

I stare in the bathroom mirror, wondering when I got so old, so tired, so useless. My roots need a touch up. Who cares? I guess I'd better care since I'll be looking for a new job. I move prescription bottles around in my medicine cabinet, find a bottle of an antihistamine that always makes me sleepy and take two pills. Maybe things will be clearer in the morning. I debate whether to set my alarm.

I awake with a start from a dream I can't remember. No light seeps through window curtains. My phone says it's five-thirty. I stare into the dark, somehow having decided not to decide or make long term plans. I will satisfy my obligations at the firm and leave before the December concert. I'll accept Diane's invitation for Christmas. Go with her and Eddie to the closing on Amanda's house.

Something will work out, or it won't.

PHILIP STANDS WITH Mark on the sidewalk in front of the farmhouse when Eddie, Diane, and I pull into the driveway. We'd talked about what we were going to do when we got here, but my resolve flees when I see a wan, disheveled Amanda watching through the front window. She looks terrible. Unhealthy. I hope the glass is distorting.

"Susan," Philip says, shaking my hand.

It hurts that he treats me like a stranger. Mark gives me a quick hug.

"Hannah made coffee," Philip says.

"Great," Eddie says, and we trudge over the frozen gravel to the newly shoveled sidewalk.

Amanda opens the door with a strained smile and accepts our hugs. Everything seems to hang from her—her limp hair, the skin on her cheeks, her faded flannel shirt. Mark's wife bustles around, taking our coats and shooing kids off the couch. I follow Amanda into the kitchen.

"How are you holding up, sweetheart?" I ask.

"OK, I guess," she says.

"Talk to me. I haven't seen you since the funeral. I can see you're grieving. I am too," I say.

"I keep wondering how long it takes for time to heal all wounds," she says. "More than six weeks, apparently."

"Are you talking to anyone?" I ask.

"Mark, mostly. Philip's having a hard time too and we end up irritated when we try to talk about it. And there's a woman in the church too."

"I meant a professional counselor."

"Mark's a professional counselor," she says, challenge in her voice.

"Of course," I say and carry a tray of coffee cups into the living room.

The sky is gray and low when we return to our car and follow Mark and Philip the short drive to the next house on the highway. Large evergreens, leafless maples and oaks obscure the small, half-painted house from the road. The roof has new-looking green asphalt shingles and a new black door. Behind the house is a barn with peeling red paint next to a rusted truck with no wheels and mounds of broken sheet rock and other construction materials half-covered in snow.

Philip unlocks the door to an empty room. It's smaller than the Vinnars' farmhouse, with a galley kitchen leading off the front room. There's a sink, but no appliances, and all the floors are plywood. It's colder inside than out.

"The bathroom fixtures come tomorrow," Philip says, "but we won't turn on the water or the heat until we're ready to move in."

"When will that be?" I ask.

"Not sure," he answers. "Spring?"

"Does it have a basement?" Eddie asks.

"Yes, and it has a tornado room," Philip says, opening a small door leading to blackness. "Mark, do you have a flashlight?"

Eddie, Diane, and I hand him our phones. He looks at us as if we're aliens. I shake my phone and the flashlight comes on.

We descend slowly. The stairs creak and crack as we peer into the dark. The center of the room is filled with a furnace surrounded by cracked concrete.

"They had an old, converted coal burner down here," Mark says. "This one is much more efficient and doesn't take up as much room. The safe room is over here." He points to a wide steel door and what appears to be a large box in the corner. Once opened, he shines the light on the box's thick metal walls, floor, and ceiling. Cabinets line the top third of the walls. "We'll keep water, food, and sleeping bags in here."

"Well, I know where to come during the zombie apocalypse," Diane jokes, but nobody laughs.

The house makes me sad. It's serviceable. It has five acres. It's near to what she considers home. But it's cold and dreary. It reminds me of that cartoon character Joe in *Li'l Abner* who always has a rain cloud above his head. The world's worst jinx. My dad loved that comic strip, would read it to us over breakfast Sunday mornings. I never got the jokes, but that dark cloud and the gentle man who lived under it sticks in my head. The most relatable character in the whole strip.

"What do you think?" Eddie asks on the way back.

"I don't see any reason to say no," Diane says.

"I agree," I say. "Although I wish there were."

"We could hold off, come back when they finish," Diane says.

I shake my head, clinging to the hope that if we make this easy, Amanda will talk with me again.

When we stop back at the house, Hannah tells us Amanda is lying down. The scowl that passes over Philip's face emboldens me. "I'll say a quick goodbye."

I sit on the bed next to Amanda and touch her shoulder. She opens her eyes and watches me listlessly.

I pull out a prepaid cellphone and hand it to her. "In case you ever need it. And call me once in a while, please?"

Amanda hesitates, then closes her eyes again. "Put it in the top right-hand drawer of the dresser," she mumbles.

I climb down the stairs, wondering if she'll ever call.

"What time is the closing?" Eddie asks.

"Tomorrow at three-thirty," Philip says.

"We'll see you and Amanda then," Eddie says, turns, and strides out the door.

"I'm not sure Amanda will make it," Philip says.

"She'd better," Diane says. "We'll authorize the money to her. Nobody else."

"She's my wife," Philip bristles.

"It's her inheritance," I say.

"IT WAS HARD to see Amanda so listless and sad," I tell Corey as we sit in my den and wait for midnight on New Year's Eve.

"Give her time," Corey says. "She always was a high-energy kid. It'll come back."

"I don't know," I say. "I found it all so oppressive. Philip thought we'd let him be on the deed. We disabused him of that pretty quick. Amanda didn't say anything at all. Just signed where she was told and shuffled out. And that house! Pretty depressing and all by itself in the middle of empty fields."

I stare at the fire, drinking champagne and trying to organize my jumbled thoughts. I sensed something weird going on with Amanda and Philip and Mark but couldn't decide what it was. I resent that they'd kept Amanda from working on her degree, that the group could decide where she would live and what she would do. But isn't that what she signed up for? The needs of the group are more important than the individual. Not so different from a family when it comes down to it.

"What I don't understand," I say. "Is why Amanda's needs weren't just as important as the commune's."

Corey seems to follow, somehow understanding what I hadn't yet said. "It should be a give and take, not a competition. But the tension's always there. Like in a marriage."

"I liked being married," I say. "Loved knowing there was someone I could count on and the comfort of working through hard things with my best friend. Until he wasn't. Until I started feeling like I was doing everything wrong, needed to tiptoe around to keep the peace. Not lovers, not even friends anymore."

"I remember," Corey says. "And I'm sure I don't know what the solution is. After the thrill of the first few months, most of my romantic relationships feel suffocating. Peculiar expectations about how often we should or shouldn't see each other, spending Thanksgiving with his family instead of mine, going out on weekends with his friends, not mine. Not to mention the jealous or controlling or gaslighting guys. Maybe the best relationships are like ours: talk, go out, but live in separate houses."

I smile. This is better than any of the relationships I've tried since Tony and I divorced. "Romance is over-rated. At least at my age. I do worry about when I'm elderly and alone, though. It doesn't look like Amanda will be around."

"We're still young and beautiful and smart. Something will happen. And you always have me."

I know that isn't a given. There have been long gaps between when we see each other, usually when one of us starts seeing a new man. I don't rely on Corey, don't feel the same confidence or ease as I did when things with Tony were good. And how did that work out?

"Here's to the New Year," I say, clinking glasses as we watch the ball drop in New York City for the third time tonight. "May it be better than this one."

"I resolve it will be," Corey says.

"And I resolve to be a better mom."

"How is that possible? You're already great."

"Amanda needs a mom who gives her more room to make her own choices and mistakes, but never gives up on her. I tried too hard for too long to protect her, and then when she shut me out, I let her. I need to find some middle ground."

"What's that old song? 'Hang on loosely, but don't let go'?"

"Pretty sure that was about romance," I say, laughing.

"Still applies." Corey stands up to leave and hugs me.

IN THE MORNING, I clear the plates and glasses and bottles and snacks scattered around the room and move knickknacks to their rightful places. I know I should get rid of some, go for a sparer look. My mom gave me Marie Kondo's book that last Christmas. But every time I try to put one of my many mementos in a box for Goodwill, I remember some place or person and take it back out. A John Prine song about souvenirs springs to mind and I sing the parts I remember and hum the rest. I pick up a scratched glass paperweight that's been sitting on my shelves in every house I've ever lived. I remember Cousin Berta and the day she gave it to me when I was ten.

Every Sunday, Grandpa drove Grandma to visit her Cousin Berta at what they called the old folks home. This Sunday was Mother's Day, and they were at our house to celebrate, so my mom offered to drive her. Sundays at my house were pretty boring—we weren't allowed to watch TV, go to a store, or do much of anything but read a book or take a nap—so I went too. The drive from the suburbs back to the old neighborhood was long. Most of the trip I lay in the back seat playing with my Barbie doll while Mom and Grandma talked softly in the front. Finally bored with that, I looked out the windows to see rows of tall, narrow brick houses so close to each other they almost seemed to touch, a big change from the sprawling ranch homes separated by large grassy lawns I was used to.

"Why does Cousin Berta always come to our house on Christmas?" I asked.

"She has no one else," Mom said. "Her parents are dead, her brother died in the Great War, and she never married. Be kind to her."

I thought about the pretty flowered dress with lace trim and a string of pearls Mom gave Cousin Berta, unlike anything I'd ever seen her wear. When Mom wrapped it, I'd asked why not give Berta a sweater since she always was cold at our house.

"A sweater would be more practical, sure. But sometimes you need nice things. Grandma told me some of the old women at the home won't sit with Cousin Berta because she's poor," Mom said, her voice soft with anger. "Mean old biddies. I hope I don't end up there."

"They don't like her because she doesn't have a fancy dress?" I asked in disbelief. "But she's so nice."

Mom sighed. "You would think Christians would be better than that, wouldn't you? But some aren't, I'm sorry to tell you."

"That's where she lives," Mom said, pointing to a square, red brick building with four rows of windows going up. I saw an old woman standing in one of the windows.

A glassed-in porch protected the front doors, and several white-haired women and men sat in wheelchairs along the side, nodding or sleeping, as two women in white uniforms sat on a bench. Inside, the front desk reminded me of school with its bookshelf and telephone and a row of square nooks behind a blonde woman with eyeglasses hanging on a cord around her neck.

"Hello, Maud," Grandma said. "Sorry you have to work on Mother's Day."

"Good afternoon, Dorcas," Maud said. "It's the Lord's work, just like the Preacher's."

We all nodded and headed toward Cousin Berta's room. I crinkled my nose at some awful smell I couldn't identify. Mom tapped my shoulder and shook her head.

Cousin Berta's room was small and dark and smelled faintly of pee. Her door seemed to be at the start of a tunnel with one small window at the other end. Another door on the side was closed. Cousin Berta gave me a hug, her face soft and smelling of talcum. Her bent shape made her just a little taller than me.

"So nice of you to come," she said. "Please, sit."

A small plate of cookies sat on a table in front of the couch, three each of windmill cookies and powdered almond crescents. She walked slowly toward a cabinet and pulled out a tin and took out one more of each.

"I thought it would be just Dorcas and Noah," she said. "This is such a nice surprise."

"I'll make coffee," Mom said, going to a counter with a coffeepot on a hotplate.

I quickly bored of the talk of sermons and relatives I didn't know, so walked around the room, looking at her few pictures, pieces of Delft pottery, embroidered pillows. On a table near the window, I found a heavy piece of scratched glass with a felt bottom. Inside the glass was a white building next to a lake.

"My dad bought that for me at the World's Fair in 1893," Cousin Berta said.

I looked at her in disbelief. How old was she?

"That's the Museum of Science and Industry now," she said.

"I've been there," I said, glad finally to have something to relate to. "I love the submarine."

"No submarine back then," she said. "But the Fair was so beautiful. All of it was just so beautiful."

When we got up to leave after what seemed like hours later, Cousin Berta picked up the paperweight and put it into my hands. My mom, standing behind her, frowned and shook her head.

"I can't take this," I said. "It's from your dad."

"Thank you, Cousin Berta," Mom said. "That's very kind, but she's too young for such a fine thing."

"Please take it. It would make me happy," she said, turning to Mom. "Really."

Mom relented with a smile.

"Thank you," I said and gave her another hug.

As I got older, I refused to go to the home, depressed by its dreariness and cloying smell. Every Christmas Cousin Berta was more and more frail. My grandparents, too, so Dad and Eddie would pick them up, and as we waited

Mom put plastic on one chair. Then she'd command Diane and me to sit on the other chairs until Cousin Berta was in her place. She would sit in that chair and smile, never talking and never responding. We tried including her sometimes, shouting across the room, but Cousin Berta couldn't hear. She became part of the Christmas decorations, a silent reminder about what it meant to be old and alone.

When she died a few years later, Mom went to her funeral with my grandparents. Eddie had baseball practice; Diane and I said we had homework to do; Dad decided we shouldn't be home alone.

I set the paperweight back onto the shelf and know I could be a Cousin Berta someday.

Chapter 29

Amanda

FOR MY NEW Year's Resolution I resolve to cheer up, be more helpful, work on the new house, tighten these flabby muscles.

"I could go back to school," I say to Philip as we get ready for bed.

"In the Fall, maybe," he says. "We'll see."

"No, I mean spring semester. It starts in a week."

He looks at me in disbelief. "There's a lot of work yet to do on the house. If you're feeling up to school, you can help us with that."

"You said I should keep busy. I could do both."

"Are you going to fight me on this again? Bring it to the Council?"

"No. I thought since I dropped out for the baby . . ."

"You know your inheritance isn't going to cover everything that needs doing, right? Tuition, books, they're expensive." Philip puts his shirt and pants back on, and leaves.

When I wake in the morning, his side of the bed is still cold. I see no reason to get up, so turn the other way.

What seems like seconds, but turns out to be several hours, later I hear a light knocking on the door and see Hannah's familiar shape peeking through a crack. I sit up and wave her in. She sits on the bed and takes my hand.

"Philip was sleeping on the couch when I got up this morning," she says. "Do you want to talk about it?"

"I said I wanted to go back to school next week, and he got angry."

"Philip's handling Iris' death in his own way. He's given you leeway, you should give him some too."

"I guess. But he's the one who told me keeping busy would help me. Now he says there's no money."

"Money is tight."

I sulk in silence.

"But if you're up to it, let's start spring cleaning."

"In January?" I say.

"It's a big job," she says.

Philip sees us scrubbing in the kitchen before lunch. He comes up from behind, puts his arms around me, and says, "I'm sorry," into my ear.

"I'm sorry, too," I say and turn to give him a kiss. Except I'm still more angry than sorry. Maybe I am a spoiled child like he constantly tells me. I say a quick prayer to be a better wife.

The afternoon passes quickly, not as quickly as when I sleep all day but quicker than I thought it would. At supper Mark tells us they'll turn on the heat, water, and electricity in the new house next week so they can finish the interior work. Several people from church had volunteered to paint the following weekend.

"If all goes well, you can move in at the beginning of March," Mark says, looking at me.

Fear runs through me.

"We'll be ready," Philip says.

"Yes," Helen echoes.

Bryan clears his throat. "People, our expenses will be going up now, so please be careful with your use of electricity and remember to turn the thermostats down. Sixty degrees would be great."

When it was sixty degrees in Phoenix, I'd wear a fleece-lined hooded jacket. No wonder I'm cold all the time.

Philip's affectionate that night as I brush my hair in front of our mirror, kissing my neck. I'm not interested, but don't resist him.

"I should get a job," I say.

He stands up straight. "What?"

"To help out with the money," I say. "That nursing home down route 52 is always looking for aides and kitchen workers. I bet they'd hire me. And it would be good practice for nursing."

Philip sighs.

"What, Philip? Tell me why that's not a good idea?"

"Everything you suggest takes you away from here. Hannah, Rachel, and Lisa need your help. Start there, not at some new project that will make you ask Mark again for relief from your obligations here."

I'm stunned. He thinks I'm trying to get away, not help. The unfairness of it stings, but part of me knows I hope getting away once in a while will make me feel less suffocated.

"You leave every day to go somewhere, do something. If I had something outside, I wouldn't be reminded all the time."

"I am constantly working around here, too. You've proven you can't do both."

Tears of outrage make me sputter.

"Waterworks won't help," he says as he leaves the room.

WE DON'T HAVE a lot of color choices for painting the rooms in the new house—we're using donated paint—but there's a nice enough yellow for the kitchen and a blue so pale it's almost white I pick for our bedroom. Anything to cheer this place up. Before we start, I show Helen, Lisa, and Trudy the tornado room.

"Philip told me my Aunt Diane said we were ready for the zombie apocalypse," I say, and we laugh as we take turns being the zombies, stopping only when we hear car doors slam.

Lots of people show up, and we finish by early afternoon. Jerry Andersson buys us sub sandwiches, and we sit on the plastic covered floors while we swap stories about painting failures.

"When I was in high school, I wanted to paint my room black," I say. "My mom said, 'absolutely not.'"

"Good woman, your mom," Jerry says.

"We settled on a dark maroon," I say.

"I'm glad you picked a happier color this time," Philip says.

"I didn't find any black in the choices," I tease.

"Thank God," Helen says.

"We should thank God for today, for this new ministry, for all we have," Mark says.

"Amen," we all say.

Mark laughs. "That will do."

MOVING DAY COMES too quickly. The air is cold and dry as we load Jerry's truck with our few boxes of clothes, a couple of mattresses and dressers. We hang bedsheets over the windows, I'm not sure why. No one is around to see in, and the trees are the only nice things here. We have the little refrigerator and microwave from my dorm room in the kitchen, but no stove or dishwasher.

"Where'd they go?" Helen asks. "We had appliances when we lived here before."

"We sold them for scrap," Philip says.

"They weren't in great shape, but they worked," Helen grumbles.

"We want you to share meals with the group," Philip says. "Trudy, let's go. We need to get to campus for the game."

Jealousy bites at me. Trudy has taken over my room with Lisa, my ministry, my place on the Council, sometimes I think she's taken my husband. Meek, mousy little Trudy.

"Don't be too late," I plead. "It will be strange staying here tonight."

"I'm not sure when we'll be back. We're taking students out for pizza after," Philip says.

Trudy never looks at me, smiles at Philip.

"Come here whenever you get back, I don't care how late," I say as he slams the door.

The house seems empty with just Helen and me. Church people brought over their old furniture, giving us a mish-mash of a blue plaid couch, a worn fake-leather recliner, a bean bag chair with a picture of a baby bear on it, three plastic tray tables, matching avocado lamps covered in gold curlicues. There are blankets and afghans everywhere when what we need is a space heater.

I didn't expect a color-coordinated living room, but this is appalling.

"Home sweet home," Helen says.

"Where is all your stuff? Did they sell that too?" I ask.

"Paul took the stuff that survived after he got kicked out of the Grange. I suppose his landlord tossed it once he ended up in jail. This is better," she says as she sweeps her hand around the room.

"Hard to believe," I say.

"You grew up rich, didn't you?" Helen asks.

I consider that. "I guess. Didn't seem like it at the time."

"Rich enough not to rely on donations and Goodwill to furnish your house?"

"Yes. Although my mom loved to buy stuff at estate sales for cheap."

Helen nods. "Not the same."

"Let's turn up the heat. This house needs warming up," I say. "Be bold. Sixty-eight degrees."

Helen needs no encouragement. "We can turn it back down before Philip gets back."

We unpack, then set up a brick and board shelf in the living room and put what books we have on it. Without a car and unwilling to cross the drifted fields for supper, we scavenge leftover pizza from the move and heat it in the microwave.

"Now what? No TV, so we can't watch the news," Helen says.

I scrutinize our books. "Any preference, fiction or non?"

"Fiction," she says, and I throw her the copy of *Great Gatsby* I used in Intro. to Lit.

"Supposed to be the Great American Novel. At least it's short." I pull out *Persepolis*, seeing that it's mostly drawings. I dropped the class before we got to that one.

I turn the heat down on the way to bed, but Philip never comes.

THE DAYS ARE gloomy and cold. Gray snow covers everything, no crocuses peeking through. Helen says the tulips and irises she'd planted last Fall should be coming up soon. She offers to pull the irises when they appear, but I say no, I love irises.

Most mornings Philip drives us to the Grange for breakfast and leaves with Trudy after he feeds the cows. When he fails to return by dusk, Helen and I trudge through the snow after supper, carrying what we can for Sue Ann who always refuses to join us, or Nathan brings us back in the truck. Nathan stays silent, his jaw set tightly as he grips the steering wheel, and I wonder if he's upset with me or Philip or something else. I'm not going to ask. Many times, Philip doesn't come home at all. Philip and Trudy always seem to have some campus event that they must attend, or someone calls Philip needing to talk.

I feel stranded. We have no car, no television or internet to let us know what's happening in the world. No telephone except the one hidden in my drawer which I know I should tell Mark about but haven't yet. Helen gave Sue Ann her cheap, no-data phone, and she's never here.

Helen and I spend most of our time together, during the day working in the Grange's kitchen baking bread and preparing meals, and in the evening sitting in our house mending socks, sewing patches onto well-worn clothing, piecing together odd scraps of leftover material church members donate to make quilts and children's clothes. Helen is funny and smart. She tells me stories of what a girly-girl Sue Ann was as a child, always accessorizing her outfits with Helen's pearls or seashell necklaces from a vacation in Florida. When I ask her if she's glad to have escaped Paul's beatings, she shrugs and says she misses him. Sue Ann misses him too, and when she's around, she's always angry. She and Helen argue about boys, about the time she comes home, about why they don't visit Paul more often, about dropping out of high school.

I keep the phone in my drawer for emergencies, but it tempts me often. I could call Mom, Dad, Felicia, Bert. But what would I say? I cast them out of my life and wasn't very nice about it. Why would they want to talk to me? They would not. OK, Mom and Dad would, but I get tired thinking about all we'd have to get through first. No simple chatting anymore, it would all be about Philip and Iris and why didn't I leave that awful place.

Despite the calendar saying it's spring, melting snow, mud, and slush makes it nearly impossible to walk between the properties. The morning after a big snow, I tell Philip Helen and I will work at our house today. We've hoarded some provisions in our pantry for emergencies—a loaf of bread, some rice and beans, peanut butter—and stashed some milk, cheese, and yogurt in the mini-refrigerator so we'll be fine for the day. He shrugs, says he may not be back if the roads aren't plowed.

That evening Philip bursts in just as Helen and I are boiling water in the microwave.

"Let's go," he says. "We can make it for supper."

Helen and I look at each other. I'm in a baggy sweatshirt and sweatpants, and she's in her flannel nightgown.

"Let me change," I say.

"No, no, you look fine. Put on a coat," he says, then looks at the slippers on my feet. "And some boots."

"I'll stay here," Helen says. "In case Sue Ann comes home."

Sue Ann had been staying with her best friend for the last week, something Philip seems not to have noticed.

"Suit yourself. Come on, Amanda."

"Why weren't you ready?" Philip asks. "We eat at six."

"We didn't know you were coming."

Philip scoffs. "I'm not gone that much."

"You are gone all the time," I say. "Sometimes it seems you've forgotten you live with us."

"Don't start," he says.

"Philip, I was perfectly happy at the Grange. You were the one who wanted to move right away and now you stay at the Grange as much as here."

"That is not true."

"Ask Helen. Ask Hannah and Mark. I assume you're staying with them."

Philip's lips clench into a thin line as we pull in front of the dining hall. I watch the animated people in the bright room through the windshield as I sit in the dark. I'm almost afraid I should stay out here, not bring gloom to them.

Philip pounds on my window. "You waiting for me to open your car door now? Come on."

He puts his arm around my shoulders just before we enter, and it reminds me to smile. Everyone greets us, asks about Helen, offers us lasagna. It's warm in here, squished between Lisa and Philip. Nathan tells me they'll lay a path to the house once it thaws so we can walk or bike over more easily. Lisa asks if we want to plant a small garden, and I nod. I carry a large portion of lasagna back for Helen and Sue Ann, but they've already eaten by the time we return. We talk as we work our way through a hamper of clothes that need mending.

Philip pretends to be sleeping when I slip into bed next to him.

INDIANA SOCIAL SERVICES threatens to cut off Helen's assistance payments after her social worker discovers on a home visit that Helen's paying no rent, turning over her food stamps to the Grange, and Sue Ann isn't here. Helen argues she's saving the State money by living here and what was she supposed to do after a tornado destroys her home and her husband gets thrown in jail? Philip calls Mark while this is happening, and when he appears, he tells the social worker our plans for a home for abused women, which leads to another tirade about licensing and inspections and how Helen needs to find a job and either have Sue Ann return or lose her benefits.

"I suppose we could charge rent," Philip says once the woman leaves. "At least on paper."

Helen stops pacing. "She's right. I should move into town and get a job. That will help Sue Ann and me too. How I'm going to find a job with no car, no phone, and no internet is beyond me. Philip, let me use the phone." She grabs the phone and makes a call as she heads for the kitchen.

"Could we have access to a car more often?" I ask. "I could get a job too." Philip stares at me.

"Not a bad idea," Mark says. "Would help with the utility bills. Not sure we can afford an extra car though." He looks at Philip. "Let's talk about it at our next budget meeting."

Helen comes back, hands the phone to Philip. "A friend in town says I can stay with her a few days while I look for a job. Philip, can you drop me off on your way to the University?"

"Please don't leave me alone," I say, looking at her. Panic rises in my throat and my heart races.

"It's Philip's job to keep you company," she says, averting her eyes. "Not mine."

"As a community, it's all our responsibility," Mark says.

"I'm not part of your commune," Helen says. "I thank you for all the help and support you've given Sue Ann and me over the last months, but this life isn't for me."

A deadening lethargy overtakes me. Another loss. Mark stays after Philip and Helen leave, holding my hand and looking at me with sad eyes.

"Things will work out," he says. "It might take time."

"I can't bear to be here alone." I can barely talk. "Can we move back to the Grange?"

"I'll talk with Philip. Make sure he understands he needs to be home in the evening, especially after Helen moves out."

"But it's clear he doesn't want to. Will resent that. It will be better if we're close to everyone. We're not ready to be on our own."

"How about Sarah and Nathan and Emma move in?"

"That would be better, but they didn't seem interested."

"Change is difficult, but necessary, Amanda. You won't be alone here for long. Soon we'll have our housing ministry going and move another couple in here."

"Can we stay at the farmhouse until then?"

"That's a lot of moving back and forth for a few months."

And my sanity, I think but nod instead. Mark puts his arms around me and slowly the panic and loneliness ebb away. "I'll keep you company this evening," he whispers into my ear.

Mark brings me back after supper. We sit together on the lumpy couch, and he strokes my arms and face as I tell him about how alone I feel. His kisses are slow and deep. His calm and reassuring voice talks about how our community is larger than a single relationship. How we should rely on each other for comfort and support. I tell him I rely on him, don't feel lonely when he's around. He says that's how it should be as his hand moves underneath my shirt and unloosens my bra and rubs my nipples with his thumb. Waves of desire pound through me, and I start to unzip his pants. He holds my hand.

"No, you're not ready," he says. "You're still too sad."

"I am so ready," I whisper into his ear and then lick it.

He stands up and pulls me to my feet and puts his arms around me, holds me until I stop shaking. When he leaves, I'm bereft.

The next evening, Hannah drives me back after supper and we spend the evening knitting and talking about what we'll plant in our garden.

Helen's friend drops her off a week later. Finding a job isn't easy without a car. The town's busses have a limited service area, and the available fast food, service station, and cashier jobs pay little and offer only part-time work.

"Whatever happened to Paul's truck?" I ask.

"Repossessed,. My social worker says I should go back to school, that there's grant money and family housing for people like me. But I've never been much for school. And it wouldn't be until Fall although I need to apply right now." Helen pulls a phone out of her purse. "My friend got me this, says I can't look for a job without a phone. I'm calling Sue Ann, see what she says."

Philip takes Helen to campus the next few days to talk to an admissions counselor and to apply for on-campus jobs. She's excited when the cafeteria calls her for an interview, then offers her a part-time job. Now she leaves in the morning with him and Trudy, and the house is empty most days. On her off days Helen looks for a cheap place to live. Her social worker gets her on a list for transitional housing, and the dreaded day comes a month later. Lightning fast, according to her social worker. There's an opening for her and Sue Ann. By the weekend she's gone, just as iris leaves start to pierce the leftover snow near the front door. I wander around the empty house all afternoon, and as the dark grows, I realize Philip won't be back until late, if at all.

A night out, just one. That's all I want. Something mindless and fun. A movie. A drink. Roller skating. Bowling. The kinds of things I did with Bert. I wonder if he's got a boyfriend yet. I wonder if he has plans for tonight. I wonder if he still has the same phone number. I dig through my plain white underwear to the lacy thongs underneath and pull out the phone from its hiding place. I stare at it for a while. Philip will be furious. I'll feel humiliated if Bert hangs up on me, which he probably will and who could blame him. But I'm desperate enough to take that chance. It rings, a good sign.

"Hello?"

I smile to hear his familiar voice.

CHAPTER 30

Susan

SINCE I LEFT my job, the days and nights have begun to blend, my only schedule my choir rehearsals, an evening Spanish class, and the very occasional times I volunteer at a food bank. I hardly ever get a phone call, and so am surprised when my phone pings as I'm reading in bed. I glance to see Bert sent a text: *Amanda is in trouble,* it says. *Call me. Please. I don't care how late.* I shake my head trying to clear my drowsy fog, and call.

"Ms. Beane. I don't mean to alarm you. Yes, I do. I'm alarmed!" Bert talks so fast I can't even say hello. "Amanda called me tonight. First time in ages. She didn't even talk to me at Iris' funeral. Says she needs a night out, would I pick her up? First I think, 'No, bitch, I got no time for you.' But I'm curious so I say OK. She gives me directions to a new place, and I think 'uh-oh.' I drive out there where it's all dark and scary and no lights anywhere. Almost miss her driveway even though it's just past that commune . . ."

"Bert, slow down," I say. "And get to the point. How is she in trouble?"

He takes a big breath. "Sorry. You have to see her to understand. I mean, it was weird her calling me at all. Figured Philip had left her or something although that would be weird too. Anyway, she says she wants to go illuminated bowling—what the hell is that? And there she is supposedly dressed to go out, in a faded man's shirt and blue jeans and you know she looks good in most anything, she even looked good in that tacky homemade wedding dress, but she always was a classy dresser. And she's all pale and too thin like she's from Somalia or something, and she doesn't have any makeup on, but I've seen her without make up before but never so pale and sick looking and I'm worried they're starving her."

"Calm down, Bert," I say, although my heart is racing. She didn't look well when I saw her a few of months ago, but she'd just lost a baby. "She might still be depressed about losing Iris. Did she talk about that?"

"Said she didn't want to talk about that. Said she needed a day off from being sad and I always made her laugh. I took some offense to that. I thought we were friends, and she could tell me sad stuff. She said she knew, but maybe later. Can you give me a preview? I asked. And she said Philip's never home and the other woman in the house moved out and everybody leaves her, and she starts to cry. Seems like you do a lot of the leaving, I think, but I'm not going to say that to her when she's crying so hard. Anyway, we go to the only bowling alley I know and guess what? They have illuminated bowling. She's terrible by the way, but we shared a pitcher with some guys in the next lane and it was funny how bad we were. Once her ball skipped into the gutter of the next lane and the manager said it was time we went home and we laughed about that."

"Bert," I say. "What worries you? How thin she is?"

"How crazy laughing she was after crying her eyes out in my car. She kept saying 'remember when' about things we did her freshman year and it was funny so we kept laughing and we went to our favorite pizza place and who should be there but her snake of a husband holding forth like a big man to several students and she goes over there and slams her hand on the table knocking over one of the cups and screams, 'I don't care if you never come home. Bert's a better friend to me than any of you.' I pull her away and decide she needs coffee so we go to Starbucks, and I say, 'Out with it.' And she starts sobbing again. Says he doesn't love her anymore. They haven't had sex since before Iris died. Never comes home. I say, 'Move out then,' and she says she can't because it's her house and she hates her house, but she has no money and no friends and somebody named Trudy has taken her place with everyone and the only reason she could call me is because you gave her a phone she hid in a drawer because she's not supposed to have it. She said they don't let her have a phone or a car or a computer and then they try to freeze her in that empty house."

"Where's she now?" I ask, afraid of what might be happening at the Grange.

"She said to bring her home, and I said no way, you're staying with me. She's sleeping in my bed while I pace here in my living room."

"I'll be there as soon as I can," I say. "Thank you."

I find a red-eye and call Tony from the airport to tell him what's going on. He's mad I didn't call him right away. I'd be mad too if the roles were reversed, but I need to not have to worry about him and all the awkwardness when we're together. I didn't want to sit with him in the airport or in the plane or share my rental car with him. I say we're boarding, I'll call when I know more. As I hang up, he demands Bert's phone number. Later.

Nervous energy keeps me awake and anxious on the plane, despite not sleeping for over twenty-eight hours now. I wish I could sleep, stop the crashing thoughts in my head. I order one of those nasty snack packs to distract me, gnawing on some beef jerky thing and greasy chips.

Bert lives in a nice complex not far from campus, four brick buildings each three stories tall and a little patio jutting out from each unit. Bert's on the second floor and opens the door immediately. Amanda's sitting at a table moving cereal around in a bowl. Bert's right. She looks terrible. She looks at me in surprise, then accusingly at Bert.

"Hi, sweetheart," I say. "Don't be mad at Bert. It was my idea to come."

"I'm not used to drinking," she says. "Bert overreacted."

I can see that hurts him. "Bert is a good friend to you. He was worried. From what I understand, calling Philip wouldn't have been a good idea."

"I suppose not," she says, then bursts out in hysterical laughter. "You should have seen Philip's face! And that damn Trudy. Almost makes this headache worthwhile."

Bert and I look at her, shocked into silence.

"Can you tell me what's going on?" I say once I recover.

"Sounds like Bert already did," she says.

"Some," I say. "I'm betting not all. Enough to get me here."

When she finishes her description of her life for the last few months, all I'm able to say is, "So what do you want to do?"

"I don't know," she says, covering her face with her hands. "Go ahead. Tell me you told me so. That I was too young. That Philip had dumped me once before. That I should finish school."

"Amanda," I say.

"Don't be nice and understanding. Tell me off. I deserve it," she says.

"No, but I hope you come home with me."

"I'm married. I chose that, it's my duty now."

Anger explodes in me, and I ball my hands into fists. "That's just fatalistic crap. Can you never fix a mistake? Take a new direction when what you're doing is crushing you? Does getting married young and joining a religious group in college determine the rest of your life? You have choices. You have things to consider. Every. Single. Day. If you're unhappy, it could be a sign you're going in a wrong direction. Gritting your teeth and pushing through isn't the only answer. Commitment is good when you're committed to the right thing. Are you?"

Amanda looks stunned. "How do you know what's the right thing? When you've made the right decision."

Deflated, my hands fall open. "Ah, there's the rub. Who can ever know? But it's too easy to say, 'Well, the church says no divorce ever so that's the end of it.'""

"Do you think your marrying Dad was wrong?" Amanda asks. She looks wounded.

"No. But the divorce wasn't either. It was sad, and hurt more people than just you, me, and your dad. But I believed then and still do that it was the right thing to do. Sometimes there are only bad choices. But they're choices all the same." I pull my chair next to hers and hold her tightly for a while. "You're welcome to come home with me. You have always been welcome."

"What a loser I am," she says. "Go home to Mommy. And much as I want to give up, it isn't about just me. Mark talks about the Spirit guiding us through the wisdom of the community. We can't make up our own rules based on what we feel right now."

"I didn't mean that," I say. "But we have to keep testing what's right in each situation, what best supports the principle, not blindly follow rules someone else pushes us toward. What are those rules, Amanda? I've never been able to come up with any that work in every situation, and I've always found people who think there is only one way—their way—to be insufferable."

"There are absolutes even if I don't know what they all are," she says. "Right things and wrong things. Good things and evil things."

I brush my eyes as I slump forward. "I hope you figure out what those are. It gets foggier and foggier to me."

"I should talk to Mark," she says.

A sizzle of anger burns through me. I hoped she would be done with them all. "How about we meet him somewhere for lunch? Anywhere you want."

I call Mark and warn him not to bring Philip. He's surprised. Asks to speak with Amanda alone.

"Up to her," I say. Hell no, is what I want to say.

Mark suggests to Amanda that they sit in his car and talk a while before going to lunch. Bert must have the same fear as I do that he'd drive off with her, because he offers to leave them alone in the apartment instead. Bert and I hang out on the balcony, stomping our feet to stay warm. Bert lights cigarette after cigarette from the one he just finished.

"Those are bad for you," I say. "Give me one."

My hands and ears feel frozen when Amanda finally opens the slider and says they're ready to go to lunch. It's close enough to walk, and as I slip on the sidewalk, hands in my pockets, I wish I'd thought more when packing this morning. My phone rings, and I see Tony's name. Later.

"Susan," Mark says after we've ordered, "you've been through a divorce. Marriage can be hard. But Amanda agrees that marriage is a lifetime commitment and when the tough times come, we need to work on it."

"Let Amanda speak for herself, Mark," I say. Bert squeezes my hand underneath the table.

"He's right, Mom. I made a promise. I want to keep it. Mark says Sarah and Nathan and Emma will move in with us, and Philip and I will have weekly counseling appointments. That'll help."

"You don't see a big conflict of interest here?" I ask.

Amanda looks baffled. "What do you mean?"

"Mark counsels you and Philip individually and as a couple? And don't forget his financial interest in your property," I say.

Now Bert has a surprised look.

"I don't care about the house," Amanda says, "and I don't want to live there."

"Then sell it. Use the money to pay for the schooling they say they have no money for." My anger and protectiveness are getting the best of me. "Amanda, how about this? Get away for a few weeks. Give yourself time to consider your options. You can come home with me or visit relatives. We could go to Hawai'i."

"Divorce is not an option in our church," Mark says.

"Another option is to choose a new church," I say, looking at him.

Amanda stays silent as Mark and I argue politely but pointedly about biblical interpretation. When we stop talking and glare at each other, Amanda seems to wake up.

"I'm going back to work it out with Philip. It's only right."

Mark smiles triumphantly.

I feel like I've been slapped, and a fierceness builds inside me. I will not give up on her. I could move here, go to their church so Amanda knows I'm there if she needs to leave again. I could live off my savings and inheritance for a while. I could hire a deprogrammer. No, that seems too much even for me. She has to leave voluntarily. Once Amanda drives off with Mark, I put my hands on my hips and say to Bert, "Well, what are we going to do about this?"

Chapter 31

Amanda

WHEN WE GET back to the farmhouse, Hannah has coffee on the table and Philip is pacing with his hands in his pocket. His face flashes anger that changes quickly to embarrassment. An awkward silence fills the kitchen nook as we all search for something to say.

"Amanda," Mark says. "Tell us why you left last night."

"I needed to get away. I was all alone and pretty sure Philip wasn't coming home. I wanted to laugh. Stop feeling sad."

Philip bristles but says nothing.

"You told me there are deeper reasons when we talked earlier. Philip needs to hear them."

I take a quick breath. "I felt like I was being suffocated and abandoned at the same time."

Philip shoves back his hair and leans forward. I can feel his anger despite his attempts to seem understanding, and I'm afraid.

"Explain that," Mark says, tenting his fingers. "Those sound like opposites."

Philip's sullen stare makes me pause. I don't want to hurt him. "It's hard to explain," I say. "Abandoned because I was alone in that cold house most of the time."

"What are you talking about?" Philip exclaims. "Helen was there all the time, I was there almost every night, and the women and Mark came over."

"Even when you were there you weren't," I shout back. "You never talked to me, just walked in the door, read a book, or went to sleep."

Mark interrupts. "We won't get anywhere by shouting accusations at each other. You are both unhappy. Instead of blaming each other, let's try to figure out what each of you needs."

Silence stretches on. I'm not sure I need or want anything from Philip. How can I say that?

"I need Amanda to be wholly invested in our marriage and our life. I need her to get past Iris' death and stop questioning everything," Philip says.

Naming Iris makes me cry.

Philip and Mark shift in their chairs. Mark looks at me, but Philip looks away.

"Changing feelings is hard," Mark says. "Name one positive thing Amanda could do to show she's dedicated to your life together. That's enough to start."

"She could be happy to see me instead of demanding to know why I was gone," Philip says.

"Happy is a feeling. For now, let's stick to actions," Mark says.

"How about she smiles, and asks me about my day—specifically, like she knows and cares what I'm doing," Philip says.

"Can you do that, Amanda?" Mark asks, and I nod. He takes my hand. "Now it's your turn. Remember, an action you need from Philip."

I grab a tissue and try to speak, but it comes out all wavery and weepy. "I need to be a part of things again. When I was pregnant, it was like I was shoved aside—no school, no car, no leadership meetings."

"And the action from Philip?" Mark asks. "We've already agreed you'll be going back to school in the Fall."

"But don't even ask to replace Trudy," Philip warns. "It wouldn't be fair."

Rage and frustration freeze my tears. "Fair. Like how 'fair' it was to keep me from school when I was pregnant."

Philip clenches his jaw. "I have another need. I need Amanda to stop bringing up old decisions."

"I need Philip to acknowledge how much his lack of support hurt me. To support me in the future." I glare at him.

"It's alright for you to challenge me, but I can't disagree with you?" Philip says.

"Stop," Mark says. "You both have a point, and it seems you've both quit listening. Philip is right, bringing up old grudges isn't helpful. Look to the future. And Amanda is right, feelings and hurts need to be acknowledged even in a disagreement. You need to see each other as part of a team, working toward the same goals."

We are silent again. As the minutes drag by, I wonder if I can.

"We share a lot of goals—we believe in community and communal life, we love the people here, we have a sense of duty and purpose in helping our neighbors. Right Philip?" I say.

"Yes," he says. "Let's face it. We weren't madly in love when we decided to get married. I'm not sure I even believe in that kind of love, although having it seems to help people through hard times. Like losing a child. No, we loved each other as friends, as part of the community. Sure I'm attracted to Amanda, but that isn't what our marriage is about."

I nod. He's right, but it hurts all the same. I was crazy about him when we first met. But it's true, our getting married was practical, the right thing to do for the community. Was I too young to settle for friendship and respect instead of passion? It should be enough. But it isn't. I want to feel about Philip the way I feel about Mark.

I can't say that.

"When we first met, I thought we would be about passion and romance, but that didn't work out. I came to agree with you that community came first. But we put expectations on each other we don't force on anyone else here," I say.

"Amanda, I sense you're having a hard time giving up the notion of romance," Mark says. "All relationships have troubles, and it takes grit to see it through. So. Back to my question. What is one thing Philip can do that will make you see him as your partner and friend?"

"How about we start with Philip sleeping with me every night, and if he doesn't want to because he's upset about something, he tells me about it?" I say.

Philip nods. "I can do that."

"DID YOU THINK about staying away?" Lisa asks as we knead bread on the cold stainless steel counters in the kitchen the next morning.

I'm silent for a while. "When my mom asked me to come home, it sounded good to sit around the pool and let her wait on me for a while. But Mark helped me see giving up was no answer."

Lisa nods. "For all its challenges, this is home. Some things here bother me too, like when I figured out that your inheritance was going to buy a house nobody wants to live in. We're all sharing, and nobody's shared more than Mark and Hannah, but I guess it got real to me then. One of the students said you accused Philip and Trudy of being together—I don't think they are, by the way, it's the way Philip is."

"What do you mean? I was angry and a little drunk when I said that."

"Philip's interest in me got me involved in the Grange too. I took a class with him—we'd both put off freshman comp. and so were a couple of the oldest ones in the class. We worked on projects together. He kept talking about this farm he lived on and the church he went to, and I agreed to go with him because he was cute and I liked him. His attention faded once I got more involved. It hurt. When I saw it happening to you and then Philip directing his attention to new students, I felt bad for you remembering how unhappy I'd been."

A realization pierces me, sending chills through my chest. Lisa, me, Trudy. Did Philip ever care about me?

"I was surprised," Lisa continues, "when all of a sudden you're made his co-leader, and then you get engaged and married and pregnant. I was envious, I admit."

I'm baffled. She's envious of my lost baby? My marriage on the rocks? My running from my commitments? How can anyone envy those things?

The room is silent except for our fists pounding dough. "I came to the Grange through Philip," Lisa says, "but Mark's why I've stayed. Everybody loves him, but there's something more. And, no, it's not that he's the father I've always wanted. It's . . .different than that."

I wonder if Lisa has the same forbidden feelings about Mark I've always had. Do I love God and the community? Or Mark? I realize Philip is barely in the mix.

"I need to figure some things out and I can't do it by running away," I say.

"Yeah." She sighs.

Chapter 32

Susan

I DECIDE TO escape the Phoenix summer, see the world, give more structure to my days, avoid obsessing over Amanda who clearly doesn't want to be rescued even if I think she should, so I enroll in a month-long summer Spanish immersion course. In Spain. Anticipation and a little fear keep me awake during the overnight flight to Madrid. On my way, on my own, to a place I've never been and know no one and where they speak a language I'm just learning. Am I crazy? Once we land, I follow the other passengers down a long corridor and drag my wheeled luggage onto a series of escalators. The lines in customs are long but move quickly, my Spanish just good enough to answer the agent's questions. After my big suitcase finally arrives, I shuffle past several guards to where a bank of automatic doors opens into a large room of windows and skylights. Crowds line a roped barrier between the arriving passengers and the rest of Spain. I scan the room twice before noticing a thin gray-haired man in a blue raincoat carrying a placard with my and one other name. I walk toward him, not sure if I can muster enough Spanish to figure out what to do next.

"Señora Beane?" the man says.

"Sí. I hope you speak some English."

"I speak much English. My name is Joe. We must await one other passenger. Her flight arrives soon. Will you sit?" He motions to a bank of chairs along a wall and hands me a bottle of water.

"Gracias," I say and take the seat at the end, surrounding myself with luggage. I dig in my purse for my last candy bar. The room is in constant movement, the automatic doors swishing open and closed as tired travelers enter, and the outside doors let in bits of the noise from the vehicles and trains and machinery outside as people leave. I'm hypnotized, unable to make sense of the excited conversations and chaotic movement around me. Soon enough Joe comes back with a tall young woman with long, blond hair who he introduces as Ingrid, an undergraduate from Minnesota. Joe drops me off first.

"Lunch is at two-thirty," Joe says. "You'll make it."

The lobby of the dorm is filled with English-speaking men and women, most of whom seem younger than me but older than Ingrid. The woman ahead of me in the registration line, Betty, is a teacher from California. This is Betty's third summer at the language program, and I gratefully listen to her explain how things work. We agree to meet for lunch after dropping the luggage in our rooms. A surge of energy spins through me. I feel adventurous.

After breakfast the next morning, the program director takes us on a walk to the classroom buildings. The air is humid, but not nearly as hot as Phoenix, and the route takes us past large trees and buildings that shade most of the way. The classroom building is newer than most and air-conditioned, with a small cafeteria on the first floor. Once the session starts, I rush there between classes for a quick hit of coffee and sometimes a potato and egg tortilla. Hundreds of students from all over the world are studying here this summer, most of whom speak English, Spanish, and whatever is their native language.

The summer is glorious. The shared meals, walks to class, excursions to investigate Madrid create an intimacy I haven't felt since college. On weekends, we travel. From the running of the bulls in Pamplona to the ancient buildings in Toledo and Barcelona, I'm in a new world. Sure, I'd read about the Moors in Spain during the Middle Ages, but I'm speechless when I see the intricate stonework of the buildings, the colorful tiles telling their stories in every city, the red and white arches in a building first used as a mosque, then as a temple, then as a church. The buildings are sacred, even to a doubter like me. Each place transports me: a cascade of lavender flower sparks joy; a stone ceiling as intricate as a snowflake, wonder; the repeating pattern of white and gold arches, awe; a gilded retablo, a sense of the holy. And the swirling, sweating, flamenco dancers stomping to their pounding, mournful music stirs a hint of long absent desire.

I want to tell someone. Everyone. I'm a convert, to what I don't know.

How had I not known? I wonder as the summer session draws to a close. How can I hang onto this elation?

I CAN'T STOP talking when Corey picks me up from the airport as I try to describe the marvels I've seen, experienced. My lingering astonishment.

"I really can't explain it," I say. "I'd live there if I could."

"And why can't you?" Corey asks as she gives the parking attendant her credit card.

Maybe I could. I look at Corey. "Come with me next year."

Corey smiles before pulling into traffic. "I'd love to. But I couldn't stay as long as you did."

"Most of the people in my dorm were high school teachers," I say.

"Probably Spanish teachers who got help from their schools," Corey says. "You want some food before I bring you home?"

"I'm beat. But let me take you out for lunch tomorrow as a thank you for picking me up."

"You don't need to, but I won't turn down a free lunch."

We drive in silence for a few minutes, my mind full of images.

"Now that you're back, what's next?" Corey asks.

Ah, reality. I know now I need the structure of a job or a class or something to give form to my days. "I need a job, for health insurance and to stop drifting. But now I want my summers off."

"You could adjunct."

"Or substitute teach. When does school start back?"

"Three weeks."

Life seems full of interesting possibilities.

"I have something for you," I say when Corey pulls into my driveway.

I open my carryon and pull out a small package wrapped in red paper with gold swirls. Corey opens it carefully, trying to save the paper. In the box is a necklace made of several linked black discs etched with gold birds, leaves, and flowers. Corey looks at me in astonishment.

"They call it damascene," I say. "I got it in Toledo."

"It's beautiful. I've never seen anything like it."

"Me neither."

Corey hugs me. "See you for lunch tomorrow. Get some sleep."

I leave my suitcases in the living room and heat a can of soup, all that's left in the cupboards I emptied six weeks ago. I try to sleep, but soon give up. I turn on my computer and scan the many emails I've been ignoring, most from online stores wanting me to order another blouse or kitchen appliance, many from charities whose overwhelming need saddens and makes me feel guilty. An email from the Community Choir tells me the first rehearsal will be the last Monday of August and this semester we will be singing Brahms's *Requiem*.

My mind flashes to the last time I sang the *Requiem*. How my roommate Mary and I cried because we'd just learned a favorite professor had died. *Can*

I do this? I wonder, wishing for that promised comfort but fearing it will open wounds. Mom, Dad, Iris. Paralyzing loss threatens the euphoria of the last month. I pull the score from my bookcase, play the scratchy recording on my turntable. From the first *Blessed they,* I know I must sing it, must uproot the grief I've tried to bury. Maybe I can cry enough at home to keep it together at rehearsal.

Blessed are they that mourn, for they shall have comfort.

I struggle with the theology of it, the promise of heaven to make up for the brevity, the vanity, of life. But I understand and need the mournful hopefulness of the music. A different kind of comfort.

Chapter 33

Amanda

NOW MY PARENTS say they'll pay my Fall tuition. I know this is a big concession, and I guess it's because of what happened with Bert. I'll bet Mom painted a grim picture of my life to Dad, and they've decided the best way to get me to leave the Grange is to give me options: career possibilities and other influences. I can almost hear them discuss it. But they didn't put any conditions on the offer, I'll give them that.

I take a couple of humanities courses during summer school, reading the texts during breaks at the Pick-n-Eat. I can feel Philip seething when Mark relieves me of jam-making duties during the last week of class and exams. He sees my taking classes as a lack of commitment, his favorite topic during our counseling sessions with Mark. I see them as a relief valve, something that makes me able to stay without going crazy.

Classes are more challenging than I remember, especially Chemistry and Microbiology. Trudy's ahead of me now, and when I struggle, I ask her for help. Another resentment. Bert and I meet for lunch most Fridays when Philip and Trudy are busy at the activity table. He can't believe I went back, but we don't talk about it much. Instead, I laugh at his jokes and listen to his latest romantic woes.

I feel adrift most of the time. Something in me died with Iris. I miss my long talks alone with Mark. Philip comes to bed so late sometimes he might as well stay away. I force a smile when I see him, and I don't berate him anymore. I hide what I think and feel, play the part of wife. Once at Bible Study I tried to get people to talk about gay marriage, but most people wouldn't, and Mark said, "It's fine for the State to make it legal, but we won't solemnize them here." Bert scowled when I told him that, said everybody needs to take a stand and it's "straight privilege" not to. The world is full of hypocrisy, I told him, reminding him who his parents voted for and how they still pay his tuition. We don't talk about that anymore.

STALKS OF CORN pierce the light fog hovering over the fields as Sarah, Emma, and I walk toward the kitchen. I remember when the sight of such beauty would have made me feel joy. I wonder when that joy might return. I'm grateful for the gravel path between our house and the Grange. I know it was an expense Bryan thought we should postpone.

Philip and Nathan left hours ago to milk the cows and get the harvester ready. They're sitting with Bryan, Trudy, and Lisa, and their conversation stops when we arrive. Conversations often stop when I enter a room.

"Oatmeal and yogurt today," Lisa says.

Philip stands to leave.

"Will you be driving us to campus today?" I ask him.

"Trudy's driving," he says and walks through the door to the kitchen, bowl and mug in hand.

I sit next to Lisa and across from Trudy.

"I'd like to leave in a half hour," Trudy says.

"I'm ready," I say.

Mark comes in with Matthew and Angela and breaks the awkward silence with cheerful talk about the weather, how the fog should burn off soon and give us many hours of dry for the harvest today and tomorrow. Matthew sits next to me and shows a picture he drew for me, mostly daisies and sunflowers but one is purple on a tall stalk and I think it might be an iris.

I love him so much.

I hug his shoulders and put my head on his.

As Trudy and I leave, Rachel and Hannah come in with books for each child. It crosses my mind that none of them are learning to use a computer. Couldn't even if they wanted to because we have no wifi. On the drive, I ask Trudy what she thinks about that.

"They're still young," she says. "They'll catch up when they need to."

"Angela's almost seven now. Maybe I'll offer to take her to the library or to Bert's to use his laptop."

"I don't know. Maybe the library."

I suppress a flash of anger. I know how she, how everyone at the Grange, feels about Bert. "I wish we did have wifi, though. It's hard to complete my work sometimes now that everything has to be turned in online."

"You just have to budget your time when we're on campus," Trudy says. "Not put things off to the last minute."

I look at Trudy, then look away. Phillip said the exact same thing to me two days ago.

I spend the rest of the drive paging through a textbook.

"Meet here at three," Trudy says as she locks the car. "We should help with dinner while everyone's working."

"Five. I have a meeting with my lab TA after class." The lie comes too easily.

Trudy shrugs. I feel the irritation coming off her in waves, and I'm glad she's too timid to fight. "Five, then. If you're done early, I'll be in the Union coffee shop. Come get me."

Maybe I will, maybe I won't.

I'M EXHAUSTED BY the time the end of the semester arrives, tired of the silent battles with Philip, tired of Trudy's simpering judgment, tired of balancing the demands of my classes with my duties at the Grange. Philip says he doesn't have time to go to the University Choir's Christmas show on campus and I hear the unspoken criticism when I say I want to go. He says I should come with him and Trudy to the *Messiah* singalong next week. Instead, I talk Bert into going. Music makes me feel alive, and listening makes me wish it were me up there. There's nothing like the energy of the crowd coming back at you. This year's show is filled with happy songs and lots of movement, and by the end I feel energized.

"Want to stay out or go back?" he says.

I take his arm. "Let's extend this a little longer."

We end up at the usual pizza place with what seems like half of all the choirs squeezing on benches, talking and laughing about nothing. I can't hear what anyone is saying but laugh anyway. It's after one and snowing, so Bert says I should stay at his house. Why not? Philip had his chance to come. I text him from Bert's phone, but he doesn't respond. As I settle in, I remember the last time I was here. How angry I was at Philip. How little I wanted to go back to our cold house. I wonder if anything has really changed.

The same question pops into my head when I wake up, but now I'm certain nothing has. I've tried, but a nagging guilt tells me I haven't tried hard enough. I make coffee and search for something to eat. Bert stumbles into the kitchen.

"Still only cereal, I'm afraid," he mumbles.

"Can I stay here through exams week?" I ask. "I'll sleep on the couch, and my last one is Wednesday."

"Sure," he says. "Do you want to get your stuff?"

"I'll need books and clothes."

As Bert showers, I write a letter. If Philip's there when I get my things, I'll tell him to his face. But I doubt he will be.

Dear Philip,

I realized last night that nothing's changed since I slept here last March. We're still just going through the motions. You're not interested in my activities, and if I'm honest, I'm not all that interested in yours. We seem to be growing farther apart instead of closer. If you want to talk, I'm at Bert's, although I'd appreciate your waiting until my exams are finished a week from Wednesday.

I don't know what I'm going to do next. Probably go back to Phoenix for Christmas if my parents haven't totally given up on me. I wouldn't blame them if they have.

I do love you and everyone at the Grange, but I need a break. I can't live like this anymore.

Love, Amanda

I have Bert read it before we leave.

"Ouch," he says. "A little cold. But good for you."

I reread it and decide it's the best I can do. "Let's go."

Philip's not around as I pack what I want to take. It's not much. I stuff Iris's urn into my roller bag. Lisa, Sarah, and Emma arrive as we're leaving.

"Just like that?" Sarah says.

"I tried, I really did," I say. "I can't seem to make it right."

"Wait for Mark," she says. "You don't need to leave just because you and Philip are having troubles. Everybody has troubles, even Nathan and me."

I find a loose piece of paper and write Bert's number, my mom's and dad's numbers. I slip it to Lisa when she walks me to the car, begging me to reconsider.

"Call me if you want to talk, OK?" I say.

Lisa looks at the ground, sticks the paper in her pocket.

I give Lisa and Sarah long hugs, then head toward Bert's car. The wind bites at my wet face.

"Ready?" Bert says.

"No," I say. "But let's go.

As we drive the desolate country roads back to campus, I feel empty. Cold. Without a clear sense of who I am or want to be.

ANOTHER GLOOMY DAY, dirt and debris pockmarking the mounds of shoveled snow as I walk to the University for my last exam. Every day, fewer and fewer people join me in this trek past the iced windows of the bookstore, pizza place, bars. A few students seem finished with exams, their drunken elation tumbling out into the street then back inside again.

I'm probably failing my exams. I have plenty of time to study at Bert's or in the library, but I can't focus. Now that I'm away from the Grange, I can see how it's all my fault. I'm the one who thought marrying Philip was a good idea. I wonder if Mark pressured him into it. And I was too needy around Mark, made him want to shunt me off to a house far away instead of keeping me close. I miss them, wish we could go back to the beginning. Mom was right about one thing: the will was stupid, controlling. If there'd been no strings, I could have given the money to Mark, not married Philip. Not had Iris. Now I'm crying again. No wonder I can't study.

Mark is waiting outside the exam room when I finish. Joy fills me when I see him. We find a quiet place in the nearly empty cafeteria, and Mark tells me what's been going on at the Grange as if I'd been away on vacation. A heaviness lifts. Helen's and Sue Ann's disdain for communal living probably colored my thinking. Mark strokes my hand, and his comforting voice calls to me, reminds me why I joined the church, makes me want that safe place again.

"Don't let a misunderstanding with Philip take you away from the great work we do," Mark says. "The people who love you. Come back."

It sounds possible when he talks to me.

Bert sees us sitting at the table and joins us, his mouth in an angry grimace. "Do we need a restraining order?"

"Bert," I say. "Mark is my friend."

"Some friend," Bert says. "Is he trying to take you back to that dirt bag Philip?"

I can't deny it. "Philip's a good man."

Bert almost stands, then I see his resolve strengthen as he folds his hands and stares at me. "Should we talk about Trudy or Lisa? How he wouldn't let you go to school or get a job? How he left you stranded night after night, sometimes with no food? That good man?"

"Mistakes were made," Mark says in a kind voice. "Let he who is without sin cast the first stone."

It's true. I'm as much to blame as Philip.

Bert leans back, arms folded across his chest. He talks to me, ignoring Mark. "All I'm saying, Amanda, is give yourself time to think. Don't go rushing back because you're at loose ends now. Take a break. Your mom wants you home for Christmas. Go there. Sit by the pool. Reflect."

That does sound good. Sleep. Warmth. No obligations. No purpose. Defeat.

I don't know what to do, what I want. I realize I agree with whoever's spoken last. I need to decide. I need to be strong. I don't know how.

Mark offers to walk me home, but Bert tells him there's no need. I walk between them, sensing Mark's unspoken pleas and Bert's silent protectiveness. It's too much. My body shakes from jumbled emotions and my mind careens from conflicting thoughts.

"I need a nap," I say when we arrive at Bert's apartment. "Please, both of you, let me be alone."

When I wake a few hours later, I hear Bert on the phone. "Christmas . . .she needs to get out of here . . .come if I can't get her on the plane . . . don't come yet."

He must be talking to Mom. I turn to stare at the wall. A week away sounds restful if Mom doesn't keep at me. If she agrees to leave me be, gives me space to think, going to Phoenix could be a good thing. I could be back by New Year's. I drift back asleep.

CHAPTER 34

Susan

I SIT WITH my cappuccino outside the airport security area waiting for Amanda's plane. Passengers come in waves, greeted by other happy family—a little girl jumps into the arms of a middle-aged woman, a young man passionately kisses a young woman. How should I act when I see her? She wouldn't come home unless I promised not to keep barraging her with questions about the Grange, or the house, or Iris. I agreed, but I'm afraid if we don't talk about those things she'll go back. A week. She said a week. I can keep my worries and questions to myself for a week.

I invited Eddie's family to come Christmas week, hoping having Nadine around will entice Amanda to stay longer. I'll tell Amanda when she gets here. Or in a couple of days.

I stand and strain to look over people's heads and see her moving slowly through the exit's point of no return. She looks a little better than the last time, but her stare has a vacancy to it. I remember the sizzling anger of her high school years. This is worse. She looks defeated now. Anger seems more hopeful. I've bought all her favorite foods, shampoo, and lotion, put new scented candles in her room. That and sun should perk her up.

"Amanda." I hug her too tightly, too long. "Your dad's meeting us at my house. We can go to lunch, or not, whatever you want."

"Can we pick up Whataburger on the way?" she asks.

"Anything and as much as you want."

"Three burgers with everything, a large fries, and a chocolate shake."

"Done."

She heads toward the exit.

"We need to go downstairs for your luggage."

"This is it," she says.

Amanda perks up when we board the SkyTrain to the parking garage, a marvel that wasn't finished the last time she was here. She doesn't say anything, but that little spark makes me hopeful. Since most of the subjects crashing my mind are off-limits, I smile.

Tony laughs when he sees us carrying three big white bags into the kitchen. "I would have taken both of you someplace nice."

"This is what I wanted," Amanda says. "I haven't had them in ages."

"What would you like to do?" I ask.

"First a burger, then a nap, and Zoo Lights in a couple of days," she says. "That's it."

I hold her close. "Sounds like a plan."

THE FIRST WEEK seems glacially long. Tony and I don't want to leave her alone for too long, so we take turns staying with her. She sleeps a lot. Cries. A lot. Sits staring at a book in a lawn chair facing the pool, but never gets in. She has no interest in calling any of her high school friends. We alternate taking her out for dinner, letting her pick a new restaurant every night, but she eats little once we're there. By the fourth night she wants to eat at home.

When I tell Amanda Nadine is coming, she agrees to stay another week. I hope they'll talk. Nadine's always had a sunnier outlook than Amanda. Than me. Amanda wants to go to a midnight service on Christmas Eve. Our old church doesn't have one, but I find an Episcopal Church not too far away that does. Tony drops her off after his parents' party and we sit in the candlelit church, first singing the melancholy "O Come O Come Emmanuel." A soprano with a piercing voice sings "Oh Holy Night." After a comforting sermon about hope and promise the service ends with "Joy to the World." I'd forgotten how calming, how freeing hope could be.

The second night after Eddie's family arrives, we pile into his rented van and head for Zoo Lights. We park in a gravel lot far from the entrance, following the crowd over berms and past cacti and juniper. Amanda's pace increases as we near the gates. Colored lights fill the park—encircling trees, creating a canopy overhead, forming all types of animals, some of them appearing to move. Amanda and Nadine rush ahead but stop often to take selfies with Amanda's new phone or to ask anyone nearby to take their picture in front of a peacock, a pride of lions, a young elephant spraying its mother, a crocodile. They want to see Dinosaurs in the Desert, something the rest of us decide to skip, so we arrange to keep in touch with cell phones and meet back at the front in an hour. Eddie, Katie, and I buy hot chocolate and corn dogs and sit on benches along the lagoon watching the musical light show. Amanda and Nadine are laughing when we see them again. They take turns showing us pictures on their phones—Amanda pretending to be scared in front of the Tyrannosaurus Rex, Nadine with her arms spread like wings in front of the Quetzalcoatl. I follow as they laugh all the way to the car, reminding each other of funny animals and people they've seen.

My beautiful girl.

CHAPTER 35

Amanda

"AMANDA, TELEPHONE," MOM says as we eat a late breakfast on the patio one sunny Saturday in January. "It's your dad."

An unspoken "again" radiates in her voice. He's gotten attentive since I got back, which is nice but so out of character I wonder how long it will last. Everyone's been attentive, Mom fighting the need to hover, Dad's daily phone call, and relatives inviting me to something almost every day. I may have to leave to get time to think.

"Hi, Dad," I say. "I'm still fine."

"Are you sure?" he says. "Or are you saying that to get me off the phone?"

"A little of both."

"Want to go to dinner tonight? Or, even better, how about you stay here for a while?"

"Dinner, yes. But I'm not sure how long I'll be here, so it doesn't make sense for me to move."

"OK. We can talk about it tonight."

Nothing to talk about, I think as I settle back into my lawn chair. It's sunny and warm. I can't seem to get enough sun and have spent the last month reading books and avoiding phone calls.

During the first week I heard Mom tell someone, probably Philip or Mark, that everyone agreed to give me a week undisturbed and to call back later. Part of me wanted desperately to hear their reassuring voices, but most of me wanted to be left alone so I didn't protest. After the week was up, Phillip called almost daily, full of questions and remorse and begging me to come back. I kept saying I needed time away from everything to think and that's easier here than at the Grange. He still calls every few days, but sometimes I don't answer. Mark called twice, and we had long talks about commitment and priorities. He says I should come back now. I say "soon."

The most surprising call is from Lisa. She says she's thinking of leaving if I don't come back.

I'm shocked. Lisa was my rock even after things fell apart.

"Why?" I ask.

I hear intermittent sniffs. "Your leaving made me see things differently. My life here is a lot more constrained than yours was, and you wouldn't stand for it. Why am I?"

Her life was constrained? I thought she was doing exactly what she wanted?

"I'm still thinking about going back," I say. "I miss everyone. And I'm married."

"After you left, we were told you would be back in a week. When that turned into three, then four I assumed you weren't coming back."

Why have I delayed? Why can't I decide one way or the other?

"If you weren't married would you come back?" she asks.

Mom and Dad asked that too, but to me it's not the issue. Life's about loyalty and keeping your promises and doing what needs to be done, every day. Sometimes that's hard, and sometimes it's not what you want to do. Mark would say it's about joy, not happiness.

"I wish I could rewind everything to when we were roommates. I was so full of joy then."

"It was great," Lisa says. "Can't we have that again?"

"I don't think so," I say.

After I hang up, I see Mom in the kitchen chopping onions, not saying anything. She's been good about only asking questions after I bring up something. She looks at me and smiles, a question in her eyes.

"That was Lisa," I say. "She's thinking about leaving too."

Mom's smile widens. "She's welcome here if she can't go home."

I wince. Mom doesn't understand that the Grange is home. So she can't understand how hard this is. "I have to decide soon what to do."

"Take your time," Mom says, throwing the onions into a huge pot and opening a large can of tomatoes. Soon I smell the onions and garlic browning in the olive oil. She's making my favorite chili.

"You can go out, Mom," I say. "You don't have to babysit me."

She stirs the pot with a wooden spoon, breaking apart chunks of meat. "I wasn't around enough when you were young. I can't change that. But I can enjoy your company now."

"You did what you thought you needed to."

"I made my choices." She puts down the spoon, dumps tomatoes into the pot, and looks at me. "Some I regret, some didn't seem like real choices. I know it didn't seem like it to you, but you have always come first."

The world shifts a little as my mind races over the concerts, the plays, the football games, the swim meets. Mom and Dad were always there. I remember the times in high school I told them to stay home, but they didn't. I think about the trips to Disneyland and the Smithsonians. The Halloween costumes. The birthday parties at Peter Piper or Chucky Cheese or at home with a huge pinata and my entire class running around the back yard. What, exactly, did I blame her for all those years? I can't remember. A chunk of ice seems to fall.

"I was a bitch to you, Mom, and I'm sorry."

She hugs me, and her tears wet my shoulder. "I will love you whatever you decide. But please don't exclude me from your life anymore."

I realize I can't promise that if I go back. Why can't my life include all the people I love and who love me? I don't want to choose. I want it all.

AFTER TALKING WITH an admissions counselor about the nursing program, I enroll in a few late start classes at the Community College. Everything is new here—the sidewalks, the administration building, the classrooms, the gym equipment, the small trees that provide little shade, and the vast parking lots. So different from the University where finding a place to park was almost impossible and where we cut across grassy lawns instead of expanses of rock. I miss the big trees and small flowers. The college is a commuter school, and by three p.m. the campus is nearly empty, most students having taken morning classes so they can work afternoons and evenings. More utilitarian, less social. A few people invite me to join their study groups, but I resist joining anything. Not even choir or a gym. I go home, read my textbooks, watch Netflix, try to tamp down my agitation.

When Mom suggests I begin divorce proceedings to try to recover my inheritance, I gasp for breath. She backs off, but it's triggered something. The room spins, and I grasp the back of a kitchen chair to sit down. Mom's eyes widen and she touches my forehead when I start to sweat and shake. I feel my heart racing and bend my head over my knees.

"What's happening?" Mom asks.

"I don't know," I whisper.

She wipes my forehead and arms with a wet cloth, and I begin to shiver. She grabs a sweater thrown over a chair and wraps me in it. I continue to shake. She calls a nurse friend who says it might be a panic attack. I lay on the couch and close my eyes as my heart and breath return to normal. Mom covers me with a blanket.

"I'm okay," I say.

"I'd like you to see a counselor," she says.

The thought of therapy makes my heart race again. What is wrong with me? Did I have a panic attack because Mom brings up what should be obvious? I remember how calm and safe I felt talking with Mark. Is that possible with anyone else? I can't imagine it.

"Let's talk about it later," I say, hoping she'll forget.

She doesn't forget. Her nurse friend comes over to try to convince me.

"How about family counseling?" Mom asks. "I'll even try to talk Tony into coming."

I laugh and say, "If you can talk Dad into coming, I'll go."

I don't know how she did it, but here we are, the three of us, sitting in a windowless room whose defining feature is brown. Brown chairs, brown carpet, brown walls, brown desk, brown jacket hung on a brown coat rack. This guy needs more books. An interesting picture. He leans back in the chair behind his desk, tents his fingers, and asks why we're here. Mom starts, then stops and asks me to say what led up to my panic attack. The counselor leans toward me over the vast expanse of his desk. I hate him immediately. Mom picks at the worn upholstery on the arm of her chair as I talk in my most cheerful voice about how going back to school was stressful after leaving my husband and moving cross-country.

"Perhaps you went back to school too soon," the counselor says.

"I think we should try someone else," Mom says once we leave.

Dad sighs. "What do you think, pumpkin?"

"I'm never going back to him, that's for sure," I answer.

I can't sleep that night. Every time I close my eyes, I see something that reminds me of the Grange. Mark, Philip, Lisa. The apple tree alongside the farmhouse. The sky darkening before a storm. The cows mooing softly in the pasture. Matthew asking for a story.

I get up and wander into my bathroom. The only razors I find are the triple bladed kind that make barely a scratch. Cutting myself may be stupid, but my life is out of control. Everything is wrong. I don't see a way out. No one understands. No one can help me.

Mom knocks on the door and enters before I can hide the razor. She sits on the tub and puts her arms around me. "Oh Amanda. Please find someone to help."

Why not? Nothing else is working. I nod.

BERT CALLS EVERY few weeks, and at the end of February he asks if he can come stay with us during his Spring Break. He's applying to law school in Arizona and found out he can interview in both Tucson and Tempe then.

"Of course, you can," I say, and Mom agrees. When I ask him where else he'd like to go, he says Disneyland. I remind him that's not in Arizona, but he doesn't care.

"Why Disneyland?" I ask.

"Happiest place on earth," he says.

Mom drives him to Tucson Monday afternoon, and I drop him off at ASU on Tuesday. We decide to leave for California on Wednesday afternoon so I'll only miss a couple of classes while we're gone. Bert's excitement is contagious. His parents thought theme parks were a waste of money, so he's never been to one.

"We went almost every year when I was young," I admit.

"Then you'll be able to show me the ropes," Bert says.

The road between Phoenix and Anaheim is mostly desert, miles of rock and sand with the occasional stunted tree. Mountains in the distance, but here, flat. I point out the sites. First, the tall concrete shell of the abandoned horse racing track, its windows blown out from when Hollywood exploded it for a scene in the movie *No Code of Conduct*. Bert looks at me as if I'm making this up. I admit I've never seen the movie either, am sharing Phoenix lore.

"We should watch it," Bert says, and I agree.

Next up, the nuclear power plant containment domes just visible along the southern horizon. I save the *pièce de résistance* for lunch. Bert sees the huge dinosaurs from the road and starts laughing. We take our pictures first in front of Dinny the giant brontosaurus and then Rex the Tyrannosaurus. Bert wants a souvenir and a post card, so we wander the cramped gift shop inside Dinny.

"It's a creationist museum," Bert says.

I try hard to suppress my laughter, not very successfully. "Oh, come on. Everyone knows the dinosaurs were created the day before Adam and Eve."

"I did not know that." He buys a postcard and a few plastic dinosaurs. "For my nephews."

"Sure," I say.

I point out the outlet mall and casinos as we pass, promising we can stop there on the way back if he wants. He shakes his head.

Our silence is easy on the drive. We take turns choosing what CD to play. He rejects most of Mom's stash—Billy Joel, Jackson Browne, R.E.M.—and mocks my high school favorites, Paramore and We The Kings. He wants to talk but is letting me decide when.

"I'm not going back," I say.

"Good," he says. "Are things better with your mom?"

"Better, but not great."

"You want to live with me if I get into law school here next year?"

I think about that. "Let's see where you get in. And who knows? You may meet the love of your life and want to marry him now that it's legal."

"You could still live with us," Bert says. "Put a little space between you and your mom."

We stay in a motel across the street from the park. It has a pool and little trees trimmed into the shape of animals. Bert says they're a letdown after Dinny.

The next morning, we eat beignets in Downtown Disney before the park opens. We take the monorail so Bert can have a view of the park. His excitement is infectious as we take pictures with Mickey and Donald and Snow White. We sing "It's a Small World" for the entire ride with the kids on our boat, despite their parents' grimaces. Bert buys a pair of Mouse Ears with his name embroidered on it. I see all the moms and dads with their children and can't help but think about Iris. My new counselor tells me I shouldn't repress these kinds of thoughts, so I watch a little blonde girl who must be about three as she stares wide-eyed at Cinderella's castle but shies away from Goofy as he lopes by. Would Iris have loved it here? Would Philip have let us come or think it a waste of money? I'll never know.

The day gets blazingly hot and the crowds make it difficult to get around by noon, but we stick it out until three, the time I reserved for the Blue Bayou restaurant. "Disney fine dining," I say. "My parents took me here for my tenth birthday." We eat to the sound of banjo music and mechanical crickets. Bert smiles the whole time, and I do too.

"You seem so much better," Bert says. "I was worried."

I shrug. "Your being here helps. Counseling and drugs help, although I hope to stop them soon."

He grabs my hand. "Whatever works, Amanda. We all need support."

I desperately want to change the subject. "My dad told me once that the Beatles song about 'a little help from my friends' is really about drugs."

Bert laughs. "Nice segue."

On the drive back to Arizona two days later I tell him about the counselor, the calls I keep getting from Philip and Mark, how Lisa decided to stay. He says he hopes it will be easier to be himself if he gets away from Indiana.

"I thought moving to Indiana would save me," I say.

"Did it?" he asks.

"Changed me, for sure."

"That might be all we can expect."

The sunset over the mountains near Mom's house is spectacular. She serves a chicken curry salad and watermelon, the orange of the tomatoes and pink of the melon matching the outline of clouds in the sky. It's lovely, but still doesn't feel like home. Mom laughs as Bert tells her about our trip, exclaiming over Dinny and the Haunted Mansion. Soon we're all three singing "It's a Small World."

"You drove all the way to California and didn't go to the beach," Mom says.

"Next time," I say.

"When I move here," Bert says.

Chapter 36

Amanda

ALL THE NEXT year, Mom and Dad and Bert hound me to get a divorce, but I resist. I know the thought of letting the Grange have all that money, of my never being able to remarry, makes them crazy. When Bert moves to Tempe, we move into a two-bedroom near the Light Rail. Studying and working at a nearby care home distracts me, keeps me busy. But every night I dream of Iris, and often when I wake the need for a baby overwhelms me. Mom calls it "baby hunger," said it hit her around my age too. I realize I don't want to be single and childless for the rest of my life. So, I file for dissolution. Philip's attorney says that since the property settlement was the biggest issue, we need to move the case to the county where the disputed land is located. Mom doesn't think that's required, then finds a local attorney when I say I don't want to fight.

I don't care if I get the money. But Mom cares. Aunty Diane and Uncle Eddie care. I guess it's a matter of principle to them. I want this to be over, and the inheritance still seems unreal to me. Not mine.

"Your grandparents wanted you to have this money, not some religious commune in Indiana," Mom says. "You need to honor their wishes. And the Trust will sue to get the money back if you don't."

I think about Grandma and Grandpa a lot after that. Finally, I agree.

Mom coordinates with the lawyers in Indiana, and I see a new side of her. Organized. Efficient. Relentless. She's hired a Professor Vozel who's written an affidavit explaining how being in a cult affects someone after she leaves. I still don't think I was in a cult, but Mom says it's the only way to explain my delay.

"We need to go to Indiana," Mom calls to say one day in March. "Philip is demanding a meeting, and they'll want to depose you. Will you be OK?"

"Sure," I say. What choice do I have?

"The church made significant improvements to the property, some right away and some since you left, so they won't just deed it over to you. We'd need to pay them for those improvements, and Dan thinks converting the barn to a dorm has made the property less valuable, not more. Dan and I think a return of the $200,000 is best, do you?"

"I don't want the house," I say.

"We should be able to resolve this by agreement, but Philip won't sign anything unless we meet."

I doubt Philip is objecting. This sounds more like Mark or Bryan to me, but I understand the Grange doesn't have the money and won't want to sell any land to get it. It's how we got here in the first place. "When's the meeting?"

"I'm thinking a week from Tuesday, and if we can't get a written agreement a hearing before the judge the following Wednesday."

"We'll be there more than a week?"

"Hopefully not. Hopefully, we'll reach an agreement, and the hearing will be waived. That's why we asked for the Tuesday during your Spring Break. To give us time to resolve the issues and draft the documents."

"I thought your law school friend, Tom, was doing that."

"He is, but I'm doing the background work so the legal bills aren't too high. I'm not sure how the court will allocate fees."

I've talked to my Indiana lawyer, Tom, many times on the phone, but I meet him for the first time the Tuesday of the meeting. His office is in one of the tallest buildings in the town across from an imposing courthouse with a large clock tower. The Indiana landscape and the emerging crocus trigger longing and loss. I wonder if I'll ever again feel that sense of belonging. Dark wood and maroon and blue carpeting soften the sounds of my shoes as we leave the elevators and enter the law firm's offices. Pictures of fox hunts and horses line the walls. A large group of people sit in the lobby's plush chairs.

"Amanda!" A young boy runs toward me. Matthew. A wave of love overtakes me. He clutches my waist and looks up. He's taller than I remember, but his softness, his smell of soap and dog, his eyes, are just as I remember. I sit in the nearest chair, unable to stand, and he jumps onto my lap.

"Are you coming home now?" he asks.

I see Philip and Mark leaning against the wall, watching. Hannah stands next to my chair and smooths Matthew's head.

"Please come home," Hannah whispers. "We miss you."

Mom is giving urgent instructions to the receptionist. Two men in nearly identical blue suits, white shirts, and red ties, appear at the glass doors separating the lobby from the interior offices. I recognize my grandpa's attorney, Dan.

"I need to talk with my clients before the conference," the man I assume is Tom says. "You're more than a half-hour early," he says to Philip, reproof in his voice.

Mark smiles at me. Philip looks at the floor.

I feel out of balance as we take our seats around an impressive conference table of polished dark wood. Mom and I sit across from the large windows overlooking the courthouse. I can tell she's angry. Aunty Diane and Uncle Eddie sit next to Mom. Tom introduces himself, shakes everyone's hand, and gives each of us his business card.

The clock chimes ten times.

"I went into that courthouse when I was here once," Mom says, and I know she's trying to regain her lawyerly cool. "It's beautiful."

"One of the best things about this town," Tom says. "That's where the hearing will be if we can't resolve this. I told Mr. Morivan's lawyer to arrive at ten-thirty, so let's quickly discuss strategy. Apparently, part of their strategy was to have the family appeal to Amanda first. They were not invited."

Mom scowls and Dan nods as Tom continues.

"Amanda's said she doesn't want the house, so we've offered to accept the two hundred thousand dollars the Trust paid to purchase the property without interest or appreciation and each party bearing their own attorneys' fees. If we go to a hearing, we'll ask for all those things plus any expert fees and the costs of bringing witnesses. They know this. There's only one issue: did Amanda gift the house to the Grange community? They're going to say she did."

Tom turns to me. "Amanda, despite our many conversations, your position on this isn't clear to me. The deed is in your name as your separate property."

"The Trust made sure of that," Dan says.

"And you never changed the deed. But you've told me everyone in the Grange shares whatever they have. That they have no individual property."

"Yes. Mark . . . Rev. Vinnar shares his property with everyone and I did too."

"The Vinnars never deeded their property to the church. They let a group of people live there. Not the same thing."

I shrug. It felt like the same thing.

"We're going to say Amanda didn't give the house, she let the group use it. I need to know, Amanda, if you agree with that. If this gets heated, they'll want to depose you and I need to know what you're going to say."

"I never intended to leave, so it didn't matter," I say.

"OK. We can work with that. We can also argue even if she did say it was a gift, the Grange community, and specifically Mr. Morivan and Mr. Vinnar, exercised undue influence, manipulated her into any gift. We think we'll win this at a hearing, but the testimony could get painful. Even ugly."

"Ugly?" I ask. "How."

Mom shifts in her chair, and Tom holds up his hand as if to silence her.

"Mostly for Rev. Vinnar," Tom says. "A reputation for improper relationships with minors and women he counseled follows him."

"I never heard anything like that, and Mark was nothing but good to me."

"You've told me things about your sessions with Mark, his displays of affection, that could further damage his reputation," Tom says. "And Detective Taylor shared what he discovered when his department looked into complaints about the Grange and Rev. Vinnar. That led us to former members with damaging information. I doubt Rev. Vinnar or the church wants any of this to come out."

A cold realization hits me. I wasn't the only one he kissed, touched, tempted. I'm not special. I never was. How many? Before or after me? Did he have sex with them? What would have happened if I stayed? My mind is a jumble of questions, but a knock at the door announces Philip's lawyer has arrived. A wave of nausea overtakes me. I pinch my arm.

A man in an open-necked striped shirt and gray blazer strides in, followed by Philip and Mark. Philip looks at me quickly and then away, but Mark holds my gaze with a sad stare and sits directly across from me.

I can't bear it. Sadness and loss overwhelm me. He knows it. He's using it. Anger and resentment punch me in my gut. I rise to leave, and Mom starts to follow. I wave her off. I run to the bathroom and throw up.

When I return, the lawyers are arguing their positions. I try to block it out, answering only when Mom repeats a direct question somebody's asked. Any time Mark tries to say something, Tom cuts him off, saying Mark isn't a party and asking why he's even here. They argue and posture for an hour. Sandwiches arrive, and we take a break. I can't eat. Tom suggests a mediation. Philip's lawyer wants to schedule my deposition.

"Stop," I finally say, looking first at Philip and then at Mark. "What is it you really want?"

Mark speaks over Tom's objection. "We want you to come home."

The room erupts, first Mom slamming her fist on the table, then everyone talking at once.

"That isn't going to happen," I say, and the room quiets. "For lots of reasons that don't matter anymore. What else?"

I hear Mom's relieved sigh.

"Philip," I say. "I don't think you want me back."

Philip gives me a stony stare but doesn't speak.

"The dissolution will be granted one way or another," Tom says, "no matter what anyone thinks they want. We're here to talk about Amanda's inheritance. That's all. This is about money, and a mediation or a hearing will only cost more."

I promised Mom I wouldn't say that they can keep it for all I care. I'm considering breaking that promise when Philip speaks.

"Let's split the money. Amanda gets a hundred thousand dollars. Move on."

"There's no legal basis for that," Tom says.

"We're negotiating here," Philip's lawyer says.

"Done," I say.

The room is silent, tense. I stand. Philip stands. We shake hands across the table. He walks out.

The lawyers start discussing payment plans and liens and selling a portion of the property. I leave the room to see if I can catch Philip. Mom starts to follow, but I frown at her.

"Let me say goodbye to him," I say, and she sits.

I stop him in the hallway before he reaches the lobby.

"I want to say goodbye and I'm sorry," I say. "Can you forgive me?"

He turns, puts his arms around me. His hurt and regret mixes with mine. "I'm thinking about leaving the Grange."

My eyes widen in surprise, and sorrow washes over me. So much loss. Hopefulness, Iris. The pain of it feels fresh. We're both victims.

"Why?" I ask.

"It doesn't matter, does it?" he asks as he releases me.

"I guess not," I say, and he walks toward the door.

I turn around to see Mark. When he opens his arms, a rush of emotions more charged than any I felt for Philip slam into me. Betrayal. Anger. Resistance. Loss. I'm aware that these emotions are stronger because I loved him more. I'm disgusted with myself.

I turn away without a word, go back to the conference room where the lawyers are working out the small details.

MOM'S FRIEND COREY picks us up from the airport. Mom sits in front and tells Corey what happened while I stare silently out the window. It's a clear day, the sky wide and blue. I know the heat and glare are coming, but they're not here yet. I relax as we pass the bushes of red bougainvillea, pink oleanders, and orange birds-of-paradise lining the freeway. By the time we reach my apartment complex, my stomach is pretty much unclenched.

"You OK?" Bert asks, taking my hand when we arrive.

I nod, and he knows I don't want to talk about it yet. Bert invites Corey and Mom for supper, says he's in the mood to fire up the grill and he bought steaks to celebrate.

Mom starts straightening the pictures and picking up newspapers the minute she enters. I give her a reproving look and she stops. She joins Corey on the brown leather couch Dad gave me when I moved in, saying Paige hated it.

"Want something to drink?" I ask. "We've got beer."

"Lemonade?" Mom asks.

"Hard OK?" I ask.

"Much better," Corey says.

I fill three glasses with ice and lemonade and hand Bert a beer.

"Can I help?" Mom shouts.

Our galley kitchen is far too small for another body. Two is too many. "No, thanks. We've got it," I say.

Bert carries his beer and a bag of chips outside to a little open area where we have lawn chairs and a small kettle grill. He piles charcoal and mesquite chips in a pyramid in the grill and lights them. The sharp smell of lighter fluid pierces then fades when Bert closes the slider and settles in one of the chairs with a cigarette. I put the lemonades on a glass table, this one a donation from my Grandma Beane. It reminds me that most of the furniture in this apartment comes from someone, not somewhere, furnished by relatives and friends eager to help.

"Think Bert would give me a cigarette?" Mom asks.

"I'm sure he would," I say, and we go outside.

Corey holds my arm before I get out the door and pulls me into an embrace. "It'll be OK," she says, and tears burn the corners of my eyes.

"I know," I say. "But today it's hard."

Mom gives Bert a peace sign, and he hands her a cigarette and the matches. Corey signals she wants one too. We stare at the fire until the coals turn gray at the edges.

A red and violet sky back-lights Bert as he disperses the coals. He hums something unidentifiable. Mom, Corey, and I are silent, lost in our own reveries.

"I'm happy—" Mom begins.

"Tonight let's pretend it never happened," I say and turn to Bert. "How's the moot court brief going?"

"Good," Bert says. "Spent a lot of time in the library the last few days and it's shaping up. Susan, would you mind looking at it when I finish my draft?"

"I'd love to. What's the question?"

While Corey, Mom, and Bert geek out on the law, I close my eyes and listen to the birds gathering, their chirps and chatters growing increasingly loud. I open my eyes to the unmistakable squawk of a grackle and see his yellow eyes watching me from a branch in an Ironwood tree. I look away first.

Bert puts on some Ed Sheeran when he goes in for the steaks. Brings us each another hard lemonade.

"This is nice," Mom says. "No Jackson Browne, but still nice."

Bert jokes about his classes and asks Corey about law school back in the day, asks her why she stopped being a lawyer.

"I couldn't take the pressure of billable hours, and after two years of feeling like nothing I did was ever good enough I gave up. Unlike Susan I didn't have a family to support, so I found a cheaper place to live and a job where every day they made me feel I was helping. Maybe I should have tried public practice, but I felt defeated. And it's worked out. I'm way happier."

By the time we're into our third bottles, Mom starts telling new stories.

"I'm glad you're enjoying law school," Mom says to Bert. "I didn't. So much competition. When you did well, you were suspect, and when you didn't, you got disdain disguised as sympathy."

"So, like life," Bert says.

"I don't believe that," Mom says. "I know a lot of kind-hearted, supportive people. Even some lawyers."

Bert laughs. "I guess so."

A chill comes on once the sun sets, and we go inside to eat.

"We should get going," Mom says to Corey after supper ends and they've loaded the dishwasher.

"Or we could watch a movie," Bert says.

"I understand you like classic movies," Mom says. "I'd stay for *Sound of Music,* which I know you have because I gave it to Amanda."

"Great idea," Bert says. "We can sing along. Come on, Amanda, don't give me that look. You like to sing."

Corey laughs. "Susan, I see you have a soul mate here."

"It'll be fun," Mom says.

I groan, but it does sound like fun. And by the time we get to "Sixteen Going on Seventeen," we're twirling and singing and laughing as we attempt an awkward little waltz.

ACKNOWLEDGEMENTS

Many people helped me write this book, and I am grateful for every one of their insights and suggestions, even those I chose to ignore. They were probably right, and I take responsibility for all questionable choices and missed opportunities. I am particularly grateful to my editors, to Julia Scheeres, whose insight into writing about religious extremism helped focus my attention on its subtleties, to Maxine Swann for the beauty of her edits and content suggestions, to Lisa Godfrey for her review, and to everyone at Bedazzled Ink for all they have done to bring the book to the world. I'm thankful, too, for the support of my mentors and workshop leaders, including Lidia Yuknavitch, Antonya Nelson, Crystal Wilkinson, Helen Klein Ross, Rick Moody, Joanna Scott, Claire Messud, and Paul Harding, whose comments pushed me to re-examine several aspects of the novel.

I'm grateful to the writing community at Writing by Writers who gave me the opportunity to work with so many great and helpful authors and to the wonderful women in my cohort there who are always supportive, helpful, and kind. Thank you too to my workshop colleagues at the NYS Summer Workshop both for a wonderful summer and their helpful advice as I worked on the final draft of this novel. I'm particularly thankful to my friends and family members who have read and commented on the many drafts of this novel: Jen McAlonan, Stacy Smith, Sheryl Austin, Meg Weber, Maggie Jansen, Tanya Friedman, Bill Hylen, Jennifer Pingeon, Marie Blanchard, Joyce Boomsma, Ann Boomsma, Dave Boomsma. And thank you to the many others who listened patiently to my whining about how hard writing is and encouraged me the countless times I considered giving up.

I couldn't have done any of this without you.

Patricia Boomsma is a retired Arizona lawyer now writing full time. She earned a master's degree in English from Purdue University, a law degree from Indiana University in Indianapolis, and an MFA in Creative Writing from Queens University in Charlotte. Her publications include short stories in *Scarlet Leaf Review, Persimmon Tree*, and *Vignette Review. Indolent Press* published her poem "Arc of the Apocalypse" both online and in the anthology "Poems From the Aftermath." Her first novel, *The Way of Glory* (Edeleboom Books 2018), won the Bill Fisher Award for Best First Book-Fiction from the Independent Book Publishers Association and a First Place/Best in Category Chaucer Award from Chanticleer Book Reviews. *Flotsam*, was published by BInk Books in 2023.

Visit Patricia's website: https://patboomsma.com